Attack of the Red Winkies

G. E. McCurry

ATTACK OF THE RED WINKIES

Copyright 2023 by G. E. McCurry

All rights reserved.
No part of this book may be reproduced, scanned, or distributed in any printed or electronic form without written permission of the publisher except in the case of brief quotations embodied in critical articles or reviews. Please do not participate in or encourage piracy of copyrighted materials in violation of the author's rights, Purchase only authorized editions. For information contact: G. E. McCurry.

ISBN: 978-0-9968016-2-1

This is a work of fiction. Names, characters, places, and incidents are either the product of the author's imagination or are used fictitiously. Any resemblance to actual persons, living or dead, events, or locales is entirely coincidental.

If you purchased this book without a cover, you should be aware that this book is stolen property. It was reported as "unsold and destroyed" to the publisher, and neither the author nor the publisher has received any payment for this "stripped book".

PRINTED IN THE UNITED STATES OF AMERICA-
PLANET EARTH
First Printing December 2024
Revised Edition with pictures by author January 2026

**This book
is dedicated to
my fun and
imaginative
nieces, nephews and grandkids
those both
family-born
and those who
big heartedly chose to
become family.**

CONTENTS

ONE
The Sneaky Invasion - 8

TWO
Tiana and Alora's Warning – 23

THREE
Rascally Rhys – 37

FOUR
Gertie's Sacrifice – 49

FIVE
Crocodiles – 78

SIX
The Mad General – 100

SEVEN
Old Town Cemetery – 127

EIGHT
Fearsome Lionesses – 149

NINE
The Flashy Castle – 161

TEN
Dungeon Demons – 192

ELEVEN
The Politically Correct Force – 215

CONTESTS

TWELVE
The Flashing Fast Ride – 227

THIRTEEN
Chief Hazelwitch Broomsky – 243

FOURTEEN
Surrounded – 261

FIFTEEN
The Fairy's Curse - 288

SIXTEEN
Angry Giants – 299

SEVENTEEN
War in the Park – 330

EIGHTEEN
Roleena's Trick - 365

ATTACK OF
THE
RED
WINKIES

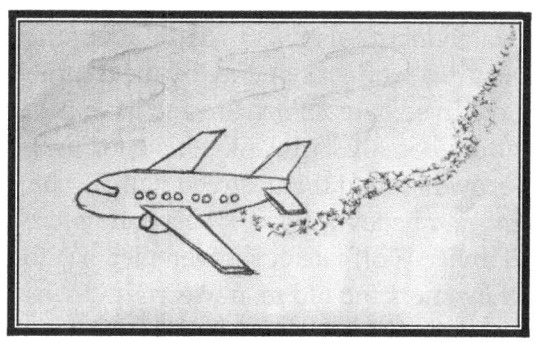

CHAPTER ONE
THE SNEAKY INVASION

A flaming red aurora borealis flashed brightly across Alaska's night sky. Local people and tourists in Anchorage rushed over to the Old City Hall Park to watch the amazing lights above its big open fields. The huge crowd that had gathered all gasped in surprise to see streams of fiery red lights streaking through its enormous broad, red glowing bands.

An elder silver-haired man in the crowd turned to the woman by him munching on a tasty reindeer sausage on a bun she had bought from a vendor in the park.

"Martha," he whispered with a shiver, "This is mind-blowing and as I lived during the crazy sixties and seventies that says a lot. What's strange is the fiery lights were all blinking together, but now the lower parts are blinking fast and then slow. Wait. They stopped. Now, the upper bands are doing this."

"It is odd, and I don't know why it's doing this but we'll ask our kids later. I'm just glad they sent us tickets to come visit them up here," she replied and he nodded in agreement.

"Here's another odd thing. May's a rare time to see this."

"Then I'm glad we got lucky."

"Are we?" he asked frowning, "Because as I watch this longer and longer it worries me to have the lights act so—"

"Look, George!" she cut in, "There's lots more of those sparkling red lights floating down into those bands."

"Jeepers! There sure are," he said scratching his head as they continued to watch in astonishment. "How about that."

A native Dena'ina woman standing by them turned to them and said, "I have lived here all my life and have never seen a flaming red aurora borealis lights like this one." Several other people in the crowd around them agreed with her loudly.

"These lights are bedeviled and it be a bad omen!" a grizzled old man in a Timber Wolf jacket shouted then he stomped off.

Little did they know the old man was right.

The night stretched on and several planes flew through the northern lights as they came in to land in Anchorage's Ted Stevens International Airport. Millions of tiny fiery red specks latched onto each flight that passed near them but no one in them was the least aware the Earth was being invaded.

**

The next day passed quietly in the north and only one local paper in Anchorage reported the red aurora borealis the night before had fiery red ribbons of lights running through its bands. One radio newscaster found this unusual enough to mention on his station in Fairbanks. Some ham radio enthusiasts then sent it on to Juneau, Sitka, Ketchikan, and way out to Dutch Harbor.

Odder news came two days later as radio stations broadcast a forest ranger reporting large wolf packs racing away from their normal habitats in Alaska. One wolf biologist said he had never seen Canadian Timber wolves, Arctic wolves, and Alaska Tundra wolves run together or in such great numbers.

Another strange report came the following day as a ranger from Kodiak Island reported two pods of humpback whales leaving the area. After many on the west coast reported this too, a renowned marine biologist went to check this out. He later said that this whale traffic was puzzling because these particular whales stayed near Alaska from May through September and having them leave when they just arrive to Alaskan waters was astonishingly. Nature lovers were worried and began to demand answers, but oceanographers and scientists had no explanation for this strange behavior.

**

One thousand five hundred air miles south of Anchorage, lies the growing city of Everett, Washington. Nestled on the east side of Possession Sound, it sits in the rain shadow of the regal, snowcapped Olympic Mountains on the northwest corner of the state. A new day dawned in Everett with rain washing the air the night before which came as no surprise to locals. The surprise was the clouds had cleared and the sun shone brightly much to the delight of two young girls living there.

**

Tiana Coins hated shopping. It bewildered her that her younger fifth grade sister, Alora, was always happy to do this. Out of school for the summer, this certain sixth grader thought she should be out enjoying this rare sunny June day by hiking around Langus Park's trails or swimming at the Forest Park's pool. Yet where did she find herself? Grocery shopping with her sister at Big Mama's Market in their neighborhood. She felt the market's name was ridiculous since it was not owned by any mama. It was owned by a big, burly East-Indian man, but he was so good-humored and kind everyone loved him.

The quirky aunt they lived with had given them money and only asked them to go buy their own cereal but it was irksome for Tiana since her sister tended to check everything out. Bored out of her mind, she tapped her foot as she leaned on their cart waiting for her sister to decide on one. She gazed around and suddenly stiffened, her eyes popping open wide to see a bizarre sight of a twinkling red cloud flashing down the aisle their direction. She jerked aside as it whizzed by her and she was relieved Alora was not in its way. As she watched it zip down the aisle, she saw it then take a turn to the right at the end.

"Wow! Is that what I think it is?!" Tiana gasped blinking her eyes in surprise. She then caught a whiff of something burned and gaped as she found a scorch mark on her jeans.

"What was what?" Alora asked vaguely as the light-hearted girl remained focused on a shelf filled with a variety of cereal boxes which she was carefully examining one by one.

"Didn't you see those flashy red lights zip right past us?"

"Nope, and you're only being silly," she said without even looking her sister's way, but then she paused and wrinkled her nose. "Ew! But I do smell rotten eggs. Did you just let off a personal stink bomb?"

"No, it wasn't me. But I do think I saw something from that watch list of Aunt Roleena's. Then again, never mind, because speaking of minds, yours is elsewhere," Tiana said dryly as Alora picked up another box of cereal and smiled impishly. "From the way you're grinning I bet that's not a cereal we're allowed to get."

Alora shrugged and flipped her long braid over her shoulder as she read the information on the box. "I think we should try this 'new' one and see if we like it."

"Why? You're rarely happy with anything we get."

"Come on, let's be adventurous!" she said mischievously.

Tiana checked the ingredients listed on the box and groaned. "This isn't healthy at all. It looks like it's got enough sugar in it to fuel an entire family for a week which would be really bad."

"You sound like Auntie Roleena when she lectures me about the evils of eating super sugary stuff," Alora said with a pout.

"Then I'm glad I do, because she's right!" She put her hands on her slim hips and looked sternly at her sister. "When I heard her do that, I looked it up and read how sugar affects our brains. To sum it up, too much sugar can make it shrivel up."

"You're just making that up to scare me."

"No, I'm truly not making it up," Tiana said matter-of-factly.

"But sugar gives me lots of energy!" Alora said defiantly.

"It can, but too much, like the hard-core sugars in candy, has a wicked backlash. You see, large amounts do give your body a rush, but after the rush your body's systems crash making you feel exhausted and can even leave you depressed."

"A little won't hut," she said clutching the box tightly.

Tiana held out her hand. "Come on, this is bad. Let me put it back." After a moment, Alora sighed and handed it to her. "Thank you. Now, if you must get something new, get one without gobs of sugar 'please', because if she saw you bring 'this' cereal home her hair would writhe like mad snakes."

"Actually, I like seeing her hair do that. It's funny!"

At first, Tiana ignored her sister's comment but then burst out laughing as she stuck her fingers under her hair and made it wiggle around. "When her hair gets snaky it does look silly. But that reminds me of her warning to keep this a secret when we first lived with her. She told us about all her quirky traits so we wouldn't be alarmed, like how if she gets mad her hair hisses like vipers, and that her kaleidoscope-colored eyes light up when she's excited. Though, until I saw those things, I thought she was kidding."

Alora nodded sharply. "Me too! I was also surprised to see if she laughs hard, she snorts then sparks fly out of her nose! She even showed us she could light a fire by doing that."

Tiana grinned. "But after that her nose smoked for an hour."

The girls began giggling loudly and Alora laughed so hard she sat on the floor holding her sides causing a lady in the aisle to come over to her looking worried.

"Are you all right?" the lady asked in a kindly way.

"We're okay. We're just being silly." As the lady nodded and moved on Tiana nudged Alora's shoulder. "We best control ourselves and not talk about our aunt's quirks in public, since as I said, we did promise to keep it a secret. I also just remembered she told us what happened when a lady ran over her foot with a cart. It hurt our aunt so badly her hair snapped at the lady. She freaked out and screamed for the police so our aunt had to limp out of there fast to keep her snapping hair from being reported."

"That's' right, and then she moved because she didn't want to risk having her alien trait exposed by this."

"It was a scary close call for her," Tiana said. "Now, please get up off the floor. It will attract too much attention."

"Okay. Okay. Help me up and I'll find a cereal for us with less sugar." Alora reached for her sister but as Tiana pulled her up, she gasped and flew into Alora knocking her back on the ground. "Hey! Why are you tackling me?" she huffed.

"Sorry, but I got zapped!" Tiana said rubbing her bottom.

"Sure, you did," Alora said sarcastically. "I think it's just an excuse for letting off another big stinky poof."

"Hey, no I didn't, and I didn't do the last one either! It was that flashy red cloud I saw streak by us before. The one I told you about a few minutes ago, but this time when it zipped down the aisle by me it shocked me so badly, I crashed into you."

"Right," Alora huffed as she got up and brushed herself off.

"Honest! That's what happened, and it was so, so creepy."

"You're making that up!"

"I'm not one who makes up silly stuff in this family. That's your thing. Now, believe it or not, that red flashy thing gave me a jolt and..." Tiana's words caught in her throat as she stared down the aisle. She grabbed her sister's arm and pulled her over with her behind a promotional stand of Paul Newman's spaghetti sauce then scrunched down low.

Alora gaped in surprise. "What is wrong with you?"

"Look down the aisle," Tiana whispered hoarsely.

Alora peeked out from behind the stand just as a glowing cloud-shaped red cluster of lights flashed by them. It whizzed down the aisle and then turned left at the end. As she looked back at her sister, her face was sheet white.

"Good grief, Tiana! What was that?" she croaked out. "Wait. Could those actually be the energy thingies Auntie Roleena told us the scary stories about? The ones she called 'Red Winkies'?"

"I think the answer to that is obvious. Yes!"

Alora bit her lip worriedly. "But I thought they were just make-believe because she always told us all kinds of wild tales about mythical gods and goddesses, and aliens or other strange creatures from far-off worlds. My favorites were the tiny magic fairies, and the mermaids and mermen living in our oceans."

Tiana nodded. "Those were good ones, but some creatures she told us about were scary powerful."

"But she said most are peaceful beings just visiting here."

"She also said some had caused a lot of trouble. But I didn't think about it much since all her alien friends we have met are nice. So, I thought the others were all from the ancient past and long gone. But now it looks like I'm wrong about that."

"Oh, no," Alora groaned. "And that means these Red Winkie troublemakers from a far-off planet have made it back to Earth."

"We should keep our voices down low," Tiana murmured. "I don't know if they can hear or understand us, but we don't want to draw their attention and find them following us home."

"Or latch onto our skin like Auntie said they can, especially bare feet. Then they can control where we go. It makes me glad we didn't wear sandals today. What's also scary is she said they can use all kinds energy to their benefit." Alora then gasped. "We have lots of electrical wires that carry loads of energy. In fact, I bet they can race along those like a super highway. Hmm, maybe if we stood perfectly still, they couldn't use us."

Tiana grimaced. "I don't think that would help, because of what I learned in biology class this year. My teacher said our bodies are full of neurons with slight electrical charges. Add an ouch to that because our bodies are never still since our blood is always moving through our veins and arteries."

"So, standing still won't help which is scary."

"Scarier yet is since blood flows to our brain which also has electrical neurons, I wonder if they can control our minds?"

"Auntie Roleena didn't say if they could do that," Alora said biting her lip worriedly.

"Let's not stay and find out. Let's get out of here now."

"What about our cereal? We told her we'd pick some up today since we're out of all of ours."

"Forget the cereal!" Tiana groaned. "She'll understand why we didn't get it, and you know what? I wish I'd listened to her more closely lately since she's been grumbling for days about feeling some trouble coming. But since she's like you and frets about nearly everything, I didn't take her seriously."

"I don't fret about everything," Alora huffed.

"Sorry to be blunt, but you two are big worry warts. And now we know the Red Winkies are real, she'd be a lot more upset if they got hold of us than whether we got the cereal."

Alora nodded sharply. "I'd be upset too!"

"Then let's get out of here before they run into us again."

"Okay, and we've only seen the one cloud here, so let's go the opposite direction of it and sneak outside super quick."

Tiana rolled her eyes and groaned. "You're kidding me, right? Our aunt told us they always travel with lots of clusters."

"Oh, yeah. I forgot about that. It seems they're too scared to go anywhere without other clusters with them."

"For good reason, remember?"

"Yes. They're so tiny we could easily squash them flat with our shoe!" she said making a crushing motion with her foot.

"Alora, don't say that so loudly right now because if they can hear you talk like that it'll make them mad."

Alora shook her head. "Nope. I just recalled hearing Auntie Roleena tell someone on her phone she found out the biggest problem dealing with the Red Winkies is they can't yet translate their language, that is if they have one. It's just a blurred noise that comes out garbled to even their high-tech alien devices."

"Still, they might sense menacing moves and what you did could make them mad. Remember, she told us you don't want to make them mad. For even though they're incredibly small, if they get riled, they're trouble with a capital 'T'."

"And like ants, zillions of them," Alora said grimacing.

"That would be disastrous for us with them being able to redirect people's movements. They could then have us walk in front of car if they wanted to kill us."

"I doubt they'd do that since she did also say that they were mostly just pranksters, not killers."

"She also said they caused several disasters on Earth."

"Oh, you're right. I guess that was super bad."

"Yes, big time, and I don't want to stay to find out if they're only pranksters or actual killers. Do you?"

"No!" Alora sputtered. "We need to go and get our aunt's help with this, because I don't want them controlling my feet or maybe scrambling my brains until they're mushy."

"Ick! That's a horrid thought," Tiana sputtered.

"But it might not be just a thought. So, you're right about us getting out of here now," she said shivering.

Tiana cautiously peeked around the promotional stand they hid behind. "It looks clear of them, but we need to be careful. They move really fast." She eased out of their hiding spot and whispered, "It's still okay. No flashy red lights in sight."

"Maybe they all left," Alora said rising hesitantly.

"I doubt it." Tiana peered around uneasily remembering all too well the jolt she got from the little red cloud. She waved at her sister to come to her, but she just looked at her wide-eyed. *I will not leave you here*, she thought and held out her hand. Alora grabbed it and Tiana felt how sweaty it was as she pulled her along with her. *She's scared, but at least she is moving.*

The girls tiptoed down the aisle and as they came to the end they stopped. They looked at each other questioningly but did not speak. Tiana cautiously peered around the corner. "It's all clear." Holding tight to her sister's hand, they tiptoed into the next aisle. They continued carefully checking each aisle and crossed over two more aisles after seeing they were clear. As they reached the last aisle by the exit, Tiana yanked Alora back before going on.

"I saw a red blinking light in that aisle riding on a little girl's shoe," Tiana said shakily. "She's standing by a woman who's likely her mom that's looking at soups on the top shelf there."

"A shoe? Don't they have to connect with bare skin?"

"I thought so, but that's what I saw. Wait. That girl had on a pair of kid's shoes that sparkle as they walk. They likely have a battery in them to make them light up and the energy in them probably drew the Red Winkies to them."

"I bet you're right," Alora said peeking into the other aisle. "And the lights on them are red even if they weren't before."

"So, since Aunt Roleena told us a hundred could fit on a dime there's likely thousands in the cluster traveling on that pair of shoes," Tiana said with a heavy sigh.

"Gracious, that's a lot, and it seems like they're super-fast at finding ways to attach to people."

Tiana peeked down the aisle again. "Crumb! Another cloud of Red Winkies just whizzed into that aisle."

"Is it headed our way?" Alora asked with a gulp.

"No. Right now it's just hovering around the woman."

"It's probably going to glom onto her so let's warn her!"

"Are you crazy?" Tiana gasped. "First of all, I doubt she'd believe us, plus the Red Winkies would also latch onto us. Then we couldn't go for help and what's more important right now is we get to Aunt Roleena and warn her about this."

"But I don't like not warning her," she mumbled.

"Me either, but we've got to consider the big picture here."

"You're right," she sighed. "The big picture is super scary."

"Frighteningly. Add to that the only way out of here is the front door and we have to go past them to get to it."

"Oh. My. Gosh. That's terrible. Find us some other way."

"I don't know of any other," she groaned in frustration.

Alora pinched her nose closed. "But their stench is getting stronger and stronger every second which means some of the Red winkies must be coming our way."

"Do you have another great idea?" Tiana asked bluntly.

"No…I guess I don't."

"Well then we'll have to use the crazy one I have now."

"What's that?"

"Run!"

Alora looked stunned. "When they're in the aisle by it?!"

"Yes, since they'll find us anyway if we don't."

"Let's wait and see if...ick! Never mind. The smell's gotten so bad I'll do it and just pray we get away safely."

"Then pray quickly, because here we go!"

"But my feet won't move," she sniffed tearily. "You go, because I just can't seem to do it."

Tiana clasped Alora's hand tightly. "You can and you will!"

Alora's eyes popped open wide for despite Tiana's smaller size she pulled her along with her past the Winkies to the door huffing like a tough locomotive. The automatic door opened painfully slow and her heart thumped so hard she could hear it in her ears. Seconds felt like hours but the door finally opened wide enough to get through and Tiana pulled her out with her.

"Come on! Snap out of it...please!" Tiana growled as she grabbed her sister's shoulders and shook her.

Alora blinked a few times then pulled away. "I'll be okay."

"Good, because we need to run. And I mean now!"

Hand-in-hand, the sisters bounded across the parking lot like deer chased by wolves. Tiana led them two blocks north and three blocks east then stopped as Alora began gasping badly. "It's only a few more blocks to Aunt Roleena's," she said to encourage her knowing she was not as athletic as she was.

"It's not this far to Auntie Roleena's house," Alora said trying to catch her breath. "But it sure is now with the crazy way you are taking us."

"That's because I'm taking us the long, indirect way there."

"Why?" she asked still gasping for air.

"I need to be sure we're not followed home by them."

"Good idea since and a super scary thought."

"It is. Now, come on." Tiana led her west several blocks but paused as her sister stopped and held her rib cage. "Side ache?"

Alora winced as she nodded. "Yeah, a bad one."

Tiana glanced around and saw thick, neatly trimmed bushes edging a driveway three houses down from them and pointed. "There!" She led her sister over to it and behind its Boxwood hedge and gently pulled her down low to rest. A few minutes later, Alora stood up to peek over the three-foot-tall shrubs.

"Just sit still," she hissed pulling her back down. "We don't want the Red Winkies to sense our movement's and locate us. Then we could get zapped...or worse."

"But I wanted to see if they're following us and just like you, I don't want them to find out where we live."

"Me either, but don't move around. Just peek through the branches," she said sharply as she scowled at her.

"Okay," Alora huffed and spread a few branches to look through the hedge. "You know, they might not have noticed we left. After all, Auntie said they don't really see things. They just use some kind of sensors they have built in to find things."

"Which means they might sense heat waves or loud sound vibrations, and they can likely detect any sudden motions."

"Why would they sense motions?"

"Because I learned in my science class sudden motions displace the air. So, if they're real sensitive, they likely sensed me dragging you out of the store when you froze up."

"But even if they did, they couldn't sense which direction we went when we left the store with them still being inside it. Not only that, you said they brushed by you twice, but didn't latch onto you so they might not be as sensitive as you think."

"Maybe, maybe not. I don't know why they didn't latch onto to me other than I was standing still." Tiana sighed and rubbed her backside where she got stung. "Maybe if something doesn't put out enough heat, they don't want to attach to it. Right now, I want you to admit having now seen them and the scorch mark on my jeans you know that's what made me fall on you."

"Okay! I admit it. So, stop being so prickly with me."

Tiana nodded then her eyes widened. "I 'had' first reasoned it didn't glom onto me because I didn't have any exposed skin. However, that doesn't explain the reason it zapped me so hard it knocked me into you and I wonder why?"

Alora shrugged. "I have no idea. I'm simply glad they didn't stick to you."

"Me too." Tiana peered through the bushes. "I don't see any Red Winkies, but to be cautious, help me out. Since you have a lot better sniffer than I do, can you smell them?"

Alora sniffed the air a few times. "No. Well...at least I don't smell any of the odors our aunt told us they put out."

"Here's another problem. They're so tiny and fast that if they were in a small cluster they'd be hard for people to spot in the daytime. In fact, I didn't notice them until we were inside and happened to look their way as they passed by me."

"Then it'll be safer to go places at night since their flashy red lights would make them be easy to spot."

"True. Good thinking."

"You know, I'm just glad you noticed them or we might both be their zombie puppets right now."

"Come on, Alora, Aunt Roleena didn't say they could turn people into zombies."

"Are you sure? I never asked her if they could do that."

"No, I'm not sure but she'd likely have told us if they could do that. Now, check again. Do you smell anything?"

"Yes. The bush, the grass, my perfume…and your sweat! Whew! You need to take a shower, sis."

"Alora! You know what I meant," Tiana groaned.

"Then, no, I don't smell them."

"No rotten eggs?"

"Nope."

"No burning rubber or foul body gases?"

"No, and as you know, I have a good sniffer."

"Yes, you do. Wait. They also can imitate a musky perfume hoping others will think they're just smelling flowers."

"As if that could ever cover the other foul odors they emit," she said making a face. "But I don't smell that either."

"And I hope we don't anytime soon." Her eyes narrowed as she studied the area again. "It looks safe to go."

"Wait! I'm going check myself, and not through the bushes."

"Alora…you know I've got great eyesight and you're not good at spotting things far away even with your glasses on."

"I know, but I need to look for myself," she said firmly but she shivered as she slowly stood up and peered over the bushes. "You're right. No tiny red winking lights at all."

Tiana slowly stood up and checked the area again. "Okay, let's go. But we'll just walk and not run so we don't make any big air waves," she said looking at her sister worriedly. "Has your side ache eased up enough to run if they find us?"

"You can bet that if I see them, I'll run like the hounds of Baskerville are after me whether I have a side ache or not!"

"Good, because really need to get back to Aunt Roleena's and tell her the Red Winkies are here," she said grimly.

As they started walking toward their aunt's home Alora slowed down and bit her lip anxiously as she glanced at her sister. "I know we have to tell her but can we wait until after the clear solar eclipse today? One she's been waiting years for?"

"Oops...I forgot all about that," she said grimacing.

"Will holding off a few hours matter? Because I don't want to say anything to keep her from making that super important off-planet call. You know how worried she's been about not being able to get a clear call out of our solar system for such a long time. She said our sun's fussy solar waves have interfered with these, and even it was calm occasionally, it was not long enough to do this due to all the super hard stuff she has to do before she can dial out of our solar system."

"It's complicated calculations not 'stuff'. Also, it's an enhanced communication system, not a dial phone like the one at her house. So, she most certainly doesn't 'dial out' to do an intergalactic call," Tiana said rolling her eyes.

"Hey, it's a fancy phone to me, Miss Picky," Alora huffed. "Besides, what's important is she said she needs to reach her off-world contacts in hopes of getting their help to heal our sick planet and in faster ways than we're doing ourselves."

Tiana sighed. "True, we desperately need to do that, or else."

"Yeah, because she said the 'or else' is it'll be too late to fix the bad stuff we've done to it before it dies and us with it. Now, I'm also scared these Red Winkies will make matters worse. Do you think it'll be as bad as the time they caused an ice age?"

"That time was long before modern humans showed up. So, I can't begin to give you even a guess without knowing lots more about these Red Winkies and their goals this time."

Alora sighed heavily. "I suppose you can't. It's just super alarming since she said once they kept firing the sun up to get more heat and could have fried everything to cinders on Earth."

"Fortunately, Aunt Roleena said the forces in what she called the 'Great Universe' stopped them and put our sun back to the way it was and now the wise aliens check on Earth more often."

"Not often enough, because they set off a big volcano."

"Oh dear, that's true. She said they set it off to draw more energy themselves, but it spewed so much ash into the air it blocked much of the sun's heat and caused another ice age."

"She also got so miffed telling us the awful things the Red Winkies did her hair writhed like a poked nest of angry snakes."

"Between firing up sun and setting off volcanoes, she had good reasons to be miffed at them."

"Do you think they're going to do one of those things again?"

Tiana shrugged. "Who knows? But let's hope they don't."

The girls forced themselves to walk and not run the last few blocks to their aunt's house to avoid drawing the Red Winkies attention. Ten minutes later, they arrived at an Edwardian era Dutch-colonial home snuggled into one of the historic districts in Everett and quickly opened the front gate. Two spruce trees trimmed in swirls were on each side it and a white picket fence surrounded an elegantly landscaped front yard. The girls raced down its red brick walkway past an umbrella-shaped lace-leafed Japanese maple tree and up to a front porch with three Skimmia bushes trimmed into domes on its left side and a big waterfall wisteria flowing over with purple flowers on its right side with all their heavenly scents filling the air.

"Yikes!" Tiana said coming to screeching halt. She then whirled around and ran back down the walk.

Alora froze and looked wide-eyed at her sister. "Did you see some Red Winkies coming?"

"No," she replied sheepishly, "I just realized we need to keep the gate shut so Paris doesn't race excitedly out the front door and into the street where he might get hit by a passing car."

"Oh! I'm so, so glad you remembered that about her pup."

"Me too." Tiana shut the gate securely then ran back up on the porch and grabbed a cloth out of a basket by the front door. They carefully wiped their shoes off for their aunt did not want anyone tracking dirt onto her lovely Persian carpet inside.

Tiana got her door key from her jean's pocket then paused to look at her sister. "We can't wait to tell Aunt Roleena we saw the Red Winkies, even with the solar eclipse coming today. I know she said making that interstellar call could be critical to our planet's survival, but this might be just as critical as that is."

"Are you sure? It's a tough to say, for even though we were told scary things about the Red Winkies, we also need to make serious repairs to this planet. She fears we won't be able to do this soon enough without her alien friends help. And maybe the Red Winkies won't do the bad stuff they did before."

"That seems like too big a risk to take. Because even though we don't know if they'll be as dangerous as they were before, if they are, it's not just going to hurt us. It could hurt everyone on Earth and we won't have much of a chance to fix this planet if they cause a bunch of catastrophes."

"Good grief!" Alora cried out in frustration. "It's like we're holding a knife blade with two sharp edges because if we're not careful about making the right decision, we're going to get cut."

"Or much worse, we could get cut out of the Universe altogether."

CHAPTER TWO
TIANA AND ALORA'S WARNING

Before Tiana could unlock the front door, it flew open wide. A short, granny-aged woman with curly white hair stood in the doorway looking at them through her glasses with eyes a mosaic of colors. Crinkles appeared around her face as she smiled broadly at them and the small American Eskimo dog she held seemed like he was smiling too. She began to speak but paused to see the girls were wide-eyed and breathing heavily.

"Okay my lovelies, what's wrong?" she asked as her brows arched up high. "Firstly, you two are never as mute as a rock. Secondly, no cereal in hand means there's been trouble."

"Um...well, a little bit" Alora said nervously biting on her lip," And maybe there won't be much at all Auntie Roleena. You see, we don't know for sure if we have a super big problem or lots of little ones."

"Hmmm, how intriguing since that's a lot of unsureness to put out all in one breath," Roleena said with a silly cackle.

Tiana leaned over and whispered in Alora's ear. "I know it might be a bad time to tell her, but we should tell her now."

Roleena's eye colors swirled like a kaleidoscope as she studied them. "I heard that, so just tell me what seems so bad?"

"It might not be as bad as we think," Alora said staring down at her feet. "So, it can probably wait until tomorrow."

"And tomorrow might be too late," Tiana said stiffly. "We need to tell her now so we'll know if it's no big deal or a matter of a fate close to death if not death itself."

Roleena's eyes began to glow. "What you're debating seems serious to me. So, out with it. Whose death is involved here?"

"Everyone's," she said sadly.

"Explain." Their aunt said nothing more though she tapped her foot loudly as she waited for them to speak.

"Tiana, can't we please wait and tell her after she's made her call," Alora pleaded. "It's super important to her."

"Yes, it is important," Roleena said nodding, "But I sense that you, my thoughtful girls, have something urgent to say that could be as important as that call of mine is."

"But you might have to wait years to make a connection as good as this one during this solar eclipse," she said tearily.

"Tell me quickly and I still might have time to make my call," Roleena said calmly. "That is if I don't have to spend a lot of time worming it out of you which you know I will."

"Let me tell her," Tiana begged her sister but Alora looked like it would kill her so she just groaned and said nothing.

"I sense this is a painful decision for you two, so I know just what to do. Let's talk over some nice hot chocolate. Then you can tell me what has you all stirred up." Roleena headed across the Edwardian foyer of the old house and opened a five-paneled wood door that led into a creamy-white 1930's style kitchen with bright red and white checkered curtains covering two large windows on its north side. Smiling Betty Boop figurines sat on all the shelves of the shaker style cupboards and a four-foot-tall Betty Boop waitress statue stood by the frig with an old floor-to-ceiling secretary desk with stained glass windows beside it.

The girls laid their coats on an antique oak church pew in the foyer. A large angel statue stood on a pedestal behind it, her wings spread out wide like she was welcoming you inside. They followed their aunt into the kitchen and slid into a shaker-style bench behind an 1830's English pub table with a round walnut top and decorative iron legs in its breakfast nook.

Roleena rummaged about in the kitchen taking a pot off one of the hooks over the stove and a frying pan from a cupboard by the sink. She set them on the stove then got milk, butter, three packages of cheese, and whole grain bread out of her old but reliable Frigidaire. After melting butter in the pan, she made toasted cheese sandwiches with slices of Havarti, pepper jack, and cheddar cheese. She gave these to the girls on silver rose Homer Laughlin plates then got out a jar of fudge from the small butler pantry and milk from the frig. She filled the pot on the stove with milk and stirred lots of fudge into it as she told them about a friend of hers. "You see, her cousin is famous for her pranks, but the one yesterday was so odd she didn't know what to make of it. I asked what it was and she said 'Gracious, Roleena, it was so strange maybe I shouldn't tell you, but since I already let the kittens out of the sack when she did this I—"

"Kittens?" Tiana cut in grinning. "That's not how you say that old expression. You say, 'You let the cat out of the bag'."

Roleena shrugged and grinned back. "Is that so? Well, 'she' said kittens then she said, 'My cousin looked like she saw a scary monster behind me and shot off in a flash yelling, 'It's them!'. This was peculiar because when my friend turned around to look, she didn't see anything unusual at all."

The girls looked startled but said nothing and just stared at their sandwiches. Their aunt then looked puzzled by this as she put a dollop of whipping cream on top of their cocoa and set the steaming hot cups by their plates. She made a cup of tea and set it on the other side of the pub table and sat on the high-backed chair there looking at the girls curiously. The girls each took a cautious sip of their hot chocolate looking at her worriedly.

"Tell her," Tiana murmured nudging Alora.

"No! You tell her. You saw them first."

"Well?" Roleena asked with a tiny smile upon seeing the whipping cream mustaches on their faces. She then lifted her cup of tea and took a tiny sip. "Saw who first?"

"The Red Winkies," Tiana blurted out. "At the store."

"Oh my!" she gasped softly. Her tea cup slipped from her hand and crashed to the floor then she fell over in a slump.

**

"Auntie Roleena! Say something…anything!" Alora said patting her aunt's cheeks as she lie crumpled up on the pub table in the corner of the breakfast nook.

"Here," Tiana said handing another cold cloth to her sister.

"Should we use one of the ammonia capsules in the medicine cabinet?" she asked worriedly and bit her lip. "She used them on you once when you fainted."

"I didn't faint! I was kicked in the head by that 'boy' as he pretended he was the 'Karate Kid'. Or maybe he thought he was 'Darth Vader' that time. Either one, I swear that 'Mr. Punch Happy' always causes us trouble but he thinks he's a hoot."

Alora grimaced. "You mean our cousin, Rhys,"

"The one and only, thank the All Mighty. Now, should I go get the ammonia capsules?"

"No…no ammonia…it might set my nose on fire," Roleena mumbled as she slowly sat up and rubbed her forehead leaving blue steaks of her natural skin showing through her makeup.

"Auntie Roleena! Sorry, but we didn't know what to do to waken you and we were super freaked out when you fainted," Alora said shuddering just to remember it. "Are you okay?"

"Yes, but you're a dear to be worried about your old auntie."

"But you're not old Auntie Roleena. In fact, someone who knew the other side of your family said you're fairly young."

"Young?" Tiana asked dryly. "He said she's 310,257,035 years 'young'."

"He was likely kidding me, but even if he wasn't it could be young for people from that side of Auntie's family or maybe years are different to them than to us," Alora said giggling then she looked at her aunt. "Are you sure you're all right?"

"I'll be fit as a faun in a minute. Just quite a shock. Yes, it's quite a shock. But now it's even more urgent to make my off-planet call for all our sakes." She used the table to get to her feet and steadied herself. "Hmmm, I can't leave you alone with those troublesome Red Winkies out and about. Much too risky. Now, who should I have come over? I know. Uncle Allen."

"Yes! He's wonderful," the girls agreed excitedly.

"Oh dear, but he's one of few who still knows Morse Code, and he's so brilliant that if they start flashing at him, he might figure out how to use it to talk to them. They'd tell him they're being persecuted and ask for his help. He's so nice he'd want to help and they'd capture him to use for their own purposes."

"But they just have flashing lights, not the telegraphing device that they used back in World War II," Tiana said. "Do you think they could both work that system out so quickly?"

"Actually, some people did use flashlights to communicate back then and he likely can do that. Then they'd make pitiful whining noises and dim their lights to look weak to tug on his human emotions and draw him close then latch onto him good." She sighed heavily. "I can't chance it. Hmm, I could ask Cousin Artemis to come guard you."

"Isn't she the amazing archer giant who visits you yearly? The one you said is a first cousin once removed making her our relative too and is from a great line of noble queens."

"Yes, and astute of you to remember the linage of our family on my distant side. That truly warms my heart," she said softly. "And I know you'll treat your great-aunt with the reverence she deserves for her many good deeds and not just for her nobility."

"Of course, and this is great! She's awesome! And it was so cool when she brought her two sweet lionesses with her and let them play with us!" Tiana said with unbridled enthusiasm.

Roleena cackled lightly. "Yes, but do remember they are her guardians and only acted like big tame kittens because she liked you which had them liking you too. Otherwise, you could have been their lunch because they're not always 'sweet'."

"Oh," Tiana said wide-eyed. "Then I'm glad they liked us."

"Me too!" Alora said. "But I'd think the enormous bow and quiver of fiery arrows she wore slung over her huge shoulders would be protection enough along with that giant spear she kept tightly in hand. What does kind of worry me is if she dislikes you, one word from her and the lionesses can turn super scary."

"Since she and her big cats 'do' like us there's nothing to worry about, so don't be acting so 'scaredy-of-cats," Tiana said chuckling at her pun and Alora stuck her tongue at her.

Roleena chuckled too then saw the irked look on Alora's face and said, "Sorry, my dear, but that play on words tickled me. However, I also agree with you in that Cousin Artemis's lionesses would be a scary sight for anyone to see."

"Mr. Hephaestus told me her aim with that big bow of hers is amazing and she's beat everyone who's challenged her."

"True," Roleena said cackling lightly to hear her call her giant friend 'Mr.' Hephaestus. "Actually, his title is 'Lord but he uses just 'Sir' thinking 'Lord' is too pretentious. Oh dear, I just remembered she can't come because she's helping relocate the wood elves since clear cutters came and took down their forest after some money moguls bought it. Such a shame."

"How about asking Mr. Adonis?" Alora asked brightly.

"Took a liking to him when he dropped by did you? Can't say I blame you. It's hard to not have a crush on that hunky male," Roleena said grinning as Alora blushed. "I suppose you are getting to that age, though it seems all too soon. And though it's quite natural, I feel it'd be best to have Tantalus come."

"The android? Cool!" Tiana said excitedly. "He brought some incredibly fun stuff with him last time we saw him."

"Oh, that's right," she groaned. "He burned a hole in my deck when he was here by setting off a rocket to amuse you."

"Aunt Roleena, please give him a break. He did have the lumber store deliver some new wood and fixed it right away."

"But the neighbors called the police about a noisy explosion over here and they came to check it out. If they'd found an android and pieces of a rocket I would've had to move again and I really don't want to. I like this place."

"But we hid him and covered the hole up fast with plywood from your shed then moved the deck's big outdoor rug over it. So, no one was the wiser. And I promise we won't damage anything this time. So please let him come he's a great guard."

Roleena nodded and called him then shook her head. "Sorry, he can't come. He and Lord Orion are searching Canada's far off mountains for a safe haven for some rare broad-horned elk," she said sighing. "There are few of the great ones left here that can help us since most have left this planet."

"Why?" Alora asked.

"I know the answer to that," Tiana said sadly before her aunt could reply. "I heard Great Aunt Artemis tell Aunt Roleena when she was last here that most off-world beings living here left being disgusted we aren't taking better care of our planet. They think most humans don't realize that without enough other lifeforms here the life cycle we all share will be shattered."

"Does that mean we're all goners no matter what we do?"

"She did say rather loudly that we're doomed."

"Not yet we aren't!" Roleena said and her kaleidoscope eyes flashed like fiery pinwheels.

"Truly?" Tiana asked skeptically. "I did hear her tell you we are close to using up our resources and that she seriously doubts we'll be able to save the Earth in time to keep it from dying."

"So, we 'are' truly doomed," Alora whispered and a tear rolled down her cheek, "Since there's no chance of—"

"There is still a chance, so stop all this negative thinking," Roleena cut in. "Be positive and believe we 'can' fix this. You must fill your mind with good thoughts, not bad ones to win the day. I for one know what my good thought is."

Alora sniffed and wiped away her tear. "What are they?"

"You two! I believe you will get other good, caring people like you to fix this by making everyone aware of why this must be done right away."

"Will you help us turn this around?" Alora asked.

"Of course, I will. This is also why it's so urgent for me to make my call to get us help to do this. But as you know, I haven't been able to send a clear message out of this solar system for a long time. So, we might have to do this ourselves."

"Auntie Roleena, can we truly do this on our own?"

"Anything's possible. Remember, believing we can do this can turn it into a reality. So, smile knowing full well it's true."

"You think smiling at a life-threatening time like this will help us?" Tiana asked her jaw gaping open.

"Yes. You see, many brave people were scared to do what seemed an impossible task. But they pushed their fears aside and took one step at a time to do the task. It also showed others how to be brave too. For an important life lesson to learn is to be brave even when you're scared out of your wits. And if you smile with confidence while doing daring deeds it confuses the enemy and makes them pause. So, smile bravely for me!"

Roleena saw the girls take a deep breath and then force themselves to smile. She choked back her urge to laugh as their smiles looked like Wednesday Addam's scary one on the Addam's Family but she applauded them. "That's my brave girls! Now, let's see what we can get done. And since it's best to do one thing at a time, let's tackle the Red Winkies first."

"That's a really silly name for them," Tiana said dryly.

"Right you are, but it fits them to a tee."

"I don't know. To me, they don't actually look like they wink. It looks like they're twinkling."

"That's how you see it. Others thought differently, so Red Winkies was the name that stuck. And trust me, from what I've heard, if they latch onto you, you'll feel them winking."

"I do trust you so I'll just take your word for it."

"Thanks. Now, back to finding someone you'd like to help protect you from the Red Winkies while I make my call. Think hard now. On your times with me, you met some of my friends here and a few aliens that might still be on Earth. Any ideas?"

"I wish the Pleiades sisters could because they're so kind," Alora said. "But they already came by and said they're leaving Earth until we can be good to it. Are there any wise ones left here willing to stay and help us deal with the Red Winkies?"

Roleena sighed. "Not many. In fact, Metis and Nereus, the wisest of the wise, left on the last big starship two weeks ago when Centauri let them know his clan made special rooms for them to provide for their needs. Since my serpentine friend, Nereus, needs a pool and a desert environment, and my Titan friend, Metis, a gigantic room, they felt it best to accept his offer. Of course, the Red Winkies had not invaded at that point or they would have asked Centauri to wait a few days to help us deal with any critical needs. Knowing him, he would have."

"It's unfortunate they've already left," Tiana said sadly.

"Yes, it is, and I will dearly miss their wise council."

"What about Poseidon's son? Is he still here?" Alora asked.

Roleena's face lit up. "Lord Triton? Of course! Why didn't I think of that?" She tapped her ear bud again on the transmission device inside it but after a short pause, her face clouded over.

"Auntie Roleena! What happened? Did you get a reply?"

"Alas, I did indeed. Lord Triton is busy cleaning out underwater caves and tunnels for Nessie because the waters are so polluted it's poisoning her. He said it will take two more days to finish and then he can come. I told him I had to find someone now and to just take care of Nessie. Hmmm, who is still willing to help us despite most ignoring the destruction of this lovely planet? Ah ha! I know who. Aunt Gertie!"

"Seriously?" Tiana asked groaning. "He's beyond weird and thinks that 'he' is a 'she'."

"That's not true. He knows perfectly well that he is a 'he'. He just likes to dress and act silly in hopes of making people laugh. He thinks people take themselves all too seriously."

"Come on, he's a lot of fun, Tiana," Alora said giggling. "And he puts on a great a tea party!"

"Yes, he's good at that," Roleena said smiling. "Oh my, I just thought of something." She jumped up and rushed to the kitchen and got a jar labeled 'Augmented Vitamins' out of the upper cupboard by the sink. She then handed the girls one each with a glass of water. "Now, take the pill I just gave you."

"I hate pills," Alora said wrinkling her nose. "And these don't look at all like the tasty chewable vitamins you give us."

"I know, but these are special ones to help protect your body, and with the stress of having Red Winkies here, we need all the help we can get," she said taking one herself.

"I agree," Tiana said downing hers with a sip of cocoa.

Alora scowled at her pill. "I can't. It's too big,"

"For heaven's sake, it's not that big and I swallowed mine easily, so don't act like a big baby and just do it."

"Fine." She held her nose and swallowed it with a big gulp of her drink. "There. I did it. Satisfied?" she asked crisply.

"Yes, and you were wrong. You could take it," she teased.

"And you're wrong about Aunt Gertie," Alora said firmly. "Like Auntie said, he doesn't think he's a she. He's just a big clown who loves to make people laugh."

"You're spot on target there," Roleena said with a chuckle. "He's a truly fun character who wears silly housewife dresses to get people to laugh or to shock those too stuffy to laugh."

"Or maybe he's in league with the Red Winkies," Tiana huffed. "They like shocking people too, just like they did me."

"Tiana!" Roleena and Alora gasped.

"He would never be in league with them or any nefarious sort!" Roleena said sharply. "Of that I can assure you."

"Come on, Tiana. He's loads of fun, so give way on this."

"Fine, I give. Go ahead and call him," Tiana said sighing. "Or just ear tap him one of your messages."

"No, I must contact him the Earthling way." Roleena dialed him up on the Mickey Mouse telephone on her kitchen counter. A moment later, she spoke on the phone waving a hand wildly around in the air explaining the situation to him. After a short pause she said, 'Wonderful!' then hung up the phone and looked at the girls. "What a relief. Finally good news. Gertie's coming over right now, and he's as clever as Earthlings get.

He's also brave and stronger than he looks so he won't let the Red Winkies get to you. Still, you'll need to help him too."

"Help him? How?" Alora asked.

"Well, his eyesight's fair at best, so how he's good at finding so many things is a mystery…like panning for gold or finding precious gems. He is well known as an amazing prospector, but he can miss things past the tips of his boots. I'm counting on your sharp eyesight, Tiana, to keep a look out for Red Winkies. If you spot them, let him know right away. Alora, use your keen sense of smell and tell him if you smell one of their odd scents."

"Like burnt rubber?"

"Or rotten eggs and body gases?" Tiana added.

"Yes! I'm relieved you both remember that," Roleena said.

"Auntie, do you really have to go?" Alora asked worriedly.

"Not if you truly believe you can't survive a few hours without me. But keep in mind it's more important than ever for me to make my call for everyone's sake."

"Since you put it like that, I'll make myself dig in and get through this," she said biting her lip to keep it from trembling.

"That's my brave girl!" Roleena then looked at Tiana. "How about you?"

Tiana stood tall and saluted her aunt. "Make your call!"

"I knew I could count on you two! I also know you'll take good care of my unique friends here while I'm gone."

"Of course, we will," Tiana said and Alora nodded firmly.

"Good." she said smiling softly.

They heard a loud, rumbling truck coming down their street and Roleena stood up. "Good, Gertie's here." She gave the girls a big hug and dashed to the back room that she called 'the cabin room' having filled it with favored items from her travels with old friends many who were miner's, mountain climbers, or woodsmen. An ancient ice axe and vintage climbing gear hung on the south wall by a painting of a wintery forest with antique railroad lanterns hanging on each side of it. An antique six-foot-long crosscut saw hung on the west side above an antler hatrack holding a Russian Cossack's fur hat, a coonskin hat, a vintage fedora, and a Muslim cap from Istanbul. On the east wall hung a large intricate wood carving of a raven, and one of an eagle's head backed by a moon. Above the door were two horse shoes. On the north side, wood shelves held complete sets of Star Trek shows, Star Wars movies, 'Big Bang' shows, 'Downton Abbey' shows, and the 1920's 'Thin Man' movies. The door rack held Harry Potter movies, Lord of the Ring movies, Jurassic Park movies, and an eclectic mix of a hundred others.

"Aren't you going to go out and greet him?" Alora asked running after Roleena.

"No time to. I must dash off." She rushed over to the backdoor and unlocked its deadbolt then left the key in it.

"Auntie Roleena, wait!" Alora called out as she opened the door. Her aunt turned around and Alora blew her a kiss which Roleena caught. She smacked it on her cheek and smiled at her.

"Lock up for me, my dear," she shouted and rushed off.

As Alora shut, locked and bolted the backdoor, she heard a knock on the front door. She ran to the front of the house and found her sister standing by it guardedly.

"Open the door," Alora said sharply when she did nothing.

Tiana shook her head and stood in the way like a roadblock.

"Argh! Move over and I'll do it." Tiana still did not move.

"Girls! It's me…your Aunt Gertie," came a masculine voice.

"Hi, Aunt Gertie, just a minute." Alora shouldered her sister aside. Tiana glared at her and stomped off into the kitchen. Alora just shrugged and undid the brass chain on the door, pulled back the bolt, and removed the heavy brace against it. Then putting on a big smile, she threw the door open.

"Rushin' to answer ain't wise to do. How'd ye know it was really me?" a brawny man said standing on the porch with his hands on his hips. He wore a polka dot dress, a flowered shawl, and a frilly bonnet topped his head. A total mismatch to his outfit was the jeans underneath and the hiking boots he wore.

"Um, well…it's because there's 'no one' that sounds like you, Aunt Gertie," Alora said.

"You still should have checked it out first through the upper window by the door," Tiana shouted from the kitchen.

"I do know his voice," she snapped and as he walked into the foyer, she quickly pulled the door shut and bolted it.

"She must be worried there might've been a sneaky, no good sideswiping varmint faking my voice. Though a voice is dern hard to fake. Still, it is best to play it safe, young un." Gertie looked around. "Where's yer sis hiding out?"

"I'm 'not' hiding. I'm sitting in the kitchen by the pub table," Tiana said taking a sip of her now cold hot chocolate. "By the way, Aunt Roleena already left."

"Yep, she told me she was skedaddling out of here straight away cuz' she needed to make that call of hers pronto like."

"Aunt Gertie, there's more going on than that," Alora said.

"Well doggies, from the look on yer face, little lady, I'd say somethin' wicked be coming so go ahead and spill the beans."

"I will, I'm just shocked Auntie Roleena didn't tell you."

"Tell me what?"

"The Red Winkies are here!"

"Dag nab it!" Gertie sat down hard on the church pew in the foyer then swiped off his bonnet and fanned his face with it. "She did say bad news was heading our way and that there's real bad news. Sorrowful bad news indeed."

Tiana walked back out to the foyer. "What should we do?"

"Lay low," Gertie said slapping his knee.

"Aunt Gertie! You can't actually mean that."

"Gee whillickers, why can't I?"

"Because we have to help get rid of them if we're going to keep Earth safe!"

"Might be too late fer that. Earth's an awful sick planet 'cuz there's too many dunderheads in charge that don't give a hoot about nothin' but their pocketbooks. Heard yer aunt say at our last roundup with her straight shootin' off-world friends that she asked the Greenie's way out yonder to pack you girls off to a safe place if it all goes down the drain here."

"Pack us off where?" Alora asked wide-eyed.

"To a safe planet if this whole shebang turns toxic."

"Toxic! You mean like it becoming deadly poisonous?"

"Yes siree, missy. Ye see, when it finally smacks the people in control here in the face that they waited too long to fix things, they'll get all lathered up and start the blame game. Then the crazy ones will blow each other up and the world with 'em."

"Then we have to find a way to stop that from happening!"

"Why go to a heap of trouble when we can up and leave?"

"Because it's our home!" Alora gasped.

"But yer aunt can find you a new one that's real purdy."

"I love this one!"

Gertie smiled at her softly. "Yer such a sweet thing you'd love anywhere you was, and yer aunt will be sure it's a place they respect and care fer the planet, not just make themselves rich and powerful. Where folks give a hoot about all the lives in God's creation, not just themselves. Still, it's a cryin' shame to lose this beautiful planet. Not many like it. You'd think the big shots running this place would reckon we need clean air, land and water to keep it going, but it seems they're just numskulls."

"But Aunt Gertie, we want to save 'our' planet," Tiana said.

"Our deck of cards is about played out at this here point…" Gertie paused as he saw the dismal look on the girl's faces. "But I be simple folk, and only the All Mighty knows fer' sure if this here games over. Who knows. With the right kind of deal, we might get a better hand and it might play out differently."

"So, are you leaving too?" Alora asked her lip trembling.

"Me? Nah, I like a good do or die fight with terrible odds. To me this one's gonna be a tougher task than hogtying a brahma bull that just ran through a spiney cactus patch."

"Aunt Gertie, I'm scared and you make it sound hopeless."

"He's yanking your chain," Tiana told her. "He already said he's going to stay and help save the planet 'and' Aunt Roleena said we can still do this. So, let's prove her right. Isn't that part true, Aunt Gertie?" She then pinned him with a knowing look.

Gertie chortled. "Yep, and from the look in yer eye if I say otherwise, you'll hogtie me and tickle my toes until I admit it."

"Count on it," she said trying not to smile but she wound up grinning and liking him a bit. "Now, what should we do first?"

"As fer me, I got to wait a bit 'cuz my mind's nagging me real hard about something important I need to be remembering."

"Can it wait? Because it's been made clear to us that we've already waited too long and need to do something now."

"True as that is, I first got to git my brain to cough up what I forgot to tell you. I know I must recollect what it is before I do anything else." Gertie scratched his head then stuck his bonnet back on. "Dag nab it. Seems like the more I try to pull it in, the further it skedaddles away. But don't you fret. I'll get it back yet. Just give me a second to lasso it."

Gertie squeezed his eyes shut and his face scrunched up. The girls then waited with baited breath for him to remember what he needed to tell them. But after a several minutes he was still silent and all puckered up.

"Well?" Tiana asked tapping a foot impatiently.

"Hold yer horses," he said when suddenly there was a hard knock, knock, knock on the door.

The girls froze in place and Gertie's eyes flew open.

"Well, howdy!" He jumped off the church bench onto his feet and stared at the tall, broad-shouldered shadow of a person on the other side of the frosted-window on the front door. The girl's gaped as he rushed to the door and unbolted it then gasped in horror as he flung it open.

"Jumpin' jiminy, I knew I plum forgot somethin'. Well, don't just stand there glowering at me. Come on in!"

CHAPTER THREE
RASCALLY RHYS

"Rhys!" Tiana hissed angrily and her hands balled into tight fists as she turned to Gertie. "What is 'he' doing here?"

"I'd say that's plum obvious. It's cuz I brought him with me," Gertie said waving the young, unusually tall teenager towards him. "It's okay, boy. Come on in."

"Yeah, come on in so I can sock you in the nose."

Rhys stood a foot taller than Tiana, but seeing her furious face he backed up. "Calm down. I'm not here to fight you."

"Too bad, because I've been preparing for the day I could pay you back for all the nasty tricks you've played on us," she said taking a defensive Tai Kwando stance.

"Pull yer spurs back, missy. There's no need to get hostile. Hmm…well doggies, maybe there is. I did hear tell from yer Aunt Roleena he's earned this a mite. Heh, heh, heh," Gertie chuckled. "He does get rascally at times. Well, don't just gawk at her boy. Come on in." Rhys didn't move so he grasped his shoulder and pulled him inside then jerked the door shut and locked it. "Trust me when I say this, young fella. It's heaps more dangerous outside than inside right now."

"Aunt Gertie, whyever would you bring 'him' here?" Tiana asked in a fierce growl. "Aunt Roleena said the river Styx down in the underworld would have to freeze before 'he' could step foot in her house again. You see, last time 'he' was here he set fire to her house and used my good wool skirt to fan the flames which turned it to ashes…my skirt, not the house."

"I wasn't trying to burn down her house," Rhys protested. "I lit a kerosene lamp in the basement and accidently dropped it. That started the fire. Your skirt happened to be in the laundry near me, so I used it to put the fire out, not to fan it!"

"Hard to believe, since before that you locked me and Tiana in the big butler pantry in the downstairs hallway when we went to get some canned foods out of it," Alora said huffing.

"I didn't know you were there when I did that."

"The screaming and banging on the door should have been a clue," Tiana said rolling her eyes.

"I'd…uh…well, I didn't see you in there as I closed it or know it was self-locking. Nor did I hear you yelling because I was in a rush to get to the bathroom," Rhys said but then he covered a smirky grin with the back of his hand.

"Aunt Gertie, he can't stay here. He has to leave."

Tiana nodded sharply. "I agree. So would Auntie Roleena."

"Hey, young fillies, hear me out. I got charge of this rascal when his folks went on a long trip and they just recently went incommunicado. Now, ye told me about them Red Winkies I fear they might've caused that. So, I'm keeping Rhys with me 'til I hear from them since I won't leave him alone and risk them messing with him too."

"It might serve him right to see what it's like to be messed with since he's messed with us so many times," Tiana huffed.

"What tomfoolery. Ye have a good heart, not a mean one, so I know ye don't truly cotton to that idea. Now, I ask ye to keep a cool head and not get your knickers in a twist."

"Really?" she sputtered. "Knickers in a twist? Where do you get all these weird sayings? We don't have any knickers. Now, make him go away. He's a danger to us all, including our aunt's dog, Paris. We're all mad at him and for good reasons."

"She's right," Alora said. "He thought it was funny to let Paris out the front gate then shut it to see if he could find a way to get back in. He could've been stolen or run over by a car. Auntie Roleena was so mad her hair hissed at him. And that's only one of the reasons she does not want him here."

"Even so, missies, there's a mess of trouble at large now. So, I know she'd rather have him safe here with me."

"No! Or 'we' won't be safe!" the girls both shouted.

"But he's family and all alone, so we need to work out a way you'd agree to let me kept him here."

"Well, since he's super sneaky and into all kinds of mischief, you'd have to keep him handcuffed to you," Alora said, "

"Or Velcro him to the ceiling like Aunt Roleena said she'd do if he ever showed up here again," Tiana said.

"Just try it and see what I do to get even," Rhys snapped.

The girls shrieked angrily then took a swing at him but Gertie snagged them away from Rhys and they only hit air.

"All of you will stop this mulish behavior! Otherwise, I will Velcro you 'all' to the ceiling. Now, go sit yourselves down in the kitchen and let's work out a truce." Gertie herded them into the nook guiding the girls to the bench behind the pub table and Rhys to a chair on the other side then stood over them. "Now, before this gets out of hand…" he paused as the phone rang.

Alora stood and reached over Rhys to pick up the Micky Mouse phone's receiver. "Aunt Roleena's residence," she said politely. "Yes, she's, I mean 'he' is here. Who's calling please? Oh my. Yes, I'll hand him the phone right away. It's for you Aunt Gertie. The lady on the line says she's Lady Maia."

Gertie's eyes flew open and he whispered, "She's a Pleiades sister and one of the head honcho's out in the stars." He then took the receiver from Alora. "Yep, this is Gertie, Lady Maia. Sure, you can shoot the info ye have straight at me." A moment later, he stumbled back sitting down hard on top of Rhys.

"Ooof!" Rhys grunted squeezing out from underneath him. As he stood up, he saw Gertie rub his forehead furiously and for several minutes all they heard him say was; 'Yep. Yep. Yep.'

"I got it, but it's hit me hard as a fry pan in the face," Gertie rasped then he hung the phone up looking dazed. "This is worse than finding an ole griz' bear had wondered inside my cabin."

"What's worse?" Rhys asked frowning.

"Sorry to give ye all bad news, but ye best be told. Yer Aunt Roleena got to her send point area and made her call but soon got cut off. They sent a big local star fella straight out there to see what went wrong but she was gone. So, now she's missing."

"Has she been kidnapped?" Tiana asked with alarm.

"It seems likely since them Red Winkies is loose here. Now, I'm so mad I could stomp me a mud hole and kick it dry."

"Would...would they kill her?" Alora choked out tearily.

"Nah, Winkies ain't that foolish. No use to them dead. And she might've seen them coming and hid somewhere safe."

"Aunt Gertie, do you really believe that?" Tiana asked and Gertie shrugged then looked away. "No, I can tell you don't. Besides, I know if she was in hiding, she would've found a way to call us knowing how worried we'd all be."

"Since she didn't, it means we need to find her," Alora said.

"Of course, we do, but we need a bigger posse and lots more protection before we can do that," Gertie said pointedly.

"But Auntie Roleena tried to find us a big-time protector and everyone was busy or gone. Oops, sorry," Alora said wincing. "I don't want to hurt your feelings since she didn't call you first. As for me, I think calling you was a great idea."

"It's all okay, little lady," Gertie said then he scowled at Rhys as he snickered. "And I thank ye for yer confidence in me and fer caring about my feelings. Truth is her star visitors have powers we aren't gifted with. Still, though I be a crafty old fella, I'll need yer help. So, let's all put our heads to good use."

"What can we do to help?"

"You can..." Gertie paused as Paris dashed out and barked angrily at the front door. Gertie clomped out to its foyer and pulled back the edge of a lace curtain hanging over the window on the upper half of the front door peeking out as the girls came up behind him. Rhys went to the first landing to the left of the door and looked out the high window there. He then gasped.

"Winkies," Gertie whispered putting a finger to his lips to show them all to be silent then waved the three cousins back into the kitchen. As he closed the door between the kitchen and foyer, Paris rushed in and growled at the windows over the sink so he pulled the curtains shut in case the Winkies came there.

"We need to lay low and keep calm 'cuz them Red Winkies are hovering smack dab in front of this house. Keep it firm in yer noggin they can sense if we get too excited, be it good or bad, 'cuz of the extra energy we give off when doing that."

"So, that sparkly red cloud is the Red Winkies?" Rhys asked.

"Yep, that be them fer sure."

"They don't look smart," he said dryly. "Even the name 'Red Winkie' is dumb. I doubt they can do much harm to us."

"They're a heap more powerful than you know, boy."

"I'm not a boy," Rhys huffed standing up. "I'm a man."

The girls burst out laughing and Gertie grinned. "Seems we disagree with the manly label ye gave yerself. Fact is, that there is something you must earn, boy," Gertie said rising up on his stout boot tips to look Rhys straight in the eye.

"I disagree," he huffed but he blushed and looked away.

"Lying to yerself only fools you. Fer no one with a lick of good sense will agree with ye yet. If I were you, I'd go about earning it 'cuz…" Gertie paused and pulled the kids down to the floor as bright red winking lights appeared outside the kitchen windows. "I reckon them purdy curtains are too thin to block the heat waves our bodies give off, so we best get to a room with thicker coverings."

"There's a heavy-duty light blocking shade in the back-room auntie calls her cabin room," Alora whispered.

"Good. Let's skedaddle over there." Gertie froze and slapped his cheek. "What am I blathering? We need to go real slow so they can't easily sense us."

They all eased their way into the back room and quickly hit the floor as they saw the window shade was still up. Worse, the Red Winkies were approaching so they hunkered down in front of the big couch under the window to hide. Gertie put a finger to his lips and they waited silently as the lights passed by what was fortunately the only window in the room. Tiana then rose and pulled the shade down and they got up. Gertie and the girls sat on the couch as Rhys sat on a rustic hand-crafted maple-framed chair with willow bough backs and seats.

"Aunt Gertie, were there any Red Winkies at your house when you drove over here?" Tiana asked.

"Nope. I'd never have endangered ye by coming here if they already were there when I was packing up to leave."

"Then how do you think they found us?"

Gertie pulled thoughtfully on his bearded chin. "That's a puzzle. I reckon they were just out trolling around this area."

"Do you think they followed us home from Big Mama's Market?" Alora asked Tiana worriedly.

"So, you two saw them earlier!" Rhys said.

"Of course, we saw them," Tiana growled. "How else could we have warned Aunt Roleena about this if we hadn't?"

"Which likely means you led them here. Real bright."

"Look 'Mr. Smarty Pants', it's a good thing Tiana did spot them," Alora said quickly defending her sister, "Or we might've become their zombies."

"They can't make you zombies," Gertie said. "Well, not that I know of. But they can control yer movements. Ye see, here's how Roleena's professor friend explained it to me. Our muscles are controlled by what he called 'electrical impulses'. Being the Winkies are electric critters, they can connect up to these and control them. Yer aunt also said the star people told her they can also magnify good or bad feelings in an unwary mind, but can't control yer thoughts or add more stuff to them."

"Hear that, Alora?" Tiana said. "I guessed right about that."

"Don't get too cocky girl. They are dangerous tricky and can control planes, trains and automobiles, even how much we hear over phone lines. Fact is, they can control anything that runs on the energy stuff we call 'electricity'."

"How about smart phones?" Rhys asked.

"Good question, and yer aunt asked the Professor about that. He said he thought they can only use them if they're attached to the one being used. Talking about phones reminds me that I need to ask ye if one of ye has a cellphone I can borrow."

Tiana looked stunned. "You don't have one?"

"Nope. Came from a time they didn't have none and haven't felt no big need to get one of them highfaluting things. Well, not until now. Do ye have one I can borrow fer a bit?"

"I do." Alora pulled hers out and showed him how to punch up telephone numbers on it. He watched closely then nodded. "This phone's called a 'smart phone'," she explained.

"Smart or not, any not hooked directly to electricity and free of having Red Winkies stuck on them will likely be safe to use."

"I've also got one," Tiana said offering hers. "Aunt Roleena got them for all her nieces and nephews so we can get a hold of her or each other if we need help."

"Yep, sounds like something she'd do to keep ye all safe." Gertie looked at Rhys. "So, young fella, do you have one too?"

"Um…yes, I do. But I need mine in case my parents call me whenever they get to a point they can reach me again."

"I surely get that," he said sincerely then turning to the girls he took Tiana's phone. "Thanks, young un, and Alora, you keep yers on ye in case we need to get in touch real fast." He winced as Rhys clutched his phone tightly knowing how worried he was after not hearing from his parents yesterday, since they had always called him daily when they were on trips.

"Now what?" Alora asked.

"I'd best look at why Paris is growling at 'this' window." He peeked under the shade and jerked back. "Whoa, time to get out of Dodge fer there's a heap of tiny red varmints churning around out there like a mad storm cloud. So, listen up. I need to lead them away from here before they find a way to get inside."

"How are you going to do that?" Alora asked trembling.

"Easy. Me and Old Faithful will scoot off and go lose them far away from here. Then just to be safe, you all get out of here fer a bit and find yerselves a place to lay low until I get back."

"Who's Old Faithful?" Tiana asked.

"That be my truck," he said proudly. "Like me, it's old and tough. Yep, sad as it is, them Red Winkies know we're here."

"I'd say from what you just saw that's rather obvious."

"True, which is why I need to get them off yer scent." He stomped to the front door flouncing his skirt like a bullfighter's cape and the three cousins followed him. "Lock this up tight right behind me, and do it quick." He then tied his bonnet tight to his head and began to unbolt the door.

"Aunt Gertie, stop!" Alora rasped like she was in pain. "Without you we'll be defenseless against the Red Winkies."

"No, you won't," an odd buzzing voice said. "Roleena told me if Gertie had to leave, to tell you she left you gifts to protect you from enemies while she was gone. Then if trouble came, to also explain that these protective devices are hidden in what you girls call 'the dungeon'. Now, go see what she left you."

"Whoever is speaking, show yourself now!" Rhys demanded as he wildly looked around the room with alarm.

"I am doing so," a high-pitched buzzing voice said.

"It's Harold!" Alora and Tiana cheered happily.

Rhys looked around but saw no one at all. "Where are you?" he sputtered angrily. Then seeing a big fly zoom past his nose, he followed it into the kitchen and tried to swat it.

"No!" the girls screamed and tackled him to the floor.

"Let me go!" he said surprised by how fast they had taken him down. "Who's Harold?"

"The one and only talking fly," Tiana said as she stood up.

"I'm not the only one. All my certain kind of kin can talk," Harold buzzed in perfect English. "We just don't speak in your language unless we want to talk to you."

"Well said!" came a lisping voice from the hallway between the kitchen and the cabin room. Paris quickly jumped up on the bench in the kitchen nook and growled towards the hallway.

"Stop fussing, little dog! Roleena forbade us from eating you," another voice rasped. "So, you can rest easy."

Rhys spun around in surprise to hear the two voices in the house's hallway. He tried spotting who was there but made no move to go look and though a foot taller he hid behind Gertie.

"Our pesky cousin grew a lot since we saw him last, for he's now way taller than Aunt Gertie. But as big as he is, he's using him as a shield," Alora said to her sister and giggled. Kassidy then chuckled and a loud raspy chuckling came from the hall.

"Not funny," Rhys said frowning when Gertie also chuckled. "Come on. Whoever is out there, show yourselves."

"Why thank you for the invitation," came a hissed reply.

Two huge reticulated pythons slithered part way into the kitchen, their long bodies stretched out across the short hall and on into the backroom. Rhys gaped and gazed at them in horror, but Gertie and the girls grinned. The pythons both hissed a snaky 'greetingsss' to Rhys but he remained speechless.

"So, human boy it seems you cannot understand us even though we spoke your language," a fourteen-foot-long albino python with purple and pink saddle marks on her back said in a perfect Bristish accent as she slithered fully into the room.

"That is why I rarely speak to humans, Dodona. It is a waste of time. Most go into shock when I do and cannot talk at all," a sixteen-foot-long brown and black reticulated python said as it joined the other one speaking in the same clear Bristish accent.

"Those…those snakes can also talk!" Rhys gasped breaking free of his trance-like state, but as they came close to study him, he waved his hands wildly at them to keep them away.

"Pointing out the obvious," Dodona said wryly, "Pythia, is he as dimwitted as he sounds?"

"Sssss," she lisped wriggling close to Rhys and arching up to look him in the eyes. "Not truly. I see he has hidden potential. He's still immature, but with hard positive work, he could bring out his good untapped talents."

"Of course I can," Rhys said kicking at the snake in alarm.

"He is rather rude," Pythia rasped jerking back to avoid his foot. "I might have given him more credit than he is due."

Rhys kicked at Pythia again and Dodona slid up next to her. "Human boy, if you do that again, you are asking for trouble and I will be sure you get it," she hissed sharply.

"Stop kicking at them!" Tiana yelled shaking her fist at him. "Come on, Alora, let's get our friends out of his foot's range."

Her sister nodded and the girls walked over to the pythons. With a big 'ooof', they each picked up one of the snakes and looped them around their necks and arms. Tiana held Pythia with her head up high, but being twelve-feet in length her tail flowed across the floor. Alora looped Dodona around her neck twice but even being three inches taller than her sister with her fourteen-foot length Dodona's tail still touched the floor.

"Sorry, Dodona," Alora said sighing. "He's just a rude boy who's being mean because he's super scared of you."

"But since he is being mean, can't I just bite him a tiny bit to teach him to behave?"

"No," she sighed. "We still need to be nice."

"Very well, but that is disappointing."

"Good females," Harold said flying over the snakes, "and I'm speaking to you Squamata Serpentetes. We must get back to business. Please go help these two Homosapien females and male retrieve their special gifts that Roleena got for them to protect them if they ran into serious trouble without her here."

"Special gifts?" Tiana asked looking surprised as did Alora.

"Yes, she told me she got them to help with a big challenge that was coming this way soon. Obviously, that is now. Still, I find it odd that she even left one for that impish human, Rhys."

"How did she know he'd be here right now?" Alora asked.

"Girls, Rhys, lady snakes, and Harold, listen up," Gertie said. "I must bid farewell to ye before ye get into that. The Red Winkies are gathering their forces outside, so I must go draw them away. Keep in mind them electric critters are dern smart and will eventually find a way in here, likely on this house's electrical wires. So, turn off all the lights or anything electric."

"What about the frig? All the food will spoil if we do that."

"No problem. Roleena put a back-up propane unit on it so I'll switch it over." He then flipped a switch on the wall by it.

"How will we see when it gets dark?" Alora asked.

"The old-school way."

"How's that?"

"Candles." he said with a quirky grin.

"Oh, I forgot about those." She ran to the butler pantry and returned with a box of candles and several candle holders.

"Good. Now, before I skedaddle, find me three big dolls or teddy bears to use. Not little ones, it must be big ones. I also want ye to give me some clothes from all three of you. Then we'll bake them in her propane oven on low fer a few minutes."

"Why do you want to bake our clothes?" Tiana asked.

"Cuz they've likely sensed our body heat by now. So, I need to dress them in warm cloths to imitate that then I'll carry them off quick-like with me."

"Oh, I get it. That's to fool the Red Winkies into thinking we're with you because they can't see us, but they can sense our body's heat."

"Yep! That's about sums it up. Let's just hope it works."

"Sounds like a dumb idea to me," Rhys said tersely.

"Then offer a better one. Well? Go on, spit one out," Gertie said pinning him with an exasperated look. "Do ye?"

"Errr...well no."

"Then be nice or I'll feed ye to pythons gals myself!"

"Okay, I will!" Rhys rasped shivering a bit as he glanced at the pythons. "Ew! You two slimy snakes can stop looking at me so hungrily. I'm not going to be your dinner."

"We most certainly are not slimy," Pythia hissed pointedly.

"Not at all, but he would be if we swallow him whole and then spit him out," Dodona replied.

"That's really creepy, so stop saying stuff like that!" Rhys said squeezing behind the chair by the pub table.

"We will if you treat us respectfully," she rasped crisply.

"Rhys, I do insist you be respectful to Pythia and Dodona, or else. Do you hear me loud and clear, boy?" Gertie growled.

"Yes," he said gulping as Gertie glared at him. "I mean, yes sir. I promise to be respectful."

"Good. Now, everyone play nice, 'cuz I truly must get going pronto." He turned to the girls. "Alora, Tiana, I need those big dolls or teddy bears now."

The girls gently set the pythons on the floor and ran upstairs. They returned a few minutes later with two three-foot-tall dolls, a four-foot-tall teddy bear, two sweaters and two pairs of jeans.

"Rhys, did you bring yer clothes in with ye?" Gertie asked.

"No. They're out in your truck. Should I run and get them?"

"No, it's too dangerous to do that. Give me yer coat."

"I'll get cold out there without that!"

"It's that or your pants and shirt. Yer choice."

"Here," Rhys grumbled but he handed his coat to Gertie.

"Girls, put these clothes in the oven away from the hot coils fer three minutes at a smidge bit under a hundred degrees."

They nodded and set the heat then carefully laid them in the oven away from the hot elements. Five minutes later with the clothes heated up the girls dressed the dolls and teddy bear in the warm clothes.

"Wish me a heap of luck!"

"Good luck!" the girls said heartily and kissed his cheek.

"From me too," Rhys mumbled to everyone's surprise.

"Thank ye all. Now, I will delegate command," Gertie said. "Rhys, you must grin and bear it since I'm putting the girls in charge. Pythia, Dodona, if he gets out of line with the girls you can set him straight. Hear that, boy?"

Rhys nodded but said nothing until the pythons hissed at him. "Yes sir, I heard," he coughed out.

"Good! Then off I go. Be careful and all of you, stay sharp."

"Aunt Gertie, when you come back, we'll throw you a super nice tea party, okay?" Alora asked worriedly.

"Of course! Wouldn't miss out on that fer anything."

Alora and Tiana then ran and flung their arms around him telling him over and over to be careful and to not get hurt.

"Now don't ye go all soft right now fer that won't cut and stack the wood. I need ye to stay strong as steel," Gertie said hugging them back then he went over to Rhys and side-hugged him. "Be nice fer a change, 'cuz honey gets ye a whole lot more than vinegar." With a wave, he quickly got the warmly dressed dolls and teddy bear then opened the front door and strode out across the porch.

Alora called out, "Wait Aunt Gertie. Catch this."

As he looked over his shoulder, she blew him a kiss which he caught in one of his big, rough hands.

"Thanks," he chuckled. "Now, lock up behind me quick."

The girls did as he asked then ran to the parlor with Rhys right behind them. They heard Gertie's boots clomping down the sidewalk as they peeked out the parlor's front window through a slit in the blinds. He briskly walked across the street to his truck, Old Faithful and as he pulled open the door of the truck it creaked loudly. He then put the dolls and teddy bear on the front seat on the passenger side next to a big backpack they all knew would be filled with items he might in an emergency. The door creaked again as he shut it and they heard the truck's starter screech sharply. Old Faithful rumbled to life and shook as the engine roared loudly. A moment later, the truck lurched away from the curb and rattled north up the street.

Two huge cloud clusters of Red Winkies then came flashing into Roleena's front yard. They quickly stretched into two long bands and shot after him like huge, red sparkling missiles.

"Wow! Did you see the way those Red Winkie clouds changed into big, blazing streaks of light and then shot off after Gertie?" Rhys asked in awe.

"Yes," Tiana choked out as she grimaced. "We saw that."

"And it was super, super scary," Alora whispered.

"Oh...I guess it was at that," Rhys said wincing to see the pain that was clearly written all over their faces.

Mere seconds later, the Red Winkies glow was out of sight. The three cousins slowly walked into the old parlor by the entryway. They slumped down onto the antique couch with its huge rolled arms, deep, thick cushions, and a crown-shaped back covered in deep red velvet. None of them said a word.

A few minutes later, a thundering boom shook them up and they all jumped to their feet. Forgetting how much danger they were in, they ran and unlocked the front door then flung it open and raced out to the sidewalk in hopes of seeing what happened.

Far in the distance, a big blaze of red light and smoke rose high in the air above the hundred-year-old elm and oak trees several streets north of them. They all gasped in fear. For they all knew the flash came from the direction Gertie had driven.

CHAPTER FOUR
GERTIE'S SACRIFICE

"Brave, brave Aunt Gertie," Alora choked out with a sob.

Tiana just swallowed hard and nodded.

"Or it was just plain crazy for him rush out to do this all alone?" Rhys growled in frustration.

"He did it to protect us!" Alora gasped and slapped his face.

"Hey, I know that so back off," he said rubbing his cheek.

Alora saw he truly looked sad and calmed down. "Okay."

"I'm just hoping it was Aunt Gertie's plan to blow up the Red Winkies and it wasn't him and his truck," Tiana said.

"Me too, because it sounded super bad."

"True, but he's a rugged a man like John Wayne was," Rhys said firmly then he smiled slightly. "Well…minus the dress."

"You think he's okay?" she asked so hopefully he winced.

"Of course." He then nudged them towards the door. "Go get your coats and some snacks since Gertie said to go somewhere else to lie low in case the Red Winkies come back."

"Okay, but you're not the boss," Tiana said. "We are."

"Not anymore, because I'm taking charge now. Face it. I'm bigger and stronger than you, so it's best that I take charge," he said boastfully as he headed back into the house.

"We cannot let him start bossing us around," Tiana spat out angrily and the girls waited a bit before they went back inside.

"Then let's ignore him and do what we think's best," Alora said and they went into the parlor seeing that Rhys had gone in the kitchen. A minute later, he came into the parlor huffing.

"Hey, like I said, I'm in charge. So, get some snack food together for us since you likely know where it's kept."

"Aunt Gertie put us in charge, so we are not going to take any orders from you," Tiana said and Alora nodded sharply.

"Then I'll make a mess pulling stuff out of the cupboards and drawers as I do it myself," he said smiling wickedly.

"Not if I take you out first," she replied pointedly as she moved away from Alora and took Tai Kwando stance.

Rhys laughed haughtily at her. "You're crazy if you think your puny attack moves could stop me."

"Stopping you can be easily accomplished," Pythia hissed sliding out from under the parlor's couch and arching several feet up in the air in front of Rhys. His eyes bulged out in shock and it was obvious that he had not seen the pythons go in there. Narrowing her eyes, Pythia leaned her head towards him and flicked her tongue. "Girls, I'd be glad to assist you with this problem boy if you need me to."

"Me too! Me too!" Dodona rasped cheerily as she slithered out from under the couch. "I want to give him a great big hug!"

"No!" Rhys blurted nervously and appeared to truly regret he had not noticed the two pythons were in the parlor with the girls. He jumped behind Alora and looked over her shoulder. "Wait! They're right. Gertie did put them in charge here."

"I'm glad to hear some good sense coming from you," Pythia said easing back, but Dodona then arched up high.

"You stay in line or I'll deal with you in ways you will never forget." She lunged around Alora and snapped her jaws at him.

"I will, I will," Rhys said moving to Alora's other side.

Harold flew into the room and buzzed around their heads. "Back to business. These youngsters need to go find the special gifts Roleena left them if trouble came their way, and it has."

"The gifts! I was so worried about the Winkies going after Aunt Gertie I forgot about them," Tiana said. "Didn't you tell us that our aunt hid them down in the dungeon?"

"Yes, I did," he buzzed.

"It's a basement, not a dungeon," Rhys said haughtily.

"But if you lock your live meals down there until you're ready to eat it can be," Dodona hissed gazing at him hungrily.

"Don't look at me like I'm on the dinner menu," he said backing up until the wall stopped him. "Be nicer."

"How about like this?" she asked batting her eyes at him.

"Enough teasing. Let's go," Pythia told Dodona firmly. "Do you want to show them the way, Harold?" she asked the fly, but the amused tone she used showed she knew the answer was no.

"Not a chance. There are too many spiders down there!" the fly buzzed shrilly. "Making it creepier for all of you as Roleena told me she hid the gifts way back under the east side."

"A nasty area," Dodona choked out like having swallowed a rotten rodent, "I already dislike how chilly it is down there."

"I find it unpleasant too, but we promised Roleena to help so we will. So, come and let us do this quickly," Pythia hissed nobly and she glided towards the back room.

Dodona began slithering after her but stopped and looked back at the girls. "And that onery boy must also come since Roleena has a gift for him too." She then waited for them.

Tiana dashed across the parlor and formal dining room to the short hallway leading into the back room. She caught up with Pythia as she slipped through the dog door and being slender, she just grinned and did so too. Alora walked to the room with Rhys shadowing her. Dodona stayed behind him to his dismay. Alora unlocked the door's deadbolt and pocketed the key. She waited for Rhys and Dodona to go through then shut the door. They crossed the wood deck and went down its stairs to a brick patio leading around its north side to a metal basement door. Pythia and Tiana had waited for them, and Tiana opened the door and went down five steep stairs into an oddly shaped basement that had a low-ceiling with exposed rafters.

She led them down a narrow corridor lined by three-foot tall concrete walls with three-foot-tall crawl spaces on both sides of it. A low-watt bulb overhead put out a meager amount of light and they could only vaguely make out that the upper areas were packed full of large boxes, tools and other tarp-covered items.

"What a mess!" Rhys griped gazing around at the boxes and other curious odds and ends. "How will we ever find the gifts Aunt Roleena left us here?"

"I will guide you to their location," Pythia rasped slithering down to the end of the corridor that ran one third of the length of the house into an open space the size of a small room.

Another dim light on the right side of the large open space revealed shelves lined the south side filled with rolled up tents, sleeping bags, ice axes, crampons, bins of mountain climbing tools, and survivor manuals. Rhys' eyes widened to also see a lot of crates there glowed an eerie green, yellow, or blue.

"What's in those crates?" Rhys asked so warily Dodona chuckled. "Come on, I heard one huff and another hum, and some are making such weird chittering noises, it's spooky."

"No need to worry. Those items are well secured," Pythia told him as she slid over to the eastern retaining wall.

Rhys followed but paused and grinned as he saw racks full of wine in front of the south wall. "This is the only good thing I've seen down here," he said reaching for a bottle.

Dodona hissed and nipped his behind so he jerked back.

"I was just looking."

"Then keep your hands to yourself and do just that," she hissed and Pythia bobbed her head sharply from where she waited at the east side of the open space by the four-foot-tall retaining wall there. An enormous, old oil furnace sat against it making grumbling noises and behind it was a dark, foreboding crawl space a bit under three-feet-high.

"How will we find the gifts when there's no light in that space at all?" Rhys asked frowning.

The girls laughed lightly and pulled out flashlights.

"Next time, you should think ahead," Tiana said grinning.

"Okay, smarty pants, do you know where the gifts are?"

"No," she said shaking her head as did Alora.

"I will guide you there," Pythia said sliding up the retaining wall and on into the crawl space.

"I'm so not going in that dark, creepy place," Rhys said shaking his head.

Tiana shrugged. "Suit yourself, but I'm not bringing your gift back." She pulled gloves from her pocket and put them on then climbed up on the ledge. The area was so low she had to follow Pythia on her hands and knees as the python slid across a thick moisture-barrier sheet. Alora followed right behind her and they went across a long, empty space until Pythia reached three small to large packages and stopped.

"These could be your gifts, but check the tags on them first before you open any of them," Pythia rasped, "Because Roleena marks everything in here so she can easily identify them."

"Okay," the girls both said but as Alora checked a package she turned to her sister. "Hey Tiana, I need your help reading this because the print's so small that with my eyesight I can't make it out. If these 'are' our packages, then if you take yours, I can probably shoulder bump both mine and Rhys' up front."

"Alora!" Tiana said, "He can very well get his own gift."

"But he refused to come and his might have something we need to help us find Auntie Roleena," she said apologetically. "Or something to help us know what happened to Aunt Gertie,".

"Argh! Rhys, get your lazy behind up here and help. Otherwise, we'll claim your box if we have to bring it out."

"Then I'll just take it from you," he said brazenly.

"As if I'd let you," came a hiss near his ear.

Rhys shrieked to find Dodona right next to him. He took a deep breath and then looked at her. "Shouldn't you be up there with your snake friend?" he asked nervously.

"No, I'll stay here and guard the girls from a poor mannered human boy," she hissed. "And after hearing the rude action you threatened to take, I might just enjoy having a nice, warm and very convenient meal if you do try to do that."

"I was joking," he lied and climbed up into the crawl space as fast as he could scrambling to catch up with the girls. He then stopped in his tracks as he neared them and began sputtering. "Yuck! There's a really gross mess of spiderwebs down here."

"You're not supposed to eat them," Tiana said wryly as she aimed her flashlight his way and saw him wiping off his face.

Alora giggled. "Looks like he's been trying to."

"As if I would ever," Rhys retorted as he crawled the rest of the way over to the girls. "That was disgusting."

"You haven't seen the worst of it," Tiana said tossing a rat cadaver aside as she checked for labels on the boxes. "I'm just hoping we don't find a rat's graveyard back here."

"That's giving me entirely too much information."

"I disagree. It's always good to be as informed as you can as it helps you be more prepared for what you might run into."

"So, are these our gifts?" Rhys asked changing the subject.

Tiana checked them all and shook her head. "No, these are marked for someone else. So, maybe it's for her alien friends."

"Right, alien friends," he said sarcastically. "I've heard of one of her supposed alien friends but never actually see one."

"I have, so someday you might be surprised to find out who our aunt knows," she said crisply due to his biting comment.

"Enough bickering! It's cold here and I wish to leave as soon as possible," Pythia hissed. "Now since it's not this group of packages, it must be the group further back on the other side."

"Further back? I'm surprised there's more since the house doesn't look like it has that much room under it," Rhys said. "Worse, the area over there's even lower than this one."

"Maybe we're heading into a two-sided dimension under here which then becomes totally flat," Tiana said spookily.

"You make up a lot of weird things," he said with distaste.

"I like studying science oddities and unusual species, so little of what I talk about is made up. It's just undiscovered as yet."

He rolled his eyes in obvious disbelief. "Whatever."

"Hey, Tiana, one thing he's right about is it looks super tight over there," Alora said. "Do you think I can squeeze under it?"

"I don't know. It is really low. But I think I can get there on my hand and knees if I keep my head down. So, just wait here and I'll go see if those packages are for us."

"I'll wriggle over with you if you want me to."

"Nah. It's okay Alora, I'll do it."

"I 'am' slender, so I'll go with you," Pythia rasped.

"Okay, thanks." She and Pythia then went over to the right side of the narrow area under the east end of the house. A few minutes later, Tiana shouted excitedly, "I found a package with a tag saying 'To Alora'!" After a long pause she added, "I found another one, but I'm too cramped here to read its tiny print, so I'll bring it out where there's more room to check it out."

Tiana crawled out of the dark corner dragging two boxes wrapped in thick, black plastic like the vapor-barrier back to the others. One box was two feet square and the other was two-and-a-half-feet-long, one-foot-wide, and one-foot-tall. "I'll need to go part-way back again, because my light caught sight of a box at the midpoint of the narrow crawl space back here," she said pulling cobwebs out of her hair and running her fingers through it to remove any hitch-hiking spiders. "But first do any of 'you' want the glory of retrieving what looks like the biggest box over there?" she asked dramatically emphasizing the question.

"No," Pythia hissed, "I'm getting too cold to go back there."

Dodona yacked with amusement from the open area's floor and the others suddenly realized she had never joined them even after Rhys had.

"It's easy for you to laugh at me while you play it safe back there," Pythia hissed at Dodona with some annoyance.

"True," she rasped without a hint of remorse. "Then again, I can be helpful since I will gladly spit on any spider bites to heal them after everyone gets out of there."

"Not heroic, but that is helpful."

"Hey Rhys, why not be a hero and go get the box?" Tiana asked him roguishly.

"No way, I'm bigger than both of you and I'd get stuck."

"Fine, then I'll go get it you big worry wart."

"And I will gladly give you the credit for doing this."

"Which I'll deserve." Tiana quickly crawled to the space at the house's midpoint. "Hey, I see a funny bump on one side of this package," she called out casting her flashlight's beam on it then she yelled loudly, "Exiting animal!" A moment later, Rhys screamed and Alora squealed as a big possum raced by them.

"Pythia, did you catch it?" Alora asked the python by her.

"No, you were blocking me from doing that with your hands flailing about excitedly."

"Do not worry. I caught it," Dodona rasped.

"Did you swallow it?" Rhys asked all too hopefully.

"No, it's a mother."

"So what?"

"It seems you are more coldblooded than any snake is," she hissed with disgust. "I have her and her babies in a gentle tail hug and I'm taking them outside to release them. For unlike what this useless male has shown us to date, they are useful."

"How?" he asked bristling mad from the insult.

"Because they catch rats and mice and don't carry all the diseases rodents and humans do." With that, she slithered off.

"So not the info I wanted to know," Rhys groaned.

The girls burst out laughing not even trying to choke it back and Pythia made funny snake yacking noises.

"What did you find?" he asked impatiently.

"A big box." As Tiana flashed her light around it, she saw a tiny box squeezed on top of it and put it in her pocket.

"Your reply not very illuminating," he said dryly.

"True," she said then they all heard scraping and grunting.

After what felt like an hour but was minutes, they saw her coming toward them from the center-back area. She huffed and puffed as she shoved a big square box forward then stopped to rest. "Sorry it's taking so long, but there's only two feet of clearance in that part of the crawl space, so it I really had to push it hard to get it past those huge wooden floor-beams that are holding this stout old house up."

"Wow," Rhys said in awe as Alora shined her flashlight at the beams. "These joist timbers are enormous. They must be half-a-foot wide on the bottom and a foot high on the sides." He then saw the big package Tiana pushed toward them was two-feet by two feet by three feet long and was even more awed.

As Tiana got close to them, Alora crawled over to her and helped pull on the big box. Minutes later, they succeeded in getting it to where Rhys and Pythia were waiting for them. As they stopped, Tiana pulled the tiny box from her jean's pocket and looked at it then shrugged. *The label on this is way too tiny to read here*, she thought and stuffed it back in her pocket.

"Holy smokes! Who's the big box for?" Rhys asked.

"I don't know. The writing was so small I couldn't read it in that dark cramped space back there." She then pointed her flashlight at it. "Ah, now I can read the tag. It's for you Rhys."

"Awesome," he said grinning.

Tiana went around Rhys's box to the other long and thin one and read the tag. "This has my name on it," she said brightly. She quickly pushed it to the edge of the open area in front of the crawl space and swung her legs over the short wall. She jumped down and stood on the floor stretching her back a moment then she picked up her box. "See ya," she said running across the basement with it and Pythia followed her.

"Hey!" Rhys shouted. "Where are you going?"

"Upstairs, where there's a lot better lighting than down in this dungeon," Tiana called back from the basement's exit.

"Good idea." Alora pushed her box to the edge of the wall and climbed out of the crawl space onto the basement floor.

"Don't leave me here alone," Rhys griped as the girls both headed out of the basement.

"You're not alone, boy," Dodona rasped with a snaky chuckle. "I'm right here with you."

"Come on," Rhys yelled his voice filled with panic. "One of you needs stay and help me get out of this...dungeon."

"Tiana! Rhys is afraid of being left alone with our darling, Dodona. So, I'll stay with him until we get his box out." Alora walked back to the retaining wall and shook her head to see Rhys and his package were still in the same place.

"He's been a thorn in our sides, so I don't know why you want to help him," Tiana said poking her head back inside the basement. "Well, don't put up with his guff, and good luck."

"Thanks," Alora said sighing as looked at Rhys. "Well, bring your box over here, and hurry. I want to go open mine." She waited but after five minutes he only moved it two feet towards the retaining wall. "Come on, Rhys, push it harder!"

"I am, but my box is really heavy!" he grunted giving it a fierce shove forward, but it just moved a foot. "I don't get how you and Tiana moved it so much faster."

Alora set her package down and scrambled over to the crawl space area Rhys was crouching in with his box. "Good grief, it's truly 'not' heavy," she said easily pushing it five feet forward. "There's only four feet to go, so put some real effort into it."

"I can help motivate you," Dodona hissed coming up to him.

"Thanks, but no thanks." He pushed harder ignoring the pain in his arms and shoulders and finally moved it to the edge of the crawl space. He sighed with relief and swung his legs over the retaining wall glad to get back to a part of the basement he could almost stand-up in.

"I'm glad you were finally so inspired you fulfilled your task," Dodona told him with some amusement,

"And you look all too delighted to have caused my sudden inspiration," he muttered. *I swear that snake is smiling.*

"What was that?" she rasped rising up to look him in the eye.

"Nothing."

"I thought so." She then yacked in her snake laughter.

"Hey, this was incredibly heavy and it was hard to..." he stopped as Dodona slid off then he noticed Alora had carried her box across the basement and the python was now by her. With a grunt, he lifted his box up and lugged it to where they waited for him by the exit. They headed out as Rhys got to them and went back across the patio then up across the deck and on into the house's cabin room.

"I'm going to find Tiana," she told him going across the room and into the short hallway with Dodona following her.

"Okay," Rhys said trailing ten feet behind the huge python.

Alora looked through the glass-paned door of the formal dining room and found Tiana. She saw the silver rose Homer Laughlin plates, Belgium crystal glasses, and the 1932 Lady Hamilton silver that their aunt had laid out earlier expecting to be back by dinner had been cleared off the French antique oak dining room table. She, Dodona, Paris, and Harold were all waiting there as she walked in the room wearing a martyr's look on her face. "Here I am 'finally'."

Tiana bit back a grin. "I told you not to baby him."

"True. Unfortunately, he met your dismal expectations."

"He can be such a pain."

"Indeed, he can."

Rhys winced to hear this as he stood in the hallway holding his box. Alora saw him and set her package on the table then went to hold the heavy leaded-glass paned door open. He came through the doorway grunting and Paris lifted his small, white, fluffy head up. He then growled at Rhys from where he sat on the couch in the parlor next to the formal dining room.

"Look doggie, I'm sorry I locked you out of the yard. But please give me a break, will you? I won't do it again."

As if he had understood, Paris stopped growling but he kept a sharp eye on him.

"Yeesh! This is heavy," Rhys said wincing. "Can one of you help me set this box down before my back breaks?"

Tiana rolled her eyes. "Oh brother! Stop being such a drama queen." She took the box from him like it was filled with air and set it on the table by the other boxes. She bit back a grin as he gaped at her with begrudged respect.

"Let's see what we got," Rhys said rubbing his hands together anxiously as he looked at their three boxes.

"Who goes first?" Alora asked.

"I will," he said bossily.

"No, you don't," Harold buzzed as he flew over and landed on Tiana's shoulder. "Your Aunt Roleena told me the order these are to be opened in."

"Well, I just made a new order."

"Oh, do tell us," Pythia hissed sliding up next to him.

"Ah...well, it's that we should draw for it," Rhys choked out and he moved a few steps away from her.

Alora nodded. "Actually, that sounds fair to me."

"Me too," Tiana agreed.

"It's not what your aunt wanted to do, but it does seem a fair way to do this," Harold said flicking his little wings.

"I'll get some paper and a pen." Alora dashed off returning shortly with the items. She then looked at boxes on the table and looked flustered. "Oh, dear."

"What's wrong?" Tiana asked.

"There's not enough gifts to go around," she said glancing at the two pythons, the fly, and the dog.

"Oh! I forgot I have one in my pocket for Paris, but I didn't find any others down there," Tiana said pulling it out.

"Then let's share ours with the others," Alora said.

"How nice, but Roleena already gave Dodona and I our special protection gifts," Pythia hissed softly.

"I also got mine," Harold buzzed.

"Okay, then I'll number the slips of paper," Alora said and tore the sheet of paper into four pieces writing one, two, three, and four on each separate slip of paper then folding them twice. "Wait a minute. I'll be right back." She ran and got a bowler hat from the vintage hats on the wall in the cabin room and put the numbered pieces in it. Rhys reached for the hat, but Dodona snatched it in her jaws and held it away from him.

"Hey! Why'd you take the hat? It was my idea," he groused.

"And a good one, finally," Pythia rasped. "However, I insist you play by the rules of proper etiquette."

"What rules are those?" he asked looking befuddled.

"Old rules, and a genteel one is 'Ladies first'."

"You can't seriously mean to stick to that old stuff," he said and she hissed at him. "Actually, that's a good idea."

"Yes, it is and it is still in all the best etiquette books."

"You are always fair, Pythia," Tiana said warmly, "But now days it is considered favoritism, and I don't want Rhys thinking we got this because we're girls. Can you let the ladies first rule slide for now since I'm okay with letting him draw first."

"I am too," Alora said.

"Very well, since I see you feel it is the wisest thing to do." Pythia said, "Which makes me think you two are part python."

"Part python?" Rhys asked like he had bit a sour lemon.

"I feel it's a great compliment," Tiana said.

"Thank you, my young friend," Pythia lisped softly. "So, go ahead and take a number, human boy. But no one unfolds them until you all have one and then we will see what the order is."

"Fine." Rhys trembled as he walked up to Dodona who held the hat brim between her jaws. He quickly snatched a number from the hat and backed away.

The girls giggled to see him so jittery and calmly went over to draw a number with Alora drawing one for Paris.

As Dodona set the hat down, Pythia rasped, "Very well, you may unfold them and look at your number."

"My luck stinks…I got the number three," Rhys groused.

Tiana then opened hers. "Wow. I got the number one," she said beaming.

"Mine is number two," Alora said grinning then she opened Paris's paper, "And Paris has number four."

Rhys gave a petulant sniff. "It seems like this was rigged."

Dodona arched up a few feet. "We all witnessed that you got to pick from the hat first. True?"

Rhys pulled out a dining room chair and sat down with a huff. "I guess so."

"Then put on a 'I am a good sport shirt' and let us continue."

"I don't have an 'I am a good sport' shirt."

"From your behavior I would say that comes as no surprise."

"Can we please start doing this now?" Alora said bobbing up and down excitedly. "No objection? Good. So, open your gift Tiana and see what Auntie Roleena gave you."

"Okay." Tiana sat on one of the elegantly carved French oak chairs at the table and pulled her two-and-a-half-foot-long, one-foot-wide, one-foot-tall box up close to her. She took a deep breath and pulled the plastic off finding it wrapped in a layer of plain brown butcher's paper. After ripping the paper off she found a layer of bubble wrap. She popped a few bubbles and Alora giggled. She then removed the bubble wrap found a layer of bright red and green Christmas paper.

Alora giggled again. "This is so like Auntie Roleena. She always makes us work to open our presents, but in a fun way."

"True," Tiana chuckled as she pulled the paper off. Her face then lit up as she gazed at an exquisite suitcase-size ebony case.

The lid was edged in a wide band of thin woven gold inset with pearls and marquis-cut aquamarine gems. A rectangular gold plaque also edged in pearls and gems was centered on the top with 'Tiana Coins' etched on it in Old English letters. Intricate enamel inlays of birds in flight covered the ebony lid. There were Giant Condors, albatross, Haast eagles, Great Blue herons, blue macaw, green Kokapo, and Cape parrots and dozens of tiny hummingbirds zipped around them. The case's sides were covered with panels of detailed scenes of inlaid woods. One of a leopard chasing a gazelle past a herd of elephants. Another of two Black Rhinoceros grazing on grass as giraffes nibbled on acacia trees. One had a brown bear and two cubs on a mountain-side with a cougar stalking elk in a valley below them. Another showed a sea with two North Pacific right whales swimming on the surface and a pod of dolphins leaping over the crests of waves. A Narwhal and two Blue Whales were in the distance. The workmanship stunned her and she heard amazed wows from her sister and cousin, soft hisses from the pythons, and soft buzzes from the talking fly, Harold as they gazed at it.

"What gorgeous artwork," Alora said with a soft sigh.

Pythia bobbed her head. "That comment sums it up nicely,".

"Yes, it does," Tiana said smiling. "And I love the humor in some scenes. Like the bear cubs doing somersaults and the baby giraffes nuzzling each other." She then felt the case's uneven bottom and turned it over. "There are also lots of panels on the bottom! One's of tiger cubs wrestling their mother, one of Giant Pandas munching on leaves in a bamboo forest, another of two Eastern gorillas in a jungle watching their little one's play, and one of a herd of Sika deer in a spruce forest."

"Hey, if you look really close," Rhys said actually smiling, "There are some flying squirrels gliding through the trees."

Alora sighed. "They're two tiny for me to make out, but I do see this one of a pack of gray wolves running across a snowy tundra with a polar bear chasing them."

"I'd be running too," Tiana said gustily then turned the box back over. As she gazed at it in wonder her eyes widened as she looked at the edges of the case and her eyes filled with tears.

"What's wrong?" Alora gasped with alarm.

Tiana was too choked up to speak. She just looked at her sister pitifully and pointed at the bottom edge of the case.

"I don't understand. You love animals, all animals. And these are beautiful inlays. So, what's the problem?"

The two pythons leaned in close to look and groaned then Pythia gently hugged Tiana's waist as Dodona rasped, "Loving all these creatures is what pains her deeply. For there are tiny engraved plaques along the bottom edges. If you know these animals' statuses now, you'll realize why seeing these hurt her."

Alora bent down close to read the tiny labels then scratched her head. "Okay, this one says 'India' in bold print the lists; lion-tailed macaques, Tibetan antelopes, and Sumatran Tigers. One titled 'Africa' says, leopards, cheetahs, elephants, giraffes, rhinoceros' and something like a Pickling Red frog. But I still don't get what's the problem here."

"That's Pickering's reed frog," Tiana said sadly. "The rhinos are Black Rhinoceros, and the plaque titled 'Russia' lists a whistling dog called 'dhole' and antelope. The one titled 'Asia' says Asian elephants and snow leopards, and another has North Atlantic Right whales, Narwhals, and Blue Whales." She then choked up again and handed the box to her sister.

Alora bent down close again to read more labels. "One titled 'Oceans and Seas' lists dolphins, porpoise, sea turtles, bluefin tuna, and manatee. Another titled 'North America' lists tree frogs, marmots, pygmy racoons, and Giant Condors." Her head jerked up and her eyes popped open wide. "My science teacher said Giant Condors are nearly extinct. Oh Tiana, I'm so sorry. I just realized these animals are endangered or extinct."

"Yes," Tiana choked out. "Not enough people realize we need these creatures to keep life on Earth in balance. Add to that crime, we are poisoning our entire world with chemical waste."

"No wonder you're upset to see this. It's a painful reminder."

"Yes, and a terrible legacy for parents and rulers to leave their children filthy water, polluted air, and trashed land."

Alora grabbed her sister's hand. "This is bad, but let's pray there's still hope for us to clean it up so we don't kill the Earth."

"I also know your aunt's purpose in giving you this was to inspire you, not hurt you," Pythia rasped softly. "Remember the Bald Eagles and Koala Bears were saved from extinction and others can still be helped. Your aunt told us it is a memory box for you to use to remind others of what we are losing. Her hope is it will inspire people to focus on turn back the deadly tide rolling across the planet, for this can yet be done but 'you' must take the first step. So why not get started now?"

Tiana took a deep breath and lifted her chin up. "Okay, but I'm overwhelmed by this huge responsibility. Can you tell me what a good first step would be?"

"To open your gifts and see what can help us start to fix it."

"Oh. Right." She forced herself to focus on what was in the case, not the extinct or endangered animals on it. She saw there were eight hinges on one side and eight hasps on the other with small brass padlocks which were all locked. She checked for a niche or loose raised panel where a key might have been tucked away and finding none went through all the wrappings. "The case is locked and I can't find any key here to open it," she said with disappointment.

Rhys smirked. "I guess you'll have to go back down in the dungeon and look for it."

"No," Pythia hissed. "Roleena would not leave anything this important where it could be too hard to find or lost. There must be some kind of a trick to opening its padlocks."

"I agree." Tiana got her flashlight out and inspected each of the locks closely then smiled knowingly. "The letter 'E' is on the back of this hasp, and the next has a R, followed by a L, D, I, E, M, and another D."

"That doesn't make sense at all," Rhys said frowning.

"That's because it's an anagram, silly." Tiana ran out of the room. She came back with a pencil and note pad and began to make different arrangements with the letters.

"What's an anagram?" he asked.

"It's a puzzle where the letters in all the words are mixed up. Hey, I got it! It says 'riddle me'. Hmmm, but riddle you how?" As she racked her brain, she recalled something. *It's goofy, but Aunt Roleena loves magic and once told me two magical words followed by a magical action always made her giggle. Could it be that simple? Do I just rub the lock and say 'open sesame'?* She shrugged and rubbed one of the locks then leaned close whispering the words softly so no one could hear her. The lock sprung open and she gasped in delight. "I can't believe the riddle was such silly nonsense."

"Whatever you were whispering might be silly nonsense to you but it worked!" Alora said clapping her hands delightedly.

"True." She held another padlock but embarrassed to use the magic command she again just rubbed the lock and whispered, 'open sesame'. Once again, the lock popped open.

Alora clapped her hands. "Let me try it!"

"I don't know because then I have to tell you the silly words I said to do this," she said blushing.

"I guess you just don't want to tell me the secret words," she said sadly.

"But it's so silly I don't want to say it out loud."

"Come on. It's okay if it's silly, since it works. What is it?"

Tiana gritted her teeth but then said, "Open sesame."

There was a stunned silence then Alora giggled, the pythons yacked hilariously, Harold buzzed zanily, and Rhys smirked.

"Sorry, but that truly is super silly," Alora said with a tiny grin. She then rubbed one of the padlocks and said, 'Open sesame'. Nothing happened. "It didn't work."

"Can I try it?" Rhys asked and Tiana nodded. He repeated the actions and the padlock still did not open.

Tiana shrugged then took the padlock in hand and said, "Open sesame." It sprang open and she sighed in relief.

"Apparently, only your voice and touch can open these," Harold buzzed as he flew around her.

"I guess that's true," she said grinning. "Which is awesome."

"Fine, but do get on with this," Rhys said impatiently.

"Okay." Tiana opened the rest of the locks and raised the cases lid. She pulled off a thick layer of scented cotton padding on the top and laughed at what she first saw.

"What is it?" Alora asked leaning closer.

"A tiny toy chair." Tiana waved a doll-sized chair around for all of them to see and they all flew backwards. The pythons hissed, Paris yipped, Harold buzzed sharply, and Alora and Rhys slowly got up off the floor. Tiana froze in place, afraid to move at all.

Alora got up and rubbed her backside. "Tiana, stay put and I'll check on the others." She went to check on them and saw they looked as stunned as she felt, but uninjured. However, Paris jumped in her arms anxiously so she gently cradled him.

"Put that away and do it slowly!" Dodona hissed.

"Sorry!" Tiana said cringing as she set it gently back in the case. "I had no idea this tiny chair would pack such a punch."

She grimaced to see the pythons still looked frazzled for they continued to hug the legs of the table with their stout tails.

"Well, now you know these are not toys, even if they appear to be," Pythia told her sternly. "They are real gifts meant to help you in hard times. So, do be careful with them."

"I will be," Tiana said contritely relieved to see everyone was okay. "Wait. I don't see Harold. Harold, where are you?"

"I got flung into the dining room curtain when we all got tossed back. So, I'm over by the south bay window."

"I'm so sorry. Are your wings, okay?" she asked worriedly.

"Yes, but I'll play it safe and watch from over here."

"Good idea, and I'll go really slow now." She reached in her case and eased out a long, stout leather sleeve that had an ornate handle poking out of its top. Three decorative bands of brass encircled it etched in ornate Celtic shield knots as was the handle. "This sleeve holds a sword," she said peeking in it.

Pythia arched up and looked in the sleeve. "Its cover is called a 'scabbard', and from the two-foot length and slight curve at the bottom, the blade is a cutlass. How quaint."

"Why do you say that it's quaint?"

"Because they were used from the seventeenth to nineteenth centuries by sailors and pirates to fight their way onto ships, and are rarely used now for anything but your movies."

"Do you think it's safe to pull it out and look at it?"

"Sssss, that's up to you to decide, but if you choose to, do it very slowly," Pythia replied.

"Wait!" Alora said blocking her sister's hand from grabbing it. "I see a small piece of paper taped under the handle."

Tiana took the note off the cutlass handle unfolding it four times to open it. "It says, 'I am the Sword of Defense. I will cast off evil thieves and killers and make way for the good of heart to escape. Warning. I will not work as a weapon, so if you try to harm anything, my blade turns into air. You can however cleave an impassable space between you and your enemies by slicing me in the air or on the ground in front of them using two hands. This cannot be crossed for four hours. Consider where you need to exit as you can't cross this space either. To hold a group in a circle for half that time, run the sword around them using only one hand'. That's all it says."

"Cool! Let me have it." Rhys grabbed the sword from Tiana and it flashed with fire. As he screamed and dropped it, the air smelled like burned flesh. The girls gasped as he sank to his knees moaning as he cradled his scorched hand.

"Foolish boy! The Sword of Defense knows its owner is Tiana, not you," Dodona hissed disgustedly as she grabbed Rhys's hand with her tail and spit all over it.

"What did you do that for?" he cried as he pulled free of her.

"Because my saliva has immense healing properties!"

Rhys looked doubtful, but as he glanced at his hand he gaped in awe. "My hand doesn't hurt and the burn's healing right up."

"It is a special gift of Dodona's," Pythia rasped then turned to Tiana. "I feel it's best you put your sword away for now."

Nodding, she put it back in its scabbard and set it carefully in her case then searched through a straw-like material cushioning the objects inside and pulled out a small thick, round case.

"That looks like a big makeup case," Alora said giggling.

"I don't know, but there's a note taped to. It says, 'A time will come you must choose who to give this to. It can 'only' be given by you to whomever you feel earned the right to lead you. If it approves of your choice, it will honor them by bestowing its powers on them when placed on their head'."

"Since it is placed on a head, I bet it's a super special hat. So, take it out of the bag and let's see." She clapped excitedly as Tiana took out a flat, ribbed silk disc and grinning she smacked it. It popped up and formed a black silk top hat. "See? I'm right, it is a hat! Can I try it on?" she asked with a silly giggle.

"No! The note said I must choose a leader to give this to and only when I know they earned it. So, I must wait and see."

"Party pooper!" she said sticking her tongue out at her sister.

"Yes," Tiana said firmly, "As it's the way it must be done."

"Alora, your sister is correct," Dodona said softly. "These are not toys. They are strong protective devices. So, I ask you to be as kind in your words as you are in your heart."

At first Alora frowned, but then she said sheepishly, "Sorry, Tiana, I was being petty and selfish."

"Thanks for admitting it," Tiana said sighing, "But you know, you were right about this being a special hat."

"So, is there anything else in there?" Rhys asked impatiently.

"I think so, but these gifts are hard to sift out of all the funny straw that's packed in here."

"It's not straw, it's excelsior and it's been used since ancient times to pack precious items up safely," Harold buzzed.

"What's excelsior?"

"Slender wood shavings, and these look old." He flew over it and took a sniff. "These still have a telling scent and came from an ancient Lebanese forest before it burned down long ago."

"How do you know?" Alora asked.

"Flies are very sensitive to scents and this is a rare one. You have a good nose, Alora. Take a sniff. What do you smell?"

"It smells like a sweetly-scented cedar," she said smiling.

"You're correct, and it's from one of their best growth years. Would you like a sniff of it, Tiana?" he buzzed eagerly.

"Sure." She smiled at how enthused Harold was and sniffed it. "It does smell nice, but now I'll see what else I have." She pulled out a silk bag with musical scores embroidered over it and a drawstring closure and looked inside for a note. Finding none, she pulled out a gleaming silver flute engraved with lacy swirls. "Look at this dazzling flute! Too bad I can't play it."

Alora grinned from ear to ear. "Come on, just try it out."

"Okay." She blew softly across the holes and an enchanting melody filled the air that was so lovely she kept blowing on it. Alora and Rhys began dancing. Paris ran in circles, and the pythons arched up several feet waving back and forth as Harold did loop-de-loops in the air. As she paused to get a breath, they all stopped and looked confused but when Tiana lifted the flute to play again Pythia hissed at her and she froze.

"Stop playing that now for it's a magical 'Charmed Flute'!"

"It is?" Tiana said wincing at the sharp orders. "But I didn't see a note on it to warn me about this."

"None-the-less I heard one before. Hold it close to me and I'll check it out." She studied it and then rasped. "Look, there's elongated writing on the flute among the fancy swirls on it."

"Yikes! I didn't see the tiny words among the swirls until you pointed it out. It says, 'I am the Charmed Flute of the Pied Piper'. Wow, I thought the Pied Piper was only a fairy tale."

"Actually, it is based on a real story of a man hired by the town of Hamelin, Germany to lure the rats away with his magic pipe and drown them in its river. I don't know if it worked, but do put it away, because that was exhausting." Pythia then curled up and rested her head on her uppermost coil as Tiana put the Charmed Flute in its silk bag and back in her wood case.

"Well, that's it for me. It's your turn, sis."

"Okay." Alora put on her reading glasses. "My gift tag says, 'Open with care'." She removed multiple wrapping layers and as she took off the last one squealed in delight as she held up a dazzling two-foot square stained-glass box for everyone to see. All six sides were a rose-colored crystal glass held together by gold joints. Wide gold bands ran across the sides and top every four inches inset with pink and white pearls. Rubies centered on gold flower petals were set on each crossing point. The top had a frosted six-by-six a crystal panel in its center surrounded by rubies with her name lacily etched there.

"That's another big wow!" Tiana said gustily.

"It is," Alora said gazing at it with astonishment.

"Well, open it up," Rhys said.

"I will, but even though it only has one padlock, it's likely as tricky to open as Tiana's." She held the lock and said, "Open sesame." It didn't open and she grimaced.

"Alora, look for a note," Tiana said.

She nodded and looked all over it then shook her head. "I don't see any note on it at all," she whispered sadly.

"May I take a look?"

"Please do," she said looking like a lost puppy.

Tiana began examining each side then stopped and grinned. "A note is tucked under one of the bottom bands of your box!" She pried it out with her fingernails and gave it to Alora.

"Thank you!" she sighed and quickly opened it. "It says, 'Do what's totally you that made me laugh and chased away my blues then this lock will open for you.' But what is totally me?"

"Just think about something you do a lot that tickles her and cheers her up," Dodona lisped softly to encourage her.

"But nothing is coming to mind," she said biting her lip.

"I know," Rhys said smirking and he made kissy noises.

"You're teasing me, even though I was nice enough to stay with you in the dungeon," Alora said shaking her finger at him.

"Actually Alora, you do blow all of us lots of kisses which is totally you," Tiana said. "Why not just try it?"

"Only if 'he' behaves and stops teasing me."

"In your dreams," Rhys said smirking again.

"Or not," Dodona said sliding over close to him. "Since I will hug you real tight if you're not nice to her about this."

"Okay, okay." Rhys made a zipping action across his mouth. Dodona nodded then went back and coiled up next to Alora.

"Well, here it goes." She kissed her hand and then blew it at the lock. To her surprise, it opened. "It worked!"

"Good," Tiana said smiling. "Now, let's see what you got."

"Okay." Alora removed the padlock and opened the top to find it full of foam chips. She reached inside them and pulled out a pink satin bag with a flower-shaped silver button on its closure flap. She opened it and peeked inside. "Oh, my stars!"

"What is it, because you look stunned?" Rhys asked.

"Look!" She took a glittering diamond tiara out of the bag and put it on her head then grinned at them all broadly.

"Take...it...off," Tiana stuttered then she just gaped.

"Why?" she asked bewilderedly. "It's just a tiara."

"Be...cause..." Dodona lisped then her voice faded away.

"Put it away!" Pythia hissed having to force the words out.

"But it is so beautiful!" She held it out in front of her gazing at it fondly. "Why look at it." They all were. *Odd, they're so quiet. Not even Rhys is making snide remarks. But this is weird. They're all fixated on the tiara.* She noticed the python's eyes pulsated while Tiana's, Rhys's, Paris' eyes were dilated, and Harold flew unsteadily around. "Oh dear, what have I done to them?" she groaned shoving the tiara back in the pink satin bag. "Hey, you guys. Talk to me. Please," she said worriedly. After a minute, that felt like hours, everyone began blinking their eyes.

"My sweet but unobservant girl, we will be fine now you put the 'Bedazzler' away," Dodona lisped lethargically.

"I'm so glad," she said with relief, "But what's a bedazzler?"

"It is an object that when worn by its owner dazzles the mind and body of anyone who looks at it thus immobilizing them."

"Oh, my gosh. I'm super sorry for dazzling all of you." Alora looked around the room worriedly. "Where's Harold?"

"Everybody, freeze!" Tiana shouted with alarm. "We don't know where he is and we don't want to accidently crush him."

Rhys scrunched up his face. "Speak for yourself. Personally, I don't like flies, and that's why they make fly swatters."

"You were right, Dodona," Pythia hissed. "Some humans are far more coldblooded than any of us in the Reptilia Class are."

"Can we even resist the urge to bite him for the outrageous comment he made?" she hissed.

"I will admit, it is hard to hold back after that one."

"Hey! I didn't move," he added quickly. "And I won't until you find him…and I won't ever try to hurt him."

"Wise decision," Pythia told him sternly then she looked at the girls. "Let's all look carefully around the room for him."

"Harold! Where are you?" Alora shouted frantically.

"I'm near one of the dining room windows because as the tiara's bright light hit my eye prisms, it blinded me. Fortunately, I bashed into its nice, soft curtains. Give me a moment though, since I'm too stunned to fly, and that's not a pun."

"Harold, I'm terribly sorry," Alora choked out with a sob.

"No tears, gentle one. I'm sure I'll be quite all right."

"Good, but keep talking and I'll come pick you up,"

"No! I don't want any big feet near me. Just give me a few minutes to collect myself and recover my senses."

"Harold, will you please let 'me' walk over and get you," Tiana said. "I can clearly see where you are. You can walk onto my finger which I'll set by you then by my shoulder. You can tuck under my hair and be safer there then flying about as we check out our gifts."

"Very well," Harold said. Tiana walked over and put her forefinger by him. He climbed up on it and she set her finger on her shoulder. He walked onto it and hid under her long curtain of hair. "I'll hang out here for a bit," he buzzed wearily.

"Good. Okay, check out your gifts, Alora, but carefully."

Alora nodded and began cinching up her tiara's bag when she heard a crinkling noise. She reached inside and pulled out a piece of paper. "Hey, I found a note on the bottom of this bag."

"What does it say?" Tiana asked.

"Oops," she said wincing.

"It says, 'oops'?" she asked frowning curiously at her sister.

"No, it says, 'Do not take this out near your friends unless they have on protective glasses. If you don't have any, warn them to close their eyes.' Sorry, I goofed up." She quickly dug through her box and winced. "And I don't have any glasses in here at all."

"Then until we can find some, before you use it, warn us to close our eyes. Now, go ahead and look at what else you got."

"I'm afraid to," she said nervously biting her lip.

"I know, but remember, I goofed up too. So, let's all do this slowly and check each other's things for warning notes before using anything in our boxes so we can hopefully do this safely."

"Okay." Alora forced herself to ignore her fears and eased a leather container out of her box the size of a binocular case. She opened it and pulled a clear acrylic rack holding four glass vials five inches tall out. "They look like what I used in my science lab but these are sealed with cork plugs. And look! Each one is filled with a different color of sparkling dust." Alora grinned broadly. "They look like the glitter I use on my art posters."

"It does," Tiana agreed as Alora began to ease a cork out.

"Look for a note before you open that," Rhys snapped.

"Oops…right. I'd better do that." She looked it all over and found a note tucked between two vials in the rack and opened it. "This says, 'One vial of magic dust makes objects bigger, and one makes them small. But if anyone but you try to use these, they won't do anything at all'. It adds in big letters; 'Warning! Use sparingly!'. Okay, that seems clear enough and there is a vial here labeled 'Big' and one labeled 'Small'."

"That sounds like a line from 'Alice in Wonderland'," Tiana said wryly and she could not help but grin broadly.

"It does, right?" Alora giggled. "And there are two more vials of sparkling dust, so I'll look and see what they do." She pulled out the next vial. "This wasn't mentioned in the note, but the label says; 'Magic Fairy Dust- use with the utmost care."

"Maybe like Tinker Bell's, it makes you fly," Tiana said laughing but then grew serious. "But is it even safe to try it?"

"I don't know," she said gulping.

"You're such a timid mouse, I bet you won't," Rhys said.

Alora flicked her hair back over her shoulder. "I'll show you I'm not timid." She opened the vial and tapped a pinch of dust on her shoulders. "Nothing's happened at all," she sighed.

"Wait a sec. Did you think happy thoughts?" Tiana asked. "You know, like Wendy did in Peter Pan."

"You two gag me with all your silly talk," Rhys groaned.

Alora huffed and scooped the dust off her shoulder onto her hand and threw it at him. Rhys whooshed up into the air and smacked his head on the ceiling. He yelped and everyone stared in awe as he floated under the ceiling like a human balloon.

"Let me down!" Rhys yelled when no one came to help him.

"Tiana, grab his feet with me and help me pull him down."

"Do I have to? This is so funny, I have to get a picture of this." She pulled her Smart phone and took a picture of him.

"Yes, we have to, so do it." As Alora grabbed one ankle, Tiana grabbed the other. They pulled him down, but as they let go of him, he shot back up to the ceiling and hit his head.

"Fix this and make this stop," he moaned rubbing his head.

"But I don't know how to fix it yet," she told him then she looked at her sister and they both burst out laughing.

"Alora, as amusing as this is," Pythia rasped with a rippled snake grin as Dodona yacked merrily beside her." You must find the antidote. It's probably in the last vial."

"I'll check it now." Alora pulled the last vial from the rack. "You're right, it's labeled 'Flying Antidote'. Now, everyone else get back." After they moved back, she opened the bottle and sprinkled a bit in her hand then tossed it up over his body. He immediately dropped down right on top of her.

"Umph!" he grunted.

"Get off me!" Alora said then seeing how shocked he looked to be laying on top of her she began laughing.

"At least we know it works," Tiana said grinning.

"That we do." She shoved Rhys aside then put all the vials in their rack and tucked them back in the protective leather case. "Why didn't it work on me?" she asked mystified.

Tiana shrugged. "I don't know."

"Your eyes are better than mine, so look and see if I missed something." She took the case out and handed it to Tiana.

"Okay." Tiana got the Fairy Dust vial out and as she read it her eyes widened. "There's tiny print here that says; 'Flying dust works if used by the owner, but not on the owner unless dispensed by a trusted family in a life-threatening situation.' I get it, otherwise anyone could make someone float off."

"Oh my, I'm so glad you saw that and I'll keep it in mind." Alora packed away the Fairy Dust and searched inside the box. She pulled out a slender, shimmering bag and looked for a note. Seeing none, she pulled a long white shining rod out of it. "This looks like a super big glow stick."

Tiana grinned. "It does. Are there any instructions on it?"

"None I can see. It just says, 'Magic Fairy Wand' in small gold letters on one side. But check it out for me." She handed it to her sister and she looked it over and shook her head.

"I don't see any notes on it either."

"Oh goody!" She laughed and clapped her hands in delight as Tiana gave her the wand back. She swished it around and to her surprise, dozens of tiny winged human-shaped fairies shot out of the tip making little pinging noises then they flit about on shimmering, rainbow-colored wings. The last one to come out chimed loudly and wore a gold ring on her head. She flew up in front of Alora's face staring at her with eyes that sparkled like emeralds in the sun. Merely two inches tall, she wore a glowing golden flower-petal dress and flew about looking in everyone's eyes then she flew back to stand on Alora's nose.

"Hello there," Alora said softly to the beautiful fairy having to look at her cross-eyed to see her on her nose.

"Human female, did you read the wands instructions?" she asked sharply in a voice as big as any humans.

"I...I didn't see any," she stammered nervously.

Tiana grabbed the bag and turned it inside out. "Oops! There is a note, but it's written on the fabric on the inside of the bag so we didn't see it," she said wincing. "It says, 'You may use this wand if you are given it but not if you are a wrongdoer of any sort, and only if you are in dire trouble' and only is underlined."

"Oh dear."

"You are a female of few words which we have heard your males say is a rarity," the tiny being told Alora. Rhys snickered and she gave him such a fiery glance he blushed and pinched his lips together. She then turned back to Alora. "You must be a good and kindly princess in your realm to have been entrusted with a Magic Fairy Wand."

"I'm not a princess," Alora said honestly. "But I do try to be kind to others."

"Good," the fairy said but looked puzzled. "To be given this wand, you must have a caring but cautious heart. However, I sense no danger here, so why did you summon us?"

"Noble fairy, the truth is it was quite by accident I did this."

"Trolls and gnomes only do such mischief!" she cried out so sharply they all winced. "You must never waste a fairy's time.

You cannot summon us for anything less than righting injustice, saving goodhearted beings, or righting a grievous wrong."

"I just goofed up," Alora said with an apologetic shrug.

"Young female, you cannot shrug this off," the Queen said so heatedly Alora's ears felt like they were burning. "Pay heed to what I now say. It was wrong of you to do. Bear in mind if it happens again, I will turn you into a wart frog or a toad stool."

"You can actually do that?" Alora asked wide-eyed.

"Most certainly!" She zipped down to Roleena's miniature American Eskimo dog and tapped his head with her tiny wand. He immediately turned into a big wart frog.

Alora burst into tears. "I'm sorry I used the wand wrongly."

"You should be!"

"I am and I promise you it won't happen again."

"It had better not for your sake. For I am their Queen and am therefore charged with guiding and protecting them from any frivolous summons, inconsequential deeds, or unworthy causes. For the light from a fairy's wand comes from magical energy from the Great All Spirit. It is only to be used to right serious wrongs or save lives. If we let it be used falsely, we die."

"It pains me to hear that. I had no idea fairies existed least of all the penalty for summoning you lightly even by accident," she said forlornly. "But I beg you if you must punish someone, punish me and restore our dog, Paris. Please do not take this terrible error of mine out on our sweet, furry friend."

"As you wish," the fairy said speaking less harshly than she had before and a curious look filled her eyes. With a tap of her wand on the wart frog's head, he turned back into a dog. To Alora's relief, she did not turn her into a frog but continued to chastise her severely. She finally stopped and waved her wand. A golden light came out of it surrounding the fairies. It drew them up into Alora's wand then the Queen burst into sparks.

"Oh no! I killed her!" Alora said sobbing brokenheartedly.

Tiana ran to her sister to comfort her but stopped as she saw a tiny scrap of paper drift to the ground underneath where the fairy queen had been. She picked it up and smiled at Alora as she read it. "I doubt you killed her, because I think their Queen left this note for you. The print's tiny, so I'll read it to you. It says, 'Fairy Queens burst into sparks when someone calls them out wrongly, but their sparks reassemble back home if an honest mistake was made,' which we all know it was. But it was truly shocking and showed me using the wand is serious business and we can't call them out just for fun."

"Me too," Alora said drying her eyes with her sleeve.

"I bet what she did was some kind of illusion," Rhys said shaking his head. "Because really, there aren't any things like fairies popping out of wands and dogs turning into frogs."

"We all saw it Rhys and it looked real to me," Tiana said. "And not wanting to live my life as a frog, I'll remember we only call on fairies if we really need to right serious wrongs."

"I know I'll sure remember that," Alora sighed. "What's more is I truly thought I had checked super carefully for a note."

"Me too, but it looks like we have to do better."

"Or you'll wind up as toad stools," Rhys said snickering.

"Hey, I saw what happened to Paris. So, you can say it was an illusion, but he looked like a real wart frog to me so we're not chancing it, right Alora?" Tiana asked and she nodded. "Okay, then we've learned we must to turn everything inside out and look for any scribbling, etching or tiny hidden notes."

"That's for sure." Alora then looked in her stained-glass box again and her face lit up. "How cute! These look like 'the' ruby slippers from Oz," she said pulling out a pair of shiny red shoes. Everyone checked them over thoroughly for notes or writing and finding none she kicked off a shoe and began trying one on when Tiana suddenly swiped the shoe away from her.

"Stop! We all missed this!" She pointed out tiny dots and dashes on the edge of the shoe's sole. Alora just looked puzzled. "It's Morse Code. Something I learned from Uncle Allen."

"But that codes so old I can't believe anyone else would even know it anymore," Rhys said rolling his eyes.

"Well, obviously someone did and so do I."

"What does it say?" Alora asked.

"Give me a sec to translate it…okay, it says; 'Caution. One-way trip if you put these slippers on. Be sure the place actually exists or you might wind up landing in outright nothingness'."

Alora gulped. "Gracious! Thanks for stopping me. I guess I'll need to be sure about where I want to go if I ever use them."

"That would be an excellent idea," Dodona hissed.

"Absolutely," Tiana agreed heartily.

"Well, I see nothing else in mine, so it's your turn, Rhys," Alora said as she put away her ruby slippers then she picked up his huge package and set it on the table in front of him.

"That box is so incredibly heavy, I don't see how you can lift it so easily," he groaned.

"It doesn't seem that heavy to me," she said shrugging.

"Well, that's just weird." He glared at the box as he stood up and lifted the bottom edge of one side grunting as he tipped it back. He ripped all the coverings off one side then did the same to the other side revealing a burnished steel strongbox. Its edges were reenforced by wide bronze Eastlake angle plates with big Eastlake corner pieces. On the top of the box was a twelve-by-six-inch platinum plaque edged in a wide bronze strip of Eastlake design inset with large square cut diamonds. On the plaque in twenty-four carat gold letters in a Rockwell Bold design it said; 'Sir Rhys'.

"Sir Rhys? Really?" Tiana asked drolly. "What a jest."

He ignored her amused comment and looked the strongbox over. "Two big old metal hasps and staples are on it, but instead of a padlock a gold bar is running through them to keep it shut."

"Then pull it out and open it," Alora said excitedly.

Rhys slid the bar out and tried lifting the sturdy lid. After five minutes of heaving on it, he could not open it. His face clouded over and he punched it with his fist. To his surprise he got flung back into the antique oak buffet behind him.

After the girls saw he was okay, they burst out laughing. He blushed but got back up on his feet then smacked it lightly. He got shoved back, but with less force than before.

"I'd say it's obvious that striking it will not open it," Tiana said pointedly. "Moreover, if you do, it throws you back."

"Then help me and try your way of opening it," he sputtered.

"This is your gift, not mine, and if you'll take a moment to recall it, neither Alora or you could open mine."

Rhys looked at Alora. "How about blowing it a kiss?"

"No way. Giving it kisses wouldn't be the right thing to do since that's 'my' way, not yours. I bet you need to find out how to do it your way, but without beating it up."

"You two aren't any help at all," he huffed.

Tiana and Alora looked at each other and shrugged.

"You're right. We aren't any help with this," Tiana agreed.

Suddenly, loudly pounded knocks were heard on the front door as they kept staring curiously at the stubborn box. They all jumped and looked at each other wide-eyed. As the pounding continued, they began to head to the front door. Tiana paused as they left seeing Paris' tiny gift still sat on the table unopened so she grabbed it and slipped it in her sweatshirt's pocket. She then ran quietly to the front entranceway to catch up with Alora and Rhys so find out who it was.

The pythons slithered along behind her and Harold flew over them and literally became 'the fly on the wall'. Paris rushed past them and got to the front door first, barking at it like he was a hundred-pound German Shepherd. No one spoke and they all stared at the door warily.

As the pounding finally stopped, the girls tiptoed up onto the stairway landing to the left of the door. They peeked out of the shoulder high Victorian diamond-paned glass window and both gasped loudly. When Rhys saw their startled faces, he squeezed in-between them to peer out the window and his eyes popped open wide. A tall, brawny policeman stood on the porch holding a nightstick in his hand rhythmically smacking it into his other hand. His lips were pursed tightly together and the deep frown on his face plus him snorting like a disgruntled bull, made it clear to the trio that this officer was in a particularly bad mood.

**

CHAPTER FIVE
CROCODILES

"We'd better see what the officer wants," Alora whispered to her sister. She tiptoed back to the front door but as she reached for the door knob, Tiana rushed down and pulled her back.

"No," she hissed like their python friends then whispered, "With all the Red Winkie tricks Auntie Roleena warned us about, he might be under their control. She also told us we were never to open the door up to people we don't know."

"Those are good points," Rhys said to her surprise. "But what if he is just a normal policeman and has news about our aunt's disappearance or our parent's silence since Gertie told me you haven't heard from your parents either?"

"True, but our parents are likely traveling in areas there's no cell reception. It's happened to them a few times before. Also, Aunt Roleena called their travel agent for us and found out ours arrived safely in Guatemala to go on their three-week Mayan temple trek. So, there's no reason to report them as missing. As for yours, even if they haven't called you for days, it could be they also have no cell reception due to bad weather or no close cell towers. As far as our aunts go, we have no proof they were abducted. So, with them just missing a few hours, the police won't take us seriously and just think we're being hysterical."

"But maybe I should ask him to check and see if any of them were in an accident and taken to a hospital."

"No, because even though we're kids, Aunt Roleena said our parents insisted that Alora and I were listed as prime emergency contacts. She also said yours did this too so any hospital would call us first before sending any police or other official here."

"I still think we should—"

"This is Officer Schmartzov with the Politically Correct Force," a man said loudly cutting Rhys off. "I know there's at least three of you in there because I heard three different voices talking in there. Answer the door for if you don't, I'll come back with a search warrant to forcefully enter this house."

"I'm not allowed to open the door to strangers," Tiana said.

"I'm a Politically Correct Force officer, PCF officer for short, so I'm not some stranger."

"You're a stranger to me, so I will 'not' open the door."

"Then you want to do this the hard way?" the officer huffed.

"No, I just want to obey my aunt's rules," she said primly.

Rhys rolled his eyes and whispered in her ear, "Why don't you just get to the point and ask him why he's here?"

"Be my guest," Tiana said then she stuck her foot against the door as he put his hand on the doorknob. "Don't you dare open that door or I'll have Pythia tie you up in knots."

"Which would be my pleasure," she hissed from behind him.

"Okay, I won't open it," he muttered letting go of the knob. "Now, hurry up and ask him what's he's doing here."

"I will. I will," she muttered back. "Officer Schmartzov, why are you here?"

"I received a call about two girls here wearing green and purple tennis shoes in public and I was sent to check this out."

Rhys glanced at the girl's feet and saw they did indeed have on green and purple sneakers. He looked at them questioningly but they shrugged and looked bewildered. "Officer, even if they dis wear green and purple shoes, why's that a problem?"

"Since by law, red must be worn on all shoes now, so I must confiscate any shoes violating this law and ticket the offenders."

"What are you then…some kind of fashion police?"

"Don't get smart with me, young man."

"Sorry sir, but I've never heard of any law like that."

"That law was instated yesterday in an emergency session of the local council. However, being it's a new law, they can plead their ignorance before a judge and just pay a fine."

"Sir, these girls are in primary school, so I think they're too young to be tried and fined," Rhys said in a respectful manner.

"I'll check my data base," he said tapping on his smartphone. "I found you're correct and the owner of this house is Roleena Bloodstone. Go get Ms. Bloodstone so I can speak to her. Then she can turn over the shoes and then appeal this to the judge."

"Sir, she left to run an errand, but she should be back soon."

"How soon?"

"I don't know exactly."

"Are you also one of her wards?"

"No, but she's my aunt too and I'm visiting here."

"Are any of you adults?"

"No, but I'm thirteen so by law old enough to babysit all day and they're ten and eleven so can be alone for two hours."

"I don't think any of you sound responsible enough to be on your own. So, I'm going to have a police matron come stay here until your aunt gets home."

Tiana peeked behind the curtains over the front door window and saw the officer tapping on his cell phone then she gulped as she saw more than that. "You guys, his car lights are sparkly red and so is the gem on his ring finger," she whispered.

"This is getting way too weird," Rhys whispered back as he peeked over her shoulder. "I don't know about your two, but I'm for getting out of here while we still can."

"But where can we go that would be safe from the Red Winkies?" Tiana asked leading them back into the kitchen.

"I say we just get far away from here and figure it out then." He headed to the backdoor and the girls followed. He tried to open the door but it wouldn't budge. He looked at it closely and groaned. "Hey, the deadbolt's locked, but the key's not in it anymore and it was earlier. Which one of you has it?"

"I certainly don't," Tiana said crisply.

Rhys then looked at Alora as she rifled her pocket. "Well?"

"I took it, but I just found a hole in my pocket so it must've fallen out when we were crawling around in the dungeon."

"It's not a dungeon," he snapped. "It's a basement."

"That's what we call it."

"Whatever. Now how do we get out of here?" he asked and as if punctuating his point, someone knocked on the front door.

"Can that be the police matron already?" Alora gasped.

"Let's go see." Tiana ran to the front door with the others but before they could peek out the question was answered.

"This is Officer Schmartzov. I'm sure you're listening so I'm informing you Officer Dwendoleen will be here in one hour with a warrant to enter this house and to watch over you. You must all sit tight until she arrives. Do you hear me?"

"We hear you," Tiana said having to shout because Paris barked madly at the officer. *But it doesn't mean we'll do it,* she thought, thankful the frosted window and curtains obscured the view of anyone trying to look inside.

"Good. Then get those offensive pairs of shoes bagged and set aside for me to take away. Keep in mind I'll be waiting by my car until she arrives to keep an eye on you three minors."

"Officer, I told you that I'm legally old enough to babysit," Rhys said, "So, call her back and tell her we don't need her."

"Law officers can decide if minors need watching and I say you need it!" he growled then stomped back to his car parked across the street. The trio shivered to see his car lights still had an eerie red twinkle to them. They also noticed he did not get in his car and just leaned against it glaring at Roleena's house.

Tiana ran to the backroom and the others followed. "It's going to be harder to get out of here with the backdoor locked, and a grumpy officer watching this house like a hawk."

"So, I guess we're trapped in here," Rhys said grimly.

Alora bit on her lip worriedly as she slumped down between the two pythons who had coiled up on each end of the cushy Southern Comfort couch in the room as her sister stared at her. Tiana then gazed up over Alora's head and her eyes widened as she pointed at the area behind Alora.

"We're not trapped," Tiana said excitedly.

Alora turned around to look and giggled. "Super idea!" she said and the girls grinned impishly at each another. "Even with the backdoor locked we do have a way out of here without the officer seeing us."

"How?' Rhys demanded impatiently.

"We simply go out this side window."

"That won't keep that officer from seeing us," he said dryly.

"Yes, it will," Tiana said. "Because his view is blocked."

"It doesn't seem like it would be blocked to me."

"Then I'll explain it to you," she said pointedly. "There's a six-foot wood fence between the front and back yard, plus a big quince tree filling the yard side-to-side. That and the bump out of the dining room bay window totally blocks his view of the backyard. So, we just keep close to the house and go through the carriage house behind it so he won't see us escaping."

"We need to get Auntie Roleena's gifts first," Alora said.

Rhys shook his head. "That police matron could be here any minute, so doing that would waste valuable get away time."

"It most certainly will not be a waste, because you will need them!" Pythia hissed and Dodona bobbed her head.

"But mine's too heavy to cart around," Ryan groused.

"Then I'll carry yours and you can carry mine," Alora said.

"You'd do that for me?" he asked blinking in astonishment.

"Of course, since we're family and all in this fix together."

"We will stay and hide here," Dodona lisped.

"Will that be safe enough for you?" Alora asked worriedly.

"Safer than leaving. If you will recall, last year a neighbor saw us out in the yard. She screamed hysterically and called the animal shelter. Animal control came over and warned Roleena they'd take us away if we were ever seen outside again."

"Sorry. I forgot about that," she said blushing.

"Hello, if anyone's interested, I'm staying here too," Harold buzzed. "It's much safer inside the house than outside of it."

"I'm so sorry for not asking you, Harold," Tiana said softly. "And if any of you think you won't be safe, I'd rather stay and be sure you're okay than chance them hurting any of you. Then Alora and Rhys can still get away and go find our aunts."

"How thoughtful," Pythia rasped softly. "But don't worry, Harold is an expert at hiding which is what has kept him alive so very long. As for Dodona and I, we can easily keep out of sight since Roleena had Sir Hephaestus make us hiding places and secret tunnels after the animal control humans came here."

"You're sure about this?"

"Yes. Now, grab your gifts and go before it's too late to get away." She then gave her a nudge with her head. "And shut the window afterwards so they think you are just not answering the door and won't know you left until they search the house. After you get safely away, we will slide over and open the door a bit so they do not break it down. Then we will quickly hide."

"Thanks for thinking of that." Tiana then looked at her sister and Rhys. "Okay, let's get our gifts and go."

As they raced to the dining room, Alora picked up Rhys's strongbox, but then set it down as she looked at her stained-glass box. "Wait! What can I use to protect this?"

Tiana frowned as she thought it over then smiled. "I've got an idea." She ran to kitchen and back in a flash. "Use this big square plastic bin Aunt Roleena puts recyclable things in, and here's some dish towels to pad it with. That'll keep it safe."

"Thanks," Alora said with relief and slid her glass box in the bin then shoved the towels down the sides to snug it in tight. "It fits perfect. Now, one more thing." She got two huge garbage bags from a kitchen drawer and put Tiana's in a bag then hers knotting both at the top. She then handed Rhys her bag and picked up his trunk by its handle as Tiana picked up her bag. "Rhys' box is tough and has a handle but ours don't, so this will help protect them and make them easier to carry."

"Good idea, sis," Tiana said.

They sped to the cabin room quickly with their boxes and Tiana opened the window then removed its screen. She set it behind the couch and leaned out to carefully look around.

"No people or Red Winkies in sight," she said as she pulled her head back inside.

"I'll look for myself!" Rhys shouldered her aside and leaned out the window. As he drew back in, he shook his head. "No way! That's got to be an eight-foot-drop down to the ground and I'd break a leg doing that."

Tiana just elbowed him aside and slipped through the open window dropping lightly to the grassy turf below it. "Will you hand me my box, Alora?"

"Sure," she said leaning over and passing it down to her.

"You know," Rhys said standing back from the window, "I think my box is too heavy for 'anyone' to have to lug around. So, maybe we should leave it here."

"No," Alora said. "It could have something we need to help us find the others, Besides, that I told you I'd carry it for you."

"But I can't even open it," he griped. "So why bother?"

"Because we might need what's in it and we can figure how to do that later." She then lifted his strong box and passed it through the window. "Tiana, can you grab Rhys's box for me?"

"Okay. No problem." She took it without any difficulty and Rhys groaned in dismay to see her do this so easily. "I got it."

"Thanks, and here's mine," Alora said handing it to her.

"Got it."

"Good. Now, here's Paris." She leaned way over the window ledge and gently passed him down to her. "Now, stand back, I'm dropping down." She slipped out the window and landed on the ground below with a thud. "Come on, Rhys, get moving."

Rhys just griped about the drop down when someone banged on the front door. He then quickly stuck his legs down over the windowsill and laying on his stomach he edged his way down but then froze. As more loud banging hit the front door, the girls grabbed his ankles and pulled him down. He gasped and landed on top of them then jumped to his feet. "That was mean," he muttered giving them a dirty look as he brushed himself off.

"Seriously," Tiana whispered angrily. "You're mad at us for pulling you down so we can all get away when officers are at the door and the Red Winkies are on that police car?"

The girls gave him a withering look then Alora turned to Tiana. With a nod, she gave Tiana a leg up and she closed the window. After another loud knock on the front door, the girls hunkered low on the ground dragging Rhys with them.

Rhys began to yell at them but Tiana clamped a hand over his mouth giving him a 'don't give me any nonsense look'. He shook her off and began to complain but stopped when he heard a woman's loud authoritative voice shout out to them.

"This is PCF Officer Dwendoleen. Officer Schmartzov had me come here to watch you until your aunt comes back. Don't be bad children, be good ones, and come open the door now!"

"Her cranky voice sounds as scary as the witches in that Macbeth play we saw," Alora whispered.

"True. It sounds like she'd rather cook us all up in her stew pot than take care of us," Tiana muttered. "Let's get go—"

"Must I force my way in?" Dwendoleen yelled gruffly cutting off Tiana's instruction.

"We can't," Schmartzov said. "The judge wouldn't give me a permit for that. She said Washington State law does allow ten-year old's to be home alone for two hours and the older one can watch them all day. So, we'll have to wait them out."

"How unfortunate."

"True, but that's the law, so be it."

"I hear you loud and clear," she groaned.

Tiana picked up her bag and waved them toward the back yard. "Let's skedaddle out of here as Aunt Gertie would say."

Alora nodded and picked up Rhys's strongbox as he picked up her bagged crate. They followed Tiana around the deck to the old carriage house behind the main house keeping as low as they could carrying their boxes. She sighed with relief to see the padlock on the rustic door was not locked. Quietly slipping it off the door, she waved the others though. After Alora, Paris, and Rhys were inside, she softly shut the door and locked it up.

They followed Tiana silently through the carriage house glad to see its back doors were still open and ran down the back alley as fast as they could with their cumbersome packages. After going several blocks east, Paris barked and Tiana turned around. Rhys was behind her but Alora was lagging way behind. She waited for her then led them two more blocks east and one north to the southwest entrance of Garfield Park. Tiana peered around relieved to see not a soul was in the park so she led them east into the shadows of a gigantic oak tree.

"Hey Rhys, you're more fit than I thought you would be," Tiana said nodding at him with some approval. "In fact, you're not puffing as hard as Alora is."

"Give me some credit here," Alora sputtered tersely. "I'm the one carrying Rhys's box which is awkward at best."

"True. I'll take it from here. You carry mine."

"No, I will," Alora insisted. "But I want to circle back later to be sure our friends at our aunt's house are okay,"

"We'd better not. That would draw attention their way. Just keep in mind they're really good at hiding. So, they'll be fine."

"Are you sure?"

"Yes. Pythia and Dodona will curl up in one of their hiding places and being a fly, Harold can hide almost anywhere."

"I know you're right, but I'm still worried."

"Good grief, Alora," Rhys grumbled, "You always fuss over the lamest things."

"I guess I do since I even worry about your safety," she said and for once, Rhys didn't give her a sarcastic reply.

"Now what?" he asked changing the subject.

Tiana peeked around the oak tree at the open, grassy fields, baseball diamonds, and large playground inside the fenced park. "I don't see any Red Winkies."

"Or those Politically Correct officers," Rhys added.

"At least for now." She warily studied the various shrubbery and trees around the park's perimeter.

Rhys looked over her shoulder. "I don't see any places to hide out here."

"True," Alora said. "Auntie Roleena said that years ago the park overseers had the big cedars taken out and thinned the shrubbery because gangs used to wreck the park at night. They wanted it more open so people could see it was clear of trouble. The police have also worked on keeping it safe for all of us."

"Good idea," Tiana said, "But let's get back on track and think of a way to find our aunts. They need our help."

"True, and I'm worried," Alora said biting on her lip.

"Me too, but for now we need to find a place to hide out of the sensing range of the Red Winkies so we can come up with a plan," Tiana said. "Hmmm, the concession stand they use for Little League baseball season is closed today so we can go back past the Bullpen and turn right to hide in the space behind it."

"Bullpen? Here?" Alora asked wide-eyed. "I've never seen them keep any bulls here."

"Yeesh Alora," Rhys groaned. "Of course, bulls aren't kept here. Watch some baseball so you don't sound stupid."

"Look, I might not know much about sports, but I'm not stupid. I just don't waste my time watching dangerous games that hurt your body like boxing and football do. I've read that those players get loads of injuries and some cause brain damage like strokes and dementia."

"Hey doofus, lots of sports don't do that like track, baseball, and basketball. I've played baseball since I was a kid which keeps you in great shape. Proof is, I ran faster than you and I wasn't out of breath, so it seems you're in rather bad shape."

"If I'm in such bad shape how come I can carry your box and you can't?" Alora asked, sharply wounded by his comment.

"Please ease up you two and stop sniping at each other." She then pointed at a long, narrow fenced in area. "Alora, that's called a 'bullpen'. They practice pitching balls in it. Now, let's go to the concession stand and hide behind it then start making plans. We can also keep an eye on the park from there."

"Okay," Alora said

"Rhys?" Tiana asked pointedly when he did not reply.

"We might as well since it's better than doing nothing."

They followed Tiana and Paris trotted along with them as they made their way to the concession stand and stood in the shadows behind it. They all were breathing heavily and Tiana guessed it was more from their apprehension than exhaustion.

"Any ideas of where to go from here?" Alora asked tiredly.

"We can go to Gertie's and lay low," Rhys said.

"Why when what we need to do is focus on finding Aunt Roleena and now probably him too?" Tiana asked bluntly.

"And just how should we go about doing that?"

"I've been thinking about that. Let's hide here until a Red Winkie cloud goes by and then follow them to their lair."

"Bad idea. Then we'll just get caught, and what did you call it? Oh yeah. Enslaved. Tell me you have a better idea than that."

"It 'can' work if we stay out of their sensing range. To start, we sneak across the field to the streets intersecting the west side of the park here."

"Why?"

"For the same reason the chicken crossed the road."

"Tell me your reason's better than 'to get to the other side'," he said rolling his eyes.

"Nope," Tiana with a sly smile. "That puts us by 23rd Street and Walnut, the two busiest roads next to the park."

"I thought our plan was to hide and not be seen by them."

"It was, but I realized that wouldn't help at all. Whatever it takes, we need to find our aunts," Tiana said and Alora nodded. "To do that we must find and follow a big group of Winkies to their hideout. I bet that's where they keep any captured people they have and we'll have a chance of finding them that way."

"That's crazy! I only agreed to do all this running and hiding with you to keep out of the Red Winkies sight. But go ahead, be my guest and do that. It's your neck, not mine. I'll stay here."

"Fine. We wouldn't want to risk that delicate neck of yours," she said dryly. "So, you can stay here and hide all alone."

"All alone?" he asked like it was not appealing either.

"Yes, by yourself since my sister and our little pup Paris are brave. They'll want to help me. Right, you guys?"

"Right," Alora choked out and even looking petrified she added, "I really do want to help find our aunts."

Paris barked gutsily and the sisters grinned knowing he wanted to show he was tough and wanted to help too.

"You can go hide now, Rhys," Tiana said waving him off.

"Argh! It's awfully stupid, but I'm coming with you."

"Suit yourself," she said shrugging then she turned away and hid a satisfied grin. "Now, let's go over there and wait for some Red Winkies to drive by."

"Can they drive now?" he asked skeptically.

"I doubt it, but we did see Red Winkies use that PCF officer and his car to come to Aunt Roleena's house. That showed me they think she's a big threat to them and so is Aunt Gertie. It also scared me to realize they can use any vehicles being driven any direction they want to go by simply riding on them."

"So. why would they ride by Garfield Park?"

"Because those officers have likely gone in Aunt Roleena's house door by now and are searching it. With it open, the Red Winkies there will sense we're not there anymore and want to find us. So, they'll start riding down the streets looking for us and 23rd is used by enough cars to catch their attention."

"Okay, say they actually do choose this street. Then what?"

"As the Winkies come by the park, I'll draw their attention and let them capture me. You two follow me to their lair which is likely where our aunts are. Then sneak in and free us all."

"That's nuts," Rhys said. "Count me out of that plan."

"No surprise there," she said dryly.

"Tiana," Alora forced out, "You'd be better at tracking and freeing us than I would so let me go get captured,".

"No. If I had a choice, I'd send Rhys because I trust you."

"Hey! That's insulting. Why don't you trust me?" he asked.

"You said to count you out, so why do you even ask that?"

"Because I 'can' be trusted if it's not some silly, sappy girly stuff to do, especially the serious stuff you're talking out now."

"You have not shown we 'silly girls' you can be trusted," Tiana sharply after hearing his snide insults about girls. She then turned to Alora. "I'm the best choice. And I know you'll be sure to find a way to get me away from the Red Winkies."

"But I'm faster than either of you," Rhys said pointedly, "I should go do it and I'll have them chase me far enough away from you two that they can't come back and catch you too."

The three cousins argued about who should be caught by the Red Winkies when a police car with sparkling red lights sped down 23rd Street near the park. It stopped at the intersection of Walnut and 23rd as the light turned red then as the light turned green, Paris shot out across the park towards the car barking at it loudly. A cloud of Red Winkies shot off the police car's upper light bar right at him and swarmed him.

The cousins heard Paris barking furiously and immediately stopped arguing and all gaped in surprise to see Paris encircled by the Red Winkies.

"Poor Paris," Alora groaned. "I can't believe we were so busy squabbling we didn't see him set out after them alone."

"Why are they corralling him? He's just a dog," Rhys said.

"The Red Winkies must have sensed his heat signature as being one of us from Aunt Roleena's house," Tiana said. "So, they likely want control of him. But the way he's fighting them, I can see they're finding it hard to do. This is great because that will slow them down. So, thanks to Paris, we can follow them as they take him back to their lair. But we'll need to do be careful not to draw the Winkies attention."

The cousins followed the Red Winkies at a distance as they were led by the furious actions of Paris towards the playground on the park's southeast corner. As the cousins carefully crossed the huge grassy field lugging their boxes, a brilliant light flashed across it blinding them and forced to stop until their vision cleared. When it did, their eyes widened in astonishment.

"You guys," Alora squealed in alarm, "This grass is turning super marshy, and I've already sunk down in it past my ankles."

"Me too," Tiana said working hard to pull her feet up out of the mud to keep moving.

"Watch out!" Rhys shouted pointing across the field that was now a watery swamp.

"Watch out for what?!"

"Believe it or not, a crocodile's swimming our way."

"Seriously?" Alora asked with utter disbelief. "A crocodile?"

"Yikes!" Tiana said. "I see it too, way out there to the right."

"Good grief, there's two more behind it!" Rhys yelled.

Tiana quickly looked around. "Follow me to the asphalt path a few yards to the right of us that goes into that playground!"

"How will that help us? Crocodiles can run on land."

"I know, but for some reason none of them are on any of the paths here. Either way, it gives us a better chance of getting away from them than slogging through this swamp does."

"True," he said nodding.

They forced their legs to work harder and got to the path in seconds climbing up on it then gasping to catch their breath. With no time to lose, they ran down the path to the playground as fast as they could. The first crocodile reached the path near them moments later snapping at them so loudly they jumped. To their great relief, it did not climb up on the path and just swam alongside it. The trio did not need to look behind them as they ran to the playground to know more deadly reptiles were coming closer as they heard them smacking their jaws loudly.

"I'm going to stand up on one of the adult-size swings to get a better look around!" Tiana yelled. She ran over to the middle one and stood on the seat wrestling her box into a position she could hold on to it with her arms looped around the swing's support chains. She saw Alora take the swing next to her and stood on it as did Rhys on the next one. But as two crocodiles swam over and stared at the path, she feared they might figure out how to get up on it and looked around again. "Hey, those crocs still aren't on the path, but it might only be a matter of time. We should jump over to the jungle gym behind these swings so we can climb high enough to be out of their reach."

Alora and Rhys just nodded as they caught their breath. But a minute later, all their eyes widened as they saw splashing near the pathway and saw water and dirt being flung in the air.

"They're digging under the path!" Alora screamed.

That moment the tip of a crocodile snout broke through the ground near them on their side of the path. They all watched in horror to see if it would pop on through, but after a long minute of waiting, it still had not gotten through into the playground.

"You know," Rhys said, "It looks to me like the ground here is too hard for these crocodiles to get through to us."

"I wouldn't count on it,' she said tersely. "I see that water is leaking in from the swamped field the crocodiles are burrowing in from. So, my fear is it is going to make the area soft enough they can break through it. To be safer, I'm going to swing up high and jump over near the jungle gym and climb it."

The very moment Tiana expressed her fear; they all saw the area around the first crocodile's snout bulge and another snout shot up by it making it look like a two-headed crocodile.

"Wow! The water's really rushing in now," Rhys gasped as the other croc's head broke through. "We need to move!"

"No kidding, Sherlock," Tiana said dryly as she swung up higher, wincing to see how dangerously close the crocodiles were to them. "I'm jumping as near to the jungle gym as I can get, because they'll be coming through soon and more will follow them. Okay, here I go." Tiana used the momentum of a high swing to toss her box and it landed by the jungle gym with a splat. She swung high again then let go and landed near it.

"Tiana!" Alora cried out as her sister climbed to the top of the jungle gym with her box. "Rhys has my box, and if he tosses it by the gym, it might break since it's made of glass."

"Hmmm...well, I heard Aunt Roleena say Rhys is a really good pitcher. Is it okay if he throws it to me and I'll catch it?"

"What if it breaks as you catch it?"

"Alora, I'd rather risk it breaking than have you eaten by crocodiles, and we could still pick out the gifts inside it."

"True." Her eyes filled with tears as she held her gift box out to Rhys. "Will you please throw my gift box to Tiana gently?"

"No problem," he said so softly it surprised her.

Tiana stood on top of the gym and steadied herself. "Okay, I'm ready." She saw him nod and he lobbed it to her gently. "Way to go. That was a perfect toss, and Alora, the glass held up great. It showed me it's tougher than we thought it was."

"I saw that and I'm super grateful to see this."

"Me too. Now toss Rhys' box near the gym and make your jump. Because from up here, I can see the ground around those two crocs is weakening and could break through any minute."

Alora threw the strongbox as hard as she could but it landed a couple yards from the jungle gym. "I'm sorry, but it was so big and bulky that's the furthest I could throw it."

"Don't worry about it, I'll go get it. You just start jumping right now!" Tiana urged as she scrambled down to get the box. She then saw her sister jump and land with a big splat by Rhys' box. "Are you okay?" she asked worriedly. Alora nodded and brought the box over to the gym where Tiana waited for her then they both climbed to the top of the gym with it.

"Jump, Rhys!" they both shouted but he shook his head and climbed up the swing's chains to the top bar.

"No way," he said focusing on the area near the jungle gym. "Those two crocodiles got through the hole they dug and swam your way. In fact, if you look closely, you can see their eyes and nostrils above the sawdust floating on the playground. So, I'm staying put. Yeesh! Two more are coming through."

"Yikes!" Tiana gasped and Alora squealed as the first two swam under the gym and stared up at them hungrily. A minute later, the watery sawdust rippled under them and two more of the large reptiles peered up at them.

"I guess my loud landing drew them to us," Alora groaned.

"Whether that did it or not, I can't land over there safely. So, you two go on without me before you lose sight of Paris and the Red Winkies," Rhys said bravely.

Tiana studied the area around the jungle gym then looked at him. "I've got an idea I think will work. But first can you jump as good as you throw?"

"I'd ask you why but I doubt I'd like the answer," Rhys said.

"Probably not, so I'll just show you," she said with a daring grin. She opened her gift box and took the 'Sword of Defense' out of it then removed it from its scabbard. After she grasped the sword's hilt firmly in one hand, she climbed down the far side of the jungle gym warily and began slicing down into the water just inside the gym's inner rim. Three of the crocs swam toward the rippling sound but one of them disappeared under the surface. It put her on high alert and not a second too soon for the submerged crocodile suddenly lunged up at her. She quickly sliced the sword in front of her and it crumpled up like it had hit an invisible wall. She then scurried around the bottom of the jungle gym to finish slicing the water just inside the rim. "Okay, I've got the crocodiles penned in, but I don't know for how long. So, jump over here and climb up."

Rhys quickly slid down the chain and swung up high on the swing then took a big leap landing within arm's reach of the jungle gym with a resounding splat.

"Move it!" Tiana shouted. "A much bigger crocodile is pushing its way through the hole!"

Rhys grabbed the lower bar of the jungle gym and pulled himself up to step on it. His foot was so muddy, he slipped and fell back in swampy playground with a splat. The girls quickly scrambled down and grabbed his arm as he reached for the jungle gym again then yanked him up on it.

"Er, thanks...again," he said climbing the top of the jungle gym with them gulping as he saw the big croc head their way.

"Rough landing followed by a big splat, so you won't make the Olympic diving team this year," Tiana said grinning.

"Maybe not, but at least I made it here," he said grinning back. "By the way, nice sword work."

"Thanks, and I will admit that you do have a good arm."

"Hey you two, I hate to stop your applauding yourselves, but where did the Red Winkies go?" Alora sputtered. "Because if you'll stop and recall it, we need to follow them and get our buddy Paris out of their clutches and find out aunts."

"Sorry Alora, we were just shelling out some much-needed positive input," Tiana said, "And I haven't forgotten Paris or our aunts. In fact, when I first climbed up here, I saw the Red Winkies rush Paris through the side entrance of the playground and out the side on 24th Street. If you look down the street you can now see their glow moving Paris way over there."

"Oh! I see that," she said as she stood up on the gym's dome. "And I can see Paris snapping at them and thrashing around furiously which is making it hard for them to drive him along."

"Good for him!" Rhys said pumping his fist in the air.

"True, but I hope he doesn't run out of energy doing this."

"Me too," Tiana said. "Let's make our way over there and get away from these crocodiles while they're penned in 'and' before more find their way through the hole. So, we won't waste any more time joking around and get going."

"I wasn't joking around. You two were!" she huffed.

"Sorry, I know that. Then let's get going before the Winkies have time to zap Paris even more or herd him out of our sight. Hey, Rhys, we'll each need a free hand to climb safely so you'll need to carry one of our gift boxes."

"I'll carry either of yours since I still can't carry mine," he said glumly.

"That's a bummer, but we'll figure that out later," she said handing her box to him. "Now, I'll climb down the gym's north side and jump over to the slide. Then I'll go up it and you can toss me our boxes, Alora, then you and Rhys follow my route.

Next, I'll go over the bridge to the knotted rope hanging off it and use it to swing as close to the merry-go-round as I can get. Then when you get to the bridge, sis, toss me our boxes again when I'm on the merry-go-round and both follow me over to it. Then being heaviest, Rhys, you jump over to the teetertotter first and I'll toss our packages to you after you've landed safely then we'll both join you. Now, the good news is the teetertotter is just one step away from the paved area around the playground which joins up to the city's street."

"But what if that one step goes watery on us and a crocodile sneaks up and grabs us?" Alora asked biting on her lip.

"Hmmm, let me think." Tiana stared at the watery bog in the playground then looked surprised. "You know what? I think the playground is returning to its solid state." She pointed to what had become a sawdust covered bog. "It must be stiffening up because I can see the crocs under the jungle gym are struggling hard to swim in it now."

"I see that, but why?"

"I think the Red Winkies used their energy to make the park a swamp and to make the crocodiles. But as they herded Paris a couple of blocks away from this area, whatever kind of energy they used to do this fell off due to their distance away now. So, I doubt the ground will give way much at all."

"There's no proof of that yet," Rhys said shaking his head. "So, I'm staying put until I know for sure."

"I think I'm right, but you're free to do as you wish."

"Wait! I'd think about that first. You can't jump there because you drug your sword in the water around the jungle gym. That pens the crocodiles in…and us for a few hours."

"That's right. Thanks for reminding me. Let me think about that," she said frowning but after a moment she grinned. "Ah, but I only sliced down in the water, and with one hand which gives its force a single direction. More proof I know we can do this is that you were able to climb up here after I did that."

"True, but are you sure about all that?"

"Yes, and I'll go first so you can see for yourself I'm right."

"Very well, but I'll wait and see what happens."

"Suit yourself. Okay, Alora, here's my plan. I'll give Rhys his box back and take mine. Then we'll carry our own boxes. Wait for me to follow my plan from the slide to the rope to the merry-go-round to the teetertotter and then a quick step over to the pavement tossing our packages as I said before."

"Okay, I'm with you."

"Good." Tiana then looked at Rhys. "Here's your box."

"Argh," Rhys groaned with frustration. "Wait! I'm coming too. But will you still carry my box and let me carry yours?"

"It must have really hurt to ask me to do that."

"Yes, it did," he said grimacing.

"I bet." She then climbed down the gym and jumped to the slide area without any problem. "See? The sword's power is just working the direction I sliced it." She went up the slide, over the bridge to the hanging rope and swung out to the merry-go-round landing in knee deep water and climbed up on it. "I'm sure glad the crocs under the gym haven't moved much now, but let's all move quickly. Rhys, you're our best pitcher, so toss me Alora's and my box from where you are. Alora, toss Rhys' as far as you can then both of you get over here pronto."

Rhys pitched the girl's gifts one-by-one right to Tiana, and Alora lobbed Rhys' big strongbox close to the merry-go-round.

"Nice throws, you two. Now, get on over here."

"Ladies first," he said surprising the sisters by being so nice.

"Okay, here I go." Alora repeated the route Tiana took and at the end she landed right by the merry-go-round.

"Great swing, Alora," she said helping her up onto it.

Rhys was seconds behind her but landed four feet away from the merry-go-round. He lunged for it and the girls grabbed his arms and yanked him up out of the sludgy ground onto it. "Hey, you two, you nearly pulled my arms off," he groaned when he heard a crocodile snap the air behind him. He turned and saw one had made it through the entrance hole from the other side and just missed grabbing him. "Yikes, that was close."

"It sure was," Tiana said as they gathered in the center of the merry-go-round. "But we still need to jump to the teeter-totter. Fortunately, it's on the other side of the merry-go-round from this crocodile. Remember, we all need to stay on the closer side to keep it low on the ground for each of us to jump onto it."

"But that crocodile will just snatch us off," Rhys gasped.

"No, it won't since it's on the other side of this merry-go-round. Not only that, if you'll look closely it's trying to move, but it's stuck and now all it's doing is snapping at us. So, I think it's safe to make our move."

"Will you show us you truly believe that by going first?"

"I would but that won't work. You must go first since you are bigger than me and Alora. Otherwise, you could toss us off when you jumped over there."

"She's right, Rhys," Alora said nodding.

"Fine, but I still don't want to do this," he grumbled.

"I don't blame you. This is all super creepy."

Rhys nodded then took a deep breath and jumped over. Then to both Tiana's and Rhys's surprise, without having to beg her to do it, Alora leapt over to the teeter-totter landing as lightly as a skilled ballerina.

"Way to go," they cheered and she bowed.

"Okay, move in front Rhys and I'll toss you the boxes one-by-one. Then pass them to Alora who can slide them up over the center top." They nodded and Tiana tossed Rhys the boxes and she eased them over the top. Then they both stood back a bit on Tiana's side to keep the teetertotter low for her to jump on. After she joined them, they sighed in relief. "Alora, you go first and I'll follow. Rhys being biggest, you need to go last so this side doesn't raise up too fast and have us sliding off."

"Got it," he said with a nod and then Alora began slowly edging her way over. But as she reached the top the crocodile behind the merry-go-round suddenly snapped loudly.

"I'm too scared to move," Alora cried out and froze in place. "I might fall and wind up in heaven sooner than I'd like too."

"You're not going to heaven yet, just over the teeter-totter," Tiana told her softly seeing how frightened she looked.

"But I'm shaking so hard I'll fall if I try to walk since there's nothing to hold onto to steady myself," she whimpered.

Tiana knew better than to argue with her when she was this scared and turned to Rhys. "Can you get past me and help her over because you're so strong that with your help I think she can move on over the top."

"You bet," he said. "However, it will be even safer if I just carry her over. Is that okay with you, Alora?"

"Are you sure you can carry me?" she asked quivering. "Because you can't even pick up you gift box."

"Which is weird because I can bench press over two hundred pounds at the gym. And if you'll recall when you two tackled me, I could lift both of you up off me at the same time."

"You're right," she said taking a deep breath. "Okay, do it."

"Here I come." Rhys slowly passed around Tiana and lifted Alora up in a bear hug. He then carried her to the other side pushing their boxes down the other side as he went. Tiana carefully kept her balance as her side of the teetertotter lifted up high. "How you doing, Tiana?"

"Fine, and I find it fascinating to see from up here that none of the crocodiles are moving at all now."

"Wow," Rhys said glancing around. "You're right."

"Finally, good news," Alora said looking at them with a silly smile as Rhys set her down. "I guess we're a lot luckier than Captain Hook was."

"True," Tiana said smiling back. "Since we all have avoided being taken in by their great big grins."

"We sure have," Rhys said chuckling. "And I also agree that the grass and sawdust do seem to be returning to their normal state and all the crocodiles seem to be stuck now."

"Actually, most of them seem to have disappeared," Tiana said tilting her head curiously.

"I don't know. They might be hiding under the surface and guessing wrong could kill us if any are close by us," Rhys said recalling the crocodile who nearly snatched him as he got up on the merry-go-round. "In fact, if I had a rifle, I'd shoot them all."

"Rhys!" Tiana gasped. "They're endangered as it is, and it wouldn't be right to kill them unless there was no other choice. Besides, it's likely the Winkie mischievous ways that turned the ground into a swamp and then somehow put them here."

"Even so, I'd rather take them out before they took us out."

"With them going away, it's no longer an issue," she said. "Plus, this might be a mind game of the Red Winkies and this all could be an illusion they put into our minds."

"It looks real to me," he said pointing at the crocodile stuck in the sawdust-covered ground by the merry-go-round. "And tromping around in the grassy swamp felt real too."

"Well, let's not waste time arguing. Whether it's real or not it won't help us to stand around debating this."

"This has been super scary," Alora said with a shiver.

"True. But we still have to get out of here. I'll go first and take step in the bog then up on the pavement. After that, you can throw me the boxes and follow."

"But one could be hiding under the sawdust and grab you."

"No, they're either gone or stuck now. Not only that, if you think about it, they never got up on any of the paths. Even by the playground they didn't try to and just dug under them. I'm guessing they had to stay in the water or it was all an illusion. As for me, I think it's safe." Without waiting for any objections, Tiana stepped into the bog and up on the pavement with no crocodiles showing up. "See? As I said, the crocs are stuck or gone. Now, toss me the boxes so we can get out of here, and please don't argue. Just do it."

Alora and Rhys looked at each other and groaned but they tossed her the boxes and stepped over to the pavement without another complaint. That moment, their heads all jerked up as they heard Paris squeal sharply.

"Don't you dare hurt him!" Alora screamed running over to the middle of 24th Street right by them to look down it. She saw the Red Winkies had herded Paris over to the park's southwest entrance by 24th and Walnut and hovered around him there.

"Alora, come back. We need to stay together," Tiana yelled.

"I have to be sure Paris is okay," she said in a manner Tiana knew not to argue with her. "Oh no! That big cloud of Winkies has divided in half, and one half is zapping Paris's behind while the other half is guiding him forward."

Tiana ran and caught up with her sister keeping her from running closer. "He's wriggling around like a mad snake, so they aren't able to move him now at all. I'd say he's giving them a tough time of it," Tiana said proudly.

"Oh no, Tiana! He turned and saw us then stopped fighting! Now, it looks like they're able to herd him across the street!"

"He's a really smart dog, so don't worry. I bet he caused this ruckus because he was waiting for us to get free of that swampy croc-filled park. That way we could follow him to wherever the Red Winkie's lair is so we'll be able to find Aunt Roleena."

"And Gertie," Rhys said surprising himself at how upset he felt over this as he walked over and joined the girls.

"Of course!"

"Paris is being such a brave boy," Alora whispered. "But I am praying super hard right now they won't hurt him."

"Me too," Tiana said as her hands clenched into fists.

"Seriously you two," Rhys groaned. "Didn't Aunt Roleena tell you that for some reason they can't do any real harm to us. At least that's what Gertie told me. But he said they can latch onto you and control your movements or zap you a bit."

"And they can obviously paralyze you like they did to both of our aunts!"

"True," he groaned. 'That was a bit of over control to me."

"Well, they certainly can't easily control Paris," Alora said.

Rhys shrugged. "Or it's hard for them to control dogs."

"Either way, he must be super tired now," she sighed sadly.

"Then let's sneak up closer and call out to him so he knows he's putting up with all this is for a good reason," Tiana said decidedly. "But we all must be careful not to attract the Red Winkies attention. That way, they'll feel they can keep moving and not spend all their energy trying to gain total control of Paris." Taking a deep breath, Tiana picked up Rhys's strongbox and strode down 24th Street toward Walnut.

Alora grabbed her box as Rhys picked up Tiana's and they ran and caught up with her. As they got closer, they saw Paris was still being zapped by the Red Winkies to keep him within their circle. Paris whimpered and the trio winced, but a moment later, he growled and snapped a the Red Winkies.

"Way to go Paris!" Tiana yelled as loud as she could.

"Good boy, we love you zillions," Alora shouted.

"You rock, little dog," Rhys added.

They then heard him give a sharp bark and they all hoped he had heard him cheering him on.

CHAPTER SIX
THE MAD GENERAL

    Tiana, Alora, and Rhys stopped and set down their bulky boxes as they neared the Red Winkies and Paris on the corner of Walnut and 24th. They watched them wait to let a car pass then they herded Paris directly across the street to a bus stop there. A minute later, a lady with a toddler walked up to the stop and the Red Winkies drove Paris behind a large bush by it. The trio then hid behind the stone wall on the park's corner topped by a large metal sign saying 'Garfield Park' and waited to see what the Red Winkies would do next. After a few minutes, Rhys started to go over to the corner, but Alora grabbed his arm and pulled him back behind the stone wall.
    "Knock that off!" he huffed. "The whole idea was to stay close to Paris so we can follow the Red Winkies to their lair and we can't see them behind that bush. So, I want to at least cross the street and stand down the block a bit to be closer to them."
    "Just stay here!" Tiana said fiercely.
    "Why? They can't actually see us."
    "But they can sense your body heat and it might attract their attention and we don't want to do that now do we?"
    "No," he growled as he shoved his hands into the upper pockets of his cargo pants. "So, I guess we just wait."
    "Yes. We stay here right across from the bus stop where we can easily see where they go when they herd Paris off again. Then we'll go shadow them."

"I bet they know we're following them since they set the crocodiles in the park after us."

"And they're likely thinking they're smarter than us by doing that and that we're still hemmed in by them," Tiana said.

Rhys shrugged then they all quietly waited. After five long minutes of watching, they heard the woman at the stop groan as she bent down to pick up her cranky crying toddler. The child then blubbered, 'Mommy set me down!' and she firmly replied, 'Not until the bus comes which will be real soon, honey'."

"I guess the bus must be coming soon," Alora said. "And Rhys is right. The Red Winkies can't see us, so maybe we should move over closer to them to see what they're up to."

"No," Tiana said firmly. "It's only been minutes since we were climbing, jumping, and running really hard so our bodies are still overheated. We should stay here until we cool off or the Red Winkies will quickly sense us being there."

"I suppose you're right," she said halfheartedly.

"Look, I know it's tough to do nothing but wait, but you aren't usually this impatient, I am. So, what do you think the Winkies are planning over there that makes you this edgy?"

"I don't know, but I have a bad feeling about this."

"Me too," Rhys said. "Whatever it is, it's likely tricky if you take in account them conjuring up that scary crocodile swamp."

"Maybe they're waiting for the bus," Alora said jokingly.

"Then they'll be in for some disappointment since dogs aren't allowed on buses anymore," Tiana replied.

"Well, I don't know why else they'd be waiting there."

Rhys and Tiana shrugged and they stopped talking as a bus came down the street. It stopped at the bus stop and the mother and child got on. As the bus door closed behind them, the three cousins sighed in relief when the Winkies didn't try to get on. But as the bus signaled to pull out onto the street half of the Red Winkies shot over to it and glommed onto its tail lights while the other half herded Paris up onto the bumper. Tiana groaned but was then shocked when Alora and Rhys ran towards the front of the bus to stop it.

Tiana grabbed hold of their sweatshirts and they jerked to a stop. "What do you two idiots think you're doing?"

"We were going to catch that bus!" Rhys yelled angrily.

"No, you weren't! You were going to become road Frisbees! The front of that bus is so tall the driver wouldn't have seen you there and you'd have been squashed flat."

"Sorry, I can see that now so you're right."

"Thank you for holding us back," Alora said sheepishly. "Now what do we do since we've lost them?"

"We go catch a bus." Tiana tapped on her cell and nodded.

"But I don't think even Rhys could run fast enough to catch up to that bus at its next stop."

"Ah, but I saw it was bus number 29 and just looked it up," Tiana said. "It comes by here every hour."

"But Paris could be in Canada in an hour if it goes north."

"Which that bus doesn't. Even if it did, the Border Guards wouldn't let a dog ride on a bumper into Canada…especially without a passport," she said with a chuckle.

"Not funny, Tiana. This is serious."

"Actually, that was pretty funny," Rhys said smirking.

"Well, I don't, because I'm super scared we're going to lose our furry buddy," Alora said and then burst into tears.

"Sorry," Tiana said patting her sister's shoulder. "I guess that was dumb to say and I'm worried about this whole thing. But if I let myself get so upset I can't think straight, I'll be no help at all. Plus, I do know they're not taking him to Canada."

"Are you sure? Because buses might go anywhere if the Red Winkies take over the controls of the bus by using the driver."

"I know, but the Winkies did not get inside the bus, so this bus will continue south through Lowell Riverside which I saw as I looked up this bus. Give me your smart phone and I'll show you." Alora pulled her phone out of her back jeans pocket and gave it to her. "See? Here's the map of the bus's route showing another bus 29 coming by in an hour and going on into Lowell."

"Oh. Yes…I see that."

"So, all we need to do is catch the next one heading there."

"Okay…but how will we know if they get off?"

"Since Paris will know we can't keep up with the Winkies since they caught that bus. So, as the bus gets to the business area of Lowell, it has to slow down. Being a tiny neighborhood, it also has very few stops. I think at one stop he'll cause such a ruckus with the Winkies he'll break free and jump off. They'll follow him, but he'll fight them until he sees we've caught up."

"I hope you're right."

"Me too," Rhys said and the girls looked at him astonished. "Hey, I like the little fuzzball too. He can be a lot of fun."

"There's hope for you yet," Tiana said with a quirky smile.

"Thanks...I think, if you actually meant that."

She just grinned. "Now, I need to look up the schedule again and find how many stops it has in Lowell." She then winced.

"What's wrong?" Alora asked worriedly.

"Your phone battery just died. Hey Rhys, can you check on the bus schedule for us?"

"Sure." He looked at his phone and groaned. "Bird dip." Alora looked confused. "What do you mean by that?"

"It's what dad says instead of swearing if something goes wrong, which it has. My phone's dead too." Rhys reached in a thigh pocket of his cargo pants and pulled out a charger then hooked it to his phone. "I've got it charging now, but it'll take an hour to do more than text."

"We can't wait that long," Tiana said frankly. "Do either of you have enough money for three bus fares?"

Alora looked in her coin purse the shook her head. "I only have enough for one bus pass."

Rhys sighed heavily. "And I don't have any cash at all."

"I have some credit vouchers, but I'll have to go to a bus station to exchange them for bus passes and the closest is the one east of here by the railroad tracks inside the train station."

Alora sighed. "That's a long way."

"Not really. It's south on Cedar here then across the Pacific Avenue overpass and then straight making it about a mile."

"That's going to be hard to do lugging around these boxes."

Tiana groaned. 'True, and not only that, Rhys' trunk is so big the driver might not let us bring it on the bus. Then we'd have to hide it somewhere since I can't just wish it smaller."

Alora smiled impishly. "Make it smaller you say?"

"Yes, and why are you suddenly grinning like the Cheshire Cat in 'Alice in Wonderland'?"

"Because you just made me remember something cool when you said you couldn't wish his box smaller. I have vials of magic dust and one of them said I could make things smaller."

"Like Alice, doesn't it just make people smaller, not boxes?"

"The note didn't say what it made bigger or smaller, so I don't know, but it's worth a try."

"It sure is!" Tiana said excitedly. "And then you can shrink all of our boxes which would make carrying them a lot easier. Plus, it won't be a problem to take them on the bus."

Alora nodded as she got out her stained-glass box and opened it. She found the vials of magic dust and uncorked the one marked 'small' then sprinkled a pinch of dust over Rhys's strongbox. It shrank the three-by-two-by-two-foot box into a smaller six-by-six-by-nine-inch box. "It worked!" she cheered.

"Awesome!" Rhys reached down to get his box, but as hard as he tried to lift it, he still couldn't. "It's just as heavy as it was before," he said with utter disappointment.

Alora bent down and picked it up. "I don't get why we can lift it so easily and you can't."

"Neither can I." He started to punch it then recalled when he did that before it tossed him back hard and pulled back.

"There's no time to fret over your strongbox now. Alora, please shrink our other boxes while I jog over to get some bus schedules and passes," Tiana said and her sister nodded.

"Let me go so I can do something useful," Rhys said.

"Do you know where it is?"

"Well, no, but I'm sure you can explain that to me."

"No. I don't want to waste any more time than we already have as I only have fifty minutes to do this. I'll go and you two wait here with our boxes. I'll be back as fast as I can."

Tiana dashed off to the bus station and fifty minutes later, Alora and Rhys sighed in relief to see her racing up Walnut towards them. But at that same moment, bus 29 came rushing up to the stop where they were waiting.

"She's not going to make it," Rhys groaned loudly.

Alora bit her lip then thought, *Somehow, I've got to stall the bus. Ah, I've got it!* She took all their boxes in her arms and clumsily climbed onto the bus. As she struggled to get her coin purse out of her jean's pocket, she dropped the boxes. As she bent down to pick them up, she let the money in her coin purse spill out on the floor. She fumbled around picking them up and then looked up at the bus driver. "How much for the ride, sir?"

"Two-twenty for a youth," he snapped. "Now, hurry it up, you're making me late on my route and no one likes that."

"Sorry," she said and to stall for time, she slowly picked out small change and paid the fare coin by coin. "There you are."

"That sure took you long enough. Now, go take a seat." He then glanced at Rhys waiting below. "Are you getting in?"

"I want to, but I don't have any cash," he said. "Do you take debit cards?"

"No, we don't. So, no money, no ride, young man."

"That's okay, sir. I've got it," Tiana said gasping for air as she got to the bus door. She slipped in front of Rhys and held two bus tickets out to the bus driver."

"Load up, and do it quick," the driver said gruffly as he took the tickets. "You know, you three are making me run late and I 'don't' like being late. So, get moving."

"Yes, sir." Rhys said and they all hustled down the aisle. As Alora took a seat in the middle of the bus, Tiana sat down by her and Rhys took the seat behind them. Alora then gave Tiana her box and passed her box to Rhys as she held his strongbox.

"Tiana, I hope you had enough vouchers to get us three extra bus passes, because if we need to get a bus outside the transfer area, we don't have the money to do it," Alora said worriedly.

Tiana shook her head. "I just had enough for two passes."

"And like I said, I don't have any money either," Rhys said. "But I do know where I can get some."

"If it requires robbing a bank, I'm out," Tiana said dryly.

"Don't be ridiculous. It's much simpler and legal. You know Gertie lives in the Lowell neighborhood on South Third Avenue across from Lowell Riverside Park, right?"

"Yes, we both know where he lives, Rhys, but what does that have to do with us getting some bus money?"

"Well, Gertie keeps emergency money on his porch in an old pair of those clunky work boots he likes to wear. He told me if I had an emergency, I could use it. Right now, I'd say this is most certainly an emergency, don't you?"

"Yes!" the girls yelled causing those nearby to glare at them.

Rhys sat thinking for a minute then tapped the girls on the shoulder and they turned around to look at him. "Hey, why didn't Paris get taken away as quickly by the Red Winkies as Aunt Roleena or like Gertie probably was?"

Tiana frowned as she mulled it over then said, "I think it's because the Red Winkies sensed Aunt Roleena's and Aunt

Gertie's heat signatures so were prepared to take them on. But they weren't ready for Paris having never run into him."

"Or could it be they just can't control dogs?"

"Maybe, but from what I saw it seemed like they couldn't get him to budge unless they zapped him with tiny sparks."

"Which would just make a cat bolt," Alora said. "But then they're feistier and smarter than most animals."

Rhys shook his head. "Dogs are smarter, like Aunt Roleena's old wolf-like dog, Centauri was. When she worked Mountain Rescue, she always took him with her to help rescue hikers lost in blizzards. Centauri always found them. Never heard of a cat being smart enough to do that."

"Then let me tell you about our friend, Thor," Tiana said.

"Are you claiming the ancient Norse god of thunder is not only your friend, but is also a cat?" he asked sarcastically.

"No, Aunt Roleena's Siamese cat. He's so smart he knows to take the high ground to whoop on bad dogs and he's good at it."

"Likely little ones. If a big one came at him, he'd take the high ground up a tree. Then he'd just be a 'scaredy cat'."

"You're wrong!" Alora said. "He fought off a mean Pitbull that attacked me and Tiana as we left Aunt Roleena's on our way to the store. Thor climbed her fence and jumped on the dog's head then bit and batted his ears until he ran off yelping."

"That I'd have to see to believe."

"Fine!" Alora huffed, "I got a picture of it as it—"

"Later, it's time to get off," Tiana cut in reaching over her sister to press the stop button for the upcoming bus stop.

"Why are we getting off here?" Rhys asked.

"Red Winkies," she said pointing out the window at a small park as the bus stopped. She took Rhys's box from Alora and handed her sister hers then strode out of the bus.

As Alora and Rhys followed her out of the bus, they saw a cloud of Winkies swarming Paris in the park across the street.

"It looks like the Red Winkies are heading for the bushes behind the park," Rhys said. "How do you want to handle this?"

"By following them at a distance so we don't draw their attention," she said surprised he had asked first before taking off. "Afterall, we don't want them zipping away so fast we can't track them. We just need to keep them in sight since it's our best chance of finding out where they stashed our aunts."

The trio checked for traffic then crossed the street and raced across the small park's grassy area toward the brush and trees at the back where the Red Winkies were herding Paris. As they neared the forested area, they jerked to a stop and gaped. Two dozen Canadian geese waddled towards them from the tree line clacking sharply and snapping their bills at them.

"Now what?" Rhys sputtered as he and Alora backed up.

"Just use your boxes as a ramrod to get through them," Tiana said walking stoutly forward. "They'll move aside."

"Are you sure that'll work? Our boxes aren't very big now."

"I'll go find out." She dashed at the geese holding Rhys' box in front of her and rammed her way through them. After a stunned pause, Alora and Rhys copied her bold move. Then Tiana stopped dead in her tracks as did they as another gaggle of geese came at them. They were even bigger and taller than the first ones all clacking and snapping aggressively.

"Yeesh! Those geese at the back look over four feet tall!" Rhys croaked out as he and Alora came to a halt.

"He's right!" Alora shouted slamming her box into a big one lunging at her. "They're getting super big!"

"I see that," she said knocking two geese aside with Rhys's box as they attacked her. She backed up to Rhys and set his box down then took her box from him and opened it grabbing her tiny lion-tamer's chair out of it. *I hope it works miniaturized.* "Alora! Rhys! Come stand close to me," she yelled and they quickly complied. She swept the chair at the geese and the ones in front tumbled back looking stunned. *Good, it still works.* The geese then honked angrily, wafting their wings to get back up and charged the trio again. Tiana swept the chair more forcefully at them and all the gaggles of geese got tossed back to the tree line. This time as they got back up, they looked bewildered and just honked at each other and to all their relief, they did not attack the three cousins again.

"Alora, give Rhys your box to carry and take his then follow right behind me." Tiana waved the repelling chair out in front of her clutching her shrunken box tight to her side as she walked toward the geese and they backed off. "It's working so stay close to me." She went through the geese as fast as they were shoved away heading the way the Red Winkies took Paris. As they got past the bushes into the trees, they found themselves at the railroad tracks. The Winkies were on the tracks struggling with Paris a mere twenty feet away, so they hid behind a tree. But Paris saw them and stopped fighting so the Red Winkies hustled him back across the park to the bus stop they had just left. The trio followed, but to their dismay another bus came to the stop and let someone out. Once more, as the driver got back on the street half of the Winkies attached to the tail lights and half of them herded Paris onto the bumper.

"Not again," Tiana groaned slapping her forehead. "And none of us has any money left to catch the next bus."

"It's rotten luck, but moaning about it won't help," Rhys said. "Let's go to Gertie's and get that emergency money."

With no traffic in sight, they crossed the street and walked over to Gertie's old Bungalow style house two blocks away from the park. They climbed up the stairs to the porch and the girls saw Rhys's eyes bug open wide in surprise.

"Where's the boots?" Tiana asked looking around.

"They're…they're gone."

"Obviously."

"I swear they were here just before we left!" he said looking stunned as he checked the porch thoroughly and found nothing. "Help me look in the bushes in case they fell inside them."

They all checked the bushes but the boots were not in them. With heavy sighs, they sat on the front porch steps in silence.

"His chair is missing too," Rhys said shaking his head.

"What chair?" Tiana asked.

"The old wooden rocker he kept by the front door."

"Another obvious point since we can see it's not here."

"Hey, you don't have to be so snarky about this."

"Well, you really left us in a fix."

"Me? You're the one who told us to get off the bus."

"That was because I saw the Red Winkies! And if you hadn't said Aunt Gertie left you emergency money here, I would not have left the bus without getting us transfer tickets to let us continue on any bus on these local routes."

"Hey, the money 'was' here because Gertie showed it to me when I came to stay with him," Rhys snapped, "But what I couldn't know was those beat up old boots would get stolen."

"You should've realized someone might do that since lots of street people wander around here and some will steal things."

"I 'did' ask Gertie about that. He said he wasn't worried at all since in the forty years he's left them out, no one has ever bothered to take his ratty old boots."

"Well, it appears they have now."

"Will you two please stop arguing?" Alora begged them.

"Stay out of this," Tiana growled.

"Yeah, this is between your mean sister and me!" Rhys said.

Alora shook her head. "You two are ridiculous." She got up and paced back and forth across the porch as they kept arguing. After pacing for ten minutes, she noticed the drapes over the front window were open a couple of inches and stopped to peek through the narrow opening. However, the light reflecting off of the window kept her from seeing inside. She then cupped her hands around her eyes to block the light and pressed her face against it. "My goodness, come look at this!"

"Why?" Tiana asked stopping in the middle of arguing with Rhys to go see what Alora was looking at.

"From the shocked look on your face, I sincerely hope it's not Gertie's dead body lying inside there," Rhys grumbled.

"Rhys!" Alora said with disgust. "I am 'not' looking at anyone's dead body. What I'm looking at is an old wooden rocker and I can also see some boots on the other side of it."

He rushed up to the porch and squeezed in front of her then looked through the narrow opening and grinned. "You're right. That's Gertie's old boots beside the rocker. He must've brought them inside when he had me go grab some clothes before we came over to Aunt Roleena's. It's odd though, since he's never put them inside the house before."

"Maybe he finally realized someone passing by could take it and didn't know how long it would be before Auntie got back."

"I don't know. Maybe," Rhys said shrugging."

Tiana tapped her toes impatiently. "Enough speculating. Let's go get the money so we can go find our aunts and Paris. So, Rhys, does Aunt Gertie leave any windows open?"

"No, and I have a back door key but forgot to bring it. I do know where he keeps a spare front door key. It's under a rock in the backyard, but there's a problem with that," he said sighing.

"Well, what is it?" Tiana asked him when he said no more.

"He's got a hundred-and-forty-pound guard dog back there."

"You must be talking about the Mountain Bernese mix he rescued from the pound last year that he named 'The General'," she said looking puzzled by his nervousness. "He is a big guy, but he's also really friendly."

"Not to me."

Tiana put her fists on her hips as she looked pointedly at Rhys. "Fess up. What did you do to him?"

"Nothing! Well...hardly much at all."

"If you don't want me to kick you in the shins, spill it."

"I can guess what he did," Alora said glaring at Rhys. "You locked him out of the yard like you did to Paris, didn't you?"

"No!" He then blushed. "But I did sort of let him out."

"Sort of? Something bad must've happened to him or that sweet dog wouldn't have stayed mad at you."

"Stop wasting our time. Just tell us," Tiana growled. "We need to hurry and track down the Winkies and Paris if we're to find our aunts. Paris 'is' a tough little dog, but he can't stall the Winkies for us forever. So, spit it out and I do mean now!"

"Well, some lady reported being terrified a big, scary dog was loose in the neighborhood," he said wincing as the girls made fists like they wanted to beat him up. "Hey, I didn't lock him out! When I opened the gate, he shot out of it and I couldn't get him to come back in the yard. So, when Animal Control got the complaint about him, they came by to pick him up."

"And you didn't stop them from doing this?" Alora gasped.

"I tried to. I told them he's a really nice dog and belonged to my friend, Gertie. So, they had me go with them into the back alley behind his house where they'd boxed him in. But as I got there, he growled and snapped at me. So, they decided he was a dangerous dog. They threw a net over him and dragged him to their truck to take him to the Animal Shelter. Gertie didn't get home until three hours later. He was hotter than a habanero chili when he found out what happened and jetted out of the house to go bail him out. When they got back here the General lunged at me, snapping his teeth so angrily he's been keeping him in the back yard."

"Something's missing here. How did he get loose when you opened the gate? Because Aunt Gertie always has us put a leash on him before we can open the gate to take him for a walk."

"Well, I was in a hurry so I didn't put his leash on first."

"You dolt!" Tiana said. "We've all been told to leash him before we open the gate. His previous owner kept him penned up and never walked him. Now, if given a chance he runs wild, which Aunt Gertie warns everyone about. Worse, it probably scared him to death to be penned up at the animal shelter."

"I know," he said sadly. "But I didn't have a problem when I did this once before so I was shocked he ran off. I tried to catch him but he dove through some bushes I couldn't get through. I looked for him for hours but with no luck. So, as I said, a lady complained about him to Animal Control. They came and when he snapped at me and I couldn't get him in the yard, they took him to the pound. So, he's mad at me for winding up in a cage."

"I'm mad too for your putting the General through that. It makes me even more surprised Aunt Roleena let Aunt Gertie bring you to her house after what you did here 'and' there."

"Actually, she did tell him I couldn't come here," he said sheepishly. "But he told her he was the only one able to take me in for my parent's vacation when their regular house sitter got sick. Her terms were conditional. I had to go wherever he went. So, even though she didn't want me here, she had no choice but to let him bring me if she wanted him to come protect you two. Worse for me was I hadn't heard from my folks for two days."

"Was he the only one who'd take you in?" she asked dryly.

"No comment," he said gruffly.

"I'm guessing with all the pranks you've pulled on everyone and your bratty attitude no one else would have you."

"Ease up, Tiana," Alora said softly, "What he did to Paris and the General was wrong, but fortunately they're okay. Also keep in mind his mom and dad haven't called him for days. I recall how freaked we got on the trip ours took to Hawaii when their hotel called us saying they had not arrived as yet and asked if they were still coming. It wasn't until the next day we found out their flight had been delayed by a bad storm that also took out the local cell tower so they couldn't call us."

"That was spooky, but this is weirder. Aunt Roleena told us today our parent's and Rhys' became unreachable at nearly the same time but she thought it was just an odd coincidence."

"Do you think all our parents are missing?" Alora asked.

"I doubt it, but if they were, we would get them back too." Tiana turned to Rhys. "I'm sorry for talking to you harshly, but it's hard not to after the mean things you've said and tricks you pulled on us." To her surprise, Rhys nodded and looked sad.

"I know," he said sighing. "But give me a chance to change what you think of me. I'll start by risking the General's wrath and go through the back to retrieve Gertie's key since I know which rock it's under. Will you two stay here and watch for any of the Red Winkie clouds while I go around back and get it?"

"Sure, but doesn't Aunt Gertie lock the gates whenever he leaves here for more than a couple hours?" Alora asked.

"Hmmm, you're right. Then I'll just climb over the fence."

"But I'm worried the General might take you down."

"Hopefully, he'll just growl at me like he's done since he got back from the pound." *Though I do hope he doesn't do what you said.* "Now, let me do it and not waste time debating it."

Tiana looked at Alora and muttered, "Just let him do it."

"Fine, go ahead. I just don't want you to get hurt," she said.

Rhys paused, stunned to hear she was worried about him. "Thanks for the thought," he said and quickly sprinted off.

"My goodness. He's fast," Alora said wide-eyed.

"Then let's hope he's fast at finding the key so we can work on getting our aunts away from the Red Winkies," Tiana said.

"And Paris!"

"Of course, but first we have to—" Tiana stiffened and Alora squealed as they heard the General snarl followed by a thump, an ouch, and ferocious growling. She looked wide-eyed at her sister then dashed around to the backyard to check on Rhys. As she got to the fence, she heard him shout, "Get off of me!" She peeked between the wood slats and burst out laughing.

Alora scowled at Tiana as she caught up with her until she looked through the slats. She then giggled to find Rhys flat on his back with the dog standing on his chest drooling on his face.

"Not funny," Rhys sputtered turning his head to the side.

"Yes, it is," Tiana said and the girls both burst out laughing.

"Don't just gawk! Help get this big brute off of my chest!"

"We will," Alora called out after seeing how worried he looked. "Tiana, come on. I'll give you a boost up over the fence and you can go pull the General off of him."

"Okeydokey," she said nodding.

Alora laced her hands together and as her sister placed her foot in them, she boosted her up. Tiana grabbed the top of the fence and lifted herself up on it, grateful the fence had a flat board along the top of it. She swung a leg over the side and the General turned his head towards her and growled fiercely.

"Stop!" Rhys cried out sharply. "When he looked at what you're doing, he lunged forward on my chest hard to growl at you. So, stop what you're doing before he crushes me!"

Tiana froze in place looking befuddled. "General! It's your friend, Tiana," she said lovingly, but he kept growling angrily.

"Tiana, look at his collar!" Alora said. "Then you'll see his collar is glowing red!"

"Wow, and it shouldn't be since his collar is leather."

"That was his old one. You must not have heard what Aunt Gertie told Auntie Roleena when he got home spitting mad from picking the General up at the animal shelter. He said they'd only release him on three conditions. First, he had to pay a fine. Then he had to put a shock collar on him 'and' place electrical posts around the backyard. That way if the gate is left open, he can't go out or he gets shocked badly. If he didn't agree to do this, they were going to euthanize him."

"What a horrible thing to threaten to do to such a good dog!"

"I know, and it's the only reason Aunt Gertie agreed to do it. So, now what do we do?"

"Well, I can't use my tiny lion tamer's chair since it would fling them both back," Tiana said frowning, "And the General would just get madder and get up and tackle Rhys again."

"You're right," Alora groaned.

"I could play my Pied Pipers flute which will entrance them into dancing around and then I could go get the key."

"You can't play and get the key too from under a rock since you need both hands to play the flute. So, when you stopped to get the key, the magic trance would end and the General would come flatten you too."

"Just do something," Rhys groaned. "He's hurting me."

"I'm sorry," Tiana said grimacing. "We're trying to think of a way to safely do this for both you and us."

"Think faster…please."

"We're truly doing the best we can!" she said wincing to see his pained face.

"Tell that to my undertaker," he moaned.

"Hey! I have an idea!" Alora said in a rush as Rhys screamed in pain again. "You take my tiara and go over and mesmerize them then push the General off of Rhys and give him the tiara. You'll get mesmerized but then he can go get the key and guide you back here."

"Okay...something seems wrong about that but I'll try it."

Alora opened her glass box and got the bag with the tiara out then got the vial of enlarger dust. She put a few specks on the tiara in the bag to return it to its normal size and passed the bag up to Tiana. Alora then closed her eyes until she heard Tiana groan. "What's wrong? And you'll have to tell me since I have to keep my eyes shut or it'll bedazzle me."

"No, it won't since it's not doing anything at all."

"Oh! That's right. In the rush to help Rhys I forgot our gifts only work for the ones they're given to."

Tiana sighed. "Me too, so it won't work for anyone but you. That means you'll have to get up here and wear it yourself." She closed her eyes to put in back in the bag and handed it to Alora which caught the General's attention. The big dog snarled and snapped at the girls then Rhys cried out in pain again.

Alora looked tearily at her sister. "This won't work since our movements upset the General which makes him hurt Rhys."

"It has to, because we've no other choice," Tiana said plainly as she reached for her sister's arm. "So, get up here now before he winds up breaking Rhys's ribs."

Alora shook her head. "I don't think I can climb it."

"I'll pull you up so stop thinking and just do it before our cousin's squashed as flat as road kill."

Alora trembled as Tiana took her hand. Pulling her up with all her might, she got her high enough to lean over the fence. With an 'ooof', Alora got up on the top, but the General snarled angrily scaring her so badly she fell back off the fence.

Tiana heard her whimper and began to jump down to help her but stopped as she saw Alora had landed in the soft grass and was just frightened. "Are you okay?"

Alora got up and dusted off her bottom. "Yeah, I'm fine."

"Then get back up here...now!" Tiana snapped angrily.

Alora's eyes widened in surprise and she burst into tears.

"Come on, I can't do this alone," she then said softly seeing how scared her sister looked. "I need your help or I'll have to go over there anyway and wrestle the General off Rhys because I can't leave him with the dog on him like that."

"No, Tiana! He'll bite you."

"Rhys or the dog?" she asked with a silly grin.

"Don't joke. This is serious."

"True, but if you won't help me, I'll have to do it. So, I'm counting on you to brave yourself up a bit and do this. As I said, I really need you to do this so we can rescue Rhys."

When her sister just shook her head, Tiana shrugged and eased her other leg over the fence to get in a position to drop down on the other side. "Okay, here I come."

"Wait!" Alora shouted.

Tiana stopped and looked back at her sister. "Why?"

"Because I'm coming up." She swiped the tears off her face and a determined look replaced the scared one. She backed up and ran at the fence jumping as high as she could. She caught the top and after a struggle pulled herself up high enough to straddle it. The General growled again, but she made herself ignore him and held on tight to the fence.

"Good job! I'm proud of you for doing this," Tiana said brightly and patted her on the back.

"Thanks," Alora said with a huge sigh. "Now, you and Rhys need to close your eyes to not get bedazzled." She then shouted this to Rhys and he choked out, 'Okay'. When their eyes were shut, she got the tiara out and put it on her head. It blazed like diamonds in the sun. "This is awesome," she said grinning then she looked straight at the General. A second later, the huge dog's eyes dilated and he became entranced. "Oh goodie, the General looks all calm and super goofy now."

"Thank heavens," Tiana said with relief. "Well, here I go." She slipped off the fence to the inside landing lightly on the ground keeping her eyes closed to not get bedazzled. A minute later, she had not heard Alora jump down. "Are you going to come down and guide me over there so we can go get Rhys?"

"I'm afraid if I move it might break the spell the tiara has on the General."

"Or you're too afraid to move," Tiana muttered to herself.

"What's that? I didn't hear you."

"Never mind," she sighed. "You stay put while I get Rhys. But you'll have to direct me since I'll need to keep my eyes shut. Then you'll have to give us both directions while he tells you where we need to go to find the stone with the key."

"Okay, but please do this quickly as you can because I don't know how long this tiara will keep bedazzling."

"Good point. Still, it might just keep working as long as you wear it. So, keep it on until we're out of there. Okay, I'm ready and I'll go as fast as I can, but it'll be tough since I'm doing this blind. So, tell me step-by-step which way to go to get to Rhys."

Tiana slowly made it over to Rhys using Alora's directions, relieved they were good ones. She petted the dog first and got a big slobbery kiss from him. *Gross, but at least he's friendly now*, she thought wiping her face off with her shirt. As she pet him, she could feel the dog's two front paws on Rhys' shoulders and gently pushed the General off him. She then nudged her cousin with her toe. "You can get up now."

"Gladly, and you don't have to tell me that twice," he said but he wobbled as he got up then groaned and fell over.

"I bet you feel pretty beat up but you have to get up again so we can go get the key to Gertie's house." Tiana felt around and found his hands then used a gymnastic trick to pull him up to his feet, relieved he remained standing this time. "Okay, Rhys, let's go." She got no answer. "Rhys, let's go!"

"Tiana!" Alora shouted. "It looks to me like Rhys must have faced my way as he stood up because now he's bedazzled."

"Great, just great," she growled. *Argh! Now what?* "Okay, I'm going to turn away and open my eyes hoping I won't get bedazzled. If it doesn't work, you'll have to come help me."

"Wait! I'm thinking." Alora looked around and then smiled. "I have a better idea. I see a big rope tied around a post on Aunt Gertie's deck. Go get that and use it to tie up the General. That way I can take my tiara off and you two can get the key."

Tiana sighed in resignation. "I'm not happy traipsing around blind, but since I can't think of a better way to do this go ahead and direct me to it."

Alora gave her directions but a few minutes later Tiana tripped and fell flat on her face. "Sorry," she said grimacing, "I didn't see the brick edging around that small herb garden in front of Aunt Gertie's deck until you caught it with your foot."

"Please, warn me if there's anything else to trip on," she grumbled spitting dirt out of her mouth as she stood. "Still, I'm glad it was a garden and not a concrete path that I landed in."

"I'm glad too," Alora said contritely "Now, it's only a few more feet to the deck so go slow and wave your arms out in front of you so you don't wind up hitting the post."

"Okay," Tiana nodded and Alora directed her to the post. As she found it, she untied the thick rope from it and Alora directed her back to Rhys and the General. Using a figure-eight knot to tie the rope to the dog's collar, she led the dog to a big fir tree nearby. She tied him to the trunk then backed out of his reach. "You can take your tiara off now, sis."

"Done and bagged," Alora said putting away her tiara.

Rhys blinked his eyes as his mind cleared a minute later, and he rubbed his sore shoulders. "What happened after you got the dog off me?" he asked bewilderedly as he dusted himself off.

"We used Alora's bedazzling tiara to daze the General, but you turned and looked at it before I could stop you," Tiana said frankly. "Now, don't go near him. He's tied up, but he's no longer bedazzled." Her comment was punctuated by the big dog lunging at them and growling fiercely.

"Right," he said with a gulp. "Now what?"

"Back to work. We need to go get Aunt Gertie's key."

"Oh, right. That part's easy since Gertie showed me the big rock he hid it under." He walked to the far-left side of the yard with Tiana on his heels to a rock the size of a big ice cooler. He shoved it as hard as he could, but it did not budge. Tiana then helped him push it, but it still would not move.

"Cripes! I saw Gertie move it, but even the two of us can't," he griped as he stood back wiping the sweat off his brow. "I really don't know what else to try."

"I do."

"What?"

"We dig under the rock until we find the key."

"I can let you know this right now. His tool shed is locked up good and tight. So, what do we use, our fingernails?"

"If we have to, yes." She went and broke a dead branch off a fir tree nearby. She began digging under the rock but found the soil around it was hardpacked. After five minutes, she had only dug a few inches out from under part of the front of it.

"We're never going to get the key at the rate you're going," he said groaning. "So, give it to me and I'll do it."

Tiana shoved the branch at him. "Fine...here! You try it." She waited a few minutes and saw he had not gotten much further then she slapped her forehead. "I'll be right back, but keep on digging." She got a startled look from her sister as she dashed back to the fence where she sat. Tiana did a flying leap and grasped the top then flung herself over it. She ran to her gift box she had left by the fence and dug around inside it.

"What are you looking for?" Alora asked curiously.

"Something better than a stick to dig a key out from under a big rock," she said with a big grin as she pulled her 'Sword of Defense' out. "Come restore it please, but also be careful not to touch it? I don't want you to get burned."

"Of course." Alora jumped down by her and got her 'bigger' dust out then sprinkled a few grains on the sword returning it to its original size. "It does look better than a stick."

"Yes, it does." Tiana heard loud gnashing noises and looked through the fence slats. "Yikes! The General's chewing through the rope I tied him off with. I have to get over there before he does or he'll attack Rhys again. So, after I jump over the fence and get to Rhys put your tiara on to dazzle the General."

"It won't work because he's not looking my way!"

"Then I'll draw his attention towards you and give you a yell when you need to put it on!" She jumped up to get on top of the fence but her sword got caught between two boards and jerked her back down. She heard a snarl and looked through the fence slats just as the General tore free. He spied Rhys and barreled at him through the yard's bushes like a speeding freight train. "Run Rhys, run!" she screamed. "The General's loose!"

Rhys' eyes popped open wide as the dog came at him but kept a cool head. He clasped the top of the big rock he was digging under and flung himself over it. The General slammed into the rock and yelped. The dog looked dazed, but as wobbly as the big fellow was, he sniffed around for Rhys.

"No, no, no," Alora moaned and began sobbing.

"Stop crying and pull yourself together. I'll fix this. Just get ready to put your tiara on and look the General's way." Tiana fairly flew over the fence waving the sword high over her head to get his attention. "Hey, you big galoot! Come get me!"

The huge dog whirled around and spotted her. He snapped the air and charged her. Rhys saw the General was going to mow her down and yelled at the dog to come get him, but to Rhys's and Tiana's surprise their cries paled in comparison to Alora screaming at the dog like an enraged winged Fury. It got his attention and he turned and started racing toward her.

"Tiana, Rhys, close your eyes!" she yelled. They quickly did so and she shoved her tiara on her head. The General became entranced within seconds, and he slid to a stop.

"Good going, sis. That was a close one," Tiana choked out. "I forgot to yell 'put your tiara on', so you saved our necks."

"Glad to," she rasped shaking so hard from the adrenaline rushing through her from her close call, she had to clasp the fence to keep from falling off it.

"We've no time to waste so guide me back to that big rock by Rhys." Alora nodded and gave her sister directions. Tiana held her breath as she passed the General as she blind-walked over to where Rhys stood staring at the rock. "Okay, cousin, let's keep our backs to Alora and our eyes on the rock to keep from getting bedazzled."

"No kidding, and since you've run yourself ragged, let me do the digging," he said taking the sword from her. Once again, the sword flashed with fire. He yelped and quickly dropped it then blew on his hand to cool it.

Tiana groaned as she looked at him. "Don't you ever learn?"

"Of course, but sometimes I also rush into things just like another cousin I know," he said smirking but then he winced.

"Yes, I know, like me...sometimes," she said grimacing to see him grit his teeth as he blew on his burned hand. "Should we take you to a hospital?"

"No, it's not as bad as last time, so just dig."

Tiana nodded then looked at the rock recalling how hard the ground was as she tried to dig under it with a stick. She took a deep breath and grasped the 'Sword of Defense' with both hands then stabbed it in the hole at the base of the rock as hard as she could. The ground rumbled like an earthquake and the stone jumped up a few feet and split in two. The energy it released tossed Tiana and Rhys back several yards and they landed on their rears with a thump as the two big stone pieces fell to opposing sides. After blinking in awe, they got to their feet slowly being a bit stunned and brushed themselves off. They checked each other for injuries, relieved to find none. As the dust in the air settled, they smiled to see a key right under the area where the stone had sat.

"Wow, that stone was in there a lot deeper than I thought it would be," Rhys said scratching his head.

"That it was. I'd say it was almost in there three feet."

"I'm glad the blast didn't destroy the key."

"Me too," Tiana said crawling down in the hole and fishing the key out of it. "Okay, let's go get Aunt Gertie's boots and see if the money's still in them."

"I hope so, but I'm worried we already lost our big chance to find our aunts and Paris."

Tiana frowned. "What do you mean by saying that?"

"Well, it's because I'm worried we won't be able to track the Red Winkies down since they're likely long gone by now."

"Somehow, someway, we will do this," she said grittily. "Now, back to it. Remember Alora needs to guide us back to the fence since we have to close our eyes as we turn around to not be mesmerized. Hey Alora, did you hear that?"

"Yes!" she shouted back. "Are you ready?"

"We are," Tiana replied closing her eyes after seeing Rhys close his. Alora then verbally guided them to where she sat on the fence. As Tiana reached it, she pulled herself up over it.

"Climbing this fence is going to really smart," Rhys said clenching his teeth as he eased his sore body up onto the fence. He dropped down with a grunt to the other side and moaned as he grabbed ahold of his sore chest. "I need to rest a minute."

"No doubt after getting pummeled by Aunt Gertie's Winkie driven dog. Maybe we should we take you to a hospital."

"No. I heal fast, so I'll be fine pretty soon."

"Tough guy, huh," she said with a wry little smile.

He shook his head. "Not so much right now, but at the moment, I'm more worried it's taken us hours to get the key."

She glanced at her watch. "Nope, it only took one hour."

"Hey, you two," Alora said. "Can I stop staring at the General now and take off my tiara?"

"Wait a sec and I'll hand you the bag for your crown." Tiana felt around on the ground and found it. "Here, sis," she said closing her eyes as she waved it in the air by her.

"Got it." Alora took her tiara off and stuffed it in its bag. "Okay, it's safe to open your eyes and not get dazzled like the dog." She slid off the outside of the fence landing with a loud plop next to Rhys. The noise caught the General's attention. No longer entranced, he charged at them and hit the fence they all leaned against like a tank knocking the three of them onto their behinds by the force of the impact.

"Sorry, I should've landed more lightly," she grimaced.

"At least the fence held up," Rhys said getting up. He then stunned the girls by taking a hold of one of their hands and gently pulling them up to their feet.

"Thanks," Alora said giving him an astonished look.

"You bet, and thank you for keeping us safe out there."

"Ditto," Tiana said. "Now, come on. Time's a wastin' as Aunt Gertie would say." She ran around to the front of the house with the others right behind her.

"I hope we can figure out where the Red Winkies went," Rhys said uneasily as Tiana unlocked the door.

"We will," she said with absolute conviction as she opened the door then everyone piled inside the house.

"How?" he asked as they all ran over to get Gertie's boots.

"Don't worry, Paris is smart. I'm betting he left clues for us. We just need to keep a sharp eye out for his trail."

"His trail or his tail," Rhys said jokingly.

"Either," she said glad he had lightened up.

"My hope too," he said sticking his uninjured hand in one boot as Tiana grabbed the other. "Nothing in this one."

"There's something in this one, but it's not money." She frowned as she fished a piece of wadded up paper out of the boot, but as she flattened it out, she groaned.

"It doesn't look like money," Rhys said disappointedly.

"And it's not. It's a note."

"Well? What does it say?"

"It says, 'Go to my disposal site, where pungent things are kept out of sight.'"

"Gross," Alora said scrunching her face up. "It's one of his super silly rhyming messages. Where do you think it is?"

"It's a disposal site so it's likely a garbage can," Rhys said.

"Okay, let's get it over with." Tiana then looked at Rhys. "Where does Aunt Gertie keep his garbage cans?"

"Out in the garage," he said wincing. "Which means this just got worse, because that's out across the yard by the garage."

"Or it could just be a waste basket," Alora said. "So, let's look inside first because I'm hoping it's in one of them here,"

"It's worth a try. So, let's start checking the rooms and see if we find anything then meet back here in five minutes."

Five minutes later they came back to the front room looking disappointed and for a long while no one said a word.

Rhys sighed. "You don't have to ask. I'll do the dirty work and go tackle the big garbage cans out by the garage."

"I'll wear my tiara and guide you over there so the General can't attack you," Alora told him shakily.

"Just a minute," Tiana said. "Rhys, are you sure there's nowhere else here to look first?"

"Nothing comes to mind," he said gloomily. "So, I'll need to look there since we didn't find it in the house."

"Then let's go," Alora said walking towards the back door.

"Wait!" Rhys said. "There is one more place to look."

"Where?" Tiana asked but he was already running down the hall so the girls followed him.

He dashed to the bathroom then paused to put burn salve and gauze around his burned hand. He then went over to the laundry hamper and pulled out a big pile of dirty clothes. At the bottom were several pairs of stinky socks and the girls pinched their noses as he held them up. "It's another kind of disposal site, and these are pretty pungent," Rhys said grinning.

"Got that right," Tiana said backing away from the stench.

He began going through them and stopped as he pulled a wad of paper out of one of the dirty socks. He straightened it out. "It's another note from Gertie."

"What does it say?"

"Antidisestablishmentarianism," he said frowning. "Any ideas what it means?"

The girls looked at each other and burst out laughing. "Yes!" they both said.

"Well?"

"It's a word game Aunt Gertie plays with us," Tiana said.

"I need more of an explanation than that for me to know what to do from here."

"Well, we played this game if we were here on a holiday like Easter. We had to figure out how to spell a word then look it up to find a clue leading to the spot he hid our Easter baskets."

"Or our birthday presents," Alora said with a giggle.

"He did try to do that with me, but I got so much from my parents I didn't take the bait and look for them," Rhys said.

"Too bad. It was fun, and now we know we're on the right trail to find the money," Tiana said. "But we need a dictionary to go any further."

"Follow me." Rhys led them down the hall to Gertie's den. Other than an old oak chair and antique schoolroom writing desk, the room had only floor-to-ceiling shelves on all the walls filled with hundreds of books. He got a Meridian dictionary off one lower shelf and paged to words starting with 'anti'. "I don't see the word here. Maybe Gertie didn't spell it right," he said showing the girls the piece of paper he found in the sock.

"Nope, it's spelled correctly," Tiana said as she pulled out a Webster dictionary to look up 'antidisestablishmentarianism'.

"Are you sure?"

"Yes, lamebrain, it's one of the spelling bee words Aunt Roleena quizzed us with since she likes word games too."

"I'm not a lamebrain," he said looking hurt. "And it was a mean thing to say."

"Tiana, it really was a mean thing to say," Alora said softly.

"Yes, it was. Sorry Rhys," she said sincerely and he nodded. She then pulled out a Roget's dictionary. "It's not in this one either, but there's loads of others so let's keep looking."

Knowing that, they paged through dictionaries on the shelves but after finding twelve others no one found one with the word antidisestablishmentarianism in it.

"Hmmm," Alora said tapping her chin thoughtfully, "When Auntie Roleena taught us to spell antidisestablishmentarianism, she told us it's now an antiquated word. So, it's likely in a super old dictionary that doesn't look like the ones today. That means we need to look at all the ancient books here to find it."

A minute later, Tiana's sharp eyes spied an enormous book shoved back on one of the top shelves. It was ragged on the edges with a cover so worn and faded she could not make out the title. She brought the chair over and stood on it. She lugged the huge book down then sat in the chair as she opened it up. A moment later, she gave an excited shout. "I found the word and this was tucked in by it!" she said waving a piece of paper at them. She then read it and looked puzzled.

"What now?" Rhys asked. "Because you look stumped."

"I am, because it just says; 'Sing the first four lines of the song 'Up on the Housetop'."

"Okay, then let's sing it," Alora said.

Rhys blushed and shook his head. "No way."

"Come on, just do it."

"You've got to be kidding me," he groaned.

"I bet he doesn't even know the words," Tiana said.

"So what. It's a kid's song."

"Tiana, ignore him and sing it with me."

"Okeydokey," she said nodding and the girls sang:
> "Up on the housetop reindeers pause,
> Out jumps good ole Santa Claus,
> Down through the chimney with lots of toys,
> All for the little ones Christmas joys."

"How's that's going to help us?" Rhys asked dryly.

"It won't until we go up on the housetop," Alora said.

"Bad idea."

"Why?"

"First of all, with his steeply pitched roof he'd know it's too dangerous, and if it rained it would ruin any note he wrote us."

"Good point."

"Ah ha! But there's only one working chimney." Rhys ran to the ancient woodstove in the kitchen with the girls on his heels. He opened the heavy iron door on the front and stuck his hand in the ashes. "Hurrah!" he shouted as his hand shot in the air with a note in it, but he scowled as he opened it and read it over.

"Well?" Alora asked anxiously.

"This note doesn't make sense at all."

"Why?"

"Because it's...well, it's written in 'Gertie' language."

"Rhys, just tell us what it says," Tiana said groaning.

"Okay. Okay. It says; 'If ye *find* yerself with a sudden loss it now be a *grave* situation. Now's the time to *visit those that first lived in house ye do now to get help* fer yer sorrows. Ye must be plucky and *look high, low and far* in *strange places,* and *'do not go back to find what's no longer there'.*" Rhys scratched his head as he showed the girls the note. "The words; find, grave, visit those that first lived in house ye do now to get help, look high, low, and far, and do not go back to find what's not there anymore, are written squiggly and it all seems nonsensical."

"It's a riddle," Tiana said pointedly.

"Okay, I can guess I can see that."

"Do you, since you said it all seems nonsensical?"

"Then do explain it to me if you're so sure of that," he said.

"I know what the part that says 'visit them that first lived in the house ye do now to get help for your sorrows' means. Aunt Roleena told us the house was built by Mr. Watson in 1906 as the old utility records show the gas and water were turned on then, and look high, low, and far comes as no surprise. What is confusing is 'do not go back to find what's no longer there."

"I get that part. Gertie didn't want us to waste our time or endanger us by us going back to Aunt Roleena's," Rhys said.

"Why would it endanger us?" Alora asked innocently.

"I bet he guessed the Red Winkies would find us there and if he had to lead them away from us, which he did, they would go back to find us. So, he didn't want us to do that. I bet he also knew they could control some people like the officer who came to ticket you for not wearing red on your shoes which is absurd. Then we gave him the slip at our aunt's house, so the Winkie run Politically Correct Officers or PCF officers as they call themselves, would keep an eye out for us going back there. So, now what do we do?"

"I know what we can do! I just remembered when I asked Auntie Roleena what happened to the original owners, she told me she found out they are in 'Old Town Cemetery' which is just a few miles south of here."

"Ah, then that would be their 'home' now," Tiana said.

"Yes, but it's a long way to walk with the Red Winkies out after us." Alora said worriedly.

"True, but he did warn us we'd have to go far for answers."

"And look 'high and low in strange places'," Rhys added.

"Low! That's it!" Tiana suddenly said brightly.

"Whatever are you talking about?"

"I know you're an A student, but sometimes you're thick as a brick. Move over." Tiana squeezed into his place in front of the woodstove then stuck her hand deep down under the cold ashes and pulled out a thick envelope after knocking the dust off of it inside the stove. "Ta da. 'Low' is one of the strange places he said we needed to look," she said grinning. She went to the kitchen and set the envelope on the counter then opened it. To her surprise a dozen quarters fell out of it. Then all their eyes widened as she pulled out a thick wad of cash and handed it to Alora. "Ick, I'm going to go wash my hands why you count it."

As Tiana went to the sink to wash her hands, Alora counted the money. "Wow! There's four hundred dollars here in ones, fives, tens, and twenties…and that doesn't count the change. That's a lot of money. So, why do you think he left so much?"

"I bet he guessed if he and Aunt Roleena were incapacitated by the Red Winkies, we'd need it," Rhys said matter-of-factly.

"He might be right for how things look now," Alora sighed.

A loud knock on the front door made them all jump. Tiana put a finger to her lips to warn them not to say a word. As they waited silently, the knocking just kept getting louder.

"Is anyone in there?" a male voice asked sharply.

The cousins all groaned and looked at each other in dismay.

"Officer Schmartzov," Tiana whispered grimacing.

"It sure is. Now what?" Rhys whispered back.

"We need to go out the back door or a side window."

"Bad idea, and you two won't want do that since…" but his words were left dangling as he gaped at the girls in surprise. For in a blur of action, Tiana grabbed his strongbox while Alora shoved the money on the table in her jeans pockets and grabbed the other boxes. They then dashed to the back of the house.

"Wait!" Rhys shouted but his words fell on deaf ears as they were already out of sight.

**

CHAPTER SEVEN
OLD TOWN CEMETERY

Rhys groaned as Tiana and Alora ran off like horses at a racetrack when the gate opened. He took a deep breath and ran after them. He found them already at the back of the house in a mudroom filled with old leather boots, buckets of rocks, picks, rock saws, and rockhounding gear. Their gift boxes lay on the ground by Alora, and Tiana had finished turning back the three deadbolts on the old oak backdoor. She then yanked on it hard, but it was stuck.

"That's a truly bad idea," Rhys said walking over to her.

"Why?" she asked turning to him briefly and as she jerked harder on the door it popped open. He grabbed her arm and pulled her back but she fought him to get free. "Let me go!"

"You'll see that's another bad idea if you look over your shoulder," he said pointedly.

She stopped fighting him and glanced back. "Yikes!" she sputtered seeing a twenty-foot drop to the ground below with only the sides of a stairway left hanging there and ending at a stone walkway on the side of the house. "The stairs are gone."

Rhys made sure she had a tight hold on the door frame then let go. "I tried to tell you that 'and' that the side windows on the house are too high to jump from or painted shut, but you two ran off before I could explain that to you."

"Thanks for stopping me," she choked out. "I could've sprained an ankle."

"I'd say that stone walkway's more of a bone crusher."

"You're right, but we need to leave and we can't go out the front door with that officer here so how can we sneak out?"

"There's only one window I know of we can use to get out without being seen."

"Where?" she asked tersely when he said nothing more.

"I'll tell you, but first listen to what I have to say before—" he stopped as the PCF officer knocked on the front door again.

"This is Officer Schmartzov. A neighbor across the street just called our station. They saw three kids enter this house and said only a man lives here. Turn yourselves over to me or I will get a warrant to enter and take anyone I find into custody."

"Rats," Tiana groaned. "It's bad luck he found us again and so quickly. Rhys, we'd better hurry and go use that window you said we could use to get out of here unseen unless either of you has an idea of how we could just get rid of him."

"I have one," Alora piped up. "Rhys, you could wear Aunt Gertie's robe and nightcap and tell that officer to come back later because you're sick with the flu."

"Seriously?" he asked dryly. "I doubt that excuse works on him, especially with his mind charged up by Red Winkies."

"But Auntie Roleena said they can't control our minds."

"Still, Gertie told me the Winkies can magnify the thoughts, emotions or prejudices you have. Especially people unaware of them. Also, he'll likely be unreasonable because he's already miffed at us for getting away from him."

"So, they can actually magnify your thoughts," Tiana said. "Interesting. Well, from what I've seen, I believe you."

"I do too and it's super scary," Alora said biting on her lip.

Schmartzov then yelled, "Open this door now!"

"Head to the kitchen," Rhys urged them. "So, we can go out the window I mentioned before he bashes his way in here."

"But the windows there look too high to jump out of."

"True, but there's a door there that leads to the basement."

"There is? I've never seen one," Tiana said with surprise.

"That's because it's so well hidden." Rhys grabbed her box and sprinted to the kitchen. The girls got the other two boxes and ran to catch up with him. As they got to the kitchen, he had opened the lower cupboard to the left of the sink. He then took out a stack of frying pans and pots exposing a modern keypad on the wall inside it. He tapped several numbers on the pad and they heard a loud click on the wall behind them then the antique china hutch sitting against the backwall slid aside. A section of the wall behind it then moved back and to the side and the girl's gaped in awe to see a landing and stairway behind the wall. He went through the opening and down the stairs disappearing into the darkness below. When the girls did not follow him, he ran back up. "What's the matter now?" he huffed.

"Is Aunt Gertie some kind of spy?" Alora asked warily.

"No, and why would you even ask that?"

"Come on, Rhys, you can guess why she asked that. I mean, how many people have secret doors behind their walls?" Tiana asked dryly. "It is a rather cloak-and-dagger thing to do."

"You're questioning a mere hidden door leading down to a basement after living with Aunt Roleena's oddballs like talking flies and snakes?" he sputtered. "She's got stranger things by far than Gertie. Let me point out that just today I was threatened by talking pythons that live in her house and had to go in her truly creepy basement that you call a dungeon. Plus, one snake said our aunt had special places made for them to hide in. So, maybe she has some too."

"She does have a...ouch!" Alora said but Tiana elbowed her and shook her head so Alora pinched lips shut.

"We can't tell you anymore until 'she' says she trusts you," Tiana said. "For all we know, it's another trick of yours. Or you are in league with the Winkies and are helping them trap us."

"That's ridiculous," he said indignantly. "I'm not in league with the Red Winkies, and it's not a trap. It's just a basement. Not only that, keep in mind I just trusted you by showing you Gertie's secret door and the stairs leading down there."

"Then after you prove we can get out of here by using the basement without that PCF officer nabbing us, we might feel more like trusting you. But you have a lot to live down since we've never tricked you like you tricked us 'many' times, like hiding and jumping out to scare us or trapping us in rooms," she said tersely as both she and Alora glared at him.

"Okay, you're right so stop trying to fry me with your eyes. Now, come on down and see for yourself that it's not a trap."

"First, turn some lights on down there so we can see where we're going," Alora said.

"But doing that will alert that policeman we're down there."

"He's got a point," Tiana said glancing at her sister.

"Maybe so, but I still won't walk down any stairs in the dark. That's super dangerous as you can't see where you're going and could miss a step and fall," she said with a shiver.

"Alora, please just do it."

"I...I can't. I might fall and break my neck."

"That's ridiculous," Rhys said. "Don't be such a baby."

"It's not ridiculous. It happened to Aunt Roleena's neighbor last winter. He fell and broke his neck going down his stairs. Since he lived alone, he wasn't found for weeks and he died."

"Sorry. I didn't know that. But it doesn't change the fact we need to leave and our escape window is down there. And if we don't get out, we'll be nabbed by that officer and put in jail."

"He's right, Alora," Tiana said frankly.

"I just can't do it!" she cried. "So, you two go without me."

"No, I won't leave you which means we'll both wind up in jail and can't go save our aunts and Paris. Let me also remind you her neighbor didn't have handrails to hold on to and we do. So, if you take hold of it with one hand while I hold your other and Rhys stays right in front of us, we can be sure you don't fall," she said holding her hand out to her sister.

That moment the officer yelled, "I called for a warrant to enter your house since you haven't responded. It will be here within the hour and then I'm coming in to apprehend you."

Tiana and Rhys gasped and looked at Alora imploringly.

"I'll give it a try," she said but did not move.

Rhys suddenly slapped his forehead. "I don't know why I didn't remember this sooner." He dashed into the kitchen and came back with two pocket-sized flashlights and handed one to Alora. "Now, you can see the stairs by using this."

"Err...thanks," she murmured. "Is there one for my sister?"

"I could only find two. Do you want mine, Tiana?" he asked.

"No, I'm fine."

"Okay, let's go." He waved them both inside the landing by the stairs and tapped the keypad on the inside wall by the opening. There was another loud click and the movable section of wall closed over the opening followed by the sound of the china hutch moving back in place then a hushed silence when it stopped.

"Wow, it's dark," Alora gasped turning on her flashlight.

As Rhys turned his light on, he saw Alora's worried face. "Hey, I had to close the wall back up so that PCF officer can't find his way down here. Now, since you're looking at me like I'm a murderous villain in a slasher movie that's just trapped you in here, I'll lead the way down. Then hopefully get us out of this house before you get all worked up into a frenzy."

"I know you're not a villain, but please do go on ahead."

Rhys led them slowly down the stairs and heard Alora sigh in relief as they safely reached the bottom. He continued going halfway across the big, open basement and stopped under a window at the top of the left wall. "This is our escape route. So, come on over but point the flashlight down so its beam doesn't draw the officer's attention." Alora nodded and did so.

"Wow. This ceiling's a lot taller than Aunt Roleena's is and that window's awfully high up but we still have to find a way to get up to it," Tiana said as the girls walked over to him, "Now, since you two have the flashlights go check and see if there's anything here to get us high enough to reach that window since it must be close to twelve-feet up from the floor to its edge."

"Goodness," Alora said, "That's going to be tough to do."

"None-the-less, it's got to be done so get looking." Tiana watched them scan the floor with their lights and saw pick axes, shovels, a big leather rucksack, and a huge, framed tarpaulin mountain climbing pack lying against the far wall but otherwise the basement was empty.

"There was a ladder down here," Rhys said with frustration.

"Not anymore," Tiana said "Alora, hold your light on the packs and I'll look for a rope we can throw over one of the floor beams here then use it to climb up to the window."

Rhys shook his head. "That won't work because the floor rafter and upper floor are joined together to tight to do that."

"Well, since that won't work, let's hope we get lucky and find something else that's useful in those packs."

Alora nodded sharply. "We're way overdue to have some luck." She guided the way over to the rucksack with her light and Tiana rummaged through it as Rhys searched the other one.

"All I found is some thick wool socks and gloves, a waterproof poncho, and a small tin of waterproof matches," Tiana said pocketing the matches.

"This pack only has a small day pack inside it with some trail maps," Rhys said. "Also, just so you know, I did check and a rope would not have helped us because there aren't any spaces above the rafters to put a rope through even if we could reach the ceiling to do that."

"Then we're trapped down here," Alora said fretfully.

"Maybe not. Why not use your magic dust to make the boxes big so we could stack them up and use them to climb up there."

"But without a rope there's no way to pull the lower boxes up with us after we all got out."

"Good point. Then how about making me fly like you did at Aunt Roleena's? Then I can fly you and the boxes out of here."

"Are you crazy?" Alora sputtered. "No way!"

"Why not?"

"Because there was a ceiling in Auntie Roleena's house."

"So what," he said shrugging. "There's one here too."

"The 'what' is that once you went out the window you'd just keep going up and up and up and might never come down."

"Oh," Rhys said scowling, "That 'is' a problem."

"Yes, it is, and I can't think of how else to do this," Alora said worriedly and she saw Rhys and Tiana looked worried too.

"Rats," Rhys said disappointedly then he felt his bruised ribs and shoulders from Gertie's dog pummeling him and sighed.

"Where?" Alora gasped looking around.

"There aren't any. It's just I realized how we'll have to do this. You two will have to climb up to my shoulders and stand up then you should be able to get out the window up there."

"Yikes! That's going to hurt," Tiana said grimacing.

He sighed heavily. "I'll live."

"But can I or Alora even reach the ledge if we do that?"

"Only one way to find out. So, I'll brace myself on the wall under the window and you climb up my back then stand on my shoulders and unlock the window. After you go through it, Alora can climb up and pass our boxes out the window to you and then climb out through the window."

"Okay, but then how will you get out?"

"I'll run and jump up and catch the ledge then you two grab my wrists to keep me from slipping off it and help pull me up."

"Even though you're over six feet tall and have a long reach you'll have to jump up over three feet high to catch the ledge."

"I'm a good jumper so I think I can do it, and if it doesn't work, you two can go on to save the others."

"No! We stay together," Tiana said firmly and Alora nodded.

Rhys looked surprised. "You two actually want me along?"

"Yes, I guess we've gotten used to you. Besides that, you're good at running and throwing so that's useful."

"Thanks," he said grinning. "Now, let's do this."

"Okay," she said and Alora nodded. "Oh, and you know, there's another good thing to doing this, Rhys."

"What?"

"You won't have to drop eight feet down like we did last time since this window is level with the walkway outside."

"Good, then it sounds like we have a plan."

"First let's empty the packs so we can put our shrunken gift boxes in them. It'll leave our hands free if we carry them on our backs." Tiana said. "By the way, Rhys, thanks for offering to do this, because with your bruises I know it's going to hurt when we climb up your back to get out of the window."

"I'll survive. Now, we need to get moving before 'the big bad wolf' out front comes to blow Gertie's door down."

"Gotcha," she said and they quickly emptied the tarpaulin pack and leather rucksack putting Rhys' strongbox in the huge tarpaulin pack and the girl's boxes in the rucksack. Rhys then got in position under the window to put their plan in action. Luck was finally on their side and it went off without a hitch.

It was just in the nick of time for as they pulled Rhys up through the window the PCF officer yelled, "I have a warrant and I'm coming in!" Then came a horrible splintering sound and they knew he had kicked Gertie's front door open.

Rhys jumped to his feet grabbing the rucksack with the girl's two boxes and throwing its straps over his shoulders. Alora beat Tiana to the tarpaulin pack giving her a 'don't argue about it' look. She nodded taking the small pack should they need it.

Rhys led them through the neighbor's backyard and the girls grinned to hear him apologize to their empty house for them trespassing. The yard stopped at the alley and as they got to the end of it, he checked to be sure no one was in sight. "All clear. Now, I just hope if we have to leave another house, we can do it by opening a door and not jumping or climbing out a window."

"I totally agree," Tiana said.

"Me too," Alora said. "But tell me how do we get to the graveyard from here? Because as far as I know, even if we caught a bus, I doubt any of them stop there."

"Let's go up to Fourth Avenue because a friend of Gertie's lives on that block. Then we'll stand on their porch to make it look like we live there, and I'll call for a cab," he said running up the sidewalk. The girls nodded and followed him.

"Will they pick up a bunch of kids?" she asked worriedly.

Rhys looked stumped and slowed to a walk. "I don't know."

"They will if we straighten ourselves up a bit and give them a good enough story," Tiana said.

"Like what?"

"Well, it's got to be close to the truth to sound plausible. So, we tell whoever comes our aunt's not well and gave us cab money to go to the Old Town Cemetery to get information she needs about the deceased owner of the house she lives in to deal with a serious problem she's caught up in. Which is true. We need answers to the riddle we got and she needs serious help."

"What if the cab driver is doubtful of our story and wants to know more about what's so urgent before he will take us?"

"Then we get teary and say we can't discuss our heartbreak with a stranger. Remember, though it's not the original tragedy of the owner's sad death in 1919, it is still heartbreaking to have had our aunts and Paris taken by the Red Winkies."

"Making it a clever cover story," Rhys said nodding.

"And with us desperately wanting to find and free them we can truly without a doubt look grief stricken," Alora said.

"Exactly."

"Not bad," Rhys said. "It might just work."

"I think it will, since we have you here," Tiana said.

"Why me?"

"Because you're so tall and solemn looking most adults take you more seriously than most kids. Plus, you're ultra-polite to adults which they like. So, just be like that and we'll be fine."

"Never thought I'd hear you say anything good about me, least of all something that nice," he said with surprise.

"Well, it's true, but don't let it swell up your head any more than it already is."

"Ouch, you just burst my bubble by adding that."

"You'll live," Tiana said rolling her eyes.

"True," he said cheekily.

"Hey, Rhys," Alora said, "Since one of Aunt Gertie's friends lives here, why not have them call a cab for us?"

"Well...I haven't actually met her. He just pointed at her house one day as we drove by it and said the great lady who lived there was a dear friend of his."

"So, tell us what you know, like her name," Tiana said.

Rhys blushed. "I don't know her name since he didn't tell me and I didn't ask. He did say she was a beautiful and brilliant lady, but not one to be trifled with. Then he began talking about rockhounding trips in Washington looking for rare 'Ellensburg Blue' gems and amethysts, garnets, and opals down in Oregon."

"But if she's not one to be trifled with, I doubt she'll like having a bunch of kids show up on her doorstep," Alora said. "So, you should just make the call from out here."

"For heaven's sake," Tiana said rolling her eyes at her sister. "Don't make such a fuss. Let's just go knock on her door and explain who we are and that we know Aunt Gertie then see if we can use her phone. She can always tell us to go away."

"But we'd have to explain why we need to do that at 'her' house when he only lives a few blocks away from her."

"Then we just use the same story we did for the cabdriver."

"She sounds too smart to fall for that," Alora said then gaped as she saw Tiana and Rhys were not even listening and were walking up to the steps of her house.

As they reached the front steps, the door flew open. A tall, dark-haired woman as grand as a goddess stepped out onto the porch wearing a golden full-length gown that glowed as if made of sunlight. "Young ones, come forth," she said majestically as she held a gold staff with a crystal orb on top up high.

Tiana backed up as Alora caught up to her and they collided landing on their bottoms on the sidewalk. To their surprise, Rhys helped them up then stood protectively in front of them.

"I expected you sooner," the woman said matter-of-factly.

Rhys bowed in a courtly manner and nearly grinned to see the girl's gape at him. "Pardon me, Madame, you say you were expecting us? But how could you be when we didn't even know we'd be coming here?" he asked astonished. "But please excuse my utter surprise and let me introduce myself, I'm—"

"Rhys, Gertie's bright but mischievous ward, nephew of Lady Roleena Bloodstone," she cut in arching one brow high. "I am Great Lady Hera. I also know the two young girls with you are Lady Roleena's nieces, Alora and Tiana."

"How...how did you know that?" Alora gasped grabbing hold of Tiana's hand. *And why did she call our aunt 'Lady'.*

"Did Gertie tell you about us?" Rhys asked with surprise.

"Yes, and sadly I do not have time to explain why I knew you were coming or why I know your aunt. For I have another crisis to tend to tend to after I speak with you so I am in a rush," she explained. "As I said, I expected you to arrive earlier today and hoped we would have more time to do this."

"We ran into a few problems."

"As have many of us, including Lady Roleena, who I am fond of. Now, since I must leave soon, just listen. I have already summoned what you call a 'cab' in hopes of speeding you on to your quest of finding your aunt more quickly."

"How did you know to call a cab for us or that Aunt Roleena needs to be found?"

"We among the stars keep a close eye on certain people on your planet. So, I was aware of this and that you must speed away from here with all due haste using this local form of transportation. But first be forewarned the Red Winkies have invaded your communication lines. They can control where your calls are sent and are rewording calls to many of your officials in a way to benefit their mission here. So, only trust what you hear from those you know well."

"Then should we trust you?" Tiana asked warily.

Hera's serious countenance fell for a second as she bit back a smile. "An excellent point, but not one I have time to answer. I hope you sense you can since I am helping you with this. Also know, when I called for a cab, I told them it was to go to Seattle to mislead the Red Winkies and that it was urgent they come quickly. So, they'll be here soon. When the cabdriver comes, I'll explain I have another emergency, which I do, and that you must go to another destination. Ah, I see your cab has arrived, so hurry. We don't want the officers that are being misled by the Red Winkies to catch up with you now do we?"

"No...we don't," Rhys said with surprise as he ushered the girls to the cab as it pulled up to the curb by her house.

"Do you have recompense for the driver?"

"Recompense?" Rhys asked baffled by her question.

"I believe you must give them a form of monetary payment which is recompense to take you to your destination," she said.

"Err...yes. I have the money to do that."

"Good." Great Lady Hera waved at the cabdriver and called out to him, "Sir, I have an emergency taking me elsewhere. So, my bright young man here by the name of Rhys, will tell you the new destination the three of them must get to post haste."

The big burly male driver growled and slapped his steering wheel hard. "Look lady, I don't take kiddies on rides."

Hera pointed a forefinger at him and her eyes glowed bright green as she told him firmly, "They have 'money' for you and you will do as I said with no more sass. Otherwise, you will pay a price I will personally exact from you and I promise it will cost you far more than a mere ride for them will."

He looked stunned but then realized she meant it and gave her a nod. "Fine lady, I don't want no trouble." He reached over and pushed open the side door where Rhys stood. "Get in then unlock the backdoor and the girls with you can sit there."

Rhys slid in the front seat and as he turned around to unlock the door, he saw Hera vanish in a flash of light. *Wow! How did she do that?* His eyes flicked back to the driver. To his relief, he saw the cabbie had not noticed that. "Please take us to the 'Old Town Cemetery's business office." Rhys then told him the story Tiana came up with as the girls got in the back seat.

"Lost somebody?" he asked actually looking sympathetic.

"We sure did," Alora said tearily and they all nodded.

"Sorry to hear that. But what're the big packs for if you're going to a cemetery?" he asked curiously.

"They're packed with important items we were given to take there with us and it's easier to carry all this in these big packs than in our arms," Tiana said frankly.

"It certainly is," Rhys said giving her a grateful look for coming up with a good answer so quickly.

"I need to let you know right off," the cabbie said, "That even though the cemetery's close by, there's a twenty-dollar minimum on any ride."

"Here you go," Rhys said but as he handed the cabbie a twenty, he noticed Officer Schmartzov heading their direction.

He came from around the corner of Fourth Avenue checking each yard he passed. "And I'll give you twenty more to get us there quickly since our things might be needed right away."

With the extra incentive, the cabdriver took off like a racecar driver at an Indianapolis Five Hundred race. Rhys glanced back at the girls and nodded at the back window. The girls turned and saw the officer spot them in the cab then he ran the other way.

"He saw us and I bet he's going back to Aunt Gertie's to get his car," Tiana whispered tersely to Alora and Rhys.

"I think he's too late to catch us," Rhys whispered back, "I just hope he didn't have the chance to get a good look at us."

"Me too," Alora said but she bit on her lip worriedly.

The cabbie pulled in front of the business office building of Old Town Cemetery in just five minutes. Rhys paid him the extra twenty and they scooted out of the cab with their packs. They had barely shut their doors when the cabdriver shot off.

"That cabbie rocketed out of here like Flash Gordon did in his spaceship'," he said to the girls with a grin.

"We didn't want him to wait, so it's a relief," Alora said.

"That it is," Tiana said heartily.

"True, I was worried he'd hang around to get more money out of us," Rhys said as they all stood in front of the business office with no one making a move to go inside. "So, where do you think we should start?"

"By finding the couple's gravesite who originally lived in Aunt Roleena's house back in 1906."

"It's a good place to start, but do you know where they are? Because this is a pretty big graveyard."

"Super big," Alora moaned. "Plus, since we lost sight of the Red Winkies and Paris and have no idea where to find them, we might never find him and our aunts now."

"We will find them," Tiana said lifting her chin defiantly.

"What makes you so sure?" Rhys asked skeptically.

"Because we won't stop until we do."

"She's got that right," Alora said. "Then how about to save time we go ask them inside where the Watson's are buried."

"Good idea," Tiana said patting her sister on the back.

They rushed inside then stopped short in surprise to find themselves in a fancy reception room. Four large sitting areas with plush, silk covered chairs sat around stylish glass-topped tables with crystal vases filled with fresh roses centered on each one. A large buffet sat along one wall with dispensers for coffee and hot water plus baskets of various teas and trays of chocolate chip and sugar cookies. But as hungry and thirsty as they were from not eating all day, they did not take anything knowing they were for the people using the places services.

"I see a restroom sign and really need to use it," Alora said.

"Me too," Rhys murmured.

"Okay," Tiana said following her sister to the women's room as Rhys went into the men's. After using the toilets, the girls washed their hands and faces in the sinks and ran their fingers through their hair to neaten it then went out to meet Rhys. They found him drinking from a water fountain between the two restrooms and saw he had cleaned up too. They saw he even washed his short hair because it was dripping down his neck.

"I'm glad we all cleaned up but I wish I had on better cloths than my Seattle Drab clothing," Tiana said with a wry grin.

"Don't you mean to say your 'grunge wear'?" Rhys asked.

"Nope. Grunge wear has holes and worn-out spots. Seattle Drab is just a dark color in a casual style like my dark blue hoodie, or Alora's black sweat shirt and jeans. As a matter of fact, both our jeans and your cargo pants are black."

"At least after brushing these off, we don't look dirty after climbing through Aunt Gertie's basement window and keeping away from the crocodiles in the park," Alora said.

"Or from scrambling on our hands and knees across the crawl space in Aunt Roleena's basement and jumping eight-feet-down out of her back window onto the grass in the backyard," Rhys added. "This has all been exhausting."

"It has," Tiana agreed. "Well, let's ask where the Watson's graves are so we don't spend all day looking for it."

Alora looked at the clock over the counter. "All day? There's not a lot of the day left. Before we know it, it'll be nighttime."

"True," Tiana said swiping her hair back as she walked to the front desk with Rhys and Alora where they saw a woman in a dark brown suit and heels with a neatly done French braid busily filing paperwork.

They all waited for her to turn around, but after five minutes Tiana asked politely, "Excuse me, can you please help us?"

"Oh my!" the woman said putting a hand on her chest as she whirled around. "You were all so quiet, it quite gave me a start to find you three nice young people standing there."

"Sorry, we didn't want to startle you."

"How thoughtful," she said in a kindly way and straightened her glasses. "I'm Mrs. Howell. How can I help you?"

"We hope you can tell us where Mr. and Mrs. John Watson's graves are. They were the original owners of our aunt's house and she told us they were buried here."

"Then I can give you copies of the map of the gravesites here and a brochure of the names and location so you can look them up." She pulled out some maps and brochures then handed them to the trio. She paused to look at them more closely and her eyes lit up. "Are you by chance the nieces and nephew of Ms. Bloodstone? Because you fit the descriptions of you to a 'T'."

"Descriptions from the police?" Rhys asked with a start.

"Gracious, no. Why would you ask that?" she asked in surprise. "The descriptions came from your aunt."

"He's just a big kidder," Tiana said as she elbowed him.

"Sorry," Rhys said blushing, "And yes, she is our aunt."

"Young man, there are places you do not jest in and this is one of them," she said sternly then turned to the girls were both mortified by his comment. "Don't worry, I have a brother who's a tease, so I'm not all that shocked. Now, it is intriguing you asked me about the Watsons since Ms. Bloodstone just recently inquired about them. She said no one in her family was buried here but she was interested in the original owners of her house. She then said her nieces and nephew would want to visit their gravesite for a research project they needed to do and she had to leave town so could not come with you due to an urgent matter she had to deal with. She also said your Aunt Gertie would be caring for you and asked if Gertie could leave some information for you here that would help with your research. I'm not sure why Gertie couldn't just give you this and she didn't say, but she seemed so anxious I just wanted help and said yes."

"Wow, you have a great memory to recall that," Tiana said and saw Alora and Rhys looked as stunned as she did that it implied that Roleena had guessed all of this might happen.

"I like to think that I do, but thank you for saying that. So, then you are indeed Ms. Roleena's nieces and nephew?"

"Yes, yes we are."

"When you asked about the Watson's I thought you were, but before I release the information do you have identification cards to prove this?"

"Yes, I do." Tiana pulled a student I.D. card out of the back pocket of her jeans and then Alora and Rhys pulled out theirs.

"Thank you," she said checking them over and handing them back. "It's always good to confirm this. I also hope you don't mind me saying how surprised I was when your Aunt Gertie came in and was…well, your aunt was a male wearing an old-fashioned dress and bonnet over army pants and work boots."

"He tends to throw a lot of people off by dressing that way."

"But he's truly a kind man and good to all of us," Alora added. "So, we don't care if he's a bit of a quirky character."

"He did seem rather nice so I can see why you would say that." She opened a drawer and pulled out a sealed envelope and held it out to them.

Tiana took it and they all thanked her, but as they started to walk out of the office Mrs. Howell called out, "Tiana, Alora, Rhys, wait a moment!"

"Yes?" Tiana asked politely as they all turned around.

"You don't have much time to work on this project of yours today, because the cemetery closes at sundown," Mrs. Howell said. "Then I also close up the office. However, if you have any more questions, you're welcome to come back and see me tomorrow. Oh, I just remembered there's something I need to tell you about their resting place."

"Is there something wrong with their gravesites?" Tiana asked warily and Alora and Rhys looked startled too as they looked back at Mrs. Howell. *This is alarming since I read about them having vandalism problems here.*

"My goodness, don't look so distraught. There isn't anything wrong that wasn't righted as best they could. You see, long ago they had to build a bigger administration building and a bigger mausoleum. Unfortunately, the expansion went into some old parts of the cemetery and the remains of the people in those graves had to be moved. I know when I looked this up for your Aunt Roleena this affected him. You see, Mr. Watson was an early burial in 1919. Sadly, he died quite young. Whether it was because of the Spanish Flu epidemic then is unknown. But his and his wife's remains are now in a columbarium niche in the newer mausoleum. So, you'll need to go there. I'll mark it on a map to show which aisle it's on since there's so many."

"That would be very helpful." Tiana walked back to the front desk and waited as she marked the map. She then picked it up from her and joined Alora and Rhys at the front door calling out, "Thanks again, Mrs. Howell."

Mrs. Howell smiled and waved at them as they rushed off. As they left the building, they dashed up the hill to the mausoleum. They followed the marked map down a maze of aisles taking lefts and rights and finally found the correct aisle.

"Gee," Alora said, "I'm glad she gave us a map marking their niche's row because this place is huge, and there are lots of rows here with hundreds of niches in each one."

"There sure are," Rhys said with a heavy sigh.

"I'll go to the end and work my way back towards you two," Tiana said heading down the aisle.

A minute later, Alora pointed at the top of the right wall and said excitedly, "I found it!" Tiana and Rhys rushed over and looked at where she pointed. They saw a brass plate with the Watson's names engraved on it and it had a piece of paper wedged under the edge of the small door covering the niche.

"Why did their niche have to be on the top?" Rhys groaned.

Tiana winced. "Sorry, but at least we know how we can get up there after you got us out of Aunt Gertie's basement."

"True. Let's just get it over with." He groaned and then faced the wall of small niches with his arms braced against it. "Well, go ahead. Climb on up."

"Thanks," Tiana said sincerely. "Here I come." She climbed up to his shoulders and pulled the paper out then eased her way down to the floor and opened it. "Okay, it says, 'Be persistent and make haste. Use the fancy stuff I left ye in a plastic crate I hid behind one of the oldest soldier's gravesites. Inside it you'll find the help you likely desperately need right now. Gertie."

Alora groaned as she looked at her map. "Oldest soldier? According to the brochure, there's hundreds of soldiers buried here but the locations aren't marked very clearly on the map. It does say there's over fifty thousand graves here so we might never find it in time to be of any help," she said wearily.

"After all we've been through and accomplished, I bet we can do this," Rhys said. "Is it okay that I suggest we take each section three rows at a time going side by-side? That will make it go faster and keep us close together,"

Tiana looked at Rhys with amazement to hear him ask them this so nicely. "Okay, where do you think we should start?"

"Let's start with the section near us and if we don't find the crate we go to the next one." He led them to the closest section and let the girls take the first two rows then he took the third. They began carefully checking the graves for a crate, but fifteen minutes later they met at the end of the last row in the section and all shook their heads.

After repeating this for three more sections, Tiana stopped and glanced around. "This place is eerie now it's getting dark."

"Yeah, it's super creepy," Alora said with a shiver. "Hey, Rhys, how are you doing?" She looked around and gasped. "He's gone! Should I shout to him?"

"No," Tiana said. "It might draw unwanted attention to us which we don't want since the cemetery is likely closed now. That means that being we don't want to get kicked out 'and' want to take that crate out with us, we need to stay low and be quiet. As far as Rhys goes, I bet he went on down the first row of the next section so I'll run down and look for him while you start on the next row." Her sister nodded and Tiana dashed off.

Two minutes later, Alora screamed and Tiana's head jerked up. She looked around but her sister was nowhere in sight. She ran to the row her sister was checking with her heart pounding so hard she felt it in her ears. To make matters worse, the sun was setting casting dark shadows across the graveyard and clouds were moving in making it much harder to see. *This is as ominous as a horror movie's setting and right about now I'd expect vampires or zombies to jump out and grab me.*

Tiana rushed down the row but could not find her sister. As she ran down the next row, something grabbed her foot. She shrieked and pulled away so hard she fell on her backside then heard chilling laughter followed by a girl's muffled scream. *That sounds like Alora!* She jumped up mad as a hatter vowing to deck whoever had her sister then realized she was standing right by an open grave. As she bent down to look inside it, Rhys jumped up from it yelling, 'Boo!'.

"Rhys, that was mean," Alora said from down in the grave and she began poking him hard in his ribs.

"Ouch, that hurts, so knock it off," he growled.

"Serves you right," she huffed. "Sorry Tiana, but he pulled me in here and covered my mouth or I would've warned you."

"Rhys! Go away," Tiana hissed so angrily her face turned red. "We don't need 'your' kind of help. Alora, raise your hands up." As she did, Tiana clasped her hands and digging her heels in to brace herself, pulled her sister out of the grave.

"Hey, give me a break," Rhys said sulking. "This has all been so dismal, I was just having some fun."

"Then go have your kind of fun somewhere else."

"Come on, what if I promise not to do that again?"

"No. Go away. Our aunts and Paris are in serious trouble and you're wasting time on stupid pranks. Do you even realize they might be dead! Right now, I wish the Red Winkies had got you and not them. In fact, after this prank, I wouldn't waste my time trying to save you from them. I'd just say 'good riddance'."

"Yeah, I've heard people tell me 'Go away' a lot," he said somberly as he climbed out of the open grave. "So, I'm good at doing just that. Bye." He slowly scuffed off with his head and shoulders slumped down in despair.

"Rhys, stop! Don't go!" Alora turned to Tiana with tears in her eyes. "I know he can be a brat, but you know very well if he'd been taken, we 'would' go rescue him since it's the right thing to do 'and' because he's family."

Tiana sighed. "True. Aunt Roleena did tell us we must do what's right even if it's hard to. Go ahead and call him back."

"No. 'You' chased him away. 'You' call him back."

"Fine!" she growled and counted to ten then shouted, "Rhys, come back! Sorry I lost my cool and took my frustration out on you because I'm worried about our aunts and Paris."

Rhys stopped and then returned but he said nothing at all to them and just stared out across the graveyard.

"Thanks for coming back," Alora said softly. "But you know Tiana's right about not wasting our time when we have serious work to do. So, no horsing around. Now, let's all start over again and go find that crate Aunt Gertie left us."

"Okay, and I truly won't horse around again until everyone's safe and sound because I'm worried about them too."

"Good," Tiana said and she went to go check another row.

"Wait!" Alora said as she looked at the map of the cemetery with her flashlight. "I just noticed some tiny notes on this map. It's on lower right section of the cemetery and I can't make them out. Since the two of you have sharper vision than me take a look to see if it's important." She then tapped the spot for Tiana and Rhys to check. "See the inky dinky print there?"

"Good catch," Rhys said eagerly. "The notations here say the northeast corner is the oldest area of the cemetery and it has a section with one-hundred-fifty civil war veterans. I bet they're the oldest soldiers here."

"I agree," Tiana said excitedly. "Let's go check it out."

"Okay, but this time we work three rows side-by-side like we were supposed to do from the start," Alora said looking straight at Rhys and he blushed as he nodded.

They dashed across the cemetery to the area of civil war veteran gravesites and started checking them. Twenty minutes later Tiana shouted. "Come look at what I found!"

Alora and Rhys raced over to Tiana and skidded to a stop. Hidden inside the foliage of a bush behind a civil war veteran's headstone was a sturdy green plastic crate with a fitted lid. She pulled the two-feet-long, one-foot-wide, one-foot-tall box out of the bush. "The label on top says; For Alora, Tiana, and Rhys."

"Quick, open it," Rhys said enthusiastically.

Tiana pulled and pulled on the top, but to no avail. "There's no latch or lock, so it must be glued on because it won't budge."

"I'll give it a go," Alora said and she yanked up on it. "Nope, I can't get it open either."

Rhys chuckled lightly and said with a grin, "Now you two know how I feel not being able to open my strongbox."

"I guess we do at that," Tiana said and Alora nodded.

"Well, lately I seem to be a sucker for punishment, so can I give it a try?" he asked them politely.

"Sure…and thanks for asking," she said surprised again he was so courteous and had not tried to grab it away from them.

After several big jerks on the box, the top popped off. A large manila envelope lay on top of some cotton batting and Gertie's familiar cramped writing on it said, 'Read what's in this envelope before removing the cotton fluff covering the fancy equipment inside this box'.

Rhys looked at the girls. "Who gets to read it?"

Again, Tiana was surprised he had asked. "What do you think, Alora? Should we draw for it?"

"No, that would waste too much time. Let Rhys read it with his flashlight and we'll look over his shoulder."

"Okay. Go ahead and read it, Rhys."

"Cool. Thanks!" He pulled a sheet of paper out of the envelope as the girls leaned over his shoulder. "It says, 'Both items in this box are labeled. The bigger one is a 'Spectrometer' which is a unique unit designed to detect energy residue left by the Red Winkies enabling you to track them. The smaller, flatter unit is a device called 'X Marks the Spot'. It works somewhat like an Earthling's compact flattop computer. It will show you the Red Winkies light trail on a live, virtual screen on a state, country or world map option. The units are interconnected. 'X Marks the Spot', abbreviated as 'XMS', collects information from the Spectrometer and shows it on the map you choose."

Rhys smirked. "They seriously named it X Marks the Spot?"

"Well, the name does make what it does pretty clear," Tiana said with a straight face but then she could not help but chuckle.

"Painfully so," he said but then he chuckled too.

"The letter did say it's also called an XMS," Alora said.

"True, which sounds better so I'll call it that."

"I don't know if you saw it but the tiny scribbled signature under the note says 'Hephaestus'," Tiana said, "And below that is Gertie's chicken scratch saying, 'Sir Hephaestus left me these units to help me find anyone abducted by the Red Winkies.

"So, did Hephaestus know about the Red Winkies and that people would be taken away by them?" Rhys asked looking at the girls for an answer.

Tiana shrugged. "I don't know. We've seen him a few times at Aunt Roleena's. He's a nice giant, but other than the time he watched us for Aunt Roleena, he doesn't say much at all. She said it's just that he's shy. However, she also said he's a genius inventor on a galactic scale. If you ever meet him, call him Mr. Hephaestus or 'Sir' and be respectful because Aunt Roleena warned us if we didn't, she'd have the pythons nip us."

"Wow, okay. 'Sir Hephaestus' it is. I never met him but Aunt Roleena blasted me cold with her kaleidoscope eyes when I went in her basement and played with one of this mechanical wizard's gizmos." He shivered and changed the subject. "So, what's he like? And what does he like to work on? Oh, and is he one of the star people still interested in helping us?"

"One thing at a time. As I said, we didn't get to know him very well because he holes up in her basement working on his projects most of the time he's there. But we did see him send off a rocket drone."

"Rocket drone!" Rhys said excitedly. "Tell me about that."

"I'll tell you later," Tiana told him firmly. "Right now, we need to work on rescuing our aunts and Paris."

"Rhys nodded and picked up the XMS mapping unit. "This does look like a laptop computer." He turned it on and grinned. "There are just five icons on its screen; a tiny planet Earth, a tiny map, a connection plug, a question mark, and a camera. It looks really simple and straight forward to me as how to use it."

"Good," Tiana said taking the Spectrometer out of the crate. "I see the keys and settings on this unit are clearly marked too."

"Hey, there's another note in this box," Alora said pulling it out. "It's from Aunt Gertie. It says; 'Alora, Tiana and Rhys, if yer reading this ye must've found all the clues I left and know I can't get back to use them fancy things myself. Good luck."

"I wish he had, because carrying our shrunken boxes is easy, but this big crate is a lot to lug around," Rhys said.

"Then why don't I shrink it all?" Alora asked brightly.

"No! We don't know what it would do to these tracking units and their programs. They might not work after shrinking them."

"But it didn't bother our other gifts."

Tiana sighed deeply. "That was just plain dumb luck that it didn't, sis. We can't chance doing that with this equipment. Finding our aunts and dog pal are far too important to risk it."

"I'm sorry if it upsets you," Rhys said sympathetically. "But as far as this goes, I agree with her this time, Alora."

"Fine, then I'll shrink our gift boxes enough to put them all in the big leather rucksack, and Rhys, you can use your belt to lash that plastic crate to that huge framed pack. Then our hands will be free if we have to climb out anymore windows," she said giving them a crooked little grin.

"Good thinking, sis," Tiana said.

Rhys took off his belt and used it and the drawstrings on the pack to tie the crate with the locating devices to the frame.

"Will one of you be able to carry the pack with all our boxes since making them smaller won't change their weight?"

"No problem, I'll carry it, because I've got super strong shoulders," Alora said with a big grin.

"That you do," Tiana said grinning back at her.

"Then I'll get busy shrinking our boxes more so we can pack up and get on with doing our rescue."

"Oh no!" Rhys suddenly groaned as the bright, red flashing lights of a police car sped into the cemetery's parking lot. "Trouble's here now."

"Yikes! You're right," Tiana said.

"But can that officer even see us in the dark from way over there?" Alora asked with a curious frown.

"Let's not chance it, so duck down!" Rhys said.

They all hit the ground behind the gravestone in hopes they would then be out of sight.

CHAPTER EIGHT
GIGANTIC LIONESSES

The three cousins grimaced as they heard the police car screech to a stop making them all too aware they came to the cemetery for a serious purpose. As the car door opened and slammed shut, Tiana peeked up over the tombstone.

"It's our die hard Red Winkie driven policeman, Officer Schmartzov," she whispered to the others and they groaned. The big as a bull man took a long look around then went over to the administration building. They guessed the door was now locked because he swore loudly after he pounded on it.

"Bummer," Alora muttered, "Just when I thought we finally got a break, our 'fashion policeman' showed up again."

Rhys sighed heavily "We have had a lot of trouble with him. But on the bright side, or the reverse in this case, now the sun has set, it's getting dark so we'll be hard to spot in what you said were called 'Seattle Drab' clothes."

"Not if he has one of those powerful police floodlights to sweep the area around this graveyard with," Tiana said.

"Well, I'm just hoping he doesn't have that on hand."

"I wonder how he found us," Alora said biting on her lip.

"I don't know," Rhys said, "But what's more important now is you stay down low as you finish shrinking our boxes more."

"We also need a better place to hide from him." Tiana said.

"Any ideas?" Alora asked uneasily as she used her magic dust to shrink their gift boxes down further.

"I do," Rhys said wincing as he added, "In the grave."

"Please tell me you're kidding."

"Not at all. It's the best place here to hide on short order."

"I don't like it either," Tiana said sighing. "But he's right."

"Then I'll do it but I'll hate every second of it," Alora said glumly shoving their three shrunken boxes in the rucksack.

Rhys quickly put on the framed pack with the crate holding the tracking and mapping units tied to it. "Come on, follow me to the grave." He scrunched down low and slowly moved off.

"That is so, so not funny."

"No, it's not, and you don't see me laughing now do you?"

"Well…no."

"Right. Do you both remember where that is in case we get separated and you have to find your way to it on your own?"

"Since I'm thinking you're talking about the empty grave you hid in when you grabbed my foot and yelled 'boo', that hole is hard to forget," Tiana said dryly.

"Sorry about that," he said sheepishly. "And it is the hole I'm talking about. Still, it 'is' a good hiding place right now."

"I guess it is at that."

"Then if you follow me, I'll take us the best way to stay out of sight getting there." He set off hunched down low as did the girls running quietly as they could with their heavy packs and only stopping as Rhys reached the dark empty grave. He set the framed pack on the ground and jumped in it landing with a soft thump. "Quick. Hand me the packs."

"But your box is in the rucksack so it'll knock you down."

"I'll just have to deal with it."

"Okay," she said sympathetically. Alora handed down the rucksack and they winced as they heard him groan. With no time to waste, Tiana handed him the other pack and began to jump in the grave but stopped as Alora backed away from it. "I'm not going in there until you do, so please just do it."

"But it's so creepy my feet won't move," she whispered.

"Then I'll help them move," Tiana said and pulled her back to the grave. "Rhys, help her down before that officer sees us."

"Come on nervous Nellie," he said reaching up for her hand. Tiana got her sister to kneel and put her Alora's hand in Rhys's then he eased the trembling girl down into the grave.

As Tiana stood on the edge watching, the ledge suddenly gave way. She crashed down hard on top of Alora and Rhys knocking them all down hard on their bottoms into the muddy bottom of the grave.

Alora began sobbing and Rhys quickly covered her mouth. "Hush," he said and she started to bite him but froze as a beam of light flashed across the top of the grave.

A few seconds later, Officer Schmartzov muttered, "I could swear I heard someone, but no one's here," as he walked over towards their eerie hiding place. A moment later, he then spoke into his com loudly, "Central, Officer Schmartzov calling in. I tracked down the kids with the shoe infraction who refused to submit to my PCF authority through a cab company they used," he said crossly. "Yes, they're the ones who snuck away from me and Officer Dwendoleen. A cab took them to the Old Town Cemetery. Don't get cheeky. They're not here because they're dead. He dropped them off alive. No, Officer Dwendoleen is not with me. She's watching their aunt's house in case they circle back. Why are they here? Well, a Mrs. Howell in the mortuary's business office said they came to do research which she told me through a speaker since she'd locked up and refused to let me inside. I pressed for more info but she pointedly told me she knew little else only adding they came two hours ago and left shortly after. Yes, I tried to talk my way in, but she refused to let me in and called that new Politically Correct Law Office. How they put that together in a day is beyond me, but I also heard lots of our new rules are being held up in court. Yes, I demanded on searching the office. She got all huffy and told me the law office said I had to get a search warrant, so I backed off. No, I don't think she has any reason to hide them. I'm going to check the grounds before I leave, but it's likely a waste of time. Of course I'm annoyed. What? You're having the Politically Correct Force send me fifty volunteers tomorrow to help search for the kids? Good. Yes, I'll still check the rest of the place here though they likely left. Over and out."

After a few minutes, the cousins heard the sound of his shoes smacking the pavement and could tell he was leaving their area. As the sound faded, they sighed in relief. Rhys jumped up high ever few minutes to see where the officer was and saw his light flashing around in the other areas. It had felt like hours passed but as he checked the time, it was only twenty minutes.

"I think the officer must be almost done," Rhys told the girls.

"Thank God," Tiana said.

"Amen," Alora added.

"You know, other than as a gag, I never thought using an open grave would be useful for the living," he whispered.

"Me either," Tiana muttered.

"Hey, I didn't see his light scouring the area anymore," Rhys said looking back at her, "But since, you have the best vision among us, can I give you a lift to see if he's gone?"

"Sure," she said and he boosted her up. "I don't see him checking anything either, but I'm know he's still here."

"How do you know that for sure?"

"Because genius, we would've heard his car start up and him leaving in it," Tiana said.

"Oh. Good point."

A half-hour later they still had not heard the officer leave in his car and looked at each other worriedly.

"Good grief," Tiana groaned, "I wish he leave."

"Me too," Alora said with a shiver.

"Look again and see what he's up too," Rhys said.

"Yes, your lordship," she said with an exaggerated bow.

Rhys rolled his eyes and lifted her up. Just as she peeked over the side, a man shrieked in terror. Tiana then laughed so hard he lost his hold on her and she dropped back in the grave.

"Geez, she must've seen something awful because she's hysterical," Rhys said glancing at her worriedly.

"No, she's not. If she freaks out, she just gets super quiet," Alora said matter-of-factly. "Tiana, what are you laughing at?"

She began to explain, but her words were cut off by gunfire. Then a car door slammed and an engine started up. The last they heard was a stream of swear words from the officer and the sound of a car peeling off out of the parking lot.

"Quick, give me a lift Rhys so I can look again!"

"Okay," he said with confusion but he lifted her up. "Come on. Spill it. What do you see?"

It took Tiana a minute to get control of herself then grinning from ear-to-ear she said, "You won't believe it, but I saw two huge lionesses chasing Officer Schmartzov's car."

"No way. That's crazy. I think you've gone loopy."

"Miss Tiana is not delusional in the least," came a loud, growling voice from above the empty gravesite.

Rhys looked up and screamed as two enormous lionesses looked down into the open grave at them. The girls merely gasped lightly in surprise and grinned.

"It's okay, Rhys," Tiana said softly to calm him down.

"It's…it's…so…so not okay. I must have gone nuts since I see two enormous lions are up there…and they talk!"

"We are lionesses, not lions. But rest easy, boy. We are not here to maul or kill you, and yes, we can speak your language."

"Then why are you here?" he asked hoarsely as he gaped at the huge tawny-colored lioness speaking to him.

"We were sent by Lady Artemis to help you get to your next destination," the other lioness replied in a low rumble and as she gazed at him, he felt like she looked into his very soul.

Rhys' eyes narrowed with a look of distrust. He moved in front of the girls and shook a fist at the lionesses prepared to fight them off. "Tell me just where is this next destination to be? In your den for a quick dinner?"

The first lioness to speak gave a raspy chuckle. "What a thoughtful suggestion."

"But not our intent," the other one said swatting the other with her tail. "We were told you will tell us where to take you."

"That had better be true, because I won't let you hurt them."

"Rhys, I appreciate you're wanting to protect us, but these lionesses are our friends," Tiana said easing his fist down to his side. "These are great-aunt Artemis's courageous companions. The stout lioness with a nick off her right ear and scar across her temple is 'Bravery'. The slender one with the piercing gold eyes is 'Justice'." She looked back at the big cats curiously. "Why were you sent here? We heard you were helping relocate the wood elves because the lumber baron's crew was cutting down their forest. Or is that already taken care of?"

"No," Justice rumbled. "She and a few others are still hiding them in a secret cave while others search for a forest safe from humans, which is getting hard to find on this planet."

"A sad fact indeed. Then why did you leave her side?"

"Lady Artemis said you needed us more urgently than she did and wished to repay your aunt for risking her life to help get her out of some serious trouble she was caught up in."

"What kind of trouble was she in?" Alora inquired.

"One a lot more dangerous and complex than yours here."

"How was it worse and more complex than ours?"

"Justice!" Bravery snarled, "We do not have time to explain that or raise their primitive levels of education here."

"I am aware of that but I wanted to tell her in a way that did not insult them like you just did," Justice told her lioness friend swatting Bravery's haunch with her tail again.

"Can you briefly say what she helped Lady Artemis with?"

"Do all Earthlings have memory problems?" Bravery asked.

"Why would you ask that?" Alora asked looking baffled.

"Because I already told you there's no time to explain this," the lioness growled. "Now, let us get you out of that hole. Then we'll race away from here and find somewhere safer to talk."

"Can't we rest a minute since the officer has left?"

"No. He yelled he was bringing lots of police back here to shoot us," Justice rumbled frankly. "Now, Miss Tiana, grab ahold of Bravery's tail, and Miss Alora, you grab mine and we'll pull you out of there." The lioness's lowered their tails into the grave and the girls grabbed onto them. The big cats towed them out and the girls thanked them profusely.

"Here, human boy, grab my tail," Bravery growled putting her tail back in for Rhys to take hold of.

Rhys shook his head. "I don't need any help." He jumped up high and caught the edge of the grave then muscled his way out of it. He then stood glaring at the lionesses, but they ignored him as they licked the mud off of the girls who both giggled as the huge cats groomed them. Rhys cautiously kept his distance.

"Come here, human boy," Bravery growled when the cats finished with Tiana and Alora. "You're dirtier than these girls were, and I won't let anyone ride on me who's filthy."

"That's okay. I'll just run along with you."

The big cat's eyes narrowed. "Can you run two hundred to three hundred of your miles an hour?"

"Well, no," he sputtered. "But what you asked doesn't fit the facts because I read lions can only run fifty miles an hour."

"We're not your planet's game-park lionesses," Bravery snarled. "We run faster than yours, boy, for we can go faster than your high-speed trains."

"Wow!"

"Your limited response shows a serious lack of vocabulary, boy. Now, since you refuse to let us clean you off, I saw a water hose on the side of a work shed by the office as we came here. Use that to wash yourself off. But hurry or we leave you here."

Rhys sprinted there as fast as his legs would carry him and rinsed himself off then ran back and stood by the girls.

"Now," Bravery grunted, "Can one of you engage enough brain cells to tell us where you need to take you?"

"I've been thinking about that having seen the Red Winkies are drawn to all kinds of electricity and red colors, especially to red lights," Tiana said. "So, we need to find a place with lots of these things because that's where they'd likely gather together."

"It's hard to narrow it down," Rhys said, "Since traffic lights are red, plus airplane wing tips, radio towers, masts on hills and buildings all have red lights. There are also millions of red tail lights on the cars and trucks around the world."

"True, but they also must find a big enough place to keep our aunts and close enough to herd a small pup like Paris to."

"Why does it need to be close if they can use buses?"

"Well," Tiana said, "We've seen the Winkies ride vehicles where they want to go. However, they had to zap Paris to get him to go where they wanted and being it was a struggle to do it, I doubt they'd choose a hideout very far from here to take him to. So, what kind of places have loads of red colored lights?"

"Aha! I know!" Rhys said excitedly. "Game stores!"

"That's a brilliant suggestion," she said with surprise.

"It is," Alora said and she quickly got her smart phone out tapping rapidly on it as she searched the web. "I see a dozen in the nearby towns, but forget the one on Whidbey Island."

"Why eliminate that one?" Rhys asked looking puzzled.

"Because it's on an island," Alora said.

"So?" he asked as he watched her scan game store menus.

"Auntie Roleena told us they hate going near any water."

"That still leaves a lot of places to check."

"I don't think so," Tiana said looking over Alora's shoulder at the different sites with her. "From what we can see, most have computerized games without flashing lights and bells, and two are too small to hide people in. My guess is they're using the game store we saw in Marysville. It's huge, with lots of old pinball machines 'and' lots of lights."

"I fear with our aunts taken so many hours ago, and though with Paris it's a much shorter time, he's had to fight them super hard, that the longer the Red Winkies have them, there's more of a chance they will find a way to control them. So, I hope you're right," Alora said anxiously.

"Me too," Tiana said. "We must free them soon, and I truly think the game store in Marysville is the best place to start."

Justice nudged Tiana with her nose. "I sense a Spectrometer and XMS are in the clear crate the boy is carrying. Have you used them to see where their trail went?"

Tiana blushed. "Not too bright of us, but no, we didn't."

"Yeesh, why didn't we didn't try using these to track them?" Rhys groaned. "The Spectrometer could've picked up their energy trail and sent it to the XMS unit's map for us."

"Well, I know why we didn't!" Alora sputtered. "We were busy hiding in a grave from that PCF officer."

"True," he sighed as he untied the box from his pack and retrieved the two units from it. He turned on the Spectrometer and as Alora stood right by him, he handed her the XMS unit.

"How do I run this?" she asked anxiously.

"The labels under the keys are straightforward," he said pointing at one of the keys shaped like a button. "See, this one says 'program on' so you tap it to turn it on. Then just check the labels under each key and choose the one you want to use."

"But I'm worried with all these keys I might accidently hit one that makes it crash like I did with my computer," she said waving a hand at the four rows of keys.

Rhys read over them quickly. "There are a lot of them, but most are not ones we need now. To start, the power button is on the bottom right edge." He pushed it and the XMS unit made a soft humming noise. "Now tap the key labeled 'locator', and do hurry since that officer will soon be back with lots of others."

"Okay." Alora nervously squinted at labels and found the key but instead of just tapping it she held it down. The unit squealed sharply and startled, she dropped the XMS, but to her relief, Tiana was standing by her and caught it.

"Would you like me to do this instead?" Tiana asked her.

"Yes! Your hands are steadier than mine right now and your eyes are far better at seeing the tiny print under the keys."

"No problem." Tiana quickly checked the labels and found three miniature map icons on the bottom row and tapped one and a Washington state map appeared on the screen. "All set."

Rhys shook his head and groaned. "I can't believe it."

"What's wrong?" she asked with alarm.

"What's wrong is I have to admit your guess was spot on," he said looking over her shoulder at the XMS map. "I sent the light trial my unit gathered to your XMS and the Winkie trail shows they are at The Flashy Castle game store in Maryville."

"Cool," she said grinning broadly.

"Get to business for it will not take long for those officers to return with guns to shoot us," Bravery growled. "Now you see where they are, show us on the map." Tiana held it up to them and the lionesses looked at it then at the trio. "We will take you to within one block of this game store, then find a place to wait for you out of sight of others. After you retrieve Lady Roleena and your two other friends, we will speed you away and find a safer place for you to decide what else to do."

"You aren't coming in with us?" Alora asked worriedly.

"No, we are not."

"I don't blame you," Rhys said. "You're probably afraid the Red Winkies could catch you too."

"Do not insult us, boy," Bravery roared at him so loudly he fell on his backside. "We already asked if we could go rescue Lady Roleena ourselves, but Lady Artemis forbade it. It seems Great Lady Hera foresaw that our intense heat signatures would alert them of our presence. They would trap us then use us as a bargaining tool to get what they want here, and you would not have a ride out of here, now would you, boy?"

"No, I guess not," he grumbled as he cautiously got back up to his feet and distanced himself from the lionesses.

Justice tilted her head curiously. "Be honest, boy, why do you stand back as if we are repugnant and talk so curtly to us?"

Rhys eyed her warily. "Can I be honest without either of you biting my head off?"

"We would do no such thing, but I see you think so. Now, please explain this to me. I promise you will not be harmed."

"Okay, here it is. It's because of the way you snap and growl at me and call me 'boy'. I'd rather you just called me Rhys."

"So that pricked you to the point of speaking bitterly to us?"

"I guess so. I know I'd do better if you didn't growl and snap at me and call me 'boy' with the same bitterness you say I use."

"Not snapping or calling you 'boy' can be omitted, but our growls come out as we speak. Can you give way on that?"

"Yeah, I can learn to handle that," he said surprising himself.

"Well, Bravery, I feel if he is polite to us, we be polite too."

"I will agree to this as long as he remains polite. But now we must go. For I sense the humans with the guns are coming."

"Now, you brought it to my attention, I do too. Miss Tiana, quickly climb on my back and then you, Miss Alora." The girls complied readily, but Rhys took a step back looking alarmed.

"You are worrying needlessly…Rhys. I will not harm you," Bravery huffed. "Now, come show me you can handle your fear and get up on me."

Rhys nodded then taking a deep breath he went over and eased up on her back. "Okay, I'm ready."

"I am glad you managed to do this," Justice told him. "Now, Miss Tiana put your arms around my neck and hold on tight. Miss Alora, do the same with your sister or the wind will rip you off me. For though I will hold my head up as I run to break the force of the wind for you two, it will be hard for you as I must go at a speed humans will only see us as a blur. Now, prepare yourselves. Here we go!" Justice took off in a flash and the girls clung to her with all the strength they could muster.

"I will also hold my head up high for you, Rhys, but do hold on tight," Bravery told him, "The wind will be fierce."

"Promise me, no biting," he said warily.

"I promise I will not bite you, so just do it."

"I'm set," he said putting his arms around the big cat's neck.

"Good. Here we go." The lioness took off and Rhys flew off her back and hit the ground hard.

"Ouch!"

"I said hold on tight," Bravery huffed padding over to him.

"That you did," he said getting up and dusting himself off.

"Well, that was honest. Shall we attempt this again?"

"Yes." He got up on her back and slid his arms around her neck gripping his hands together more firmly. "I'm ready."

"Off we go!" She then raced away at a phenomenal speed.

Stunned by the speed lioness attained, Rhys found he had to keep his eyes closed because the wind stung them. He opened them only after he felt her slow down and saw they had met up with the others who waited a block away from the game store.

"How did you catch up with your friend so fast?" he asked with awe as the lioness trotted over to Justice and the girls.

"I put on a 'burst of speed'," she replied.

"How fast did you go?"

"In your terminology, I went two-hundred miles an hour."

"Wow!"

"I am glad to hear you are duly impressed."

"Yes...yes, I am."

"Then perhaps we will eventually become friends after all."

"I'd like that," he said so sincerely the girls grinned and Justice snorted and winked her eyes in what looked like delight.

"I know he can be trying, but thanks for not eating Rhys," Tiana said jokingly, "Because we might need his gifts."

"Rhys actually has gifts?" Bravery asked in amazement.

Rhys sighed so deeply the lionesses looked at each other curiously. "I'd like to think I have at least one good one hidden inside me somewhere. However, the ones she's talking about are in the strongbox Aunt Roleena left for me."

Bravery gave Justice an inquiring look. Justice then gazed at Rhys with great intensity and a minute later she nodded at Bravery and then looked at Rhys. "You 'do' have gifts buried within you and not just those in this strongbox you speak of."

"I do?"

"Yes."

"He does?" the girls both asked with surprise.

"Yes," Justice rumbled, "but that is enough speculating. For now, just as Hercules was tasked with labors to perform, you too must all get to your labors."

"Labors?" Alora asked. "What do you mean by that?"

"You must go to work finding your aunts and dog."

"We call them missions here," Rhys said.

"Do not waste time bandying word differences. Go to that Flashy Castle place now!" Bravery roared. Without another word, Rhys and the girls raced off to the game store.

The three cousins braked to a stop twenty feet from the door as they heard loud, wild laughter coming from inside it. They then stared in amazement at the medieval castle-like façade on the front of the store. For the stones on the walls glowed in a rainbow of colors and even the mortar between the colorful stones had bright flashing white lights set in it."

"I see why it's called 'The Flashy Castle'," Rhys quipped.

"At least there's no red flashing lights out here," Tiana said.

"One saving grace," Alora added, but she grimaced as they walked to the doorway and a sound track began playing weird, spacey music mixed with pinball strikes, bells pinging, and paddles clacking, all overshadowed by a creepy crackling noise.

"That crackling noise sounds like what we heard when a tree fell down on the electric lines by Aunt Roleena's house during a wind storm."

"It just sounds ominous to me," Rhys said scowling, "And it could be an omen of the trouble we're likely walking into."

"Of course, it's trouble. What else did you expect?" Tiana asked dryly. "Because at some point we'll likely have to fight off the Red Winkies. Even so, we still have to find our aunts."

"Good point."

"Hey, we also have to find our buddy, Paris," Alora said.

"Absolutely," Tiana agreed. "Well, let's do this."

"Ladies first," Rhys said with a sweep of his hand and an impish smile on his face.

"Now, he gets super polite," Alora said groaning.

"Interesting timing too," Tiana said rolling her eyes at him then they all headed with great trepidation to the door.

CHAPTER NINE
THE FLASHY CASTLE

Tiana opened the front door of The Flashy Castle game store and cautiously looked inside. A cashier's checkout stand stood at the center of the front lobby but no one tended it. A display case beside it held boxes of assorted candies and chocolates, and a bigger case behind it held high-end games. She eased into the lobby holding the door open in case they needed to make a quick escape. Alora stood in the doorway by her and Rhys stood several feet behind them peering over their heads.

"Tell your fortune for dime, sweety!" came a woman's voice followed by shrill, maniacal laughter.

The girls jerked in surprise and stumbled inside letting go of the door. It swung back hard and hit Rhys knocking him further back. Startled by the woman's freaky voice, Tiana pulled her sister close and peered around to find the woman who again asked to tell their fortune followed by eerie laughter. With the door now shut, the girls saw it was just a female manikin sitting in a glass booth to the right of the door and burst out laughing. She was dressed in the bright gaudy clothes of a gypsy and done up with heavy makeup, rogue, and mascara.

"It's just a fake gypsy dummy," Alora said with relief.

"But the clothes look so authentic, she would look real if the plastic face wasn't as fake as a cheap Halloween mask."

Rhys then stormed into the store looking irked. "Hey, that wasn't nice of you guys to let that door swing backwards and knock me down. Next time at least warn—"

"Tell your fortune for dime, sweety!" the gypsy's voice said shrilly. Rhys staggered back a step and the girls chuckled.

Tiana gave him a silly grin. "It's just one of those manikin fortunetellers like the one Alora and I saw in Pioneer Square in Seattle last summer. At first, we didn't see her either since when you open the door it blocks the gypsy booth from sight."

"That was creepy, and having to search for Aunt Roleena and Gertie knowing Red Winkies are hiding here is creepy enough without having to listen to this Gypsy dummy."

"Come on, it's kind of fun."

"Not to me it isn't."

Tiana looked around the lobby again and called out loudly, "Hello, is anyone here?" When no one answered, she shrugged and looked at Alora and Rhys. "Hey, I wonder why the store is open if no one's here to run it?"

"The Red Winkies either scared them off or imprisoned them here with our aunts and Paris," Rhys said tersely. "After all, the tracking units showed us they came here so it's likely their lair."

"Making this super spine chilling," Alora said shivering.

"You said it."

"Well, it won't do any good to just stand here so I'm going to check out the lobby." Tiana walked over to the display case. "Hey, there's a big calendar on top of this case by the register that has a month crossed off and scribbled across it in bold ink it says, 'Yippee! Won a month vacation in Hawaii. Time to hang a closed sign and catch a plane to a sunny tropical beach'. Well, that explains why no one's here, but not why it was left unlocked and no sign on the door saying it's closed."

"Maybe they were so excited they forgot," Alora said.

"Doubtful, but not impossible," Rhys said. "Either way, I bet the Red Winkies were attracted to the lights and with it empty was a good place to hide their victims or trap people like us."

For several long minutes, the trio just stood in place looking and listening for the Red Winkies.

"Again, standing here won't help find the others," Tiana said. "Well, Alora, are you ready to start looking?"

Before she could answer a cold hand grabbed each of the girl's necks and they screamed wildly.

Rhys burst out laughing and pulled his hands away. "Geez. You two are as jumpy as a cat in a room full of rocking chairs."

Tiana punched him in the shoulder. "Hey, we have reason to be jumpy knowing the Red Winkies are here. So, knock it off or we'll hand you over to them happily."

"Okay, sorry," he said rubbing his arm as he looked around. "I don't see any, so let's go, but keep a sharp eye out for them."

"That's for sure," Alora muttered nodding sharply.

They warily tiptoed across the room inspecting the shelves on both the side walls of the lobby filled with various games and accessories priced for sale. After checking it out, they went over to a castle-like archway on the far side of it. They peeked through the opening and gaped in awe. Dozens of various game tables and pinball machines filled the big room, and most had flashing lights. To their dismay, they saw another archway on the other side of the first game room that appeared to lead into another game room. They stood transfixed behind the first archway studying all they could see and from where they stood, they saw row upon row of game tables.

Tiana felt Alora trembling beside her and took her hand and squeezed it. *I feel pretty shaky myself facing all this.*

"Well? Are we going in?" Rhys whispered to the girls.

"Yes," Tiana said straightening her shoulders and taking a deep breath. "I have to for our aunt's sake."

"And Paris," Alora choked out shakily.

The three cousins eased into the room, their eyes widening to see the huge number of games inside it. There were rows with vintage pinball machines, rows of Star Trek games, and rows with newer games like Avengers, Doom Eternal, and Mine-craft among others. They saw many flashing lights but none twinkled like Red Winkies. They crept down further passing a row with big game hunting units with fake rifles to shoot moose or elk. The next two rows had older games like Pokémon, Pac Man, Donkey Kong, and Grand Theft Auto, Doom Eternal, and Final Fantasy. Then they reached the last row across the back wall.

"This row's different. It's lined with cubicles, and some have chairs, but the bigger ones are empty," Alora said curiously.

"Those are Virtual Reality booths," Rhys said.

"Why do you say that?"

"Since the booth's bins all have Virtual Reality goggles and fake weapons for people to use in the action or combat scenes."

"Hey! Let's finish this row and get moving because we still have the next room to check out through the other archway," Tiana said briskly walking over to it to peek inside.

"Is that game room like this one?" Alora asked.

"No," she said after looking in it. "It has coin operated air hockey, foosball tables, and pool tables, and what's on the back wall mocks us, because it's lined with alien invader games."

"Rather ironic," Rhys said then they went back to finish checking the back wall booths for cupboards or doors leading into storage areas big enough to hide people or a dog in.

"Well, we're done and haven't seen any hiding places or any Red Winkies yet," Tiana said frowning. "So, let's go search that other game room."

"I suppose we have to, but it keeps getting scarier and scarier with not knowing when they'll show up," Alora whispered.

"True, but as yet I haven't seen any red winking lights."

"Me either, but not seeing them is almost more frightening."

"I'd think you'd be glad you didn't see any," Rhys said.

"I am, though I'd still rather see them before they see me."

"I 'so' agree with you. It brings to mind my watching 'The Wizard of Oz' as they merrily skip down the yellow brick road until they're attacked by flying monkeys."

"Right now, I understand why you'd say that," Tiana said.

"You know, I bet they want us to believe they've already left here. That way we'll go look for their hideout somewhere else."

"Or they're hiding as a trick to lure us further into their lair," Alora said warily. "Then they'll attack us by surprise after lulling us into a false sense of security."

Rhys stopped and smacked his forehead. "Wait a sec and I'll get out the tracking units Gertie left us. That'll show us if they are here." He set down his pack and quickly got the units out.

"Yikes! I should've thought of that myself," Tiana groaned.

"You can't be the 'only' one to think of these things."

Tiana began to give Rhys a tart retort but stopped as she saw him give her a big grin. "Right," she said grinning back.

He handed Tiana the XMS and turned on the Spectrometer as she engaged the XMS while Alora looked over her shoulder. As the tracking screen lit up, their eyes popped open wide.

"Well, that certainly clears that up," Alora sputtered.

"Yes, they're definitely here," Tiana said with a sharp nod. "And from what the tracking unit indicates there's a tiny cluster by the gypsy's booth in the lobby, two tiny clusters here, and loads of them spread out across the next room."

"They hide super well since we didn't see any winking lights near the gypsy booth or in this room," Alora groaned.

"True," Tiana said wincing.

"I wonder why they haven't tried to capture us," Rhys said.

"I don't know," Alora said biting on her lip. "Now what?"

"We still have to check the next room," Tiana insisted.

"That seems like a terrible idea."

"Which it is, but I don't see any other choice if we're going to get our aunts and Paris back!"

"Hey, I know we must do this," Rhys said, "But let's first think about ways to protect ourselves."

"Like how fast we can run if the Red Winkies come at us?"

"It won't be 'if', it will be when."

"True," Tiana said. "So, other than running and hiding, I can use my tiny lion tamer's chair to shove them off."

"That's a good plan if the Winkies attack on one front, but they might attack us from all sides or above," Rhys said.

"I can use my tiara and mesmerize them," Alora said.

"No! That would mesmerize me and Tiana too."

"True. What about using your Sword of Defense, Tiana?"

"That would make a barrier that we also couldn't get around so we couldn't look for our aunts. The only way of protecting us is to use my chair. So, if we hug together tightly, I can wave it around us without knocking you two off your feet. That'll keep the Red Winkies from getting to us."

Rhys shoved his hands in his back pockets and grumbled, "I'm not keen on the idea of us hugging up all together."

"Why, because we're girls?" Alora asked with a cheesy grin.

"Well...yeah."

"Just keep in mind as we cuddle, we're only your cousins."

"Yuck," he said grimacing.

"Don't tease him. This is serious," Tiana told her sister and she stopped grinning. "Think of it as a football teams huddle, Rhys, not a cuddle, and you're the quarterback I'm protecting."

"Okay, I can deal with that kind of thinking."

"Good. Now, Alora, enlarge our boxes to their original sizes so we can use our gifts easily. Rhys, leave your strongbox in this first game room so we don't have to lug it around."

"What if the Red Winkies take it?" he asked frowning.

"They couldn't lift Paris, so they won't be able to lift these."

"Then how did they get our aunts over here?"

"They likely zapped someone else to make them do what they wanted like they did to Paris and the Winkie driven officer. Since our packs and tracking units aren't alive, they can't do that to them." *At least I hope not*, she thought.

"Good point. Then we should all leave our packs here rather than lugging them with us while we search the next room. Then you can fend off the Red Winkies more easily as you whirl your repelling chair around."

"You're right," she said. "Good idea."

They all took off their packs and set them along the wall inside the first game room. Alora got out the shrunken boxes and set them together to restore them to their full size. She opened hers and got out her shrunken rack of magic dust. The vials were tiny and hard to hold but she managed to pull the cork out of the one marked 'bigger' and threw a big pinch over them all. She then looked up at Tiana and Rhys and gasped to see they were growing bigger too.

"Oh, no! You must've stood too close to the boxes!"

"No kidding," Tiana boomed in a giant's voice as she and Rhys grew up and up towards the tall ceiling. "Just get the fairy dust out that makes us smaller and fix this."

"But I can't reach your heads," she wailed.

"Just throw the magic dust at us as high as you can, but only at us so nothing else grows. Then stand back and we'll duck under it so it covers us. Now, hurry."

"Okay!" She quickly grabbed the vial marked 'smaller' and got a pinch in each hand. "Okay, I'm ready to throw it."

"Rhys, let's quickly scoop it over us as Alora tosses it at us," Tiana told him and he nodded. Alora then threw the fairy dust up at them and jumped back. To her relief, it worked and Rhys and Tiana shrank back down to their original sizes.

"Sorry you guys," Alora said tearily as Tiana scowled at her.

"It wasn't your fault," Rhys said elbowing Tiana and shaking his head at her. "We goofed up, not you. We were so busy watching you enlarge our boxes we didn't realize we were too close to them when you tossed the dust on them."

"You're right," Tiana sighed. "Sorry I got huffy, sis, and if we need to use it again, I'll sure remember to stand back."

"I'll also warn you to stand clear ahead of time," Alora said as she carefully packed up the vials.

"Talk about reminders, you two need to stand close by me as I pull out my tiny chair," Tiana said opening her box.

Rhys smirked. "Do you know how strange that sounds?"

"It does, doesn't it?" she said grinning. "Then again this day has just gotten stranger and stranger."

"That is so, so true. In fact, it's hard to believe it's the same day with all we've had to do."

"Also true, but nights come and tomorrows on the way. So, let's huddle and go look for a place our aunts and Paris might be hidden in the next room." Tiana slowly drew out her tiny lion tamer's chair and as they scrunched together, she saw her arms weren't the only ones covered with goosebumps.

This is beyond creepy, Tiana thought and warily led them into the next room, pausing just inside to look around. As she told them, there were rows of air hockey, foosball, and pool tables running the length of the room and the back wall was indeed lined with alien invader games. *Worse, they're now all full of bright sparkling red lights.*

"Why didn't you warn me how full of Red Winkies these games were?" Alora groused.

"Hey, we all looked at the spectrometer and XMS readouts!"

"You're right," she grumbled but then bit her lip worriedly.

Suddenly, large clusters of Red Winkies rose off most of the alien games and formed two huge clouds near the ceiling. They moved across it slowly in what seemed like a searching manner.

"They don't seem to know where we are," Tiana whispered.

"I don't care. Let's hide," Alora said breaking out in a sweat. Sensing her distress, the Red Winkies lit up brighter and came buzzing at them like an arrow to a bull's eye. "Run!"

"No, we have to stay together!" Tiana yelled but to no avail. Rhys and Alora raced down the long line of game tables. Tiana stood her ground and poked her chair at the Red Winkie cloud. Its force flung them against the back wall but in a blink, they bounced off it and came at her. Startled, she lost her grip on the chair and it skittered under a pool table in the next row. She did not have time to fetch it as she had to dive under a long line of air hockey, Foosball and pool tables. She scooted along on her hands and knees and at the end of the row was relieved to find her sister. "Where's Rhys?"

"I don't know, I was too busy running to see where he went," Alora whispered.

Tiana peeked up over the table just in time to see Rhys dive under a game table near where they first entered the room. A Red Winkie cloud then dove at him. He rolled to one row after another to evade them and wound up hiding across the room under one of the alien invader games the Red Winkies had left.

With the Winkies focused on Rhys, Tiana turned to Alora. "I'm going back to retrieve my chair so I can protect us. You can either come with me or stay and hid here."

"I'm so going with you," Alora said emphatically.

"Then let's do it." They peeked out and saw the two clouds Winkies had gathered into one at the center area of the ceiling. Keeping an eye on them, Tiana led her sister to where her tiny chair had skidded off to, scooting along on their hands and knees under the tables.

"Hey! How come the Red Winkies aren't going after Rhys anymore?" Alora asked trying to catch her breath. "They're just hovering above us."

"Maybe it's due to him hiding under one of the alien games they had already vacated."

"I guess we should've done that too."

"Maybe, or it's like Aunt Gertie told me. If you run back and forth like chickens with their heads cut off, it creates a lot body heat which attracts a predator's attention."

"So, we need to chill out," she said rubbing her sore knees.

"Not only that, we need to calm down since he also told me they can find you from the energy fear produces."

"I think I get it. You mean we produced more to attract them by running and being scared out of our minds."

"Right."

"Should we stay here and cool off?" Alora asked.

"Let me check on the Red Winkies first." Tiana slowly peeked out again. "Oh no! They're heading our way. Move!"

The girls rolled out from under the table and ran to the next row ducking under the table there and scooting down the line of them to evade the Winkies. Within minutes, Alora slowed down so much Tiana grabbed her hand and pulled her along with her.

"I do…so hope," Alora said between ragged gasps, "We can stay…out of their clutches."

"Me too."

"Tiana, I'm super sorry to be slowing you down, but my side is aching so badly I think I might collapse."

"Try taking slow, deep breaths."

"I have but it doesn't work for me like it does for you. I'm just not a long-distance runner like you are."

"That's because dad and I like to run for fun, while you and mom like to go shopping."

"I can tell you shopping is a lot more fun than this!"

"Too you, undoubtedly," she said as they ran to another row.

"They split into two groups again!" Alora said glancing up then she gasped and clutching her side, she crumpled to the ground. "That's it. I'm done for."

Tiana eased her under a table and shouted, "Rhys! Alora's got such a bad side ache she can't move. Can you help us?"

He slowly rose up from the alien invader game he was under and stood perfectly still. "I can run hard and work up some heat so they come after me to give her some time to heal up."

"Can you think of anything else so they can't get you?"

"It's the best I can come up with, and while they chase me you can get Alora out of here then go find us some help."

"You'd do that all alone for us?" she asked with surprise.

"Yes."

"Cool."

"Well, go!" he growled.

"No."

"Don't turn all stubborn on me. Just do it."

"That's brave of you, but I'm not leaving you to deal with the Red Winkies alone."

"But then you'd be rid of me, and you've told me more than once that would be a good thing."

"You drive me crazy with the stunts you pull, but I don't want to be rid of you, and I do care what happens to you."

"Why?" he asked gruffly.

"Like I said before, you're growing on me."

"Yeah, probably like a wart."

"No, to my surprise you're turning out to be a pretty good guy to have around."

"Geez," he said looking like he'd been shocked by lightning. "Then just please let me do this for you."

"No! We need…no, we 'want' you around."

"We mean it. We won't leave you here alone with them," Alora said so gustily she startled both herself and her sister.

"Then what do you want me to do? Because that big cloud of Winkies split in two again and are hovering over us. Annoying as it is, they'll be after us soon. But what annoys me more is finding out I'm not as clever as I thought I was."

"Why do you say that?"

"Because I thought I especially smart. But I've racked my brain for a way to rid us of the Red Winkies and came up with zip. It leaves me feeling really dumb…and kind of scared."

"That's super brave of you to admit," Alora said softly.

"That's so not how I feel. I feel like you said you did when you heard the gypsy dummy cackling wildly. All creeped out."

"You're not alone. I'm creeped out too," Tiana said. "Come on sis. I have to get my chair back. Then we can edge our way along the wall with you two close to me and I'll protect us while you look for a place they can hide their prisoners."

"Tiana, I can't move with my side feeling like it's going to split open. So, you two go do that while I lay low here."

"Seriously? You nincompoop. If I won't leave Rhys here by himself then you must know I won't go without you." She sat down by her sister with a heavy thump and took her hand.

Alora jerked her hand away. "Go! You must get that chair to ward off the Red Winkies and look for our aunts and Paris."

"Nope, I can't do this without you." Tiana leaned against her sister's shoulder with a resigned look in her eyes.

"Come on, Tiana. It isn't like you to cave in."

"Oh well, I'd rather go down together than leave you alone."

"Rhys!" Alora shouted then gasped in pain as it hurt her side badly to shout. "I can't move so look in your box for something to keep us from getting picked off by the Red Winkies."

"But it won't open for me," he said with frustration.

"Have you tried opening it again to see if that's changed?"

"Well...no."

"Then do it now because we need your help soon or the Red Winkies will get us for sure."

Rhys took few minutes to see what the Red Winkies were up to as they hovered over the game table the girls hid under. "Okay. You two stay absolutely still since I see both of the clouds of Red Winkie seem to be in a holding pattern."

"Why do you think that?" Tiana asked.

"It's because though one is floating way above the right side of the game table you're under, and the other is on the left, they have not moved for several minutes now. So, I'm hoping if you stay perfectly still you should be okay."

"Then we'll do what you say and stay perfectly still here."

"Good. Here I go to try opening my gift box. Wish me luck."

"Luck," the girls both said heartily.

Rhys took a deep breath and slid under the pool table near him scooting slowly from aisle to aisle on his hands and knees under the tables. *I don't want to make myself an obvious target.* As he neared the first archway they had gone through, he peered out from under the table he was under to check on the Winkies. *Good, they're still just hovering.* He held his breath and slowly commando crawled across the floor to the other side of the first game room's archway relieved to have a wall between him and the Red Winkies. *Hopefully they'll ignore me way out here.* He braced himself against the wall and then grabbed a hold of his heavy strongbox jerking it hard towards him. It moved so easily he hit himself in the head with it. *Ow. That was unexpected,* he thought rubbing his head. *Yeesh, this is bizarre because my box feels really light now.* With no time to puzzle over this fact, he tried to open the strongbox but it still did not open.

"Please, oh, please give me a hint about how to open you," he whispered in utter desperation. He then felt a slight vibration on the bottom of the box and turned it over. *Wow, now I see an etched note on the box that wasn't there before or did I miss it?* He quickly read it. 'Conditions will keep changing for the better when you learn to ask for help wholeheartedly and unselfishly'.

Odd I never noticed this. Then again, Tiana has excellent eyesight and didn't see this either. Weird. Hmm, I know how to ask for help wholeheartedly, but how do I do that unselfishly?

Rhys pushed away a wave of panic and thought it over. *I'm not sure how to ask for help in a way this note wants me to, but here it goes.* "From the depth of my heart, I ask for assistance here so I can help protect my cousins from the Red Winkies."

To his surprise, a hidden drawer on the side of the box opened up. Inside lay five pairs of sunglasses. *Sunglasses? What good are these?* He saw a note under them and opened it. 'These protect whoever you willingly give them to from the effects of mesmerizing gifts. *Wow, that gives me an idea that might help us here.* He opened Alora's glass box and got her bagged tiara out then put on a pair of the glasses and pocketed one other. "Tiana, I'm going to come near enough to toss you a pair of special sunglasses I just found and I need you to put them on," he shouted towards the back room.

"Why?" she asked.

"Please, don't make me explain it now since we're likely running out of time with the Winkies and I need to concentrate as I return to you over there." He then scooted on his hands and knees as fast as he dared through the archway toward the girls. "Just as I feared, the Winkies are slowly moving closer to the table you're under with one cloud on either side of the table. You won't be able to get away even if Alora could run. Now, Tiana, I'm going to slide some special glasses to you on top of the bag with your sister's tiara in it. Alora, put your tiara on 'after' Tiana puts on her glasses."

"I can guess why," Tiana said shrewdly as he slid the bag and glasses to her. She put on the glasses then handed Alora her bagged tiara. Alora put the tiara on and eased out from under the table. The gems brilliant rays immediately cast bedazzling light around the entire room. The clouds of Red Winkies began to wink slowly then floated up to the ceiling immobilized as did the other Winkies hiding in the games.

"I'm not mesmerized," Tiana said with delight. She turned to Rhys and wagged a finger at him. "Pretty tricky of you."

"It's truly not my trick at all, and guess what?"

"What?" Alora asked excitedly since he looked so happy.

"I got these out of my box!"

"Great! You finally got it open!"

"Well, only a drawer on the side of it so far." He then grinned. "But what's even better is the box being a lot lighter."

"Rhys, it really wasn't that heavy."

"Not for you, but it was for me."

"Alora, I think it 'was' heavy for him to lift and for a reason Aunt Roleena thought was important," Tiana said.

"Why would it be any different for him than ours were?"

"I don't know. But I do know he was strong enough to lift both of us and we're heavier than his strongbox."

"I guess that's true," she said nodding. "How odd."

"And frustrating for me too!" Rhys said.

"We could most certainly see that," Tiana said nodding.

"Now what?" Alora asked.

"We need get back to searching for where the Red Winkies stashed Aunt Roleena and Aunt Gertie."

"Obviously," Rhys said, "since it's why we came here."

"And we must also remember to get Paris," Alora said.

"I know. I know. We need to get them all out of here."

"That we do. Anybody have an idea how to do that?"

"The only one I have is to keep looking for a door leading into another room or storage closet," Tiana said.

"I didn't see any other doors when we were running around the room a while ago," Alora told her.

"I don't think you were looking for one since you and Rhys took off like a hoard of brain eating zombies were after you, and I was also busy evading the Winkies after dropping my chair."

"To me the Red Winkies are like tiny terrorists wanting to brainwash us into submission," Rhys said. "And you're right. I didn't look for doorways. I too was busy dodging them."

"Well, if we do find a door, we must be careful because they're so tiny they'd could just follow us under it," Alora said.

"Good point. So, 'when' not 'if' we find one, we need to go through with you wearing your dazzling tiara to keep them out and plug the space under the door with something," Tiana said.

"Both excellent points," Rhys said saluting the girls. "And since Alora has the Winkies floating aimlessly in the air, we can now begin searching." He then looked at Alora. "Way to go! Because of you and your tiara, Tiana and I can scour the walls thoroughly for hidden doors." With that they divided the room in two and began the search.

After a half hour passed, Tiana came up to Rhys shaking her head. "Nothing. How about you?"

"Zilch."

"Alora, did you notice anywhere we might've missed?"

She pointed to a big game board. "Yes...or at least maybe."

"I looked closely at that and didn't see a thing," Tiana said.

"But as you did that, I thought how odd it was that game had a much higher back than all the others here. So, I know Nancy would have wondered if there was a door hidden behind it."

"You and your old Nancy Drew detective books,' she said.

"Hey, don't knock them. They're fun to read. And she's a good sleuth."

"But they're so unrealistic since she can fly a plane, ride a horse standing up on it, and gets in trouble a hundred times over that would have killed her in real life the first time."

"I still like her."

"No accounting for taste," Tiana said grinning at her.

"Are you going to check it out or not?" Alora huffed.

"I will," Rhys said to her surprise.

"Err...thanks, because I do believe something's behind that one. It's also the only one that's put so tightly against the wall."

"What a waste of time," Tiana groaned. She sat down and watched as Rhys got ahold of the huge game board's front end and started pulling it out. It was so big it only moved a quarter of an inch away from the wall each time he tugged hard on it. Finally, Tiana went over to help him pull the gameboard out.

"Why are you even helping if you think this is a waste of time?" Alora asked her sister dryly.

"To help prove you and Nancy Drew wrong," she retorted.

Alora came closer to watch and as they moved the unit a few inches out, she shouted, "You're wrong! There is a door!"

Tiana and Rhys stopped pulling and went around to the back to look for themselves.

"You and Nancy Drew earned the bragging rights on this one, so rub it in all you want," Tiana said laughing.

"No kidding," Rhys said. "But we still have a long way to go to get the door to open, so let's keep yanking on it."

After much heaving and huffing, Tiana and Rhys finally got the big game board moved three feet away from the wall.

"Since it was due to your idea we found another door, Alora, you get the honor of opening it." Tiana then looked puzzled when her sister did not jump at the chance to do this.

"Well, open it," Rhys said eagerly.

"I want to but I'm afraid if I don't keep my tiara directed at the Winkies they'll come after us," Alora said biting on her lip.

"Want me to open it?" Rhys asked.

"No!"

"Hey, I was just asking."

"I do want to open it," she said sheepishly, "But I need to think of how to do it and still keep the Red Winkies at bay."

Tiana saw how anxious Alora looked and thought it over. "I'm not sure it matters, but it might. So, I'll guide you over to it backwards so you can keep the tiara focused on the Winkies."

"That would be great…and thanks."

"No problem." She walked over to her sister and led her backwards to the door. "Okay, it's right behind you."

Alora groped for the knob and tried to turn it. "It's locked."

"Can I try?" Rhys asked.

"Yes," she said disappointedly. "Go ahead."

Rhys turned the knob hard but it still did not turn. "No luck. It won't budge at all so you're right. It's probably locked."

"Which comes as no surprise," Tiana said flatly.

"Why?" Alora asked with frustration.

"Because nothing about any of this has been easy."

"True, so since I have to keep bedazzling the Winkies, I guess I need to shrink one of you to see if you can go in and find a key to unlock the door on the other side."

"But even if we do that, we still might not find a key on the other side to open it," Tiana grumbled.

"Once more, you're being negative, and I hope you will be wrong again. Now, do something positive and use that keen eyesight of yours to look through the keyhole and tell us what you see on the other side."

"Wow, not like you to get pushy. But as Aunt Gertie would say, 'Okeydokey, boss lady'." Tiana squatted down and peered through the keyhole. "It's dark in there, and I see a landing but no stairs going up. However, it might have stairs going down. Still, the way things have gone, if it does, they likely end in a dark, dank, dangerous dungeon."

"Or it might just be a normal kind of basement," Alora said.

"I doubt it."

"No surprise there. You usually take the dim view of things."

"Come on Alora, be fair," Rhys said. "Your sister is right. This scary adventure of ours has been pretty negative. In fact, little has been good in my way of thinking. Plus, the stairs could just lead to a storage room for this huge game store."

"Or it could be a way to trap us…and maybe our aunts and Paris aren't even down there," Tiana said.

"Then let's first try calling out to them to see if they answer us keeping in mind they might not be able to answer if the Red Winkies can prevent that."

"Nonetheless, it 'is' worth a try," Alora said firmly.

"Fine," Tiana said with a shrug and looked at Rhys. "Let's take turns calling out for them through the keyhole."

Rhys nodded and they began calling out Aunt Roleena and Gertie loudly through the keyhole. They shouted and shouted until they were hoarse and had to stop to rest their throats.

"I don't think they're down there," Tiana sighed sadly.

"You don't know that!" Alora growled surprising them both. "Maybe they can't hear us from up here. Or like Rhys said, the Red Winkies are keeping them from answering us."

"Now, what? Do we move on?" Rhys asked.

"No. I want to try something else first," Alora said. "Tiana, I need you to call Paris with your big, wonderfully loud voice. I haven't heard him bark, but he might if you call his name."

Tiana sighed. "That's wishful thinking on your part, and it's time that's best spent looking for them elsewhere."

"For their sakes, it's worth a try, just like the door was!"

"Ouch! That sharp remark just slapped me in the face."

"In this case, it was well deserved."

"Come on," Rhys said. "You two are rarely mean to each other, and that won't help any of us at all."

"Okay, you're not wrong," Tiana said and Alora nodded.

"Then just be your usual nice selves."

"Fine, here I go." Tiana went to the keyhole and yelled for Paris. She heard some squeaky noises but they sounded to her more like rusty hinges than a little American Eskimo pup. "Did you hear that noise? Was it him?" she asked her sister.

"It was so faint, I'm not sure."

"Come on, Alora. You have great hearing. So, if you can't tell it's him it's probably not. Let's go look elsewhere."

"No! I won't go until I know if Paris is down there," she screamed at the top of her lungs then she suddenly stopped as a loud, mournful keen came from way down below them. "That's him! That's Paris!" she shouted ecstatically.

"Are you sure?" Rhys asked.

"Yes! It's definitely his keen. So. I'll keep the Red Winkies stuck to the ceiling as you do the search. And since we don't know which gifts of ours might be useful, grab them all!"

Without question, Tiana and Rhys followed Alora through the archway and gathered up all their cumbersome boxes and packs. They then sprinted like a nest of hornets was nipping at their backsides as they rushed back to the newly found door.

"Who wants to be shrunk to a teeny-weeny beetle size to go through the keyhole to find the key?" Alora asked as Tiana handed her, her pack.

"I will," Tiana blurted out as Alora opened her glass box and pulled the vials of magic dust out from inside it. "But how will I get down from the keyhole to the landing on the other side to look for the key when I'm the size of a beetle?"

"Wait," Rhys said. "To be fair, we should draw for this."

"You're right," she admitted with a sigh and looked at Alora. "Think of a number from one to ten and we'll each guess."

"Okay, I have it," she said and they each guessed. Rhys won and to Tiana's surprise for the first time since she knew him, he did not rub his victory in her face.

"Alora," he said, "Tiana had a good question. I'll need to get bigger after I go through the keyhole so I can look for the key."

"True, so after you go through the keyhole, hang down from it on the other side and I'll blow the enlarging dust over you."

"Sounds like a good plan. Let's do it," Rhys said.

"Stand back, Tiana." Alora waited for her sister to move and put a pinch of fairy dust in her hand from the 'Smaller' vial and blew it over him. He was not quite small enough to fit through the keyhole, so she blew a tiny bit more on him until he was the right size then she gently lifted him up to it."

He crawled through the keyhole and hung on the keyhole's edge on the far side. "Okay, I'm all set," he called out in a surprisingly full human-sized voice. "Make me big again."

"It doesn't take much, so let me know if I need to blow more through the keyhole on you to get you to the right size." She then blew the dust on him and as he grew all she saw was his shirt. But a few seconds later they heard the doorknob rattle.

"Don't get excited, I'm back to a normal size and tried to see if the door would open from this side, but it doesn't," Rhys said then all they heard was the sound of his footsteps.

Tiana peeked through the keyhole and saw his shadowy form moving around the landing. "Looks like you're a bit taller than you were before."

"Yeah, 'presto-chango'," he said grinning. "I gained a few inches in height."

"Don't get used to it," Alora said sternly. "Because I'm changing you back to your normal size when you're done."

"Spoil sport," he said but then chuckled. "Okay, I'm looking for a key, but it's dark in here so I have to feel my way around."

"Why not use the flashlight you found at Aunt Gertie's house. Alora put the one you gave her in her pocket and I think you did the same thing with yours."

"Ah! You're right. That's much better," he said flashing it around. "This part of our adventure can be put in our journal as easy. I just pointed my light at the wall of the landing out here and there's a key rack by the door with seven keys on it. I'll start trying them out." He grabbed one and put into the keyhole.

Alora backed up and shouted, "Don't poke my eye out."

"Hey, I told you I was going to try the keys out."

"True," she groaned. "You did say that."

"Well, it's not this key. Now, keep back as I try another."

Rhys tried one key after another in the keyhole and when he got to the last one, he was relieved to feel it turn. "Shazam! It worked. Now stand back." He pushed the door open wearing a silly grin on his face. "Welcome to my parlor said the spider to the fly," he said like a cartoon movie Dracula.

"Thanks," Tiana said chortling knowing the funny Dracula he was imitating, but as he flashed his light across the landing, she shivered involuntarily to see an incredibly steep stairway going down and down until it became shrouded in darkness.

"Well, are you two coming in here?" The girls still did not move. "Wake up you two. You're standing there like zombies."

"Errr...okay," Tiana said so stunned by what she saw she had to pinch herself to break the grim hold it had on her. "But we need to do something else important first."

"Well, go on. Tell me."

"We still need to figure out how to keep the Red Winkies out so Alora can put her tiara away. Because we don't want to wear dark glasses to go down this dark stairwell. We also don't want them following us down inside there."

Rhys slapped his forehead. "Good thinking, and I'm sorry these stairs are going to be so hard to do. Hey, and by the way, Alora, thanks for holding the Red Winkies back for us."

"You're welcome," she said smiling as she made a tiny bow. "Now, any ideas to get me in there but keep the Winkies out?"

"Actually, I did think about it earlier and have a simple one. You two speed in here with our packs and run down the stairs like the ones behind you are on fire and I'll seal up the door."

"We are 'not' going to run down those stairs in the dark!" Tiana said firmly. "Speaking of that, Alora, will you hand me your flashlight so I can light the way?"

"Sure." She got it out of her pocket and handed it to Tiana. "Now what?"

"The what is that I came up with an idea of how to do this," Rhys said and ripped off the bottom of his tee shirt. "Now, jump inside and I'll stuff the keyhole with my tee shirt then shove my sweatshirt under the door so the Winkies can't follow us in."

"Good thinking, but first Alora has to shrink our boxes back down again to get them in the rucksack," Tiana said.

"Got it covered," Alora said sprinkling a pinch of the magic fairy dust on their gift boxes to shrink them. "Done." She then stuffed the boxes in the rucksack and put it on.

Tiana then slung the framed pack with the tracking device over her shoulders and looked at her sister. "Ready for this?"

"Ready as I ever will be," Alora said and they came inside.

Rhys slammed the door shut plugging the keyhole with the piece of his tee shirt then crammed his sweatshirt in the space under the door as tightly as he could. "Okay, now I can lift my box would you put it in the small pack and I'll carry it?"

"Actually, can you carry the framed pack with the tracking units and let me carry yours?"

"You bet." He then switched packs with her. "Alora, you can stow away your tiara now," he said turning on his flashlight.

"I will after Tiana turns ours on," she said anxiously.

"There," Tiana said turning it on.

Alora put it in its bag then stuck it in her pocket. "Done."

"Great. Let's get started," he said as he put his dark glasses in his cargo pants pocket and began running down the stairs.

"Wait!" Tiana said slipping her dark glasses in her pants pocket. "Alora's not used to the lack of light since even with the flashlight on, it's so dark it's hard to see much at all. So, she's not ready to go yet and until she does, I won't go either."

"Of course not," Rhys said walking back up to the landing. "Okay, here I am so we can stick together," He waited as Tiana tried to get Alora to move, but she just gaped at the stairs with her eyes fixed on it so warily Tiana shivered. He walked up to them and looked over their heads and realized how eerie it all looked. The stairs were uncommonly narrow being only two feet wide and they went on and on then disappeared from sight as they got swallowed up by the darkness far below them.

"Hey you two!" Rhys shouted breaking the silence. "We do need to get to rescuing Aunt Roleena, Gertie and Paris."

Tiana shook herself like she was coming out of a trance. "Yes, we do. It just stunned me for those stairs look scary and must look worse to Alora being nearsighted. Even to me, it's like entering an old Twilight Zone show where everything's shadowy and blurred. But you're right, spine-chilling as it is, we must find our aunts and Paris." She then nudged Alora. "Sis, come on, it's a spooky stairway, but 'ta da', it's just stairs."

"Or it could turn out to be petrifying," Alora sputtered.

Rhys grew impatient as Alora just stared transfixed at it and would not move an inch. *Good grief. I risk getting shrunk and enlarged, find the key to the door yet they're the ones who freak out. Well, enough of this.* He then pinched their arms hard.

"Ouch!" they screeched and rubbed their arms.

"Why did you do that?" Tiana asked glaring at him.

"I had to do something to break your fixation on the stairs," he said bluntly as he gently took the rucksack off Alora. "I'll carry both packs," he told them as he slung a strap of the other one over his shoulder. "Tiana, you set the pace, and Alora can follow you while I take up the rear."

"Okay!" she hissed then she surprised Rhys by grabbing the rucksack from him so forcefully she knocked him into the wall.

"That was mean!" he growled.

She slowly led Alora down the stairs since the flashlight only lit the stairs for a few yards ahead of them and shouted over her shoulder, "So was your pinching me."

"But I had to do something to get you two to move," he said groaning in frustration as he followed them down the stairs, but her only reply was a loud huff. *Well, at least they're finally moving*, he thought and sighed deeply.

A few minutes later, Tiana slowed down even more and called back, "Hey, be extra careful on these stairs. They're really uneven and don't have railings to keep us from falling off if we stumble. I don't know about you, but I don't want to find out how far it is to the bottom by plummeting off of these."

"Me either and I'm delighted to go slower," Alora said. "So, Rhys, you're carrying the heaviest most awkward load with those tracking units, so watch you don't slip off of these steps."

"Don't worry, as long as I keep a sharp eye on this jagged stairway, I don't see that I'll have any problem doing this."

"The key word here is 'see'," Tiana said. "It's so dark in here I can't see much of what's ahead. It might have a sharp switchback we won't see until we're on top of it and missing a turn like that could send us off a killer drop."

"Good point."

"We also need to stick close together since we don't know who or what we'll run into here," Alora said, "So stay close."

"You're such a worry wort," he said, but after he thought it over, he hustled down close to them. "Here I am. Now we're all nice and close like peas in a pod just like you wanted."

"Thanks for doing that. I don't want to lose you."

"You sure? It could be the perfect time to get rid of me."

"Don't joke like that since I truly meant it," she said sadly.

He winced to hear he had hurt her. "Sorry, I was only joking, but I guess this isn't the right time for that. I should've just said you're welcome."

"Thanks for realizing that," she said softly.

"You bet," he said and this time in a sincere tone.

They went down and down the stairs for an hour past several switchbacks when Alora caught her shoe's heel in a crack and stumbled. Rhys rushed over and steadied her but as he did the plastic crate tied to his framed pack shifted to the outside and unbalanced him and he began falling off the stairs. He tried to regain his balance but found he could not. When Alora saw this, she sat and down and braced herself against the inner wall then grabbed his legs to pull him back, but they still began to slowly slide off. Tiana turned and saw them teetering on the edge and ran up to Alora. She looped one arm around her waist and the other around the footboard of the wood stair. Then using all the strength she possessed, she held on tightly. After a scary long minute, they all finally regained their footing.

"Whew! That was a close call and it's my turn to say sorry," Alora said sheepishly. "I let my attention drift and didn't see the notch out of that step and the toe of my shoe got caught in it."

"Either way we got lucky because I can see we're just ten or so feet away from the bottom of the stairs. Unfortunately, these lead into what truly looks like a dungeon," Rhys said flashing his light around the dark cavernous area to show it to them.

"Are you sure that isn't just a bigger landing with the stairs hiding somewhere off to the side?" Tiana asked.

"I doubt it, since it's many times bigger than any landing we've been on. But we need more light to check it out."

"This area's flat, so I could put my tiara back on light it up," Alora said. "But wearing dark glasses might wash out its light."

"Well, let's check it out." Tiana got her glasses from her front pocket and put them on as Rhys donned his. "Okay, we're set and I hope it still looks lighted with our glasses on."

"Me too," she said getting out her tiara. "But as you said, it's worth a try. Okay, is everybody ready for the light?"

"Yes!" Tiana and Rhys shouted eagerly and Alora set it on her head. It instantly glowed brightly casting back the darkness.

"Good heavens," Tiana said with awe. "Even wearing these dark glasses, I can see lots further now."

"We should have tried this in the first place," Rhys said shaking his head. "Then we wouldn't have had to creep as slow as a slug to get down these stairs 'and' it would've helped us go down them more safely."

"That water's gone under the bridge. What's more important is we all got down here in one piece. Not only that, you or I could've asked her to try using it with our glasses on, but none of us thought of it because we were all feeling a bit stunned."

"Good point, and more than a bit I'd say," Rhys said. "So, like you said, it's water under the bridge and we got here safely.

Now, I'm just feeling like we should all keep in mind how stressful this is and remember to go easy on one another."

"Gracious, that's super cool of you to say that," Alora said.

"It is?"

"Yes, and you bringing that up is a good surprise," Tiana said smiling warmly at him as did her sister.

"Thanks," Rhys said smiling back then he looked around. "Shazam! With this lit better I can see a cavernous hallway here. There's also a road starting at the bottom of these stairs about thirty feet wide that looks made of concrete…and the walls on the sides are so tall I can't even see the ceiling."

"Me either, and it's hard to guess the height of these since they look made of black obsidian and seem to disappear into the darkness above them."

Alora wrinkled her nose as she looked around. "You know, those stairs were super creepy, but the blood-red slashes across these walls tops is even worse."

"No kidding," Rhys said. "This is even spookier than Aunt Roleena's basement. Hey Tiana, you've got keen eyesight. Can you see any end to this two-lane-street sized hallway?"

"Nope, but if its end point is as black as these walls, it would be hard for anyone to see it."

"Well, it's not helping us to just stare at it. Let's move on."

"Okay," Tiana said and after a pause, Alora nodded.

They walked warily down the broad lane checking around them like a monster was going to jump out at them any second. Several blocks later, all they found was more gloomy black walls with dark red slashes on them. No one spoke for a long time until Rhys cleared his throat loudly and Alora jumped.

"Sorry to startle you," he said sincerely. "Are you okay?"

"Yes…well, truthfully, no," she choked out. "This is a super sinister place."

"It is pretty dismal down here."

"You can say that again," Tiana said.

"It is pretty dismal down here."

"Funny guy."

Alora burst out laughing. "Actually, that was kind of funny."

"Don't encourage him."

"Why not? I'd rather laugh than cry while we walk down this spooky lane."

"Then laugh if it helps," she said but again, no one spoke.

Twenty minutes later, they came to a massive pair of iron gates blocking the hallway and stopped and gaped at them.

"Looks like the jail bars they use in the old westerns I watch with dad," Rhys said. "Except these are the size of water pipes. It makes it seem like they're made to keep in 'or' out a herd of elephants or another big beast."

"I do hope it's not because of that," Tiana said.

"Me too," Alora whispered.

Rhys frowned as he studied the gates. "Ditto, although its colossal size suggests it's keeping back something big, which makes me glad your tiara lights things a good distance away. What's also curious is the concrete road ends here and the other side is made of huge, rough, square slabs of granite."

Tiana nodded. "You're right, and that is curious. Another curious thing is the walls further down are inset with iron-barred gates like this one, except much smaller and appear to be the size used in older zoo cages."

"It all looks like a set in a scream-theme film," Alora said.

"It does, with cages for the big creatures Rhys mentioned."

"Do you think these gigantic gates are locked?"

"I'll find out." Tiana walked up to the pair of gates and pushed on one hard. It squeaked and moved a bit then stopped. "It moved, but not far. Help me shove on it to see if it opens."

Alora shook her head, but Rhys walked over to help her. As they pushed on the gate as hard as they could, it moved a few inches making a loud rusty squeal and then they heard a high-pitched keen in the distance. Rhys's eyes widened, but the girls looked at each other and shouted excitedly, "Paris!"

"You're sure?" Rhys asked skeptically.

"Absolutely," Alora said running over to them. "Come on, I'll help you push."

"They all dug in and shoved on the gate with all they could muster and it gave way so fast they fell flat on the ground.

"Ouch," Tiana groaned scrunching up her face. She then got up and began picking bits of gravel out of her palms.

"Is it an ouch of pain or embarrassment?" Rhys asked with a wry grin as he wiped his hands off on his cargo pants. "Because I bet we look pretty silly after falling on our faces like that."

"So, so, true, so it seems you're changing your attitude from 'Big-Pain-in-the-Rear' to 'Best Dungeon Clown'."

"Well, at least I'm a tall clown, which is more than you can say... 'shorty'," he said with a mischievous grin.

In a flash of motion, Tiana did a jujitsu scissor sweep and upended her six-foot-two-inch-tall cousin. "I might not be as tall as you, but I'm quick on my feet."

He sat on the ground glaring at her then burst out laughing. "Not bad." He reached out to shake her hand and as she clasped it, he flipped her over on her back then pinned her.

"No fair! I was just going to help you up!"

"Hey, from what I've heard about Jujitsu, it teaches you to always be ready for your opponent's tricks," he said laughing as he let her go and stood up.

"Right," she said dryly and quickly used a leg to sweep him off his feet again but Rhys jumped up to his feet.

"Nice demo, you two," Alora said with a giggle.

"I guess so," he groaned then he grinned like a Cheshire cat.

"Thanks for the laugh. I needed that."

"Me too," Tiana said, "But let's get to back to our search."

"And go off to follow the rough granite road," Rhys said.

"That doesn't sound nearly as nice as that song in the Wizard of Oz, 'Follow the Yellow Brick Road'," Alora said.

"No, not as nice at all," Tiana sighed.

"Then let's nice things up a bit!" She hooked an arm around Tiana's and one around Rhys's then pulled them along as she skipped and sang, 'Follow the Yellow Brick Road'.

Tiana and Rhys only slogged along with her until she gave them a sad, disappointed look. They then grit their teeth and skipped and sang with her. After doing it twice, they walked arm-in-arm silently staying as far away from the walls as they could. They passed several barred doors leading into drab and dreary cells but they were empty. They also passed niches in the walls with various statues of death that made them shiver.

"Some statues look inspired by that gruesome plague long ago called the 'Black Death'," Rhys said, "And those holding a scary scythe in their hand look the 'Grim Reaper'."

"It makes this place even more depressing," Alora muttered.

"I'll second that," Tiana said.

"Ditto." Rhys agreed then looked puzzled. "But I'm thinking this part of our journey has been too easy." As if proving his point, a large, dark, elongated globule the size of a car whisked by high over their heads. They froze and gaped at it as it sped down the passageway into the dark shadows beyond moving so fast, they only saw it as a dark blob. "What the devil was that?"

"It might be just what you said."

"Huh?"

"The devil," Tiana said flatly.

"You don't really believe that's what it is, do you?"

"Well, we've met a lot of unusual beings at Aunt Roleena's. Hers have all been good ones, but this could be a bad one even worse than the Red Winkies which would explain why we haven't seen any of them down here."

"Wow. I never thought about it until you said that. You're right. We haven't seen any Red Winkies here at all."

"True," Alora said biting on her lip nervously.

They crept warily along for an hour searching for their aunts and Paris finding only empty cells when they came across one with straw strewn across the floor that looked lived in, then one with piles of straw covered by rough wool blankets, then others with trees, or big piles of rocks, and one had a large pond in it.

"Ew!" Alora said pinching her nose shut as they came to the next cell. "This is the first one that stinks super bad."

Rhys scrunched his face up in disgust and pointed to the back of the cell. "That's because there in the far corner you'll see a huge urinal and poop bucket. At least I'm guessing it is from what's spilled out of them onto the floor."

"Ick! I see that, but I don't see anyone or thing in there."

"Maybe they got hungry and ate what was in there."

"Rhys! You said Aunt Gertie told you that Red Winkie's won't hurt anyone," she said slapping his shoulder.

"I know, but we don't know what happened to who or what was in there, or who or what might have put them in there in the first place," he said shrugging. "It might just have been a cow."

"Just?" Alora gasped. "I doubt a cow or any animal wants to get slaughtered and eaten any more than I do."

"Good point, you animal lover softy and Aunt Roleena feels the same way so avoid that. None-the-less, we live on a tough predatory planet where carnivores eat other living beings."

"Ew. Thinking of it, I might not eat red meat now either."

"On to the next cell," Rhys said changing the subject. "Those cells with straw piles covered by a blanket seemed odd. I mean I can see covering a prize horse with a blanket to keep flies off it, but I don't think they'd give them blankets to sleep on."

"Maybe it was a super special pet horse," Alora said.

"I doubt it, because these aren't fancy stables down here," Tiana said as they walked on to another cell. "Here's an odd one. It's a huge pile of straw with an indentation in the middle of the blanket like that of a giant human, or the size of one of the space faring giants that come visit Aunt Roleena."

"But the ancient humans called those visitors 'gods and goddesses', and most thought they were," Alora said.

"True, but she told us it was due to them having powers humans don't possess, as well as starships and loads of other devices far more advanced than any we humans had."

"Maybe these were humans from the future that came back to study us which is why they're shaped like us," Rhys said.

"Only some look similar, and of them are much bigger than us, with appendages we don't have, like wings."

"That's enough speculating for me. Let's pick up the pace so we can find our aunt and Gertie...and Paris of course," he said to Alora then they began swiftly walking down the passageway.

They passed four more empty cells then as they got to the next one Rhys braked to a stop. His jaw gaped open wide and they saw why. At the back of the cell a man lie on top a huge blanketed pile of straw draping over it all the way to the floor.

"That's Gertie!" Rhys shouted excitedly.

"How can you tell for sure?" Tiana asked dubiously.

"Because I recognize the dress and bonnet he's wearing."

"Oh. My. Gosh. You're right. Aunt Gertie!" Alora yelled.

"Good grief, sis, don't call up the demons that might have gone by us," Tiana growled. "Or be here, for this pile of straw is floating in the air, so don't draw the attention of whatever put him in there and dial it down now!"

"But we have to wake him up!" she yelled frantically.

"Alora, please don't shout," Rhys said so gently she stopped and nodded. "What Tiana is trying to get across to you is we need to be cautious, calm and quiet since we don't know what we're dealing with. High-pitched screams could set off energy-sensitive beings like a match sets off a firecracker."

"Oh…sorry, I guess you're right, it could." She squinted to check out the cell and did see that it was indeed floating a foot off the ground. "It must be Red Winkies!"

"Calm down. They can't do this or they would have floated Paris away with them. We also would've seen a twinkling red glow under that straw pile, and there's not one," Tiana told her.

"But what else can make a straw pile float?"

"It might be enchanted, like your magic dust."

"Maybe, but with the way that big blanket is draped over the side I can't tell if anything's hiding underneath it or not."

"How about we just call Gertie calmly until he responds?" Rhys asked and the girls nodded. "Okay, here we go."

"Gertie," they called and called but after ten minutes they stood back sadly disappointed for they got no response.

Alora suddenly arched up. "I heard Paris keen again."

Tiana looked at her sister sadly. "I didn't hear him."

"Me either," Rhys said shrugging.

"I know I heard him," Alora said defensively.

"You likely did, because you certainly heard him before. So, now we know he's down here after we get Gertie out of this cell we'll go find him."

"Do you think he's okay?" she asked. "He sounded super upset which scares me because I'm afraid they might kill him."

"They can't kill us, so like you said, he's upset," Tiana said.

"Okay…but how about Aunt Gertie? Since it's not the Red Winkies holding the hay up then whatever's doing this might hurt him or Auntie Roleena or Paris."

"She's right," Rhys said. "We need to find out what we're dealing with. So, let's forget about being quiet and shout at Gertie to waken him." The girls nodded and they all shouted until they were hoarse. "Now what?" he rasped.

"I don't know," Tiana croaked. "But I have to rest my throat a minute before I can yell again."

"Yelling isn't working anyway. We need to go get him out of there!" Alora managed to shout angrily at them.

"Of course we do, but you need to get a grip first," Tiana said firmly, "So, stop yelling at us, for none of this is our fault."

"Aren't you both forgetting something?" Rhys asked.

"What?" she snapped so aggressively he backed up.

"Geez, don't bite me."

"Sorry. this place is getting to me."

"Me too, but it's important to remember we're all stressed out so we decided to treat each other kindlier."

"You're right," Tiana sighed. "Sorry."

"Thanks for reminding me of that."

"Me too," Alora said taking a deep breath. "This is a terrible place to have to search, but now I'm calmer and wearing my tiara I am realizing whatever's holding the pile of straw up shouldn't be able to stop us from getting Aunt Gertie. Right?"

"Oh, that's right," Tiana said. "That slipped my mind."

"There's something else we forgot," Rhys said flushing.

"What's that?"

"None of us has even tried to see if this door is locked."

Tiana smacked her forehead. "Good grief! We didn't." She pushed on the cell door. "Hey, it moved. Help me push it open."

Once again, the trio pushed on the door. It moved a tiny bit and then stopped. They tried again with no luck.

Rhys then jerked the door back and forth hard. "I hear the latch inside hitting the strike plate so it's loose, but definitely locked which is now obvious and not helpful at all."

"No, it isn't," Tiana sighed. "Well, genius, I hope you have a bright idea about how we go about opening this."

"Maybe. I do see a hook on the wall by this cell, but don't get excited. There's no key hanging on it. Still, it might've fallen off the hook so let's look around and try to find it." With that, they searched every nook and cranny around them.

"You guys, I don't know if I found it, but come look," Tiana called out from a few yards down the hall from Gertie's cell and Alora and Rhys ran over to her.

"I think it's in there." She pointed inside a barred closet-sized nook with an empty key rack high up on its back wall.

"I don't see any keys anywhere around there," Rhys said.

"It's easy to miss because the key is in the shadow of that wooden stool under the key rack. If you look closely, you'll see it's down in a small crevice under the stool."

"Oh! Now I see it." He laid on the ground and stuck his arm in between the bars as far as he could but was a foot short of reaching it. He got back up and dusted himself off and looked at Alora. "Why not use the fairies in your wand to go get it?"

"No, it's not life threatening so the Fairy Queen would be mad if I didn't try other ways to do this and turn me into a wart frog. But I could use my magic dust to make one of you small to go get the key. Then I could make you big again."

Tiana shook her head. "No, from the size of the keyhole this key will be big. That means it'll be too heavy for us to wrangle it out of that deep crack in the floor it's stuck in to drag it over here when we're in a shrunken form."

"Then use your sword to poke it out and pull it over here."

"That won't work since it's wedged deep and my sword's really broad. So, it won't work well for snagging a key."

"Don't be such a pessimist. Give it a try it," Alora huffed.

"Ok," she sighed, "But first you need to get your magic dust and enlarge my sword to its normal size." Alora nodded and did as she said. Tiana then used her sword to reach inside the nook and was able to knock it out but it skidded into the wall behind it. "I told you it wouldn't work. Now, it's out of my reach."

"My arms are longer than yours," Alora said. "Let me use it to get behind the key and drag it forward."

"Are you crazy? Do you want to get burned like Rhys did?"

She quickly backed off. "No, that looked painful."

Rhys nodded sharply. "It was. Now what? Shrink us?"

"Yes, I'll have to use my magic dust and shrink you both. Though I'm getting worried because I'm getting low on it. Still, we'll have to chance it if we're to free Aunt Gertie since it will take two of you to drag that big key out here."

"What if it's the wrong key?" Tiana asked gloomily.

"For once can you just say something positive?"

"Okay. What if it's positively the wrong key?"

"Argh! You drive me crazy when you're so negative."

Tiana sighed. "I know. So, here's a positive idea I thought of to save on magic dust. Let me get all our shoe strings from our tennis shoes and tie them together. Then just shrink me and I'll pull one end of the string over to the key and lasso it and you pull the key over here. Hopefully, it will unlock the door."

"Since Rhys is bigger and stronger than you, let him do it."

"It truly hurts me you think I'm not capable of dragging a shoestring over there," she snapped and her nostrils flared.

"Tiana, this kind of risk scares me badly," Alora said sadly. "If something attacked you in there neither Rhys or I could get through the bars to help you fight it off."

"It's a risk for either of us, but from my climbing experience with dad I can tie great knots and I'm fast. And just as I have the courage to do this, you have the courage a task far more important than mine."

"What task?"

"Bravely wearing your tiara which is likely keeping what's under that straw pile from becoming a problem for us."

"I should shrink myself and do this to keep you both safe."

"That won't work. If you'll recall, when you picked up any of the fairy dusts, they didn't affect you at all."

"Oh. That's true. The magic dust didn't change me at all."

"Tiana's right," Rhys said. "Holding these other threats at bay here is of the greatest importance to all of us right now."

"I still don't like doing this," Alora huffed but as she picked up the shrinking dust Paris keened even more sharply. "Paris!"

"I heard him too!" Rhys looked the direction of the keening and his eyes widened. "Wait!" he hissed grabbing Alora's arm.

"Why, since we settled this?" she asked a bit miffed.

"Alora, look up to your left and you'll see why!" Tiana said.

She gazed up and saw a huge, black, jellylike blob rushing towards them high in the air churning about like a pulsing tub of gooey black butter. "Should we run?"

"As fast as it's moving, I doubt we can outrun it."

"Then what should we do?"

"Just brace yourselves!" Rhys put his arms around them and they watched in horror as the enormous blob flew at them.

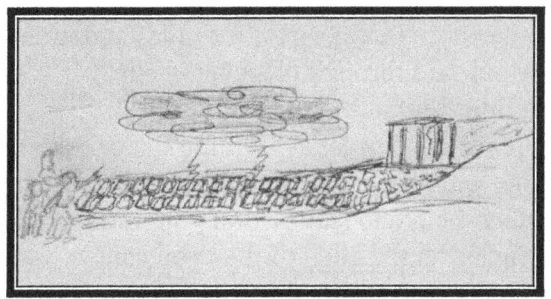

CHAPTER TEN
DUNGEON DEMONS

The dark gelatinous blob boomed as loud as thunder as it flew the trio's way. They clung together not knowing what else to do. After a minute later, Rhys stood back from the girls and studied the dark blob looking more curious than scared.

"This is odd," he said scratching his head.

"Odd? It just looks wickedly dangerous to me," Alora said.

"That it does, but what I also saw as it came at us was this big angry sounding blob hasn't just slowed down, it's stopped. In fact, now it's backing up, and if you look closely, you'll see it's moving out of the halo of light coming off the tiara."

"Cool!" Tiana said. "See Alora? Your tiara's protecting us."

"Good," she sighed and relaxed a bit. But then she heard Paris bark angrily and the blob sped back down the hall. "Oh no! That blob shot off the direction I heard our Paris barking!"

"And he sounds closer than I thought he was," Rhys said.

"I have to go save him!" Alora shouted frantically.

"No, it's too dangerous to go chasing after that thunderous blob without scoping out the dangers first."

"I don't care. I'm going. We'll come back for Aunt Gertie." Alora then ran as fast as she could down the wide granite street.

Rhys and Tiana ran hard to catch up with her knowing they had to stay close to her to be in her tiara's protective sphere of light. After dashing half-a-mile past ten empty cells, they caught up with her as she stopped to catch her breath.

"No one would believe me if I told them there's a tunnel under this game store that goes on for miles and miles like this one does," Alora said through clenched teeth.

"It's more like a mile," Tiana said.

"Must you always correct everything I say?" she huffed crossly. "Now, get out of my sight until I calm down."

"I can't since I have to stay within your tiara's light ring."

"Then go as far to the edge of it as you can."

"Fine. I will."

"No! Like it or not, we stay together," Rhys said so forcefully they gawked at him. "And do stop snapping at each other, though it does come as a surprise since you usually snap at me."

"Then come close and I'll snap at you instead," Tiana said.

"No way. Now, chill off. This is depressing enough without you two going after each other's throats. Besides, Alora has a point. This dungeon's road has gone on a long, long way."

"True." Tiana sighed and looked at her sister awkwardly. "Sorry for being such a picky thorn in your side."

"And I'm sorry for being a drama queen," Alora replied.

"So can we get to looking again?" Rhys asked.

The sisters nodded and they continued their search. As they came the next cell, the girl's eyes lit up when they heard a muffled keen. They looked inside it and their eyes widened in fear to find a layer of black goo covering the top of Paris' body.

"This is why we could rarely hear him," Tiana said.

"Except for his keening," Alora said, "That sharp sound of his got through the black blob that muffled our small buddy."

"Which is likely what choked him off most of the time."

"Then I bet the reason he could finally bark loudly was that dark glob left him to come investigate us," Rhys said.

"And look at the bars on the bottom of his cell. It's covered with a thin sheet of this black blob so Paris can't slip out through them." Tiana kicked the cell door in frustration and gasped as it swung open. "It wasn't locked!"

Alora did not even pause to think, she quickly went inside.

"I'm coming with you," Tiana said following her sister, but Rhys stayed outside. "Aren't you coming with us?" she asked.

"You guys need to watch more spy thrillers. Then you'd realize there might be another glob or a worse menace that would come by now and lock us 'all' inside this cell."

"Yish, I should've thought of that," Tiana groaned.

"Then it's a good thing I did," he said with a wry smile.

"Actually, yes, it is." She and Alora then went on ahead.

"I'm now thinking of why this glob didn't lock this cell, but did lock up Gertie's. It's because they sensed that he's a bigger threat to them and they also hoped to trap us in here with Paris."

"Aunt Gertie would've been a bigger threat. Plus, I do agree that as you said, it counted on us coming in here to get him. But now thanks to Rhys thinking ahead, it can't trap us."

"And it was right about us coming for him, since we would never leave him behind," Alora said looking at her sister and Rhys in a way that let them know they best not think otherwise.

"Of course not. What they didn't expect was for Rhys to stand guard outside the door." Tiana then saw her sister walk towards the dark blob covering Paris and scooted after her.

An eerie howl shot down the hallway from far in the distance and Rhys braced himself. "Might be more trouble," he groaned.

"Is it another blob thingie?" Alora gasped and the girls froze.

"I don't know, but whatever it is I bet it's up to no good," he said as they stared nervously the direction of the bone-chilling noise as it moved closer and closer to them.

To Tiana's surprise, a minute later Alora boldly walked on. She followed her keeping a wary eye on the dark blob over Paris for it boomed louder the closer they got. "Alora, if that thing attacks you, I'll grab you and pull you out of here."

"Not until I free Paris."

"I will if I feel I have to, to keep you safe."

"As if. I outweigh you and can out wrestle you."

"True, but you don't outweigh Rhys. So, I'd switch places with him and have him come get you for me."

"He'd better not before I get Paris or I'll knee him in that sensitive guy spot," she snapped and Rhys winced. "Because I'm going to get my buddy out of here one way or another."

"Who's taken over my shy sister?" she asked shaking her head. Suddenly, the globule boomed louder and Tiana grabbed Alora's arm but she gave her such a furious look she gaped.

"I will not leave anyone I love behind!" She firmly removed Tiana's hand from her arm and strode over to the rumbling blob over Paris with her hands in tight fists. As the brightest area of her tiara touched it, it lifted off Paris leaving an acrid smell in its wake like heated ammonia. After it rose in the air, Paris then jumped in Alora's arms licking her face all over. Giggling in delight, she carried him out of the cell with Tiana on her heels and the dark thundering blob shot off up the boulevard.

"You did it!" Tiana said with utter astonishment.

Alora nodded firmly. "Yes, I did, and do try not to look so surprised." She turned to Paris as he wiggled around to get down and laughed. "I guess like any scared little boy, you want a hug to make it better then want to be free to run around." She set him down and he ran around her in circles barking happily. A moment later, Alora's eyes lit up. "Come on you two, with Paris funning around just now it just gave me a fantastic idea."

"What?" Rhys asked.

"I'll show you when we get back to Aunt Gertie's cell. Then Paris and I will play a game that's super fun."

"What game?"

"Like I said, I'll show you," she said impishly but then she gasped and raced up the granite street like a wild fire with Paris on her heels. "Run, you guys, run! I just realized as that mad blob left it headed the direction of Aunt Gertie's cell!"

Rhys looked stunned. "Holy smokes, I didn't notice that."

"Me either," Tiana groaned as they dashed after Alora and Paris working hard to stay in the tiara's light.

"I didn't know your sister could run this fast," Rhys gasped.

"That's because she never has," she said panting.

As Alora and Paris got back to Gertie's cell, she stopped so fast she slammed into the iron door's frame. She winced and rubbed her shoulder but as she peered in the cell she grimaced. The dark sludgy blob had indeed returned. "This keeps getting worse," she huffed as Paris barked at it furiously. She searched to find Gertie through the black churning mass in the cell and finally saw him inside it then noticed a black lining under the pile of straw. "Oh my gosh! There's a layer of the dark blob under Gertie holding this up!" she shouted to Tiana and Rhys as they caught up with her. They then looked bewildered as she raced off with Paris to the nook with the empty key hooks. "We need that key!" she yelled and they ran after her again.

"Come here, boy," Alora said to Paris. He trotted up to her and she knelt down on one knee. She feigned taking an object from her pocket and pretended to throw it in the nook under the wooden stool. Paris perked up and squeezed through the bars scampering the direction of her throw then got down low and wiggled under the stool. A moment later, he brought back the key. "Good boy," she said ruffling his head.

Rhys gaped. "How did you get him to do that?"

"It's just a silly game we like to play."

"Oh, you mean like fetch?"

"Not exactly. It's invisible fetch. I throw a pretend item a fake direction and he has to guess what he needs to pick up."

"Okay, that's cool, but again, how did you get him to—"

"It's just good that she did, which she can explain later," Tiana cut in. "Right now, let's go get Aunt Gertie."

Alora nodded and raced to Gertie's cell door then stuck the key in the keyhole. To her relief it turned and unlocked the door. She pushed it open and studied the black blob. "Paris, you sit here and stay," she said and he sat. "Now, as I said before, I've had it with waiting." Alora took a deep breath and marched toward Gertie keeping a close eye on the dark gooey blob.

"Rhys, will you…" Tiana paused thinking of how to ask him the ridiculously selfish request she wanted as a favor.

"Yeah, I'll stand guard at the door with Paris so you and Alora don't get locked in...and pull you out if things go south."

"Thanks!" She dashed over to her sister as she walked up to the stormy blob. As the brightest light of Alora's tiara touched it, the blob shot to the ceiling as did the one under the pile of straw and joined the big one high up on the tall ceiling. Gertie and the straw pile then landed on the floor with a thump. Alora gently took ahold of Gertie's hand as Tiana kept a sharp eye on the enormous black globule over them.

Alora bit her lip and frowned. "His hand is cold as ice."

Tiana began to reach for him but stopped as she gazed up. "Look! That black gooey blob is shaking." A second later it shed what looked like yellow hail then it flew out of the cell.

"Whew! Those things stink," Alora said wrinkling her nose.

"Yeah, it smells like it peed its pants," Rhys said pinching his nose shut as Alora turned back to Gertie and shook him.

"Aunt Gertie, wake up!" Nothing happened so Alora shook him again. "Still nothing, and he's cold as ice," she cried. "Are we too late? Did that awful thing kill him?"

"He's not dead since I see his chest moving up and down," Tiana said. "So, let's do what we learned in first aid for people with hypothermia and rub his limbs to get his circulation moving." The girls then began massaging his arms and legs.

"I wonder if the Red Winkies did this to him or if the that dark angry blob did it," Alora said worriedly.

"I don't know. Either way, we're taking him with us, so let's use the blanket he's on to carry him out of here." Tiana took a hold of both sides of the top and cradled his head and Alora did the same to his feet. With a nod at each other they started lifting him off the straw but quickly set him back down.

"He's a lot heavier than he looks. Rhys!" Tiana called out to him. "We need your help to get Aunt Gertie out of here."

Rhys ran over with Paris and tried lifting Gertie off the straw pile but could not. "Wow! He is heavy. I know, we'll slide him on his blanket down this straw pile to the floor then tie the ends of it around his feet so he doesn't slide out the bottom. That way two of us can pull him along in a sitting position. We can then also rotate positions since this will be really tough to do."

The girls nodded and they all proceeded to do so, but when they got him lying flat on the floor they gasped for he bulged a foot up in the middle. Rhys rolled him onto his side to check it out and chuckled as he laid him back down.

"I see nothing funny about this," Tiana said tartly.

"You will when you see why he's so lumpy."

"Don't keep us in suspense. Just tell us."

"He's got his emergency pack on," he said chuckling again.

"Then stop laughing and get it off him since dragging him like this will likely wreck his back."

"Okay." He turned him on his side and loosened the pack's straps. "Can one of you please hold him after I sit him up so I can pull his pack off?"

"I will," Alora said kneeling down to brace Gertie.

Rhys lifted him into a sitting position and Alora held him there as he slipped his pack off then he rummaged through it. "Whew!" he said waving a hand over his face as he pulled out some used underwear and socks. He threw them at the girls and they squealed, but as they scolded him, he just grinned. Next, he pulled out a rope, four big packages of beef jerky, six chocolate bars, a canteen, a first aid kit, and several waterproof matches.

"He certainly was better prepared than we are," Tiana said.

"No kidding," he said nodding. "I know it adds more weight but we should keep all but his stinky underwear and socks."

"I totally agree about these," Alora said pinching her nose shut and throwing them as far away from them as she could. "And keeping the food, water and matches is a good idea. But that big rope is super heavy, so maybe we could leave it."

"Actually, I think we should keep it," Rhys said.

"Why? We haven't needed a rope."

"True, but with all the weird things that have happened to us today it might come in handy."

"Tiana, what do you think?"

"Since we're not out of here yet, and we don't know what we're going to run into, I think we should take it with us."

"Then I guess I'm outvoted." She gave them a tired smile and her sister gave her a sympathetic look.

Rhys pocketed the matches then put the rope, food, water canteen and first aid kit back in Gertie's pack and set it on top his chest. "Who's taking the first shift with me?"

"I will." Alora then looked at Paris and said, "Heel."

Rhys got out his scout knife and cut off part of the rope then tied Gertie's pack to his chest. "Okay, looks like we're set, so let's move him on out of here." Rhys and Alora lifted him up in a sitting position on the blanket. They worked hard to pull him out of the cell then headed toward the stairs to the game store.

"Stop! You're going the wrong way," Tiana said. "We have to find Aunt Roleena before we leave."

"No, we don't. She's not down in this dungeon." Alora said.

"What makes you say that?" Rhys asked unsure what to do.

"Because if she was here, Paris would not be willing to go head out with us. He would have gone off to track her down."

"He might not know she's here since she was taken first."

Alora shook her head. "That wouldn't matter."

"Why not?"

"Because his sniffer is forty times better than a human's," she said pointing at her nose. "He'd easily have caught her scent if she had come through here and would go find her."

"Actually, she's right," Tiana said. "We watched a dog show about their tracking abilities and they're amazing. Plus, after seeing him get the key, I think he could easily find our aunt."

"Okay, since you seem so sure of it," he said. "Then I have a suggestion. Why don't we check and see if there's a faster way out of here further down this boulevard?"

"No!" Alora said kicking his shin.

"Ouch! Knock it off. I was just asking."

"And I was just answering. We don't know what else we might run into here. So, we're going back the way we came."

He nodded and they began dragging Gertie up the boulevard changing positions each hour after a short break. Four tough hours later, they finally saw the stairs leading up to the Flashy Castle game store. Sweating and feeling exhausted, they rested a few minutes. Then tired as they were, they drug Gertie to the foot of the stairs, all groaning as they looked up at them.

"How will we ever get him up all those stairs?" Alora asked.

"I don't know," Tiana said frowning.

Rhys sighed. "I do. We go up a step at a time, and one of us should hold his feet up to be sure he can't slide out of blanket."

"Then Alora and I will need to take the top end or he'll tip to the side because of your height."

"Good point," he said but no one moved.

"Guys, these are super, super steep," Alora moaned stating what they all were thinking as she rubbed Paris' ears.

"They are, and I forgot how narrow they are," Tiana said. "It also shows me we have to all have the same positions since you and Rhys couldn't fit side-by-side to pull Aunt Gertie up this,".

"You think I'm that fat?" Alora asked looking wounded.

"Good grief. No. The stairs are the problem, not you and I should've said I'm glad you and I are small enough to do this."

"Oh...okay," Alora said mollified. "But are we strong enough to get him up all these stairs?"

"We have to be. Or do you want to try Rhys's idea and go back through the dungeon to find an easier way out of here?"

"No, I'm just worried we won't be able to do this."

"I get it, and I admit I'm also bothered by how steep this is and how far we'll have to carry Aunt Gertie. It could take days and I'm worried someone might faint or even die of thirst or extreme exhaustion."

"Well, if someone does, we'll have extra food and a liquid available to us," Rhys said dryly.

"I can see being able to divvy up more food but why would that give us more water?" Alora asked looking puzzled

"Not water, another liquid," Tiana groaned as she rolled her eyes at Rhys. "Think about vampires and you'll get it."

"Ew! That's super, super gross."

"It is, but you're the one who just had to ask for an answer to his disgusting comment," Tiana said shaking her head.

Alora grimaced. "I guess I did."

"Well, let's go." She grabbed her side of the blanket to lift Gertie but as Alora lifted hers, she pulled him up higher than Tiana could raise him. He tipped off the other side and his head hit the wall as his body collapsed across the stairs.

"Alora, you're a walking accident," Rhys groaned.

"Me? If you had held his feet up properly, he wouldn't have fallen out!"

"No way. I saw what happened. Tiana lifted her side as you did but you lifted your side of the blanket up so high it tossed him off and he crashed into the wall. I'm just glad we had just taken our first step and he didn't have far to go."

"Sorry. You're right," she said tearily as Tiana checked Gertie out. "It was tough lifting him, so I did pull up hard."

"He got a little lump on his head but otherwise he looks okay," Tiana said with relief. "Though I did pray it might jar him awake. It didn't, so let's get him back on the blanket."

Rhys and Alora nodded and they all gently set him back on the blanket. They began to lift him up when they heard a chilling howl from way down in the dungeon and froze.

"That was 'not' a dog," Tiana said tersely.

"Let's get moving before it gets any closer," Rhys said staring into the dark dungeon, but then they heard a groan and looked down to find Gertie blinking his eyes.

"Aunt Gertie!" the girls shouted happily.

"What in tarnation is…" he began but the light of Alora's tiara hit him and he quickly became mesmerized.

"Rhys! Quick. He needs a pair of your special dark glasses!" Tiana said getting his gift box out of her pack.

He got out his shrunken strongbox and retrieved a pair of the glasses that blocked the gift's effects. It was too small to use, so Alora got her vial of enlarging dust out and put a couple grains on it to return it to its normal size. He then put the glasses on

Gertie and a moment later he looked bewildered, but no longer bedazzled and the three cousins cheered loudly.

"Ouch," he groaned. "Ye best talk soft or yer gonna make my head explode faster than a short-fused stick of dynamite."

"Sorry," Alora whispered as Paris sat on him licking his face. "We were worried since you fell off the blanket we were carrying you on and hit your head on the wall."

"Thanks fer comforting me, little fella," Gertie said to the dog then he looked at the kids. "How come yer carrying me?"

"Because when we rescued you from the dungeon cell you were in, you couldn't talk least of all walk, and we wanted to get you out of that cell as fast as we could."

"Rescued, ye say? From them Red Winkies?"

"No, from a wicked flying dark blob that imprisoned you."

"Well, howdy, since I don't see one now, ye succeeded. But then why'd ye yell so loud at me 'cuz that really hurt my head."

"Actually, your head hurts because I accidently dropped you on it," Alora said sheepishly.

"Then why were ye yelling at me?"

"Because we were thrilled to see you finally wake up."

"So, why'd ye drop me, little lady?" he asked Alora.

"I just slipped up and I'm truly sorry about that."

"Or are ye tryin' to bump me off so ye can lay claim to my gold mine?" he asked narrowing his eyes as he looked at her.

"Of course not!" Alora said.

"You can't steal what he doesn't have," Tiana told her sister seeing she had not yet realized he was teasing her.

"Ye got me there." Gertie chuckled then winced in pain and stopped. "I bet ye hoped it'd knock my senses back into me."

"Yes and no," Rhys said when no one else replied.

"That's a dumb as a stump answer. Which is it, yes or no?"

"Yes, we wanted to wake you up. But no, not that way. So, since we couldn't wake you up, we had to get you out of this dungeon the hard way. We also had to find the key to get you out of the cell you were in and away from a mad thundering blob that had caged you and Paris up. Then with you out cold, we had to pull you all the way back to the stairs leading up to a game store called 'The Flashy Castle'. Before that we had to fight off big clouds of Red Winkies up there to not get taken over by them. Then earlier we couldn't find you until we found the tracking units you left us in the graveyard Sir Hephaestus made for you. We used them to find the Red Winkie's hideout, but that took time since we had to dodge a Winkie controlled PCF Officer and—"

"Whoee, young buck," Gertie cut in, "That there story yer rattlin' on about took oodles of energy to spit out and now yer starting to look a bit peaked. So, with all ye done and all ye jest put out, rest yer lungs a spell and let the girls talk a bit."

"That almost sums it up other than we also had a tough time tracking the Winkies from Everett to Marysville," Tiana said. "And a near heart attack making adventure before that when they turned the park we were in into a crocodile filled swamp."

"Sounds like ye had a devil of a time and what ye went through's worse than when I got chased by jackals during a bad sandstorm in the Sahara Desert. So, I owe ye a heap of thanks."

"Can you move at all yet?" she asked worriedly.

"Dunno, I was listening to you so to reckon how I wound up here in the first place and haven't tested these ole body parts of mine as yet. Here I go. Nope. Dag blast it! 'Cept fer my head, I'm limp as a beached jellyfish. Can't even raise a finger or wiggle a toe. But my mind's finally firing up 'cuz I recollect now I gave them Winkies a fitful time as they zapped me as I stopped fer a redlight near Roleena's home. Truth is, I don't recall nothin' after that so they must've knocked me out. I also don't see how they got me through that game store ye spoke of, or got me packed down here and shut up in a cell."

"They knocked you out?" Rhys asked with alarm. "I thought they didn't do things like that would hurt us."

"News to me too and it is a bit aggressive fer them. Truth is, it didn't hurt me none 'cuz I can't recall feeling no pain at all."

"I'm glad of that," Alora said.

"Me too, but right now, we need to figure out how we can get you up those stairs," Rhys sighed but then his eyes lit up. "Hey Alora, I wish I'd thought of this sooner, but can you use your fairy dust on Gertie to lift him up the stairs?"

"Why, yes, I can and I wish I'd remembered that before we tugged him a couple miles back over here," she grumbled.

"We all could have but we were incredibly tired and stressed out," Tiana said with a shrug. "But now it's a good thing you and Rhys voted for us to keep Aunt Gertie's rope since we'll need it to keep him from floating away."

"Dern tootin' it is. A rope's essential," Gertie said. "Ye never know if you'll need to get out of troublesome places, like now."

Rhys opened Gertie's pack and pulled out the rope then got out his scout knife. He cut long piece off of it and tied it around Gertie's torso then around his waist. "Okay, we're set."

Alora got the magic flying dust out of her box and giggled as Rhys backed away from her. "Don't worry. I won't throw any at you or use as much as I did on you."

"Good. I don't want him rising to the top of this cavernous ceiling and then having to find a way to bring him back down."

"Nah, I know my sweet niece here wouldn't let that happen to this crusty old feller," Gertie said.

"That's right," Alora said as she looked at him adoringly.

"Your sweet niece is the one who dumped you on your head," Rhys said with a mishievous grin.

"I didn't dump him on purpose. It was an accident!"

"Of course, it was," Gertie said gently. "So, don't worry that pretty lil' head of yours about it."

"Thanks, Aunt Gertie, and don't worry. I'll only use a speck at a time and stop when you're floating a foot off of the floor."

"I'd like ye to raise me higher than that, so no one accidently kicks me in the head. That would ease my mind a lot 'cuz my head's still a mite sore after saying howdy to that wall."

"I'm still sorry super about that," she said wincing. "And I'll raise you up until you tell me you feel high enough to be safe."

"Okay missy, then let's get to it."

Alora turned to Paris. "Go to Tiana." After the pup got off of Gertie and trotted over to her sister, she opened the vial and put a pinch of flying dust in her hand. She sprinkled it a tiny bit at a time until Gertie told her 'Stop' when he was floating three feet off the ground. "Does this feel like it's a safe height to you?"

"Yep, ye done good girl," he said cheerily.

"Then shall we get going?" she asked smiling when an eerie howl came down the dungeon's street sounding closer this time.

"Yes!" Tiana said sharply "And none too soon for me."

"Me too!" Rhys said and he quickly pulled Gertie up a few steps. "Hey, he's floating as light as a balloon, so I won't need help from either of you to take him up the stairs."

"You sure?" Tiana asked. "Because my sore feet recall that it was a long, long, long way getting down here."

"Yeah, this will be no problem at all."

"Lead on then," she said. She and Alora then followed Rhys and Gertie up the stairs, but as they came to the first switchback fifty feet up, Rhys took the corner so fast Gertie floated several yards out over the deep abys below.

"Whoee, young un," Gertie hollered. "Don't fly me like I'm a kite. Keep it firmly in yer head, I'm a land lover at heart."

"Sorry," Rhys said contritely. He pulled him in and quickly shortened the rope to keep them closer together.

"You should be!" Alora said severely. "None of us knows how long the magic in the flying dust lasts. So, if he comes down, we want him to be on the stairs and not in a dive that could crash land him on the bottom below."

"I know that now, and I'll go around those switchbacks a lot slower now."

"Good, but I think I should tie Aunt Gertie's feet to my waist so he can't swing out like that."

"Trust me. You don't need to since I cinched him close up now. It was just that it had more slack in it than I realized."

"Trust you?" Tiana asked dryly. "I'm not sure how much to trust you yet with all you've done in the past. You see, our dad taught us that trust must be earned."

"Come on, you know I've changed. I worked hard to nicer and fairer with you during this weird rescue of ours."

"At the beginning you weren't."

"True," he said sadly. "Not at first. But I had a change of heart when you were finally nice to me. Now, I've tried really hard to show you I 'can' be a good guy."

"He has been super helpful and reliable…even pretty nice," Alora said. "He's also been super fair to us."

"Only for two days."

"Tiana, other than joking around, he's worked hard to not be, well, not be…" she paused looking for the right word to use.

"Onery and rebellious?" Gertie said with a quirky grin.

"That's it, and he hasn't been that at all," she said grinning.

"Then I say ye should give the lad a chance to prove his worth to ye."

"I'm okay to do that if you are, Aunt Gertie. So, are you willing to risk your life on him helping you?" Alora asked biting on her lip as she saw Tiana was still frowning at him.

"Yep. I know his hides worth more than ye figure it is. Besides that, yer forgetting somethin' grave here."

"What's that?" Tiana asked.

"The fact is, if I go plummeting down there, he'll get dragged down with me. So, this will be risky fer him too."

Rhys' eyes widened hearing Gertie's comment but then he began laughing. "You're right, Gertie. That 'is' a rather good incentive to keep you safe here with me."

"Darn tootin'," he said, "So girls, what ye say that we let him lead on and get out of this dismal abyss of misery?"

"I'm totally with you on that," Tiana said and Alora nodded.

Rhys led the climb at a slower pace using each switchback to take a short break. After a long, arduous climb past six more switchbacks, they finally reached the landing leading into the Flashy Castle's game store.

"Do you think the Red Winkies are still waiting for us?" Alora whispered as they all came to a stop.

"Probably," Tiana said grimacing.

"Ye can bet yer best boots they are," Gertie said.

"How about we all take a break before we confront them?" Rhys asked looking around at the others.

"I figure if yer not too tuckered out, we should blaze on through and get this part over with."

"Aunt Gertie," Alora said shyly, "If you don't mind, I'd first like to eat a bit of chocolate and drink some water."

Tiana's stomach growled in response and she patted it. "Traitor," she said laughing. "I guess I need to eat something too. But I'd rather have some jerky and so would Paris."

"Me too," Rhys said.

"Ookeydokey, Rest stop it is then," Gertie said agreeably.

The three cousins slumped off their packs with relieved sighs and Rhys opened Gertie's pack pulling out the food and water.

"Hey there, young'uns, since yer stoppin' to chow down, I'd like some vittles too. My stomach's rippin' me a good one since I ain't ate since yesterday. Fact is, I could eat a mule about now. Heh, heh, but not my mule, Betsy. She's as good to me as gold. So, just give me a chunk of that jerky and chocolate bar."

Alora grinned. "Right now, those sound heavenly, right?"

"Absolutely," Rhys said enthusiastically.

"Well, siree," Gertie said. "There's a bit of a catch to this fer me. As ye tear into all this can ye help an old geezer out."

"Sure, we will," Alora said. "What do you need?"

"It be mortifying, but I need one of you to play mama bird and drop food and water in my mouth since my arms are as useless as an unstrung puppet."

"I'd be delighted to help you, Aunt Gertie." She got some beef jerky and chocolate from Rhys and then periodically gave him pieces of each and sips of water.

**

Thirty minutes later the trio stashed the remaining food and water in Gertie's pack and prepared to leave. As they put on their packs they groaned and were dragging their feet as they walked to the door leading into the back room of the Flashy Castle. Gertie looked sympathetic but Paris just dog grinned.

Rhys got to the door first and looked at the girls. "Ready?" he asked and got no reply. They just stared at the door as if it was the gateway into the devil's den itself.

"Well, don't stand there like a bump on a log, get on in there. It ain't gonna get easier by frettin' about it," Gertie said seeing how much they were all dreading going through the door.

"True," Tiana said. "Okay, Alora. You have to go first since you're wearing the tiara that immobilizes the Red Winkies."

"Then it looks like it's yer turn to wrestle the wild bull."

"I know," Alora whispered, "but my feet won't move."

"Ye did this before didn't ye?"

"Well…yeah, I did."

"Then ye know ye can, so do it again," Gertie said firmly.

"But even knowing that doesn't make me any less antsy."

"And nothin' will, so git yer big girl britches on and do it."

"Okay. Okay."

"Rhys, I ain't able to move yet, so be a proper gentleman and open the door fer yer cousin."

"On it." He bent down and got his sweatshirt from under the door then grabbed ahold of the door knob.

"Remember, we all need to stay near her," Tiana said.

"What fer?" Gertie asked as Alora came and stood by Rhys at the door.

"Because we have to stay under the protective halo of her tiara's light. It does reach about thirty feet out but it gets weaker the farther you get from it so we like to stick close to her."

"Good thing to keep firmly in mind," he said.

With a nod from Alora, Rhys opened the door and stood together like pickles in a jar in the game rooms doorway. Within seconds a cloud of Red Winkies zoomed towards them like a bomber to a target. Paris barked, Tiana gasped, Rhys groaned, and Alora screamed and covered her eyes.

"You can uncover your eyes now," Tiana said a few seconds later. "The Red Winkies anywhere near us have been stunned by your tiara's light and are just floating under the ceiling."

Alora peeked through her fingers. "But there's a big cloud of them on the far side of the room buzzing like mad bees."

"Just remember what happened to the evil dark cloud," Rhys said. "It tried to resist the light, but when you got close to it, it didn't matter. The light of your tiara forced it back."

"But will that still work? Because it looks to me like there's millions more of them here now than there were before. This makes me afraid that they're going to zap all of us."

"I know that ye can be brave when ye must, my sweet lass," Gertie said seeing her freeze up. "And this be one of them times ye got to take a big sip of courage and push on."

"But I'm so scared I can't get my feet to move."

"Then let's do it together," Rhys said softly, surprising her by taking ahold of her hand and guiding her into the room.

To her relief, the tiara's light kept the Red Winkies at bay as they walked across the room but when they got to the archway, Alora stopped again. "Auntie Roleena! We still must find her!"

"True, but she wasn't in these rooms," Rhys said.

"Are you sure?"

"Yes, as scary as it was being chased by the Red Winkies, we searched these rooms thoroughly for her. You even had us move an oddly tall game table on one wall to look behind it. Which thanks to you is why we found the door to that dungeon and rescued Gertie and Paris. But we also know due to Paris coming along with us Aunt Roleena wasn't down there either."

Gertie chuckled "Ye know from an outsider point of view yer yarn spins out like a comical dark monster movie."

"But ours wasn't funny at all!" Tiana huffed.

"Only in the tellin', my feisty young filly. Yer gonna see as ye spin it out later when yer all safe and sound, it's a mighty comical story," he said with a quirky grin.

"I guess given enough time, we might," Rhys said nodding.

"I'm still want to check these rooms again and I won't leave until we do," Alora said so adamantly they knew she meant it.

"For you, of course we will," Tiana said surprising her.

"Then git to yer redo, if ye feel ye must," Gertie said.

"I will!" Alora stomped into the back room but she was pale and shaky. Rhys followed pulling Gertie with him as Tiana and Paris took up the rear. They rechecked every nook and cranny looking for another hidden door Roleena might be stashed in but did not find her. They were well aware the Red Winkies were following them but also saw they were being forced to stay at the outer edge of the tiara's light.

"Could it be any more menacing than this?" Rhys asked.

"It would if that thundering dark blob joined them," Tiana said as she scowled at the Red Winkies.

"This is creepy enough without you two reminding me of that awful gungy blob," Alora said crossly.

"I was just making a point."

"Alora's right. Best be careful about filling yer head with scary thoughts," Gertie said somberly. "Cuz' thinkin' it might attract it your way like carcasses attract vultures."

"Aunt Gertie," Tiana groaned. "What a gross thing to say."

"Yep, but it's best I warn ye to not draw trouble yer way."

They said no more as they finished up the room then went on to inspect the other game room. As carefully as they searched, they still could not find Roleena. They all sadly went on to the front lobby and stood glumly by the checkout register.

"Not a thing," Tiana groaned.

"We did check these rooms thoroughly, so did you really think she would suddenly show up in them?" Rhys asked.

Tiana just shrugged.

"Well, I did," Alora blurted out. "Auntie Roleena's here somewhere. I know she is." Paris then barked as if agreeing.

"I don't know why you even think that," Rhys said bluntly.

"Well, it's a strong feeling I have and…" she paused and her eyes brightened. "How silly of me not to think of this until now. Paris can sniff her out! Paris! Paris, come here boy."

They heard his sharp bark, but no matter how loudly they called him he did not come to them and just kept barking.

"His bark's coming from somewhere in this room," Alora said. "So, I'm going to go find him and see why he's barking."

"Since your tiara is protecting this entire room, we'll stay in here with you," Rhys said. "And since it's a fairly small room and I have Gertie, we'll just hang out by the archway leading to the back rooms and keep an eye on the Winkies for any trouble. Then you two can focus on seeing what's up with the dog."

"Thanks," Tiana said. They followed his barks and quickly found him wedged behind the fortune teller's booth.

"So, hiding behind the booth's why we couldn't see you," Alora said reaching behind it to get him but he backed away from her and kept barking.

"Paris, it's just a dummy," Tiana said with a groan.

"And it's just as creepy as the rest of this place," Alora said.

"True, and the mannikin isn't nearly as lifelike as the ones at Madame Tussaud's Wax Museum. It's just a cheap Halloween mask of a gypsy face put over a dummy and topped by a wig with long wavy red hair with makeup that's way overdone."

"But she's got lots of great looking gypsy clothes on," Alora said, "And the crystal ball she's holding is super cool."

Tiana nodded. "I do like all the layers of colorful silk shawls around her shoulders and tied around her long skirt with swirly patterns or peacock eyes on them. And the bright yellow scarf on her head in red paisley print is wild. Still, I think she's gaudy and the mascara on her lashes looks like they used tarantula legs to make them," she said scrunching her face up in distaste.

"I bet it's to impress their customers since most portrayals of gypsy women are showy and eccentric like this one is."

"Her costume reminds me of the gypsy woman in that old were-wolf movie we watched," Alora said. "Though that was in black and white so I don't know if it was this colorful."

"I bet Gertie's an expert on any old black and whites," Rhys said grinning. "He likely saw them when they first came out."

"Dern tootin' I did, but don't get cheeky about it. Fer they weren't like yer newfangled movies nowadays. That's when the actors captured the audience by grand acting not just by using explosions, flashin' skin, and heaps of violence."

"Aunt Gertie, not all our movies use that," Alora groaned. "Besides, dad said what's good is a matter of opinion. I like our modern ones, not those silent films or talkies in the 1920's."

"Heh, heh," he said chuckling, "I do like those. Still, my favorites weren't that early. I best like the movies betwixt the 1930's to 1950's. But ye weren't even on the planet then."

"Not even close, and those movies are super ancient to us."

"True, but keep in mind, ye might jest live to be old and crusty as me and have young'un's say the same about you."

"You're not crusty, you're wonderful," Alora said warmly.

"Good knowin' I have a fan," he said smiling fondly at her.

"I'm a fan too," Rhys said surprising them all.

"Well, howdy, ne'er thought I'd live to hear that," Gertie said chuckling as Rhys blushed. "T'was good to know. Real good. So, thank ye young fella."

"Moving on from the Elder's History Channel," Tiana said to get the spotlight off of Rhys seeing how embarrassed he looked, "We need to go search elsewhere for Aunt Roleena."

"I still think she's here," Alora said with a stubborn pout. "And I can't go until I get Paris from behind the gypsy booth."

"Then go on and get him out of there," Rhys said gently seeing her pained face. "Because we really do need to go look for our aunt in some other places now."

"What do you think Aunt Gertie?"

"Well, siree, that gypsy doesn't look a bit like Roleena, but with my mind still fuzzy, I reckon you three should vote on it."

"Then I vote we go look at another game store," Tiana said.

"Me too," Rhys said looking apologetically at Alora.

"Looks like this time I'm out voted," she mumbled sadly.

"If it doesn't pan out you can always back." Gertie said.

"Okay, but I don't like having to do this."

"I know," Tiana said. "But let's at least try another place." She then went to the door and opened it. "Wow, you guys, it's getting light outside."

"We have been down in the dungeon a while," Rhys said.

"A long while I guess, which means we've gone into another day. No wonder I'm so tired."

"Yeah, it can't be due to running, dodging, and hiding from the Red Winkies 'and' that weird, globby dark menace."

"Good point. Maybe we should find somewhere to rest a bit," Tiana said holding the door open wide for Rhys so he could pull Gertie through too.

Alora gave a last look around the room then shuffled to the door. She held it open and called for Paris but he stayed behind the Gypsy's booth barking. "Paris, come," she commanded.

Paris kept barking and stayed where he was.

"Hey buddy, I don't want to go either. But I was outvoted. So, we have to go look for Auntie Roleena somewhere else." To her surprise Paris shot out from behind the booth and began to run around it fast. "Tiana! Come here and help!" she shouted.

Tiana rushed back inside. "What happened? Are you okay?"

"Yes, but now Paris is running in circles around the gypsy booth like crazy which is making it hard to snag him."

"Want me to come catch him for you?" Tiana asked.

"No, I will." Alora tried grabbing the dog as he rushed by her but missed him. She then caught him as he ran past her the third time and he cried sharply like he was in pain. "Paris! Did I hurt you?" She loosened her hold and he wriggled out of her arms and dropped to the floor. As he hit the ground, he clawed madly on the gypsy's booth.

"What's wrong?" Tiana asked as she and Rhys stood holding the door open as they waited for her.

"It's Paris. Now he's clawing madly on the gypsy booth."

"I'll get him." Tiana came to the booth and tried to pick him up but he snapped at her and ran to the other side. She followed him but he kept out of her reach. "Head him off, Alora."

After a few rounds, Alora managed to catch him but again he keened in pain and wormed his way out of her arms. "Help me," she said getting down on her knees with her arms spread out. Tiana did the same and they sandwiched him between their two kneeling bodies as he went by again.

"Got him," Tiana said grabbing his ruff and he squealed.

"Stop hurting him!" Alora said crossly.

"I don't want to but I have to keep him from slipping away."

"Then let me leash him up then you can set him down and I'll just pull him along," she said and Tiana nodded.

Tiana held him tight as Alora got his leash out of her jean's pocket but as she began to hook him up Tiana loosened her grip. Paris then popped up over their heads like a greased pig. His sharp dog nails hooked onto the top edging of the gypsy booth and he scrambled up on top of it. The girls groaned as they found the booth was so tall, they could not reach him. They tried jumping high as they could to grab him but he evaded them like a boxer in a fight ring dodging an opponent.

"Get on my back and grab him," Alora said.

"Okay." Alora got on her hands and knees and Tiana stepped onto her back. As she reached out to nab Paris, he backed into the far corner so she lunged over the booth to grab him but hit the top of it hard. It began tilting over and her foot got caught in Alora's hoodie dragging them both with it and they wound up falling on top of its side. It landed with a resounding boom and sent Paris skidding across the floor. The top of the booth then fell off and Paris dashed over and sniffed inside it.

The girls looked at each other in awe, relieved no one was hurt. They got to their feet relieved to see the booth had not shattered, but as they checked it out, they realized why. The walls of the booth were made of a plexiglass. They saw Paris peering inside the booth that now lay open on the floor. With a sly nod at each other, the girls sneakily went on either side of him to catch him. Paris spied their tricky move and dove into the booth. Rhys then walked over pulling Gertie with him and saw the girls reaching into the gypsy booth over and over.

"What in tarnation is goin' on you two?" Gertie sputtered.

"We're trying to get Paris out of this booth, but he doesn't want to be caught," Tiana spat out as they tried to get him out of the jumbled-up piles of clothing the gypsy was dressed in.

"This should be as easy as shootin' fish in a barrel."

"Do be my guest and show us how it's done."

"Can't hardly fish him out with my teeth," he told them.

To the girl's astonishment, Paris began jerking the scarves off the gypsy. They tried to snag him again, but he dove among the multitude of huge scarves and billowing skirt to evade them.

"Why not just pull the gypsy out of there?" Rhys asked casually as he tried to bite back a grin and failed.

"As I told Aunt Gertie," Tiana said tersely swiping back the sweaty hair that had fallen across her face. "Be my guest."

"Okay. Then if you two will get out of the way, and then tie Gertie to you, I'll be happy to go do it."

Alora and Tiana backed out of the booth and stood up looking as rumpled as the manikin and glared at Rhys with exasperation. Tiana huffed and went over and undid the rope tying Gertie to Rhys and tied it around her waist.

"Well, go ahead," she said waving her arm at the booth.

With just a nod, Rhys walked over and grabbed ahold of the gypsy manikin under its arms and pulled it out of the booth. The thick plastic face mask came part way off and Alora squealed. Then to their surprise, she threw her arms around the manikin as Paris came and nuzzled the gypsy.

"Have you and Paris gone wacko?" he asked.

Tiana looked at Gertie who looked as stunned as she felt to see them behave so oddly. "Alora, what's going on?"

Alora looked up as if just remembering they were there, her face covered in tears. "It's...it's Auntie Roleena."

Tiana dashed over pulling Gertie with her as Alora pulled the mask all the way off and saw it was indeed Roleena. "She's as pale as a ghost," she gasped turning pale herself. "Is she dead?"

"Speak up girl! Is she breathin'?" Gertie asked Alora sharply when she did not answer.

"Yes! I can see her chest rise and fall," she said and leaned down close to her face. "I can also feel her breath on my cheek. But she must be knocked out like you were, Aunt Gertie, since she's not coming around at all as I pat them."

"Well, I'll be hog-tied and gagged," Gertie sputtered. "Even in a glass booth under a heap of cloths that little critter of hers knew she was in there and tried to wake us up to this fact."

Alora looked at Paris as he came over to her and ruffled his fur. "Yes, he did know. He's so, so wonderfully amazing," she said giggling as Paris wagged his tail happily as if agreeing.

"Well, howdy! Thanks, little fella fer finding Roleena fer us," he said beaming at Paris who went and sat on Roleena's chest as if also aware he was her champion.

"So, how do we wake her up?"

"Let's put on our thinkin' hats on first and figure out how to do it more gentle-like than I had done to me, cuz' I don't want ye crackin' her on the head."

"Aunt Gertie, you sliding of that blanket truly was just a very unfortunate accident!" Tiana said in defense of her sister who looked at her gratefully.

"I know, I know, but we sure as shootin' don't want to repeat that. Ye also got to figure if ye can't wake her up, you'll need to find a way to lug her around like yer doing with me."

"Actually," Rhys said pointedly, "With her crashing down in that booth like she did it would've woken her up if she was just dazed like you. So, Alora will need to use her flying fairy dust to lift her up like she did for you. Then we'll pull her along with us after tying her to one of us to keep her from drifting away."

"Then it's good that the booth's walls are a thick plexiglass because we can use one to lay her body on," Tiana said.

"That's a grand plan 'cept fer one more thing," Gertie said.

"What's that?"

"Well, I reckon it'll draw some mighty unwanted attention to be pulling two floating bodies down these here city streets."

"And wait until dark to do it then sneak down the back alleys to make our way over to your house secretly."

"No!" Rhys shouted but as they all looked at him, they saw he was not looking their way at all.

"Come on, with a little luck, it might work," Alora said.

"So not why I said that. Look!" He pointed at the edge of the window where the artwork on the blackened window did not cover it completely and a tiny sliver around it was clear.

Alora ran over to him and looked out through the thin space and groaned. "We're not having much luck here at all."

"So, what's got you two in such a lather?" Gertie asked.

"It's because there's a bunch of trouble heading this way."

"Trouble with a capital 'T'," Rhys said as Tiana pulled Gertie over to where he could peek out the pencil thin space around the edge of the window.

"Dag blast it, if that don't beat all. The Mounties are coming with their posse in tow," Gertie sputtered.

"Mounties?" Alora asked looking confused.

"Yep, or whatever ye want to call these here lawmen."

"It gets worse. We know the two in that police car because we've had a run-in with them before. In fact, we're fugitives and for no other reason than not having red on our shoes," Tiana said tersely and Alora and Rhys both nodded sharply.

"Doesn't that jest beat all for being plain dumb as a stump."

"It certainly does."

CHAPTER ELEVEN
THE POLITICALLY CORRECT FORCE

"Tarnation! Having these here Mounties show up puts us all in a sticky wicket," Gertie huffed. "And as much as I want to help you, I'm as limp as a wet noodle."

"They're called Mounties in Canada, Aunt Gertie," Tiana said frankly. "They're just called policemen or officers here."

"Same hill of beans, cuz lawmen are lawmen whatever ye call them. They're good fer catching bad guys 'cept fer times like now when they're misguided and on the wrong trail."

"Either way they're driving the direction of this game store, and though I hope they'll pass us by, I doubt they will. But I might be wrong since they're driving at a snail's pace. Maybe they're just looking for us and don't know where we are."

"Is that why you think they're driving super slow?" Alora asked as she sprinkled a pinch of flying dust on Roleena.

"No. Look down the street and you'll see why," Rhys said.

"It's a waste of time being I'm nearsighted," she told him keeping an eye on Roleena as she sprinkled flying dust on her until she rose three feet in the air. "By the way, I put the mask back on Auntie Roleena so she will still look like a mannikin, and I'm draping the gypsy scarves across her so they hang down to the floor to hide the fact she's floating. There, I'm all done."

"Good thinkin', little darlin'," Gertie said.

"Thanks," she said smiling.

"Since you're done will you come take a look?" Rhys asked.

"Okay, but I doubt I can see what you want me to see."

"Trust me, even you will be able to see this."

Alora got a cloth belt off her aunt's skirt. She tied it to one of Roleena's belt loops then to her own belt loop and pulled her over to the window. "I do see lots of people by the car out there, but they're just standing around it in the middle of the street all wearing some super freaky fire-red outfits."

"That's because the officer has stopped his car a block away and rolled down his window. Now, it looks like he's talking to the crowd since they're all nodding."

"What a bunch of ninnies," Gertie said with disgust.

"Ninnies?"

"Short fer 'nincompoop' which is a word Job used in the Old Testament fer foolish people."

"That silly word does fit their outrageously red clothes and shoes as well as their hotheaded shouts," Rhys said nodding.

"If the officer's here for us, why aren't they coming over to bang on the door like the ones in Everett did?" Alora asked.

"Well doggies, maybe this one heard ye slipped the others twice which be awful embarrassing," Gertie said. "So, this one gathered up a big rowdy red posse to help find ye and is likely telling them how to keep ye from sneaking off again."

Rhys huffed loudly as his hands clenched into fists. "Good grief, this is eerie. They look like a lynch mob being escorted by a mad sheriff, and their loud hollering sounds like thunder."

"But how did these local police know to come look for us?" Alora asked wide-eyed. "Did we trip an alarm when we tipped over the booth Auntie Roleena was in which drew them here?"

Tiana shook her head. "No, that's an Everett police car, not a Marysville one. I bet someone saw us go in the Flashy Castle game store last night but didn't report it until this morning. So, I bet this is 'our' Red Winkie driven officer who found out about it and asked the Marysville police to let him handle this even though it's not in Everett."

"I also bet it took him a lot of hard work to round up all these 'Winkied' Politically Correct Force people," Rhys said.

"Winkied?" she asked with a quirky grin.

"To be fair to the people the Winkies glommed onto, that's what I call the people like these officers and the crowd who probably don't even know what's got ahold of them."

"Actually, it 'is' a fair-minded way to describe them," Tiana said looking impressed and Alora nodded.

"Ye know these lawmen?" Gertie asked looking surprised.

"Sadly, we do," Rhys said. "That big, beefy guy behind the wheel is Officer Schmartzov. The woman next to him is Officer Dwendoleen. What's odd is I can see that he's not wearing any red clothes like the crowd is wearing."

Tiana studied him. "Ah, but if you look closer a red stripe's running down his uniform sleeves and pants. Another's around his hat band. Yikes! Look what else they're wearing."

"Sunglasses!"

"Do you think the Red Winkies gave them these to keep my tiara's light from bedazzling them?" Alora asked nervously.

Tiana shook her head. "No, Winkies can't see and since the glasses don't emit heat, I doubt they know about them at all."

Rhys nodded. "I bet the officers saw we wore sunglasses and got to thinking they should too. And since they haven't seen your tiara at work, they don't know theirs won't protect them."

"Are you sure?" Alora asked biting on her lip.

"Pretty much." *And I'd better be right*, he thought.

"As fer me, I'm a might fretful about the sounds comin' from all them folks stompin' around over there," Gertie said. "It sounds to me like they're angling fer a fight."

"What's more chilling to me is after the news catches on to this there will be a lot more Winkied people coming to—"

"Seriously? It's so not the time to be adding that to our stress list," Tiana cut in. "It's time to move into action, not freeze in fear. I'll lock the door and put up the closed sign. Rhys, you tie up to both our aunts and take them as far away from the window as you can. Alora, turn off the lights. Then we'll all lay low and hope they go away and don't break down the door to arrest us."

"Tiana, turning off the lights won't help since I have to wear my tiara to keep the Red Winkies at bay."

"Silly me, I didn't think that through. Thanks for reminding me. Then we'll just scrunch down low behind the counter."

"Okay, Captain Bossy," Alora said saluting then she grinned.

Tiana grinned back then crept over to the door and opened it an inch slipping a closed sign on the front of it. She locked it as Rhys pulled Gertie and Roleena to the back of the lobby behind the freestanding shelves to keep out of sight. Tiana then went and sat on the floor with Alora behind the lobby counter.

"Tiana, what about my tiara's light? It's going to draw the officers and mob's attention," Alora asked looking terrified.

"You're right, so give me a minute to think."

Tiana quickly looked around the lobby's shelves and grinned. She dashed over to a shelf and picked up three various laser light shows that were for sale. She plugged them in and faced two at the window and one at the door then lie on the floor.

"Ta da! That'll either confuse them or blind them."

"Thanks," Alora called to her. "That was a great idea."

"Then let's pray with the door locked and the closed sign on it, no one will break in here to get us," Tiana said uneasily.

"I doubt anyone will do that with officers present since they know it's against the law to do that," Rhys said.

"And with these here windows painted dark as night, and those flashy lights pointed at them, it'll be dern hard to see anything in here," Gertie said. "That oughta buy us some time to figure how to slip out of here without getting nabbed."

"Only if no one gets worked up enough to break a window."

"Don't appear they're to that kind'a boiling' point yet."

"I hope you're right," Alora said biting on her lip again.

"I am, missy, but then yer over there protecting us all alone which is mighty noble of ye and real brave too."

"Thanks, but it is super scary sitting here alone."

Tiana groaned and quickly crawled over to her sister. "Sorry I forgot to come back, but I'm here now so you're not alone."

"Good," Gertie said then he looked at Rhys. "What I can't figure out is why they're so fired up over three young'uns that's done them no harm at all."

"The truth is so crazy it's hard to put into words," Rhys said. "You see, it's…well, it's…well, it's just too weird for words."

"It is, but it started when Officer Schmartzov came to Aunt Roleena's to enforce one of the new 'fashion laws'," Tiana said when he said no more. "He threatened to arrest me and Alora for not obeying a new red shoes law."

Gertie laughed so hard he began choking like a cat hacking up a fur ball so Rhys sat him up and patted his back. "That's enough, young feller. I'm fine as frog's fur, 'cept fer being stiff as a body in the morgue's cooler."

Alora gasped. "Aunt Gertie! It's not funny after all we went through, especially in that old cemetery. You know we had to go into an open grave to hide from Officer Schmartzov. And just hours before that he came to Auntie Roleena's lit up by Red Winkies to arrest for us for not having any red on our shoes."

"Sorry to laugh," Gertie said seeing how upset she was, "But that is crazy, even though it was a scary thing to be caught up in. So, that's what's happening to folks as Winkies get hold of them. It chills me like an Arctic night fer it shows they can now hide on red getups, not just red lights. It also shows they can be smart little critters that work all crafty-like to control folks."

"There's more to the story, for after another Winkied officer came, we had to go out the back window to escape from them. So, we ran and hid in Garfield Park, but the Winkies came by soon after and Paris helped us by running out barking to attract them his way. They surrounded him and drove him across the park turning the grassy fields into a crocodile filled swamp. It was hard to evade the crocs, but we did and caught up to the Red Winkies. But they got away with Paris by making him ride with them on the bumper of a bus. We caught the next bus and found them in Lowell Park but they caught another bus, and we had no bus money left to follow them. Rhys told us you left him money for emergencies so we went to your house to get it and found a clue you left us with the cash. Then Officer Schmartzov showed up and we escaped out your basement window. Rhys led us to a friend of yours house a few blocks away. There, a super regal lady came out on her porch saying she was Great Lady Hera. She must've been psychic for she had already called a cab to take us to the local cemetery which was exactly where we needed to go. We then found the units there you left us to track the Red Winkies that was given you by Sir Hephaestus."

"Bless her kindly soul. Great Lady Hera's one of the finest omnipotent beings here, and even being true royalty, she cares unselfishly about all life-forms unlike some other royals."

"Omnipotent beings?" Rhys asked in amazement.

"Yep, she's what ancient Earth people called a 'goddess'."

"Are you pulling my leg?"

"I can't be pulling yer leg when I can't even twitch a muscle. Now keep in mind, she's powerful and could slay us all with the fire in her eyes if she deemed us to be evildoers. So be good."

"Wow! That's mind-blowing," Rhys said wide-eyed.

"Back to my story, that's how we wound up in the Old Town Cemetery," Alora said. "Officer Schmartzov then drove into the cemetery an hour after we got there so we had to run and hide. But we got away from there with Bravery and Justice's help—"

"Holy smokes!" Gertie cut in and his eyes flew open wide. "That news ye just spit out nearly made my head explode. Yer sayin' Lady Artemis's lionesses helped you?"

"They most certainly did."

"Whooee, makes me believe pigs can fly and pots of gold are buried under rainbows."

"Can I tell part of the story now, Alora?" Tiana asked.

"Sure, but do it quick before the officers bang on the door."

"Okay," Tiana said. "After the lionesses sped us away from the cemetery, we used the tracking units you left for us. Using the spectrometer, we found the Red Winkies light emission trail on the XMS unit's interfacing mapping device. It showed their trail ended at the Flashy Castle store in Marysville. We then found you, then Paris, and then he found Aunt Roleena."

"Tiana," Alora sputtered with exasperation. "You skipped the parts about how we had to thwart the Red Winkies."

"Thwart?" she said smirking. "I think more accurate words are how we had to dodge, dive, hide and evade them."

"I think thwart was a perfectly good word to—"

"No need to squabble over the best words to use, cuz both ways clearly said ye ran into a peck of trouble," Gertie said cutting off their dispute. "Lets' figure on a way out of this."

"Any ideas of how to do that?" Rhys asked eagerly.

"Yep. If I wasn't limp as a rag, I'd face this mob all chipper-like and they'd be confused from their nose to their toes. They'd get brain fog just trying to figure out why I was happy to see them. That way they wouldn't shoot me straight off."

"Aunt Gertie, I doubt they'd shoot any of us."

"Yer likely right, but they might toss us all in jail and bein' I just got out of one cell, I don't fancy being locked up in another. So, maybe I can smooth talk em' to keep them from doing that."

"There's no way you can do that once they see you're flat on your back floating on a pile of hay," Tiana said dryly.

"I can fix that." Rhys stretched out the blanket Gertie was lying on until it was down to the floor to cover the empty space.

"That won't work, because those officers will look under it."

"Why would they bother to do that?" Alora asked.

"You've never liked to watch true crime shows, and I have. The police always check under things that are covered up."

"I feel like all you want to be is negative about this."

"It's better to prepare for the worst, than be caught with—"

"Put a sock in yer muzzles, you two," Gertie said. "Instead of butting heads, put yer clever heads together and figure a slick way we can deal with this here situation."

"Yeah," Rhys said. "Like coming up with a good story for being here with two people who look like they're on stretchers."

"I don't know what kind of story would cover this," Alora said glancing at Gertie and Roleena. Then her face brightened as she looked at Tiana. "You made up a good story to tell the cabdriver. Can you do one for this?"

Tiana frowned as she thought it over. "How about we tell them Aunt Gertie's a repairman that came to fix the broken gypsy fortuneteller. Even if we stop the lights from flashing at them, with as little as they can see through a pencil thin clear strip around the window, it should look to be true if we leave the mask on Aunt Roleena then lie her next to the tipped over booth with Aunt Gertie sitting up by it like he's working on it."

"Okeydokey, that's pretty slick," Gertie said, "But if ye talk they'll know yer in here fer sure. Do ye want 'em to know that? Fer they might just arrest ye fer breaking that shoe color law."

"Good point," she said sighing. "So, how else can we get out of this you guys. Think."

As they looked at each other worriedly, there was a loud rap on the door. They all jumped and were alarmed they had not noticed the officers and crowd were now at the game store.

"This is the PCF police. Open the door!" a man said firmly.

"Yikes!" Tiana said. "It looks like we've run out of time."

"I know someone's in there because the lights are on, so come open the door now!" Schmartzov shouted angrily.

"Sounds like yer gonna need me to wing it and get to tellin' a story to keep us all out of the lockup," Gertie said.

"Okay by me if it works," Rhys whispered and the girls nodded in agreement.

"Tell ye what. I'll spin the officer a quick story that'll put him off 'til we can figure a better way out of this."

"What can you say to him to do that?"

"Dunno, but I got me an idea that might work, and I'm good at spinnin' yarns, so leave it to me. Now, I need each of ye to give me a nickel or dime and ask me to watch this place. Then tell me to let no one else in here while the place is closed."

"Why do you want the small change?"

"Because after that, I'll tell them I got paid to guard this here game store. Now, don't bog me down with questions. Just fork it up, fer I got to be talking all confident and sound true blue."

"Okay." Rhys got some change from his upper cargo pant pocket and handed a coin to the girls and kept one for himself.

"Now, hand me yer coin and each whisper to me yer hiring me and not to let anyone in. And no more questions, just do it." All three of the cousins quickly did what he told them to.

"Next, hitch my rope close to this artsy painted door and plug the keyhole so's they can't see through it. Then you all hunker down behind the counter so I can't see ye at all."

Rhys nodded as he tore off another piece of his tee shirt and plugged the hole. "I'm glad it's hard to see anything through these painted over windows."

"Darn tootin' it's a good thing, and I'm—"

"This is PCF Officer Schmartzov," the officer cut in," And I know someone's in there because I heard someone talking. So, let me in or I'll get a warrant for a forcible entry."

"No need to go to a heap of trouble, officer, and yer right, there is someone here. Me. I was contacting my employers to see what they want me to do and they told me. So, now I'm done with talking to them, I can talk to you. I'm Mr. Ruff, the guard here today," Gertie said in a tough no-nonsense way. "Now sir, what brings ye here?"

"Let me in, Mr. Ruff, and I'll explain," Schmartzov said.

"I can't rightly do that, Officer Schmartzov."

"That's absurd. Of course, you can."

"No siree, I can't. My employers gave me strict orders that I was not to let anyone in. You see, these owners are on a sorely needed vacation. Besides that, ye ain't said one word about why ye want to get in here so bad in the first place."

"We got a call from a citizen today who saw three kids enter this store yesterday. They were up all night and said they never saw them come out. They might be ones we're looking for."

"I didn't see no kids come in here last night and I was here all that time. Why are ye looking fer them, officer?"

"They broke some newly instated laws."

"What laws?"

"Several. Can we discuss this after I look for the kids?"

"No reason to since I don't see anyone else in here but me."

"Just let us check to make sure you didn't miss them."

"Are you accusing me of being so blind I can't see three young rascally kids?!"

"Mr. Ruff, that's not what I meant."

"Then ye need to be clearer about it. Besides, to do this proper like, ye need to get a legal search warrant to do this."

"To be candid, the Politically Correct Force people helping us with this search are fired up. They could resort to breaking in the store if you don't open up and let us look for them."

"If you let that happen, the owners would sue you for any damage done by yer people as well as any injuries. I reckon ye also know breaking and entering is 'not' the correct thing to do. I think right now, ye should be reminding yer crowd of this."

He then heard Schmartzov repeat what he said to someone else.

"Mr. Ruff, enough of your stubbornness. Just open up," the officer said gruffly smacking the door hard with his hand.

"Sir, I nice and po-lightly explained I won't disobey orders from my employers especially fer the no-good reason of a mad crowd's curiosity."

Rhys commando crawled over to Gertie and whispered in his ear. "I think you need me and you can argue it out with me later if you want to, but I'm not leaving you alone here."

Gertie began to protest then paused and whispered. "Truth is, yer right. I could use yer help to check on the situation outside."

"On it." Rhys crawled to the front door and unplugged the keyhole to see what he could. Schmartzov stood so close to the door all he saw was his slacks. He heard him grumble a bit and then go and stand by Dwendoleen. She was crouched down two feet from the door looking ready to pounce inside if it opened with a huge crowd behind her. Rhys then went and told Gertie.

"To be a good citizen," Schmartzov bellowed as he came back, "You should cooperate with us, because you'd be just plain crazy to keep officers of the law from doing their job!"

"I ain't crazy. Truth is, seems crazy to me ye want to break and enter fer no good reason. As I told ye, I'm doin' my job and keepin' a sharp eye on things in this here fancy game store."

Schmartzov backed away flinging his arms up in frustration. Rhys peeked through the slit around the window and saw the front of the crowd behind the officers held a 'Politically Correct Force' banner up. He ducked down as a few came right up to the window. They pressed their faces against it trying to see through the thin clear area around the darkened window but quickly backed off after getting blinded by the laser lights.

Rhys leaned close to Gertie and whispered, "I noticed a screen next to the cash register shows there's three security cameras covering the front area. You could let him know this is all being recorded. Maybe they'll back off and—"

"Mr. Ruff," Schmartzov growled, "I'll give you one more minute to open the door then I'm coming inside. Now, open up!" The crowd then chanted, 'Open up! Open up! Open up!"

"Ye best not do that, fer that be illegal. I know the law and first ye have to get one of them warrants sayin' ye can lawfully enter these premises without my or the owners say so." Gertie was met with silence.

"It'd waste the taxpayer's money to make me get a warrant."

"Then ye best all smile real big now, fer this here is all being recorded as we speak. If ye break-in I'll have videos of you doin' it and send it to the news station straight away. It'll show your disregard fer the law even after bein' told ye can't come in. Folks won't like that ye didn't even try to do this properly. So, I truly believe it's best ye leave and take that angry mob with ye or I'll have to send this to the news people right now."

"You want to play tough, do you?"

"No, siree. Not at all. I want to do what's right. And what yer planning to do is just plain wrong. So, think it over."

Rhys saw Dwendoleen look up at the cameras and whisper in Schmartzov's ear. He looked disappointed, but he nodded.

"Have it your way for now, but I guarantee this. I'll soon be back with a warrant to enter this place."

"That'll be fine as long as it's done up all proper and legal."

"It will be," Schmartzov huffed then Dwendoleen whispered to him. He nodded then he stood up tall and spoke through his megaphone to the crowd. "Politically Correct Force people, we thank you for coming. But we must leave this area now until we get permits to enter and picket. Do so quickly and peacefully."

Rhys' eyes widened in surprise as the officers led the crowd away from the Flashy Castle without any more trouble. After they left, the cousins surrounded Gertie all clapping joyously.

"Way to go," Rhys said clasping his shoulder.

"Don't let yer guard down, 'cuz we're not clear of this yet. Those officers will be back and bring a warrant to enter this place and that silly politically correct squad will be with them."

"What should we do now?" Alora asked.

"We va-moose."

"Va-moose? Do we need to find a moose to do that?"

Gertie laughed so hard he shook. "Nah, it just means to git while the gettin's good so things don't go south on us."

"What do you mean by that?"

"Good grief, don't they teach nothin' useful or practical in school? It means we need to git before this shebang goes bad."

"Oh. I get it. So, do you think it might?"

"Dunno, but if it does it can go bad fast. So, let's—"

"Vamoose!" Alora cut in with a silly grin.

The cousins ran and grabbed their packs from where they laid them by the back wall. They strapped them on tight and sped out the front door with Gertie tied to Rhys and Roleena tied to Alora. Tiana and Paris ran ahead to scout out the best alleys and side streets to use to avoid any of the Politically Correct Force or others that might report them.

"This side streets good," Tiana said running back to them with Paris after she had got them down six blocks of ones she found clear. "So, do we go to your house or Aunt Roleena's?"

Gertie scratched his head. "That's a mighty good question."

"We should go to Auntie Roleena's," Alora said. "She'll have something there to get your bodies working again."

"Likely so, but there's a burr under my saddle about that. Ye see, after I led them rascally Red Winkies away from her house, ye told me that officer showed up there and gave ye trouble. So, I figure they have someone watching her house. Then the same officers came to the game store bringing a posse with them. Tells me they be on the watchout fer ye. So, we best head fer mine and use my secret gizmo to get us to Roleena's unseen."

"What kind of gizmo can get us there like that?' Rhys asked.

"I told ye it be a secret," Gertie huffed. "So, I can't tell ye."

"Okay, but the Red Winkies were at your house too."

"How'd ye figure that if ye just got the money and note I left then skedaddled when the Mounties came?"

"Aunt Gertie," Tiana said as Rhys blushed and said nothing else. "He feels bad. You see, he didn't have your key with him. So, when he went into the backyard to get the spare front door key you left buried under that big rock the General attacked him and laid him flat like he was a burglar."

"Saints alive, that old fella must still be riled up at him fer causing him to wind up in the local dog jail."

"Actually, he wouldn't let me or Tiana in the yard either which truly stunned us," Alora said. "Then we saw his new shock collar twinkling bright red and that it was Red Winkies causing this. So, I had to use my tiara to mesmerize him so we could get the key."

"Winkies! Dag nab it. Gettin' in will be a real prickle then."

Rhys groaned as he studied a map on his smart phone. "That is not our only problem. It's seven to eight miles to get to either house. That leaves us vulnerable for long stretches where we could be nabbed by people controlled by the Red Winkies."

"Aunt Gertie," Alora said biting on her lip, "You did warn us things can go bad super-fast, and it looks like it has."

"It does look that way," Tiana said sighing heavily.

"Fraid' so," Gertie agreed. "But even if it'll be tough to pull off, we got to get to my house first. So, we're gonna do it."

"Then we all need to pray for a miracle…again," Alora said.

"That's for sure," Rhys said emphatically and as he uttered a prayer, they others did too.

CHAPTER TWELVE
THE FLASHING FAST RIDE

Tiana, Alora, and Rhys snuck down back alleys and side streets to avoid being seen, pulling Roleena and Gertie behind them like floats and Paris trotted along right next to Roleena. Four blocks later, he growled as some dogs in the distance who had begun to bark fiercely.

"Hush Paris," Alora commanded. He obeyed, but the other dogs kept barking and the trio stopped to look around. "Do you think those officers brought guard dogs over here to find us?"

"No," Tiana said. "I saw a show about police dogs and how their handler had to show them the scent to follow and it took a lot more time than has gone by."

"Yep, a lot more time," Gertie said. "I figure what we have is some overexcited dogs that caught the scent of a raccoon. Fer now, I'm just de-lighted them Winkied officers chose to be law abiding. But make no mistake, they'll come back with a search warrant to look fer ye in the game store."

"I hope when they do, we're so far away they can't find us," Alora said shivering. "And that those dogs stop barking soon."

"Me too, but whatever's causing them to bark, we need to keep moving." Tiana then froze as did Rhys and Alora, as a deep growl came from behind the tall hedge they were walking past and by Paris jumped up into Alora's arms.

"You truly should keep moving," a gravelly voice said from behind the hedge. Then two giant lionesses leapt over it and sat down in front of them. Rhys gasped and the girls just laughed.

"Justice!" Alora squealed clapping her hands delightedly.

"Bravery!" Tiana said grinning broadly.

"You two felines are a pair of show offs," Gertie chuckled.

As the golden eyed lioness padded over to Alora, the lioness with the scar on her face sat by Tiana, and Paris leapt up onto Roleena's floating body looking warily at them. The girls were so happy to see them they gave them a hug around their necks and had to stand on their tiptoes to do so.

"Rhys, ain't ye gonna give em a big hug too?" Gertie asked choking back his laughter as Bravery looked at Rhys with a grin so broad it exposed her huge, sharp fangs.

"I'll pass…but it's good to see you both," he said politely.

"Likewise," Bravery replied batting her eyes at him sweetly.

"Now, don't be a tease," Justice grunted.

"Are you speaking to me or him?" she asked in an amused tone, smiling like Wednesday did on the Addams Family.

"Bravery," Gertie said shaking his head, "Do stop toying with my lad here. He's been a heap of help to me today."

"I'm heartened to hear that, but you are spoiling my fun," she huffed. "Nevertheless, my playing with him must wait, for from what I hear now, we must leave this area immediately."

"Is trouble heading our way?" Rhys asked tersely.

"Did you humans not hear the sound of sirens starting up? They are quite loud and are definitely coming this way, and they are getting closer and closer by the second."

"Nope, we can't hear them sirens yet," Gertie said frankly.

"Be fair," Justice told her companion flicking her with her tail. "We were told humans cannot hear as well as we do."

"I did read lions have great hearing, but that range is five miles and the police station is further than that," Rhys said.

"But we're not an average lioness from any Earth pride."

"True, which shows us your hearing is superb since it's seven miles from here to the Everett Police station," Tiana said. "Now, since at high speed they could get here in ten minutes, will you two lionesses quickly take us away from here?"

"Yes," Bravery replied. "Tie Sir Gertie's tether around my waist and I will pull him. Next, put the dog in your small pack then you and you sister get up on my back holding him between you two. Rhys, tie Lady Roleena's rope around Justice's waist then you get on her back." They all quickly did what she said.

"Where are we going?" Rhys asked he got on top of Justice.

"To Sir Gertie's house," Justice replied. "We will cross the bridge over the sloughs between Marysville and Everett then again use alleys and side streets to get there and hopefully we will avoid being seen by other humans."

"But Aunt Gertie's big dog won't let us in the backyard," Tiana said. "You see, the Red Winkies found his place before we got there yesterday and attached onto his shock collar. Now, they control his movements, and as grouchy as he with them doing this, we can't go in the back way."

"Right!" Rhys said looking at Tiana gratefully and silently mouthing, 'Thank you for not telling them it's also because the General hates me for letting him be taken to the pound."

"Hold yer horses!" Gertie said. "I have a key in my back pocket to the front door so we can go in there. Now, before ye kids start whining about being seen, I'll remind ye Winkies can't see at all. So, we sneak in calm and cool like so we don't put off a lot of body heat and our talented lionesses can sense if anyone's hiding nearby wanting to nab us. Then no one has to fend off the General who ye say is all stirred up by Winkies."

"What if they do sense us and come after us?" Alora asked.

"I saw yer tiara knock back millions of those tiny varmints. That means it won't be no problem at all to use that fer a few."

"Oh my," Alora said nodding. "Of course, you're right."

"Then let's git. But instead of going over the slough, let's use the big I-5 freeway. Then we'll be at my house in a snap."

"But we can't," Tiana said. "People will see the lionesses."

"Not as fast as these gals go. They'll only see a blur."

"Actually, even so, we still we can't do that," Rhys said.

"Why? Are the fires of Hades blocking our way?"

"No, but close. When I checked the WSDOT site I saw the police now have check points on all the freeway exits leading into Everett. I'm looking at a local map for the least traveled roads and alleys and it looks like the least used roads are near Aunt Roleena's house. It's also closer than yours is, Gertie."

"Rhys, since I know this area better than you, can I use your phone to map out a route for us?" Tiana asked.

Rhys nodded and handed her his phone. "Be quick as you can about it, or they'll have time to nab us."

"Sure, no pressure," she sighed. Within minutes she mapped out a route and slipped off Bravery to show it to her and Justice.

"It looks good to me," Justice rumbled and Bravery nodded. "Sir Gertie, this puts us at Lady Roleena's house, not at yours. Will this be all right with you?"

"Yep, right now it seems like a better plan. Let's skedaddle."

"Here Rhys, and thanks," Tiana said handing him his phone back then she leapt back up on Bravery.

The lionesses shot off fast as bullets with the girls holding on tight to Bravery and Gertie tied behind them. Paris peeked his nose out of the pack between the girls, while Rhys held tight to Justice with Roleena behind them. As the felines ran, Roleena and Gertie looked like banners flying behind two golden blurs as they flashed through southeast Marysville moving like a jet stream across it and over the slough into Everett. To outsiders, they were just a blur. The lionesses only slowed as they got into Riverside neighborhood then made their way warily across the freeway overpass and sniffed around. To the kid's surprise, they went a little further then leaped high over a tall fence of a large house close by so they all cleared it and then stopped.

"Did you see what I saw?" Alora asked biting her lip.

"Dag nab it, I'm dern sorry to say I did," Gertie groaned.

"As did I... unfortunately," Tiana said sighing heavily.

"It was all a blur to me, so I didn't see anything," Rhys said hopping off Justice. "What did you see?"

"A nightmare," Tiana said flatly and Alora nodded.

Lacking a clear answer, Rhys climbed up and peeked over the fence then quickly dropped down. "A human nightmare."

"Yep, all stompin' around like a herd of angry heifers and bulls," Gertie said. "Worse, that herd is blocking our way."

"Hey everyone, lay low or someone here will see us," Alora whispered pointing to the house of the yard they just entered.

"Actually, I bet these two clever lionesses sniffed this house out and chose it because they know no one's home," Rhys said.

"His intelligence level is rising," Bravery grunted.

"Come now," Justice said, "Just admit it. He is correct and smarter than you thought he was."

"Or it was just a lucky guess."

"Quit giving him such a hard time."

"I will when I feel he's earned that."

Justice shook her head then joined the girls as they looked through the spaces between the six-foot-tall boards on the fence.

The people all wore red clothes and some held up a Politically Correct Force banner shouting, 'Correct the politically wrong. Applaud the politically correct' as they marched in a circle in the intersection far below them.

"This can't be real," Rhys moaned flopping onto his back.

"Evidently, it can, 'Detective Ostrich'," Tiana said dryly.

"Ostrich? My heads not stuck down in the ground."

"They don't really do that. They lie flat on the ground if they feel threatened by a predator hoping not to be seen by them."

"Wish that'd work fer us," Gertie said. "Cuz, they sound like hot oil in a pan and might find it fun to tar and feather us."

Alora shivered as she gazed at them. "They do sound scary."

"And we cannot take you by them," Justice sighed.

"You can't be serious," Rhys said gaping at her.

"I am. Lady Artemis told us after the officer saw us that we can help you but 'only' as long as no other humans but you see us. We cannot avoid that if we go past all of them."

"Tell us what you can do," Tiana beseeched her.

"We can take you back the way we came and search for another way to reach the house unseen by others or find you a place to hide. However, we must be quick about it because we can smell more humans coming, so must leave soon."

"Tiana, why did you take us through an area that is so crowded?" Rhys snapped.

"When I looked at it, Rhys, it had the least people around for us to get to Aunt Roleena's. So, it was the best I could do."

"Of course you did," he sighed. "Sorry I snipped at you."

"I get it, especially since I'm feeling a bit uptight myself."

"Thanks for that, and it's not your fault the crazies are here."

"You are all justifiably upset," Justice rumbled, "But Tiana did well to find us alleys with no traffic or streets we could flash down fast enough to be unrecognizable blurs."

Tiana then groaned loudly. "Rats! I just realized we could have taken East Grand and cut over by the old Co-op then used the back streets of Lowell to get to Aunt Gertie's house."

"If we move quickly, we can still do that," Bravery grunted.

"Good." Tiana leapt up on Bravery and pulled her sister up behind her with Paris who still peeked out of the small pack.

Rhys stood on the ground staring at the girls with his arms crossed over his chest. "No. The Red Winkies are obviously directing people to block the streets around here. I bet it's also like this around Aunt Gertie's house and no matter where we go, we'll run into them. So, instead of running from them," he said lifting his chin up, "It's time to just push past them."

"That sounds crazy," Tiana said frowning.

"Not if we turn the tables on them by using our gifts."

"Okay…go on, I'm listening."

"If you'll recall, we got away from the Red Winkies at the Flashy Castle by using your gifts and later from the officers and crowd using our wits. So, let's use both our wits and gifts. Let's go over what we can do to get by these Winkied people, and think of ways we can free them from being under Red Winkie control. I hope like me, you'll see this is the right thing to do."

Tiana sighed and nodded. "You're right," she said and got a shocked look from Alora as she jumped off the lioness. "It's time to either wake them up or drive them off to get by them."

"Have you two gone totally loopy?" Alora gasped.

"Maybe, but we can't keep running. It gets nothing done to fix this, and we've been given lots of gifts to do this."

"Then let's get to using our gifts to help our aunts 'and' these Red Winkied people," Rhys said turning to Alora. "Will you please restore our gift boxes to their original size now."

"But it's utter madness to try doing this," Alora groaned then Paris wiggled out of the small pack he was in. He jumped down and went over to Tiana and Rhys. "I see Paris also agrees it's the right thing to do. So, I'll help," she sighed sliding off of Justice. She gathered up all their boxes and got the enlarging dust from hers then normalized them all. "I'm done, but let's move further away before we make a plan," she said but Tiana was busy pulling her gifts out of her box as Rhys just looked at his sadly. "Hey, are either of you listening to me?"

Rhys looked Alora straight in the eye. "I know this is scary, and I'm scared too. We can run and hide, but they'll just track us down. It's better to deal with this now. I also promise you both this. I will go test this group out first. If it goes badly take off on the lionesses with Aunt Roleena, Gertie and Paris to find a safe to hide until you come up with a better plan."

"You…you'd do that for us?" Tiana asked wide-eyed.

"Yes, we've faced a lot of serious stuff together these last couple days and I've learned a lot. You took the trouble to get me out of some bad few fixes like with the General and that showed me you care about me even if I sometimes annoy you."

"Sometimes?" Tiana asked but she grinned at him broadly.

"Well, maybe more than sometimes," he chuckled.

"That's for sure," Alora said giggling.

"Okay, don't flog the sacrificial lamb," Rhys said kiddingly. His eyes then narrowed and a serious look came over his face as he studied the angry crowd. "Now's my chance to show you I care about you too. All of you. And since you said I'm a smooth talker with adults, I'll talk them into being sensible. If I can't, I'll ask for a set of their new rules and ask for some time to look them over. My goal is to get them to calm down enough to get by them. Then since it is closest, we can go to Aunt Roleena's house to find something to remove her and Gertie's paralysis."

"Not a bad plan, young fella, not bad at all, fer I sure cotton to the idea of you fixing us," Gertie chimed in.

"Rhys seems to be taking after you, Bravery," Justice purred.

"I was thinking that myself," she replied padding over to him. For the first time, Rhys did not back away in fear when the lioness came up to him face to face. To their surprise he stroked Bravery's neck. She actually purred then licked the side of his head and he laughed heartily.

"Thanks. I'll work hard to live up to your name," he said.

"I suspect you will," she rumbled flicking him with her tail.

Tiana went over the gifts in her box staring at one item long and hard as she looked at Rhys then nodded to herself. *Now I know what to do with this.* She pulled the silk top hat out of its bag and handed it to him. "I have decided to give this to you."

Rhys chuckled as he saw what it was and popped the top to restore it to its full shape. "Why do I need a fancy top hat?"

"I have no idea. But on the inside brim of the hat is a note Aunt Roleena wrote to me so please read it out loud."

"Sure, I'm game. It says, 'Dear Tiana, give this to who is first willing to protect you against greatest odds. Doing so earns them the right to wear it into battle'." He looked at her gaping. "Seriously, you want me to have this?"

"To my surprise, yes, I do. What do you think, Alora?"

"Yep. He is first to ask to defend us against huge odds."

"True, so go ahead, Rhys, and put it on."

"This is kind of weird, but okay." He stood and waved the hat about then gave them a deep bow. "I shall work hard to live up to this honor, milady's," he said and set it on his head. It then flashed brightly and turned into a bejeweled gold crown.

"Cool!" the girl's gasped in astonishment.

"What's so cool about it?" he asked taking the crown off to look at it. As he did, it flashed again and became a top hat.

"Rhys, as you put it on it turned into a fabulous gold crown set with a zillion diamonds," Alora said with awe.

"You must be pulling my leg," he said scratching his head as he looked it over. "It's just an old-fashioned silk hat."

"I'm not kidding! Put it on again and leave it there. Then reach up and feel the shape of it with your fingers."

With a shrug, he put the hat on and it flashed. Seeing the girl's eyes widen again, he reached up to feel it. First a look of shock filled his face and then delight. He could feel that the hat had indeed become a crown. "Awesome!"

"That it is," Alora said giggling delightedly.

Tiana nodded. "And very regal." She then looked at his gift box curiously. *I wonder?* "Rhys, try opening your strongbox."

"Why? Do we need more sunglasses?" he asked jokingly.

"I'm not talking about the drawer on the side. Try lifting the top." She grinned as he hesitated. "Come on, I dare you."

"Oh yes, please do," Alora said clapping her hands excitedly.

"Okay, but no laughing at me if it doesn't open." He grasped the lid of the strongbox astonished to have it open up easily.

"See? It did open!"

"Yeah…it did!" He grinned broadly and reached inside it.

"Check for notes! Because the times I forgot to remember to do that I accidentally stunned everyone with my tiara and then I made you fly in the air with my magic dust."

"I won't forget that anytime soon," he said rubbing the spot on his head he had smacked on the ceiling.

Alora winced. "I'm still super sorry about that."

"Don't sweat it. I'm fine. Besides I deserved a knock on the head for all the tricks I played on you and your sister."

Tiana jumped up to her feet and put her hands on her hips. "Wait a minute, who is this nice guy sitting here with us, and what have you done with my cousin Rhys?"

"Wow," he said dryly. "You're such a…now what did you call me a while ago? Oh yeah, a comedienne."

"No, she's terrible at telling jokes. So, don't encourage her or she'll quit to school to become one," Alora warned him but then she giggled and they all laughed.

"Okay, back to the business of seeing what I have that might be useful to deal with the tough stuff ahead." He reached inside his strongbox and pulled out a three-foot-long staff, but as he checked it over, he looked puzzled. "I don't see a note. Will one of you inspect it for me in case I missed seeing one?"

"I will, but just a look in case it's like my sword and doesn't want anyone else touching it and retaliates," Tiana said warily.

"Sure, and thanks," he said holding the bottom end near her.

Tiana leaned as close as she dared to inspect it. "It looks to be carved out of ebony with a smoke-colored stone set into the wood knob on the top that looks like a big glass eye."

"It does, and what's odd to me is I'd need to be a lot shorter to use this stick," he said scratching his head.

"Then there must be a notation here somewhere. Oh! I found one etched on the side. It says; 'Stand and lightly bump my tip on the ground and I fit you perfectly and help keep you safe. Warning! My eyestone's power is engaged by striking my tip on the ground hard. Point me only at wrongful beings to repel them or if you are assaulted.' See, it does say it's an eyestone."

"Okay, this seems simple enough." Rhys stood up tall and tapped it lightly on the ground. The staff immediately grew to the exact height needed for a six-foot-two-inch-tall person.

"That height looks perfect for you but wait before you do anything else for there's another note etched on its extension."

"Can you read it to me?" he asked checking out the stone.

"Sure, but the print's really tiny so hold it up close to me."

"Okay," he said staring fixedly at the eyestone for it seemed to be eerily staring back at him. But he misjudged the distance to her face and she grabbed the tip to keep from being poked with it then gasped in pain. "I'm so sorry! How can I help you?"

"Thanks for asking, but I'll be fine. It just gave me an awful shock," she said rubbing her hand.

"Should I take you to a doctor?' he asked worriedly.

"No, it just smarted and that's going away now," she said rubbing it briskly. "But don't ask me to read it again, because

I'm not going risk it. The results might be as bad as when you grabbed my sword and it burned you."

"You have good reason to be cautious after that." He looked at the staff squinting to read the note on its extended part. "It's labeled 'Leader Staff' and says, 'This will empower you if you are on the right path and make a point if it is seriously needed'. "Point? Like a spear?" He looked at the lionesses. "Do you know what this staff does?"

"We don't know all it will do, but we have seen what it 'can' do when Lady Artemis uses hers," Bravery growled. "It should amaze you to know this. One of the times we saw her use it she swept a garrison of four hundred soldiers off their feet as they attacked the animals she was protecting just by waving its point across them."

"Did it kill them?" Alora gasped.

"No," Justice replied. "It tossed the garrison backwards and they landed on their posteriors a hectare away."

"What's a hectare?"

"To give you a familiar frame of reference, the length is more than two of what you call 'football fields'."

"Wow! That must have shaken them up," Rhys sputtered.

"It did more than that," Justice said. "For we heard from two crows later who circled over the fallen army after Lady Artemis left that they were knocked out cold for an hour."

"Then it's an amazing defensive weapon!"

"Yes, it is, and Great Lady Hera has a more powerful one and the strength to wield it. For staffs vary in strength as do all beings. However, we don't know how yours will work for you."

"But take warning," Justice rumbled. "Great Lady Hera did warn a goddess who dearly wanted a Leader Staff of her own it can backfire and kill you if you choose a bad path to follow."

"Bad path?" he asked gazing at his staff warily.

"The path of evil and wrongdoing or one to acquire riches or power for wicked or self-serving reasons."

"Gosh," he said with a gulp. "This is quite a responsibility."

"Yes, it is."

"Excuse me while I check the crowd." Rhys looked at them through the fence slats and frowned. "It's odd the Red Winkies haven't made this crowd make any move towards us."

"I suspect after Alora's tiara kept them away from you at the game store, they let the other Red Winkies know this. So, they are likely being more cautious and holding the crowd back until they see what else you might use."

"Good, that will give us more time to think of ways to get past them and their possessed crowd, and hopefully find a way to free the people from the Red Winkies over there."

"Those are just and noble thoughts," Justice purred heartily.

"And amazing," Tiana said wryly. "Especially for a guy who went from being a self-centered cocky scoundrel to being a good guy…at least for the last couple of days."

"Let's both give him a break," Alora said. "He's been super cool lately and he's come up with some great ideas."

"Hey! I admitted he's recently turned into a good guy."

Rhys sighed heavily. "Alora, it's okay. For now, it's the best I can expect from my back history." He slid his staff through a belt loop on his cargo pants and reached in his box. His eyes widened as he took out another item. "Awesome! Obviously, it's for protection purposes." He held up a platinum shield. A gold overlay of a dragon with ruby eyes was centered on it standing up on powerful legs with its wings fanned out.

"Does it have a note?" Tiana asked.

"Yeah, it does," he said pulling the note off the back. "This says, 'This Dragon Shield will cover and protect any good being that cannot protect themselves'."

"So, it's not to protect people able to defend themselves like us, but for good people like our aunts who can't do this."

"I think you're right."

"Then I'm thankful ye have that fancy shield," Gertie said. "Cuz with yer Aunt Roleena froze up like a statue and me limp as a rag, we sure as shootin' can't help ye deal with this riled-up crowd until we get fixed and can move again."

Rhys slapped his forehead. "That's it. I should've realized it right away. And what a relief it is to me too."

"What's a relief?" Alora asked.

"I'll show you." He slung the shield over his shoulder then untied the tethers on Roleena's and Gertie's floating bodies attached to the lionesses then took them over to a stout bush near the fence and tied the tethers to it.

"We are not leaving our aunts behind!" Alora sputtered.

Tiana echoed this and they both ran over to their aunts.

"Of course not," Rhys said. "That would be absurd."

"Stand down!" Gertie said sternly and the girls backed up a few feet. "Let the fella show us what he's got in mind."

"Okay, here it goes." Rhys set his shield between Roleena and Gertie and stepped away. It magically lifted in the air above them, but did nothing else.

Alora frowned. "I don't see how it's going to protect them."

"Sorry, I thought I had this…or them, covered."

"Rhys!" Tiana said. "I see words etched around the rim of the shield that say, 'You have but to ask for help to receive it'."

"Thanks for noticing. I'll try asking. 'Protect our friends'." Nothing happened and Rhys's shoulders slumped.

"Try it again, since if it's like my Smart phone I often have to change to way I ask my question until it gets what I want."

"Yeah, I've had to do that too," he said brightening. "Okay. Here it goes. Dragon Shield, please protect our paralyzed aunt and friend that are underneath you."

A blinding flash of light shot out the edges of the Dragon Shield and they shut their eyes. As the light dimmed, they opened their eyes a glimmering, transparent, silvery-blue dome under the shield now completely covered Roleena and Gertie. Rhys reached out and touched it and a wave of energy tossed him on his backside.

"That felt like a hundred bees stung me," he said wincing.

"At least you didn't get tossed back two field's lengths and get knocked out like Artemis' spear did to those attacking her animals," Alora said as she and Tiana got him up to his feet.

"Yeah, I'm glad it didn't do that. It also shows me they'll be safe under it." He then paused to think. "You know, I could ask the Dragon Shield to protect all of you while I go confront the Red Winkies and Winkie run people down in Garfield Park."

"We thank you for the kindly offer, but must refuse," Justice purred, "And if you do not need us to take you somewhere now, we must go help Lady Artemis with her task."

"Of course, and I won't need to stay and protect Alora and Tiana since I can extend my shield to protect them too so they'll be safe no matter what while I confront the crowd."

"Rhys, I'm coming with you," Tiana said firmly.

"Me too," Alora said.

"Why? We don't know what these people might do with the Red Winkies controlling their movements."

"Rhys, we're in this together, like it or not," Tiana said. "And to me, it would just be like sealing us up in a safe prison."

"Is it open for debate? Because then at least I would know I was keeping you safe like I promised you."

"No!" they both said sharply as they scowled at him.

Rhys watched Alora gather up her tiara, magic dust, and fairy wand and put them in her glass box as Tiana put her Sword of Justice, pied piper flute, and doll-sized lion-tamer chair in her wooden one. He then nodded to himself. *I promised to go first and protect them so I must do exactly that.*

"Dragon Shield, please extend your protection over my two cousins here and the little dog Paris who's sitting by them."

"No!" Tiana and Alora shouted as the shield covered them and Paris. All three of them then slumped down fast asleep.

"Sorry, but I had to do this to keep my promise to you. I hope you'll realize how important this is to me and will forgive me for doing this without your permission."

Rhys winced and had to turn away from their tear-stained faces. He quickly closed his box but bumped it as he did and heard a tiny rattle. Curious, he looked to see what made the noise. To his surprise he found under all the packing straw was a tiny object in the shape of an ancient 'Scales of Justice' inside a clear capsule. *No wonder I missed this. It's the size of a pill.* He picked it up and found a note tied to it with thread that said, 'If you wish to be just, swallow me. But be warned. Only do so if you want justice to be the ruling part of your soul. From this point on, all things big or small must be weighed according to their merit or lack of it. Remember, and matters not its size'."

Wow, another big decision. Or is it? Above all else I truly do want to be just, so weird as it seems to do this with a pill, here it goes. Rhys put the capsule in his mouth and swallowed it.

"Rhys!" Justice growled sternly, "Why did you take that 'Scale of Justice' without thinking it over thoroughly?"

He turned and saw both lionesses looked shocked to see he had done this. "Well," he said blushing to see how intensely they were staring at him. "I didn't need to think about it longer because being just has become of great importance to me after what has happened these last few days. Please realize I truly sense this is right, and…whoa…this is weird. My face is tingling." He stopped talking as a prickling sensation rushed through him from head to toes. A minute later he gasped as a clarity of mind came to him like a cleansing tide washing away the clutter that had mired his prejudiced thinking before.

"Justice, you and Bravery are amazing. I thank you ever-so-much for all your help," he said sincerely. "I now clearly see what is happening here is my people's responsibility and know what we must do. It is we that must battle for the Earth, not you. So, as you return to Lady Artemis, please tell her that somehow, we will get the Red Winkies to leave. Then we'll work hard to save the planet and all life on it from our damaging ways." Rhys then stood up taller. "It can't be put off a second longer and I must start with this first mission right now."

"May we see you off, Master Rhys?" Bravery asked.

"Master?" he asked with surprise and the lionesses nodded.

"Lady Artemis heard your heartfelt words," Justice purred. "She passed this on to Great Lady Hera who foresaw you will become a true master of justice, so gave you this title. She also saw your cousins and close friends will also do this and other brave feats. We among the stars are heartened to see this and wish you great success."

"Thank you." He bowed politely and strode briskly off.

"Wait!" Bravery roared and Rhys froze in place.

"Why?" he asked curtly then slapped his cheek. "I'm sorry to have spoken so sharply, but I'm really tense right now."

"Understandable," Justice purred to help calm him.

"Thanks for knowing that," he sighed. "I now also realize you would not have stopped me unless it was important. So please tell me why you wanted me to wait?"

"It is because you are so busy bracing yourself to deal with this angry Red Winkie driven crowd, you did not realize you have another critical matter to tend to. For now, if anything dire befalls you on your task, Roleena, Gertie, your cousins, and the dog will remain in the shield's protective dome which will hold them in a sleeping state for centuries if needed. They will not starve or die if you do not return, but your cousin, Tiana, was correct in saying the Dragon Shield would be a prison for them as they cannot live real lives like that. Since you want to be a just, you will not wish to leave them in a trap like that."

"Of course not! That's so repulsive a thought it hurts me," Rhys said rubbing his temples as his head began to throb. "Thanks for making me aware of this. So, being you're wiser and more knowledgeable than I am, will you suggest a way to be just 'and' fulfill my promise to them?"

"Change your shield command," Bravery grunted, "Let it release them all if you are taken hostage or killed. For though she sensed you will succeed, the future is not always fixed and sometimes changes. If your current plan fails, you should have this backup plan. Then the girls can call out to us to take them all to a safe place to plan other ways to solve these problems."

"That sounds both fair and wise. I will do so," Rhys said nodding. "Dragon Shield, I ask you to release all those under you if I am killed or captured by the Red Winkies or crowd as I strive to talk some good sense into them. Then go with them and the lionesses as they take them to safety somewhere else."

"As you wish, it shall be done, Master Rhys," came a deep rumbling dragon-like voice from the shield.

He gaped in awe as the shield not only spoke, but called him, Master Rhys. Stunned, it took him a moment to reply. "Thank you," he finally said then he looked at the lionesses. "May your journey back to Lady Artemis be a safe one. I'd say more to express my gratitude but I must go and work on a way to protect my friends and free the others."

"Master Rhys, are you sure you want to face this alone?" Justice asked with concern.

"I honestly can't say I want to go alone, but I know I must do what I promised them."

"Understood," Bravery growled with a deep nod at him. "I am proud of you, young Earthling. Now, I will share what we just received from the High Council. Lady Roleena planned ahead in giving you your gifts. Your crown, Tiana's 'Sword of Justice', and Alora's tiara are protective items that will keep the Red Winkies from gaining total control of you. They were only given and recently empowered for use because the Red Winkies do not belong here and are not part of the natural scheme or order woven into being by the Universe."

"That's great news. But do my two cousins know this?"

"Yes," Justice replied, "We linked up to their minds so they can hear all we have said to you even in their sleep stasis."

"Wow! It's amazing you can do that."

"It is indeed. Also, know this. We and many others in this galaxy believe or hope that you, your cousins, and your friends find a way to resolve the Red Winkie problem in a fair way and go on to save your planet."

"I know it will be hard work, but somehow, we will do this. I promise I will endeavor to be fair to the Red Winkies, but I also can't just let them take us over."

"True. Farewell." The two lionesses gave him a nod then flashed off in a blur of speed.

"Well, here I go." Rhys took a deep breath and walked down toward the angry mob marching in circles in the northwest intersection by Garfield Park. As he drew close, he grimaced to see tiny red sparks swarming around all the people there.

Drat. The Red Winkies are on them as thick as flies at an outdoor barbeque. It likely makes these people even madder. I hope I look impressive enough with my crown and Leader Staff to get these Winkied people to let us by them, and maybe I can even free them of the Winkies. If that doesn't work, I'll wave my staff at them to push them back, but more lightly than Lady Artemis' did. At least, I'll see how far this moves them. Then if it looks safe enough to get by, I'll go get my cousins so we can take Aunt Roleena and Gertie past them...and our little furry friend, Paris, he thought with a smile. *However, if we can't get by them,* he thought taking another deep breath, *We'll have to backtrack and go to Gertie's house for that secret item he has he said can get us to Aunt Roleena's house invisibly so we can find her cure for their paralysis.*

The entire crowd suddenly turned Rhys' way and began yelling angrily at him and furiously shaking their fists.

"This just gets worse and worse," he muttered as he braced himself and marched on towards them.

CHAPTER THIRTEEN
CHIEF HAZELWITCH BROOMSKY

Rhys saw it was going to be tough to get the Red Winkie driven people to let them by. Still, he thought by using his powerful gifts from Roleena it would convince them it was best to let them pass. But would the Winkies let the people do this? As he got closer, the fury he felt coming off the crowd made him realize it had all been foolish thinking on his part.

He reminded himself again he had promised his two cousins to try to do this alone. But now he was close enough to see the faces in the crowd, he saw how angry they looked and hearing their furious shouts at him he was filled with doubts. *Looks like it was rash of me to insist on doing this alone, but that insight came too late. What's done is done. I must try to find a way to get Gertie, my aunt, cousins, and Paris by them without being Winkied ourselves.* He stopped thirty feet away from the tightly-knit crowd walking in circles in the intersection shaking their fists at him. *I'm going to have to scream like a banshee to be heard over their jeers and hisses.*

"Your attention please!" he yelled holding his staff high and to his and the crowd's surprise, his staff's orb glowed as bright as the rising sun. It caught their attention and they quieted down to whispers. "Will the person in charge please step forward?"

A tall, husky woman stomped over to the people holding the 'Politically Correct' banner at the front of the crowd and stood sideways to avoid the staff's light. She clapped her hands loudly and everyone stopped moving or speaking. Rhys warily lowered his staff and its light dimmed. The woman walked towards him stopping ten feet away and set her fists on her broad hips.

"I am Chief Hazelwitch Broomsky," she said gazing snootily down her nose at Rhys, "Head of the Politically Correct Force for this section of Everett, and leader of this newly formed PCF unit. You may address me as Chief Broomsky."

"Chief Broomsky, I'm fortunate to meet you so quickly," he said bowing deeply to hide he was biting back a grin after hearing her name. *Broomsky fits her perfectly since she looks and acts like a Halloween witch. It would not surprise me to see her fly across a night sky on a broom. But now, with the amount of Red Winkies I see around her the speech I had planned to give now won't work. Yet I must try something, so, here I go.*

Broomsky kept looking down her long pointy nose at Rhys and studied him. "You certainly are fortunate," she harrumphed with a sharp lift of her pointy chin.

"Yes, I am, and being you are the Chief here, I bet you can tell me what this new force of yours is all about. You see, I'm just visiting and want to know what the rules are here."

"Before I answer you, I must correct your way of thinking right now. We do not allow betting, so you must stop that bad way of thinking while you are here. I will also inform you that it is my duty to be sure these offenses are corrected promptly."

"Thank you for informing me of this, Chief Broomsky. Now, do let me introduce myself. I am Master Rhys," he said nodding sharply and as his head snapped up his crown flashed and sent flames over the crowd. *Holy smokes! That was a surprise. I'm just glad my crowns sudden fireworks went over them and not at them or someone might've been fried!* he thought with alarm and forced himself to look calm as everyone had gasped at the brilliant spectacle, except Broomsky. She stood boldly in place with her arms folded in front of her.

"Young man, your flashy stick and trick crown that shoots off fire doesn't impress me. My grandsons have much better toy gimmicks than that one," she huffed indignantly. "Now, state the business that brings you here today."

"Does it matter if all I need is to walk by all of you with three of my family and a friend so we can get home safely?"

"One moment!" she snapped eyeing him suspiciously. She got out a cell phone and tapped on it then looked all too pleased.

"It does matter for you're likely one of the troublemakers I was told to watch out for, and I don't want your kind in our town."

"So, why in your opinion am I a troublemaker? I did nothing but walk over and ask to walk by. I haven't caused any trouble."

She paused looking baffled by his inquiry. "It's insolent of you to question my judgment when you don't even live here!"

"Why is it insolent to ask you that?" he asked softly.

"I can tell you are indeed going to cause me a lot of trouble."

"I truly am not trying to be any kind of trouble. In fact, I am trying to prevent it."

"Ah ha! But you 'are' giving me a lot of trouble now by arguing with me," Hazelwitch said with a sniff of disdain and then spoke to the crowd. "See? He 'is' being a troublemaker."

"Chief Broomsky, I am not a troublemaker. I simply want safe passage by you," he said repeating this wholeheartedly to the crowd. He saw he reached some people despite the Winkie's influence as some nodded or smiled at him but most of them still scowled. *Yeesh, with the clouds of Winkies around the folks here, most will likely support her bad treatment of me. So, how can I keep her from making me out to be a troublemaker?* he wondered with dismay and his shoulders slumped down.

"Young man, stand up straight! That is not the correct way to stand. You must also not talk back to your elders, for that is also an incorrect thing to do."

"Chief Broomsky, we were simply hoping to find a peaceful way to pass by your group," Rhys said straightening up.

"We? Don't you mean you? I don't see any 'we' with you even though you mentioned having three of your family and a friend that needed to get by us. So, where are they?"

"They're still far away, because even out there we heard the furious shouting over here. So, I asked them to wait there until I checked it out. I came down and found angry people blocking the streets here. I don't know why that is, but can we have a brief truce with you here and simple go by you safely?"

"A truce? We are not at war with you," she said dryly.

"Good. Then will you please let us pass by you here?"

"No, you are on my troublemaker's list now, and I have reported you as such for having improper ways of thinking."

"I'm sorry you feel my thinking is not as proper as you want it to be. I will ask nicely one more time. Can you make a brief exception for the sake of a peaceful resolution and let us pass by you? I promise we'll do this quickly and respectfully."

"I will not make an exception!" she said stamping her foot.

"Then you leave me no other choice but to clear a path through your crowd so my small group can go by you safely."

"Officers! Come at once. This brazen boy just threatened us. Take him to our detention cells this instant."

Rhys was sad but not surprised to see Officer's Schmartzov and Dwendoleen bulldoze their way through the crowd toward him being they were both still swarmed by Red Winkies. They looked all too delighted to get to put someone in a cell.

"Stop!" he shouted tapping his staff on the ground. It flashed brightly again and the officers paused. "Think this over. I have done you no harm, nor have my cousins. However, I will do what I must to protect my family and friends though I prefer to simply pass peacefully by you."

"Chief Broomsky, what this young man said is true. He has done nothing to harm us," Dwendoleen said. "So, what is he charged with that gives us any legal grounds to take him in?"

She stabbed a forefinger Rhys' direction. "To start, he has blatantly ignored my authority by not turning back when I told him his group cannot pass by us. He just now threatened to clear a path through us, likely by using his fire shooting stick. He also could be of one of three youngsters reported for not obeying our new rules that got away from you officers yesterday."

"I don't know. We never really saw them," Schmartzov said.

"Well, he's also not wearing any red! Those three things are more than enough broken Politically Correct laws to give you the right to take him in. So, do it or I'll find officers who will."

"Yes, ma'am," he said regrettably and with a nod at Officer Dwendolyn, they both headed warily towards Rhys.

"Chief Broomsky, I'm sad you chose not to let me resolve this peacefully. I'm also shocked you're violating my rights by ordering an officer of the law to take me in without just cause, which I've given you none and force me to protect myself." Rhys lightly waved his staff at the officers and it pushed them back ten yards as well as those near them. *It worked! But I'm glad to see doing this lightly harmed no one at all and they just look embarrassed at getting shoved back.*

Broomsky gasped and looked stunned until another cloud of Red Winkies swarmed her. She then jerked like she had been shocked. "Politically Correct Force people, go take that boy down before he swings that stick again!"

"We can't take down a kid for no good reason," a man yelled and most people nodded so no one tried to do so.

A huge swarm of Red Winkies then came and zapped their behinds until they went for Rhys. He quickly swung his Leader Staff in a sweeping motion at them and they tumbled back ten yards all piled up on each other. Again, to his relief, no one was hurt, but they looked startled, as did the bystanders. After a moment, those toppled got up and brushed themselves off.

Rhys was glad to see that instead of attacking again, they backed off. He also saw some of the people were leaving. *Good. Despite the Winkies, a few regained their senses and left.* He then heard a noise right behind him and the hairs on the back of his neck prickled. Before he could turn around and look, a rock hit him on the back of the head. He sunk to his knees groaning and those close by gasped. Four men near him then made a grab for his staff and crown but as they touched them, they blazed outwards. Two jumped back and blew on their hands as the other two ran off screaming and the entire crowd pulled back.

Rhys rubbed his sore head and slowly got up to his feet but everything seemed to swim all around him as pain and dizziness swept through his body. He bent down and vomited but to his relief he managed to stand up straight again.

**

Far up the hill near the overpass, Alora and Tiana were still in their sleeping state but dreamed that something bad had happened to Rhys. Even deep in their slumber they silently prayed for the Dragon Shield to release them so they could go help him. But it did not do so and held firm.

**

"Don't let him get away with that! Go bash him again!" Chief Broomsky yelled at the men blowing on their hands after getting burned as they tried to steal Rhys's crown and staff.

One man shook his head looking at her like she was crazy and left. The other one got out a pocketknife then went and cut a small branch off a nearby tree. With a smug smile, he reached out with the branch to shove the crown off Rhys' head. As he touched it, the crown shot out flames that singed his clothes and hair and the branch caught on fire as did the edge of his shirt. He screamed and ran away patting the fire on him out.

"You pathetic wimp!" Broomsky yelled shaking her fist at his retreating backside, "You can't even take down a boy." She glanced at Rhys and saw him tip his crown back a bit to rub his injured head. Her eyes lit up and she smiled wickedly as she picked up a big rock on the ground near her. She then tiptoed up behind him and smacked him on the back of the head. Rhys cried out in pain and fell on the ground. Grinning smugly, she grabbed for his crown but to her surprise a red beam from the center stone on the crown struck her body. She dropped to the ground like a sack of potatoes and the crown turned into a hat.

**

As Rhys fell to the ground unconscious, part of the Dragon Shield's dome by Tiana and Alora pulled back. The girls felt a slight shock and jerked awake. Alora lay there dazed, but Tiana shook her head to clear it and jumped up then helped Alora up. Tiana then slowly reached out her hand to test the area of the dome that now looked clear instead of silvery-blue.

"Part of the dome's shield opened up," she said worriedly.

"Then something bad has happened to Rhys!" Alora cried out and she saw the same thought mirrored in her sister's eyes.

"Let's go help him!" Tiana shoved all her gifts but her tiny repelling chair in her box which she put in her jeans pocket then slipped on the frame pack. "But first shrink our gift boxes."

Her sister nodded and seeing Tiana keep her chair out she slipped her tiara in her hoodie's pocket. She quickly shrunk their boxes and stuffed them in the rucksack and put it on.

They raced towards 23rd Street to help Rhys in Garfield Park but seconds later, Tiana grabbed Alora's hand and stopped. "We forgot to be sure our aunts and Paris are still protected," she sputtered. Alora gasped and nodded. Their faces showed how desperately they wanted to help Rhys, but they also knew they had to check on their defenseless aunts first. They ran back to the dome and to their relief their aunts and Paris were safe for the open section of the Dragon Shield had sealed over. They spun around and raced down the hill praying the people there had not harmed him…or two things worse. The angry crowd had killed him or the Red Winkies now had control of him.

"Put the protective glasses Rhys gave us on!" Alora shouted fishing her tiara out of her hoodie's pocket and Tiana pulled her glasses from her sweatshirt's pocket. As she put them on, Alora got her tiara out of its bag and stuck it on her head as they ran to Garfield Park. They reached the crowd a few minutes later and saw how tightly packed together they were. "They are trying to block us from getting through, but will soon find they can't," she said assuredly to her sister and as the light of her tiara touched them it immediately mesmerized them allowing the sisters to easily slip through them. The girls quickly found Rhys in their midst and were thankful to find he was still alive.

Tiana checked his pulse and found it was steady so went on to check the rest of his body for injuries. "Though he's alive, he has two big knots on his head and it's likely why he's out cold."

Alora looked worriedly at both Rhys and the angry crowd. "What do we do now with him 'and' his crown and staff?"

"Fortunately, he's still clutching his staff to his chest so it will protect him, and since the crown got knocked off, it turned back into a top hat. I'm hoping it'll be safe to put back on him." She gritted her teeth and picked it up then gently set it on his head thankful it became a crown without harming her. "Okay. Let's drag him back up to the dome and hope that crowd doesn't follow us."

"Then what?"

"I don't know," Tiana groaned. "I'm making this up as I go. Can you come up with any ideas that might help us get away?"

"Nothing comes to mind," Alora said as they each looped an arm under one of his arm pits and began dragging him toward the overpass. As they got two blocks up the hill with him, she looked at the crowd and saw people blinking their eyes like they were waking up. "Tiana, look! I'm getting too far away for the tiara to work. I have to let go of Rhys and go hold them back."

"But he's too big for me to carry up there all alone."

"Do the best you can to drag him back to the Dragon Shield while I dazzle the crowd again," she urged her. "When you're there, give me a shout and I'll come join you. Then we'll call out for the lionesses and ask them take us all to a safer area."

"I don't like leaving you here alone," Tiana said frowning.

"I know, but it's all we can do under the circumstances."

"Okay," she grumbled.

Thirty minutes later Alora heard Tiana shout, "I'm here!" *Thank heavens, she was able to make it up there alone.* She ran up to her sister but screeched to a halt as she got to the fenced yard the lionesses had left them in. She blinked in surprise to find her sister sat by Rhys's unconscious body which now lie against the outside of the fence.

"I couldn't get him up over the fence," Tiana said bluntly.

"Oh, my gosh, I forgot he wouldn't be able to do this since he's out cold," she said apologetically. "I'll get out my flying dust and put a bit on him so we can float him over the fence."

"Okay, but let's make it look like we're all climbing over it together so no one in the crowd sees any more than that."

"Good point." Alora got her flying fairy dust out and put a tiny bit on Rhys. As he rose, they held him between them and pulled him over the fence with them to the other side then sat on him to hold him down. "Whew, we did it, but now what?"

"I don't know. Give me a moment to think."

"Okay, but I hope it's only a moment because it sounds like companies already coming." She sighed and swiped the sweat off her face then gasped as her tiara fell off.

"What's wrong?" Tiana asked looking at her stricken sister.

"My tiara's light is barely flickering," Alora said her lip quivering as the tiara dimmed and slowly went out.

Tiana put her arm around her sister to comfort her. "It's okay, sis. I'll think of something." *Did you hear that brain? Think of something and you'd better do it fast.*

**

"Hey everyone!" a man shouted as he pointed east up the sidewalk on the northeast side of the park. "I saw that girl with the mind-numbing light on her head go up towards the overpass and it looked to me like her light was starting to go out. Let's go check it out and see."

With the crowd out of the tiara's mesmerizing range, its effects had worn off and they began debating whether to go after the girls or go home. Most said they thought they should just go home. But Chief Broomsky overheard this and quickly moved into action to stop them from leaving.

"Go bring back those naughty kids!" she commanded. When no one obeyed her, she snatched Officer Dwendoleen's bullhorn away from her. "Come follow me! We must go catch those bad troublemakers before they do anymore harm!" she yelled so loudly they all cringed. She then ordered her Politically Correct Force assistants to break up the people debating this and she was able to guilt most of them into helping round up the kids for everyone's safety. After a sizable crowd of supporters had been gathered together, she led them like a storm trooper as she stalked up the hill after the kids with them behind her.

**

The girls heard Broomsky on the bullhorn all the way from the park telling the crowd to follow her up the hill and groaned as they peeked over the fence and saw them coming.

Tiana quickly pulled Rhys over to a tree in the yard and used her belt to tie him sitting up to it then got her tiny chair out of her pocket. "Hey sis, I'll need your help to keep them away. Will you kneel down so I can stand on your back to reach over the fence to use my chair to repel these Winkie driven people?"

"Sure," Alora choked out looking terrified, but she took a deep breath and knelt on the ground next to the fence.

Tiana stepped up on her sister's back grasping the top of the fence with one hand to steady herself as she held the repelling chair in the other. As the crowd approached the fence, she waved it vigorously at them. It pushed them back twenty feet, wishing it had been further. A few minutes later, a few people figured out by crawling over and lying low on the ground, they could avoid the chairs thrust and peek through the fence slats. But after a few minutes, they shook their heads and returned to the group. The girls then heard them tell the others that all they saw was three kids hiding in a yard, and likely to avoid their assault and they did not want to trespass to try to get them. The majority agreed, one man saying he did not want to risk a lawsuit and it was not worth his time or effort.

"My goodness sakes. So, they truly can't see our aunts and Paris inside the dome like we can," Alora said wide-eyed.

"I guess not," Tiana said, "And I'm glad they decided it isn't worth the risk of climbing over the fence to get us."

"Me too," Alora said with relief. "But do you think they'll give up now and leave us alone?" The answer to her question came all too quickly.

**

Broomsky stabbed a forefinger at three men standing near her. "You, you, and you. Get over that fence and grab those children by their necks and shake them until they promise to come out of that yard and give themselves up!"

"No, Chief," a lady said walking over in front of her. "By law we can't shake these children by their necks as you so indelicately put it. That would be both illegal and politically incorrect to do. Also, those children are on privately owned property. We must first get permission from the owners to enter it. I know this to be true because I am a real estate attorney."

"Well, don't just stand there spewing legalities. Go do it!"

"As our leader, what is correct is for you to go speak to the owners of this property, and you above all should know we must follow the correct rules and actions here."

Broomsky's nose flared and she swore nastily at the woman until she saw all the people with them staring at her in utter shock. They no longer looked at her as their champion but like they were questioning her sanity.

"Of course, I should do this, and I will," she said then she stomped up the sidewalk to the front door and knocked on it. No one answered but she just kept knocking and knocking.

**

Tiana sighed and got off her sister tucking her tiny chair in her jeans pocket. "Well, at least the crowd's backed off for the moment and their Chief's just still knocking on the door. But as unfortunate as this is, I just realized we can't let them get into this backyard or they'll find our aunts."

"How? They aren't visible to them under the dome."

"I know, but if they got in and searched it, they'd run into the dome and get thrown back. Then they'll call those officers over here who will then call in the FBI or Homeland Security and we don't want to have to deal with that kind of mess."

"Then what should we do now?"

"Not we, it is you that must now do something tricky."

"Me? What can I do?"

"We both know a huge crowd followed their Chief up to this fence. So, I need you to float the three of us into the backyard next door. We then go out the far side of that one since it's further away from the crowd. Then we'll make a lot of noise as we run east up 23rd to draw them away from this yard. I've also seen that these Winkied people seem to walk really slow. So, they won't be able to keep up with us if we run. After we're out of sight, we'll use that other route to get to Aunt Roleena's then hopefully find something to fix our aunts and bring it back."

"Okay," she choked out shakily and got her magic flying dust from her pack as Tiana checked along the adjoining fence.

"Wait!" Tiana said dashing back over to her. "I just found a slim front gate on the side over there that was obviously made to blend in. Let's use it then tie Rhys to us and tote him along so we don't risk someone seeing us all floating over the fence."

"Good. I was also afraid if I put the flying dust on all of us at the same time, we might drift off and land in Snohomish or the Cascade mountains if the offshore wind picks up. After all, I don't have much experience with all this stuff."

"Maybe not, but I think you've done a fantastic job with it," Tiana said looking at her proudly.

"Thanks." Alora smiled a bit to get the compliment then she grew serious. "We'll have to take all the packs because we can't chance someone getting a hold of them."

"You're right, but it's my turn to carry that awkward framed one with the Winkie trackers this time. So, since you've already shrunk our gifts boxes we should be set to go.

Alora shoved the little pack into the rucksack and put it on. Tiana put on the frame pack then undid her belt tying Rhys to the tree and put it back on. Alora put a pinch of floating dust on Rhys until he rose up three feet then they each grabbed one of his hands and rushed through the hidden gate. They shouted as they ran up 23rd to draw the crowd's attention and led them on a merry chase through the neighborhood until they lost them. But as they began to use the other route to Roleena's they got cut off by buses full of Politically Correct groups forcing them to over to Summit Avenue to 22nd Street to avoid them. They ran west and then south on State Street back around the far side of Garfield Park to head towards their aunt's house.

"Holy smokes," Tiana said. "No one's in the park now."

"That's super weird," Alora said as they then cut through the park to the exit near Walnut and 23rd Street. But they braked hard behind the park's big sign, stunned to see the street's buses were now filled up again with Politically Correct Force people and they all began pointing at them. They ran to the south side's exit and found those buses were filled with PCF people too.

"Crumb," Tiana growled. "These crazy Red Winkied people tricked us by getting back on the buses and they're blocking all the streets. So, it looks like we've been, well, we've been…"

"Surrounded," Alora finished for her and bit her lip.

"Yes," she said sadly. "I'm going to need to fend them off so let's get back in the field so I'll have more room to swing my lion tamer's chair around while I think of a way out of here."

"What about the crocodiles?" she asked worriedly.

"We won't find any since the crowd here is a Winkied one."

"You know, I can still get us out of this scary jam we're in if I use my fairy dust to float us all out of here right now."

"Can we use that as a last resort, since we don't know where the wind will have us float off to if we do that?"

"Okay," Alora said as they walked back to the grassy field.

"Talking about floating off, I need you to sit on Rhys so he doesn't float off. I'll stand right by you so I don't knock you down as I whirl my chair around when the crowd comes."

"Maybe they'll stay in the buses."

"My guess is they're just waiting for their Chief's orders."

"Then close your eyes a sec. I'm going to see if my tiara is working yet." She looked in its bag out and groaned. "Nope."

"Sorry, sis, just put it away so I can get ready to defend us."

"Just did," Alora said pushing Rhys down to the ground. She sat on him just in the nick of time as they then heard the chilling voice of Chief Broomsky as she marched into the park with her Winkied followers behind her.

"Here they come, and here I go." Tiana held her repelling chair at shoulder level and began twirling around. People began coming at them from all directions and the chair easily pushed them back. But she found what seemed like hours was just ten minutes and she began to wobble as she turned in circles.

"Alora, this is making me really dizzy," Tiana said between clenched teeth. "What scares me is I don't think I can do this much longer without falling on my face."

"I bet all this twirling is super hard to do," she sympathized. *And it scares me that I've never seen you look this frightened. But I know all too well how that feels.* "I think you're incredibly strong to be able to do this. If it were me, I would be flat on my face in a minute. So, whatever happens, just remember I know you did the best you could to protect us."

"This might be the end for us," Tiana said feeling nauseous.

"And with you twirling that chair my fairy dust would just be blown away if I try to use it," she said pained to see a tear roll down her sister's normally stoic face. "But if this is it for us then at least, we'll go together."

"No!" Rhys spat out from where he lay underneath Alora.

"You're awake!" she screamed excitedly.

"Obviously," he grunted. "And it's 'not' the end for us."

"Thank heavens," Tiana sighed in relief.

"Now, please get off of me, Alora."

"I can't, I put flying dust on you so we could take you with us since you were unconscious when we found you in the park."

"Take me with you? But I'm still here," he said befuddled.

"We'll explain later, if there is a later," Tiana said.

"There will be. But right now, neutralize this flying dust, and I emphasize the now!"

"Okay." She wrangled her pack around to her chest then got the neutralizer dust out. She sprinkled a bit on him and eased off his back looking relieved he did not float off.

"Thanks." He got up on his hands and knees, but as he stood, he got knocked down by the force of Tiana's lion-tamer's chair.

"Rhys, stay down!" Tiana yelled. "I have to use my repelling chair to keep this Winkied crowd away from us. So, if you get higher than my arms holding this chair, it'll flatten you again. To catch you up a bit, when we got you away from this frenzied crowd blood ran down your face from two big lumps on your head. So, we knew you'd been smacked hard a couple of times. You're likely concussed and probably woozy too, so as I said we'll explain the rest of what happened later. For now, just sit back and know we're doing our best to protect you."

"I see that, and thanks," he said sincerely. He then felt the lumps on his head and moaned, but seeing the girls worried faces, he forced himself to smile. "Hey, I'll be fine, and I bet it's not as bad as it looks. Head wounds bleed a lot which I know after I saw what happened to my buddy as he skied down a steep slope near the tree line and hit a sink hole. He sunk into it and cracked his head. Trust me, he was a lot bloodier than I am and lived to tell the tale which most people don't."

"That story did nothing to cheer me up," Tiana said dryly.

"Hey, I'm just trying to reassure you, so give me a break."

"Someone beat us to that and nearly broke your head open. So, for now, you need to let us handle it."

"No, I'll help…and I should've listened to you when you told me earlier, we're all in this together. You were right and I should've given way and asked to retract my promise to you."

Alora and Tiana both just pinched their lips tight together.

"Come on, I did say you're right."

"And you truly should've listened to us," Tiana huffed.

"I did admit that so please ease up, because I can see you're so dizzy from spinning you're turning green. Let me help, and don't argue about it. I'm not going to back down on this and it'll just make my head ache worse if you do. From now on, we will fight this together whether we go down trying or not."

"I don't know," Tiana said frowning deeply.

"Tiana, you are the one who made him the leader by giving him that top hat, so I'm sure you meant to say, yes," Alora said looking at her sister pointedly, "So, let's not fight about it since we don't want his head to hurt worse. Right?"

"Okay," she forced out too nauseated from spinning with her chair to squabble over it any longer.

"Good," Rhys said. "Now, let's stand back-to-back with the repelling gifts we have to fend off the Winkied people here and then we discuss how to get past them."

"I can't help because my tiara fizzled out," Alora said sadly.

"That doesn't surprise me with all you've had to do with it. So, I'm just glad for what you were able to do."

"Thanks for saying that," she said with a grateful nod.

"You earned it. Now, you stand between us as I use my staff on one side as Tiana uses her lion tamer's chair on the other so she won't have to spin in circles anymore. Sound okay, Tiana?"

"Yes, because I'll be really glad to stop spinning."

"Great, let's do it. Then we'll figure out how to get by this Winkie mad crowd. Alora, first you and I need to stay down low to get up on Tiana's backside safely with you in the middle and me on the outside. Then we'll stand up and I'll wield my staff as she wields her chair."

"Got it," she said and they quickly moved into position.

"Alora, can I lean against you for support?" Rhys asked.

"You can lean on me all you want. In fact, I'm super glad you thought of a way for me to help out here."

"Which you will by helping me stay upright," he assured her and within minutes, they saw they were keeping the crowd back without any difficulties. "This is working so well I want to open my strongbox if you have it and see if I have another hidden drawer with something in it to help get us out of here."

"It's in the rucksack I'm wearing. We didn't want to leave it in case that mob got in the yard with our aunts and took it."

"Good thinking! You guys, are awesome," Rhys gushed with such enthusiasm the sisters blushed.

"Thanks, but there's a problem with you that," Tiana said.

"Your negativity is a real downer," Alora groaned.

"Hey, I'm not being negative. I'm being logical. Tell me how is Rhys going to get in his pack while he wields his staff?"

"Oops. I guess I hadn't thought that one through."

"Me either," Rhys said frowning. "Alora, do you think you can get my strongbox out of the rucksack and enlarge it then hold the box open behind my back so I can reach inside it?"

"I don't have a problem lifting it so I'm sure I can do that."

"Great. Then please do it and I'll feel around inside it."

It took some finagling but Alora did as he asked but as he groped around inside it hoping to find another hidden gift, he accidently knocked it out of her hands. It hit the ground and was thrust away from them by the repelling staff he was using.

"Cripes!" Rhys said. "That was a terrible slip-up of mine."

"Tell us something we don't know," Tiana said dryly.

"There is some good news," Alora said pointing at the box.

"What?!" Rhys growled.

"Don't snap at me. I didn't drop it. You knocked it away."

"I know, and I'm not mad at you. I'm mad at me," he sighed.

"Well, as our sweet Gramma Betty used to say there's no use crying over spilled milk, so, what's done is done."

"True, and I bet there wasn't anything else in there anyway. I'm sorry. My goof-up puts me short on gifts until I get it back. That makes me anxious to hear your good news."

"Your strongbox's top slammed shut as it tumbled away."

"What a relief! At least that means they can't get into it."

"I hate to rain on your parade of happy thoughts," Tiana said. "But I saw another Winkie cloud swarming their Chief.

She's now focused on the strongbox and going over to it faster than I thought was humanly possible for her to do."

The three cousins watched as Broomsky ran over and sat on the strongbox then gave the trio a nasty sneer.

"I now have something you most likely want to have back," the Chief called out to them smugly.

Rhys just shrugged and whispered to Alora, "Act like you don't care if she has it and ask Tiana to do this too."

Alora nodded and whispered to Tiana what he said.

"Got it," she whispered back and yawned dramatically.

"Chief Broomsky," Rhys called out loudly, "It really doesn't matter if you have it since it's locked and you can't open it."

"We'll see about that!" She got off the strongbox and pulled up hard on its lid. When it did not open, she kicked up on the top hard and got flung back ten feet. With a snarl, she grabbed the handle to take it with her but it did not budge. She stomped over to the crowd and pulled two strong-looking men over to the box then told them to open it anyway they could. They went to check the buses and came back with a crowbar and hammer. They both looked shocked as they failed to open it or even dent it. They shrugged and walked off. Broomsky yelled insults at them as they left and they looked back at her with disgust as did most of the people around her.

Tiana turned her head to Alora. "Let Rhys know I see people pouring into the park my direction and heading our way. Also, remind him we not only need to get his box back and find a way out of here, we also have to go get our aunts and Paris."

"I hear you loud and clear," he said glancing her way and he winced to see how pale she still looked from twirling her tiny repelling chair in circles for so long to protect them. *Wait a sec! I now recall what that note on the bottom of my strongbox said and wish I had sooner. It said things will change for the better if I ask for help unselfishly.* He searched his cargo pants pockets with his free hand hoping what he had would help them. "I'm working to find something to get us out of the mess we're in." *And right now, as cool as all these pockets on my pants are, I wish I didn't have so many to fish through right now.*

"Good, and I hope you find it soon because it looks like half the city of Everett is heading here," Alora said gulping.

"Unfortunately, I see that too," he said grimacing. He then grinned as he found his smart phone in his lower left pocket. He used his fingernail to flick off the protective tab on its side that covered a red button and tapped it. "I hope what I did will soon solve our problem, but it could take a while to know for sure."

"I hope it's a 'short' while," Tiana groaned as the crowd got thicker. "Because I'm still queasy from all the spinning I did, and my hands are nearly numb from waving my little lion tamer's chair at the crowd for so long."

"I understand all too well, because my banged-up head is letting me know I could use a break." *Well, Aunt Roleena, you told me this was an 'emergency only' button you had installed on our smart phones and to 'only' use it if we were in dire trouble. This sure looks like dire trouble to me. So, I hope this actually gets us the help we need before it's too late.*

Thirty long minutes later, sweat ran down Tiana's and Rhys' faces as they winced in pain from continually waving their repelling gifts at the crowds to keep them back.

"So, tell me what's going to be the solution to our problem?" Tiana asked forcing herself to be calm and not tap her toes so as not to worry her sister more than she already was.

"I was counting on my solution to come our way soon, but it hasn't," Rhys said sadly. "I'm really sorry since I might not be able to keep my promise to protect you then."

"Hey, you tried super hard to do that, and got bashed on the head twice for it. I'm just glad we still have you," Alora said.

"You are?" he asked with surprise.

"Actually…I am too. It was brave of you to try talking this cranky crowd into letting us go by them, even if it was kind of dumb to do," Tiana said sternly but then she grinned at him.

"As dumb as knocking my box out of your sister's hands?"

"No comment seems to be necessary on that one."

"True," he said peering up at the sky every few seconds. "I know we can blaze our way over to my gift box, but as we got near it our gifts would just push the box away from us again."

"As much as I hate to say this, we might have to leave your box for now and make a run for Aunt Roleena's house to look for something to fix our aunts."

"But the way it packed here now, I don't think we can get through this huge group of people," Alora said biting on her lip.

"Don't say that," Tiana sputtered. "We have to! Still, I see why you said that since I see that hundreds have crowded into this park. Maybe we should blaze a path through them to the bus station near Pacific Avenue and catch a bus to Aunt Gertie's house. Hopefully, we can find his invisibility device. We could then catch a bus back to Everett Avenue and dash over to Aunt Roleena's unseen and find what she has to fix them up. Next, we could return here unseen and grab your box then dash back up 23rd to unfreeze our aunts in that yard near the overpass."

"It exhausted me just to hear your plan," Rhys moaned. "But maybe we should do it since we'll soon be so exhausted waving our repelling devices at the crowd we'll drop in our tracks."

"You two decide, I just can't do this much longer."

"Yes, you can," Alora said. "You're amazingly strong, and it's not like you to doubt yourself. But I know you're tired, so I'll tell you what you'd usually tell me. Draw from the powers in the Universe to garner some of its strength."

Tiana smiled wryly. "So, we'll all draw from the Universe and magically get away from here then we'll be able to easily figure out how to get the Red Winkies the leave."

"Yes!"

"And save the Earth, of course," Rhys added getting in the spirit of their wild imaginings.

"Most certainly."

Tiana then grew glum again. "I don't know. Right now, what scares me more is this. What if these Red Winkie run crowds are now all over the Earth? That would mean the entire world could is being controlled by these zap-happy tiny aliens."

"That's a horrible thing to say!" Alora gasped.

"True," she said grimly. "Let's pray it's not so."

CHAPTER FOURTEEN
SURROUNDED

"Good grief, Tiana, saying the Red Winkies are in control of our world is too frightening to even imagine and definitely your most pessimistic comment to date," Rhys groaned then turned away from her and stared hard at the distant sky.

"Or is it just the naked truth? Look at all the busloads of PCF people coming here and expand it to all the world's cities. That makes it look all too probable to me, and yes, it is quite scary."

"Good grief, Tiana, snap out of your gloom and doom stuff and let's make sure it won't happen," Alora said then looked at Rhys curiously. "Why do you keep looking up at the sky?"

"If I knew the answer to that as yet I'd tell you."

"Whatever do you mean by saying that?"

"It's just that I've been expecting something and I thought whatever it was would have come by now. Wait!" he shouted excitedly and pointed at the sky. "I think it's finally here!"

"Why? Is Superman or Captain Marvel winging their way over here to save us?" Tiana asked dryly.

"No, but I think something is," he said looking southward.

"Fine, I'll play along." She glanced at the sky and scowled. "Okay, I do see a couple of objects are heading our way."

"Finally." Rhys said sighing in relief. "This is great."

"Why do you say that since it sure doesn't look like any super heroes are coming." Tiana's eyes then widened. "But it does look like huge winged-creatures are flying our way which might cause us even more trouble than we have right now."

"No, I bet these 'winged-creatures', as you put it, are not coming to cause trouble, but are coming to help us."

Tiana squinted her eyes to focus on the two objects. "Look Alora, there's two crows…wait, these have a broader bill so they're ravens, but they're the biggest ravens I've ever seen."

"Ah, now I can see a see them and they 'are' super big."

"Look again! Now, you can see people are riding on top of them," Rhys said elatedly. "But I can't make out who they are."

"I see that too!" Tiana said enthusiastically.

"Did you know someone was coming?" Alora asked.

"In a way, because I did expect some kind of help."

"Why?" Tiana asked.

"Because I called for emergency assistance."

"I didn't see you make any calls."

"That's because all I did was tap the red emergency button Aunt Roleena had installed on our smart phones. She said it would let her know we had an emergency so serious we could not even talk on the phone. Well, this looked serious to me."

"That's putting it lightly, and I just hope these people can help us so we don't wind up Winkie puppets and—"

"Hey, look!" he cut in smiling broadly. "It's our cousins! I see Lani and Kira on the back of one of those big ravens, and Shaw and Wain are on the one beside them."

The gigantic ravens swooped over the crowd cawing so loud everyone covered their ears. The trio saw Lani and Kira, their older girl cousins, wore packs on their backs as did their older male cousins, Wain and Shaw. The frowns on their faces made it apparent they knew the trio was nose deep in trouble.

"I'm thinking they're carrying gifts in those packs that were given to them by Aunt Roleena," Tiana said matter-of-factly.

Rhys nodded sharply. "Little doubt in my mind about that."

"Me either," Alora said.

The ravens cawed loudly dipping down low at the crowd surrounding the young trio until they cleared an area fifty-feet around them then landed in the big open space. Lani, Kira, Shaw, and Wain jumped off of the huge birds and they flew off. The older cousins began walking towards the trio but with the birds gone, the Winkie controlled crowd quickly got between them and their younger cousins. With the trio no longer being able to see their cousins with the crowd in the way, they quickly shouted warnings out to them telling them to protect themselves from having the Red Winkies latch onto them to control them.

Rhys began jumping up high to see over the crowd and then told the girls, "If you jump up high, you'll see that our cousins are walking through this Winkied mob like a hot knife through butter and are somehow keeping out of their reach."

The girls jumped up as high as they could, but to no avail.

"I can't get high enough to see a thing," Tiana huffed.

"Me either, can you tell how they're doing it?" Alora asked.

"I don't see them holding any repelling gifts do this, but maybe the glowing headbands they're wearing are doing this."

"Since I can't see a thing, I'll have to take your word for it," Tiana said disappointedly.

"Hey, shortie, even if you can't jump high enough to see over the crowd, you wield a mean chair," Rhys said grinning.

"That I do," she said grinning back at him.

"I'm just super jazzed they came to help us," Alora said beaming happily, but then she looked seriously bewildered.

"Why are you frowning?"

"Because I'm puzzled. Aunt Roleena can't have told them we had an emergency being she was taken and frozen up by the Winkies. So, since it wasn't her, who else could respond to the emergency call sent to her since Aunt Gertie also taken? The only ones who knew about this were the lionesses, but they had to go help Lady Artemis with the emergency relocations. Still, maybe they told her we were still in serious trouble and she thought it important enough to send us additional help."

"It's possible," Tiana said. "Aunt Roleena did tell me Lady Artemis has command of many animals, but they were all land creatures, not those of the sea or air, and it was gigantic ravens who brought our cousins here. Hmm…our aunt did mention that Lady Athena can command those in the air, but only mentioned owls and raptors, not glider-sized ravens."

"Then she must have known someone with raven friends."

"But who would help us? Our aunt said most were in a rush to leave this planet knowing its ecosystem was collapsing, and they were disgusted by the poor care most humans were taking of Earth and had had enough of us."

"Gertie told me he heard the same thing," Rhys said, "And with the dirty state this planet is in with us polluting the land, air and water, I don't blame them. He said even our oceans have become overused garbage dumps."

"Then I'm grateful that despite our bad galactic reputation, someone cared enough to get us some desperately needed help," Tiana said and Alora nodded vigorously. "Hmm... I do recall reading a book of Greek Myths that said ravens and crows are sacred to some deities, and can guide those needing help. So, maybe one of them had their ravens bring our cousins to us."

"And whoever did respond to this emergency call knew when Aunt Roleena didn't answer it something was terribly wrong, and that not only I desperately needed help, but she did too since she didn't answer it."

"Likely true, but I'm surprised someone was willing to help three 'very' distant Earth relatives of Aunt Roleena's."

That moment the trio's faces lit up hearing familiar voices as their four cousins came through the front edge of the crowd.

"Looks like you could use our help," Shaw said grinning.

"You think so?" Rhys asked grinning back.

"Ah, but first we have to solve a possible problem between you three and us four," Kira said matter-of-factly.

"What's that?"

"We might not be able to get any closer to each other with our protective devices on, which is why we're standing ten feet away from you."

"Are you sure it's a problem?" Rhys asked. "Because you're just ten feet away from us, but the two repelling devices we're using keep the crowd twenty to thirty feet away. I also don't feel yours is pushing us back like I saw them do to the crowd. Do you feel ours pushing you away at all?"

"No, I don't," she said with surprise and glanced at her other cousins. They shook their heads and looked surprised too. "Interesting." She cautiously walked over to the trio and had no problem doing this, so the three other cousins followed suit.

"I'm so glad to see that your gifts and our gifts from Auntie Roleena can all work in harmony together," Lani said smiling.

"Me too," Rhys said heartily. "So, how did you find out we needed help and then get here so quickly?"

Shaw laughed heartily. "Due to two super cool ravens, but I'm surprised you asked since they're pretty hard to miss."

"Thanks, Mr. Obvious, we did notice that," he said dryly. "What I meant is you must have been able to drop whatever you were doing to get here this fast."

"That we did, but it isn't every day a horse-sized raven lands on your doorstep," Wain said shoulder bumping his brother and big grins spread across their faces. "In fact, it's actually 'never' happened to us before."

"True, and we opened the door rather fast due to them beak-rapping it like a rock hammer," Shaw said. "Then they cawed roughly in English a crowd was bullying three young people in a park which was great timing since I'd been wanting to learn how to do crowd control with all the riots happening lately."

"For me, this was more exciting than my plans today."

"What about you two?" Tiana asked Kira and Lani.

"We were out on a run preparing for a Ten-K race and were shocked as a huge raven flew down in front of us," Lani said. "We thought we were goners until it cawed in English the same message Wain and Shaw got. It also said that on its way to get us it heard a flock of goldfinches twittering about being scared off by a big angry crowd as they attacked three young humans in the park they were roosting in. So, we wanted to help."

"We didn't know it was you," Kira added, "But they said they were in serious trouble and we felt the right thing was to go help them. It also gave us the opportunity to finally put to good use the cool gifts Auntie Roleena recently gave us."

"The raven also heard some squirrels say the same young humans ran into crocodiles there earlier."

"We wish you'd called us then so we could've helped you deal with them. You see, we dealt with some in Kingsgate Park years ago, but ours was a game we played with Auntie Roleena and she showed us how to have fun keeping away from them."

"It was 'not' a fun game for us," Tiana huffed. "It was bad."

"I'm sorry to hear that," Kira said wincing.

"Me too," Lani said.

"What's interesting," Wain said, "Is our raven told us an owl of Lady Athena's heard another owl tell her that people called Roleena and Gertie were captured by Red Winkies, but three kids then rescued them. Was that you? If it is, are they okay?"

"Yes, it was us," Rhys said, "And they are alive, but the Red Winkies paralyzed them, so we have to find a way to fix that."

"We most certainly do. How can we help?" Kira asked.

"We need to find a way to get past all these 'Winkied' people which we haven't been able to do as yet."

"The four of us are raring to help you with that," Wain said.

"Thanks!" Tiana said gustily. "To start, how much do you know about the Red Winkies and the trouble they're causing?"

"Aunt Roleena warned us about them if we ever saw them, but until now we hadn't. So, the first time was seeing the clouds of them as we flew here and hearing you warn us about them."

"Then at least we don't have to explain that. Right now, we need help getting to Aunt Roleena's to get the fix I mentioned. As you can see, we're really overrun by Red Winkies."

"We could all definitely see that as we flew here," Lani said. "But where are our aunts because I don't see them here?"

"They're hidden in a fenced yard up the hill by the overpass under the protection of my Dragon Shield," Rhys said.

"Dragon Shield?" Shaw asked. "What's that?"

"I'll explain later, but for now it's keeping them safe."

"Good, and I'm guessing the shield must camouflage them since the ravens didn't see them and they have keen eyesight."

"Yes, my shield hides them from all but we three. So, right now, I'm just extremely thankful you came to help us."

"Me too," Alora said elbowing her sister.

"Right, thanks," Tiana said rubbing her ribs. "So, what kind of gifts do you have that could help us out here?"

"You mean besides our good looks, charm, and brilliance?" Shaw asked jovially as he wiggled his eyebrows at her.

"Seriously?" she snapped. "You're cracking jokes? Rhys got brained, and we ran ourselves ragged to keep free of Winkies and their control, like of the people, the officers and their entire Politically Correct Force. We also had to fight off horrendous dungeon demons to get our aunts back. So, no joking. We have a lot to do to fix our aunts, get rid of the Red Winkies, and save our planet or we and this magnificent die!"

"Okay, but jokes beat griping, which won't help at all."

"I'm just want you to realize how serious this is."

"It's been super bad, so go easy on us," Alora said wearily. "But what's good is our protective gifts can all work together."

"And it's good they do or we'd get tossed on our backsides, mesmerized, or stunned along with the crowd," Wain said.

"Which is curious," Tiana said, "Since before you got here, we had to protect ourselves from each other's gifts."

Rhys's eyes popped open wide. "That's right. We did."

"So, why don't we have to do that now?"

Everyone's eyes widened and it was quiet as they thought.

"I know what's different!" Kira said. "You don't have the protective headbands Aunt Roleena gave us. They must be programed in a way that allows our gifts to co-exist."

"I bet she did that so we could all work together," Lani said.

"Smart of her to do," Wain said.

"It sure was," Shaw said nodding.

"Then let's be smart too," Tiana said studying the crowd, "And what would be smart is to get away from here now. Look around. The Red Winkies are zooming around people faster and sparkling even redder as they do. I think they're making this mob even more frenzied than they were just minutes ago."

"Keen observation," Kira said, "And now I see that too."

"Then let's get going," Rhys said. "But first, get out as many protection gifts from your packs as you can carry in your hand or a pocket that might help us, and do it pronto."

Kira, Lani, Shaw, and Wain nodded sharply and quickly got the items they deemed to be the most useful out of their packs.

"Look!" Alora squealed pointing at the sky. "Zillions of Red Winkies are gathering together into a super big cloud over us."

They looked up and gasped to see a glowing red cloud over them covered the entire park. A section of the cloud then broke off and swarmed the crowd. They screamed like people on a runaway roller-coaster and ran toward the park exits but were blocked by more of the Red Winkies and forced to retreat.

The seven cousins stared at the crowd shocked to see Red Winkies moving in crackling red streams around the crowd. A small cloud then broke off and dove at the cousins who braced themselves for the worst. Seconds later, they sighed in relief. For though the Winkies flew at them hard, they bounced off as if hitting an invisible shield because of Rhys' protective staff, Tiana's repelling chair, and the older cousin's headbands.

"The Red Winkies couldn't get to us!" Alora cheered.

"For which I thank the Almighty's grace for," Kira said.

"Me too," Rhys said and everyone nodded. "Now, let's get while the gettins' good as Gertie would say."

"Tell us where we need to head to get to Aunt Roleena's house and how we keep them from following us," Wain said, but as Rhys began to answer, he was cut off by a woman screaming louder than the entire crowd. "Good grief, that woman sounds like she could be Saruman's mate."

"Actually, that role would fit her well," Rhys said dryly.

Tiana and Alora nodded in agreement, still grimacing after having recognized the voice of the person shrieking.

"Why doesn't that woman look scared like most of the others here look?" Lani asked.

"I don't know, but she's scary," Alora said biting on her lip.

"And I dared to hope things would change for the better after you four showed up," Rhys said sighing heavily.

"No such luck yet with 'Ms. Misery' herself bulldozing right towards us," Tiana groaned. As if to prove it, Broomsky popped through the crowd shaking her fist at the seven cousins.

"The Ms. Misery title does seem appropriate," Wain said.

"No kidding. Who is she?" Shaw asked.

"None other than Chief Hazelwitch Broomsky, leader of this areas Politically Correct Force, PCF for short," Rhys said dryly.

"Is 'Hazel-witch' 'Broom-sky' her real name?"

"Yes, it is," he said, "Weird as that is."

"So, you three are all familiar with this woman?"

"Unfortunately, we are, though we only met her today."

"And she's truly the head of this PCF group here?"

"Yes."

"That's wild. She's more whacko than any of the others are."

"Aces more," Tiana said, "In fact, she embodies the word."

"Officers!" Broomsky yelled angrily as spittle flew from her mouth. "Arrest these seven troublemakers! They are responsible for the terrifying assaults on us! You saw how these four new arrivals flew down on monster-sized birds knocking us out of the way as they joined them!" She then hissed and shook her forefinger at the at the seven cousins so furiously she truly symbolized a scary witch. "And that the tall boy who came to us first with his fire stick just threatened us again! He told the four new ones here to get any weapons they could use on us from their packs. So, arrest them and lock them up!" she shrieked.

"Chief Broomsky," Shaw said pointedly, "The fact is we haven't harmed anyone. You have. You ordered this angry mob to attack our young cousin with rocks then you yourself bashed him on the head with one. You're the sickly violent one."

"Nonsense. It was just a light tap that was necessary to stop him from using his weapon," the Chief snorted disdainfully.

"Light tap?" Alora said heatedly. "Look at the blood and huge knots on his head! You nearly killed him!"

"Ridiculous, they're just little bumps, nothing more."

"No, his bump is not little. This a serious injury," Tiana said.

"It was also super scary to have you threaten us and have the crowd attack us like you have," Alora said tearily.

"What utter twaddle," Broomsky huffed.

"We should take him to the hospital to have the injuries you gave him documented and treated," Wain added gravely.

Officer Schmartzov looked at the genuinely worried cousins, then at the angry mob, and lastly Rhys' wounds. "Those lumps look bad to me, too," he told Officer Dwendoleen.

"They do," she said looking at their Chief doubtfully.

"Chief, this young fellow has bled a lot and those are pretty big lumps on his head," Schmartzov then told Broomsky.

"Frankly, if I were in their shoes, I would've been scared out of my mind to have hundreds of people yelling threats at me and then attacking me." Dwendoleen said.

"You fool! These delinquents made us resort to doing this," Hazelwitch shrieked waving her arms at the kids wildly and repeated their violations but the officer backed off. Part of the Red Winkies circling Broomsky then went and circled the officers and zapped them and the Chief smiled to see this. "I demand you arrest them or I'll find officers who will do so."

"Yes, Chief," Schmartzov said reluctantly, wincing as the Red Winkies kept zapping him. He stiffly nodded to his partner and she nodded stiffly back then they walked jerkily toward the seven kids like dysfunctional robots.

"Quick, form a circle with our backs to the inside," Rhys said. "Alora since your tiara isn't working stay in the middle, "Tiana and I will face the officers since our gifts repel people further than your headbands will and give us more protection."

They all agreed and Alora moved to the middle. The cousins all held their breath as the officers moved towards them. But try as they did to reach the cousins, the force emitted by Rhys's staff and Tiana's lion tamer's chair kept them thirty feet away.

"You imbeciles. I ordered you to get those delinquents!" Broomsky shouted. "Do it!"

"We're trying to, Chief, but we can't get close to them," Schmartzov said wincing as the Winkies kept zapping him.

"Don't act like puppets on strings. Try some other way."

"I don't like her orders because doing this to these kids just isn't right," he mumbled to Dwendoleen.

"Me either, but orders are orders," she groaned.

He nodded and unclipped a police bullhorn hanging from his waistbelt and shouted at the crowd. "Now here this! I need all of you from the Politically Correct Force to push me and Officer Dwendoleen forward as hard as you can!" he called out and the huge crowd covered with Winkies pushed the officers forward and they slowly inched their way toward the youngsters.

"Officer Dwendoleen, get your Taser out in case we need to use them," he said pulling his from the holster on his belt. She followed his lead and they continued moving closer to the seven cousins by the sheer mass of people in their united assault.

Schmartzov saw the people at the front faint from the staff's forces as they got to within twenty feet of the cousins and yelled through his bullhorn, "Stop pushing and stay in place!"

The crowd stopped so suddenly it amazed the seven cousins, but the pile of unconscious bodies in front and the pressure of the crowd packed so tightly together made people madder and the jeers rose to a higher level.

"Wow. The way they jerked to a stop really did make them look like puppets on strings," Rhys told his cousins.

"Yeah, and their Chief is their super-mean puppet master," Alora said her face puckering like she was sickened by her.

Tiana shook her head. "Actually, I think the puppet masters are the Red Winkies."

"The way the Winkies are swarming these people to move certain directions, I think you're right about that," Kira said and the others nodded. "But I wonder what they'll do next."

"But look at the change in the way those officers are staring at their mad-as-a-hatter Chief and crowd," Lani said. "In fact, now they're looking at each other like they're shocked. Maybe they're beginning to realize what they're doing is wrong."

"They must have good minds and strong bodies to fight the effects of the Red Winkies then," Rhys said.

"So, deep at heart, they're good people?" Alora asked.

"Most likely," he said, "But with Red Winkies controlling them, I'm worried they still might push their way over to us and then we'd get zapped by the Winkies."

"Not going to let that happen," Wain said. "Right?"

"Absolutely," Shaw said. "Because we still have a few tricks left up our sleeves and won't let it get to that point."

"Like what?" Rhys asked perking up.

"I'm asking for you to trust us on this," Wain said.

"I know I can count on you, so of course I will."

As they stood still waiting, they heard Schmartzov growl to his partner, "I think we're going about this wrong."

"What do you think we should do?" Dwendoleen asked.

"Well, being told to arrest a kid who got clobbered just for asking to go by this angry crowd with his friends doesn't seem right. I'm going to try doing this another way."

"Whatever you think's best, I'm with you," she said.

Schmartzov gave her a nod then looked directly at the seven cousins. "I'm asking you youngsters to voluntarily come to the station and explain to our judge what happened to get all these folks so upset with you so we can help get you back home. So, set your weapons down and step away from them and don't make us Taser you to get you to cooperate with us."

"Threatening to Taser us if we don't go with you is a threat in itself. It does not make it seem like you want to help us get back home. It makes it seem you either want an easy out or else shoot us," Rhys said frankly and saw all his cousins nod at him sharply. Curiously, he then heard whooshing sounds near him and though he kept his eyes trained on the officers, out of the corners of his eye he saw Shaw now held a compacted staff similar to his in hand that he carefully hid from the officer's views as did Lani, Kira, and Wain.

"We've got you covered, fearless leader," Wain whispered.

"That's for sure," Tiana muttered behind him.

Rhys felt a lot more confident than he had seconds prior to the other staffs appearing. "What you're asking does not sound good under the circumstances since you just tried assaulting us again using this mob of angry people, and all we've ever done is defend ourselves. So, our answer is 'No, thank you.'"

"Then you're forcing us to stun you with our tasers since you refuse to come with us," Schmartzov said then he turned to Dwendoleen. "I have two backups, do you?"

"Yes, sir."

"Good. Stand behind me and on my count of three, shoot over my shoulder. If I go down, you can use me as protection and then taser them until they're all down. I'll start with the one called 'Rhys' as you take down one of the males by him, but wait for me to count to three first."

"Yes, sir," she said engaging her taser.

"Engage your staffs," Rhys said as the officers raised their tasers. His older cousins tapped their staffs on the ground which instantly became full-sized staffs. They flashed so brightly the officers paused in utter astonishment.

"Rhys," Wain whispered, "Can your staff's stone block a taser like ours can?"

I don't know if mine will do that, so I'll just have to hope it does, Rhys thought and whispered back. "I've pushed a lot of angry people away, but haven't needed to do that. Still, Aunt Roleena's note said this is a 'Leader Staff, so I'll go with yes."

"Rhys has the Leader Staff!" he gushed out to Lani, Kira and Shaw and they wowed as then told Rhys, "Aunt Roleena said one of us had a leader staff more powerful than all the others and now we know it's yours. But she also told us if the person receiving the Leader Staff got power hungry, or used it wrongly its power was set to automatically cut off."

"That was a wise thing to do and I'll be careful using it."

"Good."

"It's time to act," Rhys said. "So, let's push the crowd out of our way and ease our way through them and get out of here."

"We're all set to go, but remember to point the stone eye on your staff at the crowd, not at us or we'll shoved off too. You see, our staffs won't block the power of a Leader Staff."

"Got it. Now, let's tighten our circle with our backs towards the center and then follow my lead. Bear in mind I will be the one to head right towards the officers and Chief Broomsky."

"Why?" Wain asked quietly. "We know what our staffs can do and how to use them and you're new to this."

"True, and though I haven't used mine against a taser, I did push back an enormous crowd. I have faith I can do this since I was chosen to wear the leader hat. I truly feel that I must be the one to be facing off with their leader and these officers."

"You feel that strongly about this?" Shaw asked.

"Yes, I do," Rhys said firmly.

"Okay, fearless leader," he said but Wain looked doubtful.

"I'm not fearless," he said candidly, "But I must do this."

"We agree," Tiana said firmly and Alora nodded sharply. "When I chose to give him the Leader Hat, it became a crown. That meant it also accepted him as our chosen Leader, not just me. Not only that, he's become a good one," Tiana added and from the look on Rhys' face the compliment surprised him.

"Fine, I concede that since he won the crown, it's his call," Wain said and Lani, Kira, and Shaw echoed this.

"Staff bearers engage staffs," he said like a commander.

Without question, the four older cousins struck the ground again. Their staffs flashed brightly again and Rhys' was the brightest of them all. As Rhys faced Schmartzov, Dwendoleen, and Chief Broomsky, the four others spaced themselves out around the circle facing outwards four other directions.

"Chief Hazelwitch," Rhys said firmly, "I'm giving you and all present fair warning to back away this minute and let us by."

"You can't seriously think those silly sticks can stop all of us?" Broomsky replied with utter contemp.

"You're about to find out if you don't all move right now," Rhys told her with grim determination.

"Everyone, stay put!" Broomsky shouted but she then went and stood behind the two officers.

Rhys waited a minute, but no one moved. "On the count of three, tap your staff gently and point it at the crowd. Take care to not tap hard. We want just enough power to drive them back. We don't want anyone hurt. We just want by. Ready?"

"Ready!" Lani, Kira, Shaw and Wain said sharply.

"One, two, three!"

"Fools," Broomsky huffed. "Shoot them, officers."

As the officers aimed their tasers at the cousins with staffs, the staff bearers tapped the ground with them. The stones atop their staffs blazed even brighter than before and the cousins all waved their eyestones at the taser shots and it absorbed them. The cousins then pointed their staff's eye towards the crowd. The force coming from the staffs pushed the people who had not fainted back, only stopping when they reached the fence lining the parks boundaries in in each direction.

"We still have a problem," Tiana told the others. "Because even though the crowd has been pushed back to the fence line, we're still surrounded by those outside the park.

"Only 'a' problem?" Rhys said dryly. "Let me explain then. First, we must get by the Red Winkies and this crowd. Next, we need to go Gerties to get his invisibility device to travel unseen by others. Then we need to go to Aunt Roleena's to get a fix for our aunts Winkie paralysis and come back to repair them. After that, we need to find a way to get rid of the Red Winkies. To top it off, we must restore our planet's entire ecosystem that's being poisoned to death by we Earthlings or we're goners."

"Right, there's definitely more than one problem," she said wincing as did all the other cousins.

Rhys grimaced and took a deep breath. "Okay. Let's take on one at a time and get past this crowd to get the cloaking device at Gertie's house, and do it without these people following us. Does anyone have an idea of how to do that?"

"I do," Alora said excitedly and turned to her sister. "You can play your Pied Piper flute. It'll make this crowd dance to your music and they'll only follow you as long as you play."

Tiana frowned. "But if I do that, I can't go with you."

"Oh dear. That's true, but we must get to helping our aunts. Still, I don't want to leave you alone, yet I can't help protect you since my tiara doesn't work. Rhys, you have a Leader staff so you could do that while I go find a fix for—"

"Whoa, girl, as Gertie would say," Rhys cut in. "Sorry to stop you in the midst of your plan, but it already won't work."

"Why not?"

"Because Gertie's keyed his security pad with my genetics as a backup for him if he got disabled. Since he is disabled, I'm the only one who can open the safe his device is hidden in."

Alora sighed deeply. "And I have to go open the hidden nook with Auntie Roleena's miracle medical fix-its if Tiana's here."

"Then I'll go with you to Gertie's and Aunt Roleena's house with Lani and Kira coming as added protection. Then Wain, you and Shaw can stay here to protect Tiana. Is that okay with all of you?" Rhys asked the four older cousins.

"Sure, sounds like fun," Lani said wryly and Kira nodded.

"And it'll be our pleasure to guard our magic flute player," Shaw said and Wain echoed the sentiment.

"Good. Then it's settled," Rhys said. "But first, I need to see if Tiana's magic flute keeps all the crowd dancing 'and' that it doesn't make us dance too."

"But our headbands will protect us from the flutes effect," Shaw said. "And our staffs will protect us from the crowd."

"Probably, but I don't know as yet with her playing the flute how the headbands will work and on so many people."

Lani turned to Tiana. "Since we don't know for sure if our headbands will do that, can you briefly play your flute? Then if we can walk and not waltz it will settle that. Right, King Rhys?" she asked grinning broadly as she curtsied to him.

"That's 'Sir' Rhys, Milady," he replied with a courtly bow to her and she laughed. "If it works, that'd be great." He looked at Tiana. "Okay, try it, but just for one minute."

"Yes, 'Sir' Rhys," Tiana said smirking as she got her flute from her gift box. "I'll start by playing jazzy music to keep everyone hopping." She blew into the flute and fluttered the keys and it came out as an east coast swing tune. *Wow, that sounds great, but why? Hmmm, it must just play whatever I say since I've never played a flute before yesterday. I wonder if it's a device like 'Siri' and automatically plays anything I mention.* A minute later, she looked up and saw all the crowd in the park were dancing with each other, and her sister, Rhys, and four older cousins were grinning because none of them were.

"This looks good," Rhys said gratefully, "So, it looks like you can turn off your staffs, but keep them ready to blaze as I walk through the crowd to see what they do. If they just dance and ignore me, we'll know my group going to Gertie's can slip past them. If they come at me, I'll dash back and we'll know this won't work." Rhys walked through the crowd and they kept dancing so he walked back to his group smiling. "It's working, so we'll go. Alora, follow me closely and I'll reach back and hold your hand. Then you and Kira do the same to link us all together so the Winkie's can't split us up. Shaw, you and Wain go position yourselves by Tiana in case she needs protection."

"Will do," Shaw said and Wain echoed this.

Rhys, Kira and Alora then walked toward the park's exit as Alora nervously checking for crocodiles. They easily walked through the crowd, but there were so many they had to dodge about to avoid them as they swung around, but Rhys's crown and Lani and Kira's headband kept them from getting struck.

"This might not work," Kira said sadly. "Because now we're near the exit, I can see the sidewalks are filled with people outside the park and they're barely dancing at all."

"True," he said disappointedly. "I see that too."

"And there's so, so many of them," Alora said shivering.

"Also true, so let's head back and rejoin the others."

They worked their way back and the others could easily see by the looks on their faces how disappointed they were.

"I'm sorry to say the flute's magic only works for a bit over a block," Rhys said sadly. "We need to think of another way to get out of here without them following us." They remade their protective circle and engaged their staffs again. "Okay, Tiana, you can stop playing, but thanks for doing this for us."

She sighed and put her flute away. "I'm just sorry it didn't work far enough away for you to get free of them."

"Me too, but it was worth a try." Rhys then looked at Lani. "I know what Alora and Tiana have in their gift boxes, but do either you or Kira have a tiara that can mesmerize crowds like Alora's tiara used to do before it lost its power?"

"Yes!" Lani quickly looked inside her pack and laughed merrily as she pulled out a silk bag. "We both have tiaras but never used them after reading the warning on them, but we keep them with us in case we might need them."

"We sure do," Kira said smiling brightly as she got hers out of her pack.

"Stop!" Rhys said holding his hand up to them. "Don't open those bags! I don't want you turning us all into zombies."

Kira rolled her eyes at Rhys. "They don't turn you into zombies. Aunt Roleena's note said they just mesmerize you."

"We also have special glasses that came with it to protect us from that," Lani said. "Shaw and Wain have them too."

"That's right, we do," Wain said and Shaw nodded.

"Kira," Alora said seriously. "Please don't roll your eyes at Rhys because there's a good reason for his alarm. When I first used mine, its dazzling effect did sort of turn him and my sister into zombies, as well as Auntie Roleena's python friends and talking fly. We didn't find the protective glasses until later."

"Oh, sorry Rhys," she said and he gave her a knowing nod. "I bet Pythia and Dodona were irked about that."

"They certainly were and Harold nearly got hurt," Tiana said wincing. "Now, I suggest you try yours out on the Red Winkies and crowd after we all put on our special glasses to protect us from their mesmerizing effect and see how well they work."

"Sounds like a good Idea," Rhys said.

They all put on their special glasses, but as they did three big clouds of Red Winkies zipped down and buzzed around the crowd so tightly it agitated them into a near state of frenzy.

"Should we put our tiaras on now?" Kira asked.

"No. Let me see what the Winkies are up to first," Rhys said.

"My guess is they're up to no good," Tiana said.

"True, but I want to wait and see why they're doing this for I suspect they're doing this for a reason. We can always surprise them later with what you girls have in store for them."

Seconds later, Chief Broomsky pushed through the crowd all aglow with Red Winkies. "Everyone, get back to pushing your way over to those troublemakers!" she yelled. "Show them their fancy sticks, glowing head bands and wearing sunglasses won't stop us from getting them. So, get mad and get even!"

The crowd shouted at the cousins angrily and pushed hard against the force of the cousin's defensive gifts. All seven of them looked worried as they began inching closer to them.

"We'll reach you yet then my officers will arrest you and take you to our detention center!" the Chief yelled gleefully and a cheer of approval came from the crowd.

"You're wrong if you think we'll let that happen," Kira said.

"Wrong to the max degree," Rhys said. "Put your dazzlers on, ladies, and stand on each side of our circle so you'll effect the most people." He saw them nod and move in position.

Lani and Kira quickly pulled out their tiaras and set them on their heads. In seconds the Chief and crowd were bedazzled and stood still as statues as they stared transfixed at the tiaras as the Red Winkies merely floated lazily about.

Alora then gasped as the bag in her pocket with her tiara began glowing brightly. She giggled happily and pulled it out. "My tiara must've recharged because it lit up again!"

"That's great news," Lani said smiling. "And the more the merrier. So, put it on and come join us."

"I'd love to." She quickly shoved it on her head and beamed proudly as she stood in the circle with them.

With the tiaras mesmerizing the crowd they stopped pushing and the force of the staffs began moving them back. Those far outside the park still tried to get in, but upon reaching the tiara's light, they became bedazzled too. To the cousin's relief, ten minutes later the people outside the tiara's influence began to shake their heads and leave.

"Hey, you guys," Shaw said cheerily. "This is working and we're finally gaining control of this crowd because we have the crowd in the park under control and most outside of it left."

"Well, working on crowd control is what you told us earlier you wanted to learn to do, and you did," his brother jested.

"True," he said grinning.

"This is super," Alora said beaming happily.

"It sure is," Rhys said. "But let's not congratulate ourselves yet. I need to go to Gertie's with one of you girls to mesmerize the crowd we go past so they can't follow us. Then we'll catch a bus to get to his house quickly and find his cloaking device. As we do that, and since no one should go anywhere alone, Alora, I want you and Tiana to get Gertie, Aunt Roleena, and Paris and bring them here. Then we'll all be in the same spot. And I know you'll be safe with Alora's mesmerizing tiara working again, and your repelling chair, Tiana. Then when we all get back, we can all leave under the cloaking device to go to Aunt Roleena's and find her cure for their paralysis. So, let's get to it. There are likely more busloads of Red Winkie controlled PCF people on their way here. Remember, even being invisible they'll still feel us if we have to squeeze through them."

"Sir Rhys," Tiana said and seriously this time. "There's a problem with doing it that way."

"Tell me, but spit it out fast because we need to get going."

"We can't get our aunts without you since only you can ask your Dragon Shield to drop the protective dome over them."

"Oh, that's right," he said slapping his forehead. "I forgot."

"Can't imagine why," Wain said wryly waving a hand at the Red Winkie covered crowd. "Now, what can we do to help?"

"Can you four hold the crowd back while I go remove the protective dome from our aunts and Paris? Then I can help Alora and Tiana bring our aunts back and Paris can follow."

"No problem," Shaw said.

"Seriously?" Wain said. "Come on, this is 'all' a problem, but of course we'll do it so you can go take care of business."

Rhys gave a grateful nod to the four teens then he, Tiana, and Alora ran up the hill near the freeway to the fenced yard where they left Roleena, Gertie, and Paris under the protective Dragon Shield. As they reached the yard, they raced around to open the hidden front gate and sped over to the shield.

Rhys guardedly stopped shy of its stinging energy barrier and called out, "Dragon Shield, I bid you to pull back your shielding so we can take those under it to a safer place."

"As you wish," it replied withdrawing into its original shield shape then it hovered in the air above the three bodies under it."

"Good grief, it's about time ye did that," Gertie grumbled as the shield withdrew and Paris barked in agreement. "Even in my sleep state, I was figurin' ye plum fergot about us."

"Aunt Gertie, we would never forget you," Alora gushed to the crusty old miner who she knew was a softy at heart.

Rhys quickly tied Gertie and his floating straw pile to his waist as Tiana tied Roleena's body on the floating plexiglass sheet to hers. They quickly ran back with Pairs trotting beside them to join the four cousins waiting for them in Garfield Park.

"Heh, heh, heh," Gertie chuckled as noting the trio kept him and Roleena protectively close to them. "Good to see ye all. I prayed to the All Mighty ye was gonna come back fer us."

"Your prayer worked, because we did," Alora said smiling.

"No time to chat," Rhys puffed out as he set a breathtaking pace for them. "Because I bet these Red Winkies are bringing even more Politically Correct Force people here to snag us."

They ran briskly, with Alora's tiara mesmerizing any who came at them as Rhys' staff and Tiana's tiny lion tamer chair pushed them back making a six-foot-wide space cleared for them to go through. But as they got to Garfield Park it became harder to get through as more buses had arrived unloading more of what they saw was PCF people from the banners on the buses. Now, not only Alora frowned worriedly. They all did.

"Yikes," Tiana said glancing at the special watch Roleena had given her. "It took ten minutes to go a hundred feet through this park since the people are now packed in here as tight as sardines in a can."

"If not for our gifts they'd be crushing us," Alora moaned.

"Hey!" Rhys said brightly and as he peered over the crowd he waved. "I see the rest of our motley crew inside an open area created by their staffs and it's just twenty-feet ahead."

Five minutes later, Tiana, Alora, and Rhys finally made it to their older cousins and Kira, Lani, Wain and Shaw sighed in relief to see them return safely. Rhys and Tiana put Roleena and Gertie in the middle of their circle and Alora giggled as Paris took a fierce guard dog stance on top of Roleena's prone body.

"Alora, you weren't kidding when you said the whole city of Everett was coming out here to see us," Lani said sighing.

"It does look that way."

"That's painfully true, but we 'will' find a way out of this for everyone's sake," Rhys said so staunchly they looked up at him.

"Then do enlighten us great and wise leader with a brilliant escape plan," Shaw said with a deep formal bow to Rhys.

"That's so not amusing. Being your leader is tough. In fact, more so if you study the sea of people inside and outside the park. You'll see those at the far edges aren't affected by our gifts. The people out there are also trying to get at us over here." Rhys then looked at Shaw. "So, even with our powerful staffs, mesmerizing tiara's, repel chair, and my crown we can't get rid of them. So, tell me, do you have a new kind of crowd control you want to try?"

"Not that I have thought of as yet," he said apologetically.

"Then a good idea better come to us before they do."

Shaw sighed sadly. "Wow, you guys. I thought we had this."

"Not yet, but I know that somehow my dear cousins, we will figure a way out of this mess," Rhys said so encouragingly his crown glowed brighter. "I'm counting on all of you to help me think of a way to keep their mad Chief and Red Winkie run group from taking us down."

"But it looks like we're going to be swallowed up by them," Lani said with a shiver.

"No, we won't!" Rhys said. "So, don't even think that."

"Sorry to say this," Alana said, "But it's worse for you, me and Tiana since we've fought off Winkies or Winkie run people for two days. I'm getting too tired to fight them."

"Tarnation girl, of course yer tired. But there be a fierce fighter deep inside ye, so you can do this," Gertie said and she smiled a bit. "Fact is, all you young'uns are a lot sharper, brighter and smarter than most. So, I know ye can do this."

"I don't know, since I'm about to cave in," Tiana groaned.

"But you can't!" Alora said shocked it was Tiana and not her wearing out first. "And Aunt Gertie's right. We can do this. In fact, my amazing sis, you'll be instrumental in helping us, pun intended." She untied the bag on Tiana's belt loop the Pied-Piper's flute was hanging from and handed it to her. "Let's try something new. Since we have staffs to keep the crowd at bay, put your chair away and we'll take off our tiaras to save their power. Then you play super loud rock-and-roll on your flute. That should reach further than our other gifts do and maybe we can get by this crowd if you get them dancing."

"Oh, okay," Tiana said blinking as she had nearly dozed off. She put her tiny chair in her jeans pocket, took a deep breath, and played a rock tune on her flute. A minute later, the crowds near and far began dancing. Then to her shock and dismay she saw her sister and cousins were dancing too and nearly dropped her flute. *Now what do I do? Their headbands should have made them immune to my music. Bless the Almighty, I'm just glad those with staffs are still holding on to them.*

Alora giggled as she danced beside her sister. "I guess my idea of you playing the magic flute backfired on us."

"But why has it?" Lani asked dancing up to them. "Because when we four came our protective headbands kept our gifts from affecting each other's."

"My guess is the massive amount of energy the Winkies are using to control the crowd is weakening our gifts," Rhys said.

"Now what?" Tiana said pausing to take a deep breath.

"Just keep playing while we think of a way around this."

"Think fast," Wain said, "Because dancing this fast will wear us out sooner than later and then we'll drop."

"There's an idea that might work!" Kira said excitedly. "Play an even faster tune until all the crowd has to sit down and rest."

"But then so will we," Rhys said. "Come on everyone, think! I'm open to your wildest suggestions." No one spoke.

An hour passed and Tiana felt her lips going numb from her playing the fast, gusty notes for so long. She had been heartened at first as lot of people became so exhausted they sat down. But as they did, the Red Winkies whisked over and zapped them which jolted them back up to their feet to her dismay.

"Sorry everyone, but this is getting us nowhere," Rhys said.

"Yeah, we noticed," Shaw said and the others nodded.

"True," Alora said then she sighed deeply. "So, I've made a super serious decision that might help us."

"What?" Lani and Kira both asked eagerly.

"I'll show you, otherwise I might lose my nerve." She pulled her backpack around to her front and got a long silvery bag out of her shrunken box along with her magic fairy dust vials.

"Wow!" Rhys said excitedly. "Do you have enough fairy dust to fly us all out of here and then bring us all back down?"

"Sorry, I don't have enough to do that," she said sadly.

"Seriously, you have magic fairy dust?" Shaw asked.

"Come on, you must be kidding," Wain said.

"No, she's not," Rhys said bluntly, "And I've personally experienced the magic flying dust." He then looked at Alora. "So, what else are you planning to do with it?"

"I'm using enlarging dust to normalize one of my gifts," she said sprinkling some dust on a long, thin wand she had pulled out of the bag. "Now, I'll shake the magic fairies out of my wand and ask their queen for help."

"No!" Tiana yelled dropping her flute and everyone stopped dancing and began to look angrily at the cousins.

"Tiana!" Alora said, "Play your flute or the crowd will turn back into a mad mob and stomp all over us!"

"Right...sorry!" She scooped the flute off the ground and played it, but was so upset she blew too gustily and the crowd jerked around wildly. *Yikes!* She then played Beethoven's Moonlight Sonata and everyone began waltzing serenely.

"Good, you calmed them down, but you're good at keeping your cool," she said dancing near her sister. "It's something 'I' must do now. So, even though it scares me, we're truly in a tough spot and I simply must ask the Fairy Queen to help us."

"Alora...what if...she turns you...into a toad?" Tiana asked in tiny pauses she put between the notes. "She did... threaten to do that...when you first...shook the fairies...out of your wand."

"But that time she did it accidentally, not for a good reason," Rhys said. "Now, we are seriously in big trouble."

"He's right!" Alora said so forcefully Tiana looked stunned. "Besides that, I'm so tired I might drop any minute and the Red Winkies could come get control of me. So, it's worth risking that our cause is just and the Fairy Queen will want to help us."

"She might not…want to," Tiana rasped out between notes.

"This time I think she will," Rhys said softly. "And Alora's right about it being worth a try, since it looks to me like we're all close to dropping. So, let me suggest this. Alora, first, you shake the fairies out and then let me ask for help instead of you. It might stun her into saying a quick yes."

"It also might make her angrier and have her turn you into a wort frog," Alora said utterly horrified by his suggestion.

"No, I'd be a really handsome frog and some princess would kiss me and turn me into a prince," he said smiling broadly.

Alora shook her head. "No. Auntie Roleena's note warned us that our gifts won't work if someone else tries to use them."

"Truly?" Lani asked wide-eyed. "I didn't get that note, but then again we don't use each other's gifts."

"Yes," Rhys replied wincing. "It's something I learned when I tried to use Tiana's 'Sword of Defense'. It flashed with fire and singed my hand." His eyes then lit up. "Hey Tiana, I forgot about your 'Sword of Defense'! It cleaves a barrier in front of attackers like it did with the crocodiles that appeared in this park, and it gave us a safe way to escape."

"I can…try to…but it's a big park…full of people to circle."

"And both a ridiculous and dangerous suggestion," Alora huffed shaking her finger at him. "She is certainly not going to try that! You can't possibly expect her to do that around blocks full of angry people before one of the hundreds here hit her on the head with a rock like they did to you, Rhys."

"You're right," he sighed and looked contrite for suggesting this as the rest of them agreed loudly it was too dangerous.

"Don't look so gloomy. We've reason to hope," she said brightly. "I believe the Fairy Queen will help us, and even if she winds up cursing me, maybe it'll be fun to be a frog," Alora said with a goofy but uplifting smile only she could pull off.

"I want to say you shouldn't rush into doing something this risky," Lani said anxiously. "But there's more buses coming in that are all probably filled with Red Winkie controlled people. But can even your magical fairies deal with so many?"

"With the magic they possess, I believe they can," Alora said confidently. "That means it's time to get help to stop the Red Winkies and Winkied crowd before it's too late."

"Now you choose to become a hero at the most perilous time in our lives," Tiana said with annoyance as tears filled her eyes. "That drives me crazy."

Alora gave her sister a tiny smile. "Only because you thought it would be you saving the day."

"You bet I did." Tiana then surprised her sister by grabbing her and hugging her hard then she began playing the flute again.

"Cousins, to be fair," Rhys said pointedly, "I first must warn all these people that Alora will be calling on magical fairies to make them leave if they don't go home immediately."

"You truly are getting all noble and just," Lani said softly.

"What's important is it's the right thing to do."

"I agree," Kira said," But when you mention that we're using magical fairies to do this they'll think you're crazy."

"Quite likely, but I still need to do this," he said firmly.

"How will everyone hear you?" Wain asked. "Because even if you shout, I doubt the people outside the park will hear you."

"Good point," Rhys said dancing in place as he studied the crowd. "Ah ha! The officers are still at the front of the crowd so that gives me an idea, but first has one you girls learned to use your tiara on just one person?"

"I can do it," Lani said, "If I just put it on right in front of someone and then cup it with my hands."

"Great. Then will you dance over to Officer Schmartzov with me so I can borrow his bullhorn?"

"Sure," she said grinning as they danced over to Schmartzov and Lani focused her tiara on just the officer to bedazzled him.

"Sir, I need to borrow your bullhorn a moment." Unhooking the bullhorn from the dazzled officer's belt, Rhys waltzed back to Alora and handed it to her. "Here, this ought to do the trick."

"You just took it off that officer," she gasped in surprise.

He and Lani grinned at each other. "He didn't object."

"Because he couldn't," she sputtered.

"True," Rhys said simply as Lani just smiled and shrugged.

Alora stood staring at the bullhorn until she saw her cousins look at her expectantly but 'um' was all she could choke out.

"Since it's your fairy wand, I thought you'd want to be the one to warn them," Rhys said gently. "But if you want to give the bullhorn back to me, I'll do this for you."

"No!" she shouted then winced. "Sorry, I didn't mean to yell at you, but you're right, I should do this myself." Alora took a deep breath then faced the officers, Chief Broomsky and the crowd. "All of you people need to go home now!" she shouted through the bullhorn. "Look for the closest exit and dance out of here. I warn you, for those who do not, I will release magical fairies to deal with you as they see fit 'and' when I tell you they can turn you into a frog if you refuse to do this, you may rest assured it is true. Now, it is up to you, but you've been warned of the risks. So, please go home now."

Laughter filled the air only stopping as the stout Chief of the Politically Correct Force stomped up to Alora. She clapped her hands to silence everyone then pointed her finger right at Alora.

"Shame on you," Broomsky said sharply. "You should know there's a new law against calling anyone fairies."

"But the pretty little ones I'm talking about truly 'are' called fairies, and I did say they are 'magical' fairies."

"Child, you must address me as Chief Broomsky, and pretty or not, you must not call anyone fairies. I am appalled you did so. You also need to first ask my permission to speak," she said snootily then went on about how despicable the kids all were.

"Hey, cousins," Wain said as he danced near them ignoring Broomsky's tirade as it went on and on. "Why isn't their Chief dancing like everyone else? She shouldn't be immune to our gifts like we are…or at least like we used to be."

"It's weird, but that's been changing," Kira said. "Like we now have to dance to Tiana's Piped Piper flute and shouldn't have to. So, several things are being thrown off kilter here."

"That is puzzling," Rhys said perplexed. "I bet something the Winkies are doing is keeping her from being as affected by our gifts as all the other people are."

"I think I know why," Alora said. "I've noticed there are lots more Red Winkies swarming her than anyone else. So, maybe they're able to kill the effect our gifts should have on her."

"Good point," he said and the others nodded.

"Silence! How dare you talk amongst yourselves without asking my permission!" the Chief shouted angrily. "You must be possessed by demons. Yes, that's what's wrong with all of you. I should have guessed it from the start."

"We most certainly are not possessed!" Rhys said.

"Yes, you are and it's plain to see as the nose on my face," Broomsky huffed but as she mentioned this, a man guffawed loudly and most near her snickered as this drew attention to her huge hooked nose. Then a wave of people began laughing so hard they could barely stand up and dance. Even the cousins could not stop themselves from grinning because with the Red Winkies lighting her up it spotlighted the witch-like facial feature looming so prominently on her face.

"Enough! Anyone who continues to laugh will be fined for abject rudeness," Broomsky growled as she glared at the crowd then turned back to Alora. "Look at what you've done! You made everyone behave incorrectly. This proves you are a bad influence, so no one will fault me for having you throttled."

"As you would say, that is incorrect," Alora said primly. "For you made the comment about your nose, not us. Moreover, you are the rude one for constantly threatening us. Now, you and your people must leave or I will release the fairies."

"You awful girl, I told you to stop calling them fairies!"

"No, for it's the truth. These tiny people do call themselves 'fairies', just like those you hear about in fairytales."

"Poppycock! I've heard enough of your drivel. Officers, take this mentally unsound girl away."

Rhys danced over in front of Alora moving back and forth facing the Chief and the two officers. He held his staff high to make it clear to all he was protecting her. "Chief Broomsky, it's in everyone's best interest for you to send them home 'or' to let us go by you all safely so we can end this peacefully."

"No!" she screamed and shook her fists wildly at him. "I will do no such thing, you wretched boy!"

"Watch out, Rhys. I don't know if the Red Winkies are causing this or not, but either way, I can tell she wants to deck you," Shaw said and he was not grinning as he said it.

"Officers!" Broomsky shouted so shrilly their ears hurt. "Take him away with this girl and her pretend fairy wand. In fact, take all seven of these insolent youngsters directly to jail."

The cousins all saw the officers were too busy dancing to take any action against them at all. Broomsky did not seem to realize this at all and kept repeating herself over and over again like a CD player stuck on repeat.

"She's made it obvious that she's unwilling to discuss this," Rhys said sadly as he glanced over his shoulder at his cousins and Gertie. "Is that how all of you see it?"

All the cousins nodded sharply then looked at Gertie.

"Yep, I agree fer this here filly calling herself a 'Chief' that's been spouting all this muck about you is more onery than a bad-tempered mule."

"Then are we all in agreement that it's time to take action?" Rhys asked glancing at them again.

"Yes!" his cousins all shouted and Gertie shouted 'Yep!'

Rhys then turned and looked at Alora. "So be it. We did try hard to be fair, but the Chief in charge of this Politically Correct Force group refuses to be reasonable so leaves us no other choice. Go ahead and release the fairies, Alora."

"To be clear, you want me to take fairy action now?"

"Yes," he replied firmly.

"Okay then, here I go," Alora said then she leaned in close to her sister and whispered, "But I'll tell you this first, I truly am hoping the Fairy Queen doesn't turn me into a frog."

"I know," Tiana whispered softly. "But if you are turned into one, I'll take good care of you because I really love frogs."

"Thanks…I think," she said with a tiny crooked smile.

"Sis, before you do this, I want you and everyone else to know I think you're amazingly brave," Tiana said loudly so her whole group could hear her and they agreed heartily.

"Thanks," she said a bit more brightly, but as she undid the string on the bag holding her wand, her hands were shaking.

CHAPTER FIFTEEN
THE FAIRY'S CURSE

Pangs of fear ran through Alora as she pulled the fairy wand out of its slender bag. She vividly remembered her first meeting with the fairies and the curse the fierce Queen put upon Paris when Alora used the wand frivolously. It resulted in Paris being turned into a wort frog. *Please don't turn me into a toad,* she prayed and gripped the wand firmly. She took a deep breath and shook it briskly. Fairies instantly streamed out of it making tiny pinging noises and kept coming and coming. Her eyes popped open wide to see so many more coming out this time. Within minutes, the glittering fairies covered the area over the crowd and Red Winkies like a bright, iridescent sheet. The last fairy to come out chiming loudly and glowing like a tiny twinkling star was the Fairy Queen. Alora bowed her head and curtsied like she had seen ladies in the movies do before royalty.

"Fairy Queen, I don't know how to properly address you because I don't know your name," she said biting her lip to keep it from trembling.

"I am called the Fairy Queen as my title is my name," she said in a regal manner as she floated in front of Alora's face.

Alora glanced around and saw the crowd staring in awe at the fairy queen for she sparkled like diamonds which threw off rainbow-colored lights. *She's certainly grabbed the attention of everyone here because they're all captivated by her. They've also stopped talking...or has she silenced them?*

"Fairy Queen, why is your title a name?"

"My fairy people believe giving a name to a queen or king diminishes this exalted position. Know that when this noble title is earned by one of us, we must from that moment on be totally and impartially fair, and immune to bias in all our judgments and works," she said in the grand manner a ruler of this magical realm explained this to those outside their kingdom.

"That sounds super wise to do," Alora said sincerely.

"It is. For these are not idle words. It is a fact."

Wow, I can tell she truly means this. "Yes, I see that."

"No, you do not see this clearly as yet. But you will in time. Now, explain why you brought me and my fairies forth."

"First, allow me to introduce myself for I do have a name. It is Alora, and I'm ever-so humbled and honored to have the opportunity to meet you now properly, good Fairy Queen."

"Human girl, do not waste time showering me with praises. Why did you bring us here? Wait. Before you speak, I do hope you paid heed to my warning. It must be for a worthy cause this time or you will pay serious consequences."

"Yes, your majesty, it is indeed for worthy reasons," Alora said gulping nervously then told her what happened to her aunts and the people on Earth due to the Red Winkies coming. At the end she added, "We are in desperate need of your help to get free of their control which is why I called upon you and your people. I pray it is the right thing to do during this dreadful time of ours and dearly hope you can see it's truly justified."

"I will look into this myself." She gazed deeply into Alora's eyes then her cousins and the crowd her wings moving fast as a hummingbird's. Next, she studied the Red Winkies and began glowing more brightly. She then looked back at Alora. "I see the Red Winkies are using their energy to direct these people to do their will. I also know they did great mischief here before."

"My two aunts lie paralyzed because of them," Alora said pointing at their prone bodies encircled by her group. "Our aunts told us they came here before and caused trouble, but this time differs. This time they're making our people act strangely and even angrily who did not act this way before they came."

The Fairy Queen wagged a finger at Alora. "From what we have observed, many of your people were prone to these kinds of behavior before they arrived."

Alora sighed heavily and nodded. "True, but most of us are working on not doing embarrassing or mean actions anymore."

"Then I pray you do so soon, especially your tendency to act violently and wage war."

"Yes, we have much to improve upon, but in time we will."

"We shall see, and I truly hope you succeed in doing this."

"Me too, but for right now, I just hope you feel it was right of me to call upon you this time."

"I do," she said softly instead of like an angry judge as she had before. "I also find you are a good Earthling to face me as kindly as you have knowing I might turn you into a frog or a toad stool if I found you lacking sincerity in your cause."

Alora sighed with relief. "Thank you. Now, do bear with me for I must go straight to the point. My cousins and I are at our wits end with worry. Can you help us 'de-winkify' ourselves?"

"De-winkify?"

"Sorry, de-winkify is a word that came to me as the best way to describe this. What I mean by it is how do we get the Red Winkies off our people and send them back to where they came from so everyone altered by them can go back to normal?"

"Hmmm, de-winkify. Interesting word choice, and it does in essence convey the idea of the removal of the Red Winkies. I like that word. May I use it?"

"Certainly, I'd be honored if you did."

"Good. We shall use that from now on. Thank you."

"You're welcome…but please help us. How do we do this?"

"I sense you and the six humans here you call 'cousins' do truly wish to stop them from controlling your people. But even with your gifts, you do not have the ability to do this. So, with your permission, we will 'de-winkify' your people for you."

"Can you and your fairies do this without being harmed? Because your tiny people look fragile," she said anxiously. "I don't want any of you to get hurt due to us and our problems with the Red Winkies here on Earth."

"So, you are worried about us?" she asked and Alora nodded vigorously. "Again, how kind. Yet another reason for me to like some humans. It leads me to think there is hope for your people and more reason to help you. For though we are small compared to your kind, we are not fragile, and our tiny wands have more power than your gifts do, so can rid you of the Red Winkies."

"Your wands can truly do that?" Alora gasped.

"Yes."

"Wonderful!"

"First, know this. You must formally give us permission before we can remove the Red Winkies from your people. We will then contain them while the Universe's overseers decide their fate. Now, since you were given charge of your Earth Ambassador's Fairy Wand, your say in this will be taken into consideration. They do handle urgent matters like this swiftly so be aware their decision might be put into action today."

"Today? That's an awfully quick judgement to make."

"It is, but it will be done fairly by beings with infinity more knowledge and wisdom than your Earth people currently have. So said, do we have your permission to begin this process?"

Alora bit her lip and thought it over. "This might be odd of me to ask, but can this be done without hurting them?"

"Are you telling me as troublesome as the Red Winkies have been to your people, you are even worried about hurting them?"

"Well…yes, I am."

"Then be at peace for they will not be harmed."

"That's good to know, but can you first tell me more about these overseers of the Universe who will decide this?"

"They come from the most learned and wise of our Universe, but I have little time to expand on this. In brief, they are noble judges of the highest power in existence. For now, we must act before the Red Winkies incite this crowd enough to overwhelm you and your cousins. Do we have your permission?"

Alora took a deep breath and nodded. "Yes, you do."

"Good. Now, we need you and your cousins to put your gifts away for they will hinder our ability to separate the Red Winkie beings from your highly 'winkified' crowd of humans."

"Is it safe for us to put them away without this angry crowd then hurting all of us?"

"Yes, we will keep you all safe from harm," she replied then smiled. "I wager most here will be glad to stop having to dance. The crowd will also be glad to not be dazzled by your tiara's or shoved by your staffs, headbands, and tiny lion tamer's chair."

"So, we can trust you to protect us from this crowd?"

"Yes, and keep in mind we showed faith by coming both times you beckoned us, even though the first time was done wrongly. You must have faith in us to do this. Just know the magical power the Creator of the Universe gave us is strong."

Alora nodded then said solemnly to her cousins, "I do so believe her. Now, as you heard, the Fairy Queen said we must put all our gifts away so they don't interfere with theirs as they remove the Red Winkies from all these folks so please do this."

"Are you sure putting them all away is wise to do?" Shaw asked and the other older cousins also looked skeptical. "Rhys did get hit from behind by that Chief of theirs and she's still telling others to attack us. I think we should discuss this first."

"Come on, be fair to Alora with what she risked for our sakes," Rhys said, "We need to show we'll stand behind her in this. So, I'm going to show my faith in her for what she's been able to arrange with the Fairy Queen." He laid down his staff and took off his crown which turned back into a top hat.

"Yes, you've done good, sis," Tiana said putting her flute back in its bag and setting it on the ground.

"Thank you," Alora said softly to Rhys and her sister.

"For you three showing your good faith I will give the others an act of good faith," the Fairy Queen said waving her wand. A soft golden light flowed from its tip widening into a low rolling mist that billowed softly across the entire area. To the cousin's amazement, the crowd stopped dancing and none of them tried to attack the cousins. Seeing this, the four older cousins looked at each other and nodded then set all their gifts down. As they did this the Fairy Queen gave a nod to her fairies. They waved their wands over the crowd bathing them in an iridescent glitter and the people no longer looked mad, just baffled. They stood in place calmly, even Broomsky to the cousin's surprise. The thousands upon thousands of tiny flittering fairies lined up row upon row creating a tall sparkling wall around the seven cousins, their aunts and Paris as another wall of fairies formed around the crowd covered with Red Winkies.

"My fairies are now protecting your group while others hold both the Red Winkies and crowd in place," the Fairy Queen said to Alora. "Now, to keep your group away from the power we must use to contain the Red Winkies, I need you to move your group five blocks away from here. My fairies will protect you as you do this, but do so now for it takes a lot of power to hold them. Then we will remove the Red Winkies from this crowd."

"Tiana, let's go to Summit Park, it's near here," Alora said.

"Good idea, since it's four blocks east and three blocks north of here it should be far enough away for us to be safe."

"Yes, that is a safe distance away," the Fairy Queen said.

"Then we'll head over there right now," Alora said.

"Good, and do so quickly due to the energy we must expend to control the Red Winkies and this huge crowd."

"We'll need your fairies to let us pass through their wall."

"Of course, and twenty will come with you to protect you then fly back to me to let me know you arrived safely." With a flick of her finger, the fairies opened a space for their group.

"Thank you so much," Alora said with a curtsy to the queen then she turned to Rhys as the Queen flew off. "Will you, Shaw and Wain take Aunt Gertie to Summit Park?"

"Sure, no problem, and we can take Aunt Roleena too."

"No, we girls will be taking her, because if she wakes, she'll be less confused with us there."

"Okay," he said without argument to her obvious relief.

"You can either get going or follow us for Summit Park is easy to find. It's the long, skinny park right along the freeway."

"Got it. All right, you guys, let's do this," Rhys said. Shaw and Wain nodded and Rhys hooked Gertie up to his waist.

The four girls tied one of their hands to a hand or foot on Roleena's floating body using her numerous gypsy scarves. As they finished, they found the boys waiting for them with twenty fairies. They joined them and all walked up to Summit Park. As they got there the fairies told them their Queen would let them know when they were done and flit off.

A minute later, the cousins and Gertie saw a bright glow over Garfield Park and the surrounding area. Ten long minutes later, the brilliant Fairy Queen rose high above the big cloud of fairies that covered the park like a gleaming blanket. She then flew swiftly over to Alora.

"My fairies scooted all the Winkied people in 'and' around Garfield Park into one large group inside it. So, gathering the Red Winkie infected crowd together is complete," the Fairy Queen said hovering in front of her face.

"Wow, that was fast!" she said and the queen smiled.

"My people are gifted, swift, and efficient, for which I am grateful. Now, may we will begin the next phase?"

"What exactly is the next phase to be?"

"We totally separate the Red Winkies from your humans."

"Which we will all thank you immensely for doing."

Suddenly they heard a woman's angry shriek coming from the lower park even though they were seven blocks away and the Fairy Queen sighed. "It seems not all of you are."

"No, not all, and I know who that is," Alora said groaning for the scream came from none other than the irate PCF Chief. "However, I 'am' super grateful as are my cousins and aunts."

"I am glad to hear that. Now, prepare yourselves, for after we remove the Red Winkies you will have many people feeling bewildered and may even wonder how they got to the park."

"I understand being confused since these last two days have been mind-boggling for my sister, cousin Rhys, and me after all the strange things we've seen and been through."

"With just what I have seen here, I can understand that. Now, shall I give the order?" the Fairy Queen asked.

"But how can they possibly hear you from way up here?"

"The same way the crowds heard us even though some were blocks away. For as small as we are we can make our voices travel through the air more easily than you can. So, if we want, we can be heard by people miles away."

"Amazing!"

"A concise comment, but not an answer. May I continue?"

"Can I first ask my cousins and Aunt Gertie so I have their agreement on this too?" she asked glancing at them.

"That's a good idea, and a fair one too," Rhys said.

"Do as you wish Alora, but decide quickly for every second drains our power," the Fairy Queen said, "And only you can give me permission as you are the one given the Fairy Wand."

Alora turned to her cousins and Gertie. "Should I give her permission to do this?" They all immediately shouted, "Yes!"

Alora looked back at the Fairy Queen and nodded. "You have my permission to give your fairies the order to do this."

"As you wish." The Fairy Queen rose high in the air calling out loudly to her fairies and in a way everyone in Garfield and Summit Park could hear her. "My dear fairy folk, we will now use our wands to whisk all the humans in the lower park with our blue lights to immobilize the Red Winkies around them.

Then on my say we will flush them off with our rainbow lights." The Queen then flew off to Garfield Park to join them.

Those in Summit Park could not see Garfield Park, but did see flashes of blue lights over the area. Those in Garfield Park saw a blazing Fairy Queen leading tens of thousands of fairies into flashing their blue lights over all the people there.

After the fairies immobilized the Red Winkies, the Queen rose high in the air again. "Now, we are going to flush the Red Winkies off of you humans," she said and those in Summit Park also heard her. She pointed her wand like holding a hose and shook it. A rainbow spray of light fired out of its tip like a July Fourth fireworks finale and with a nod to her all her fairies, tens of thousands of them fired off their wands and rainbows of light showered the people like a cleansing spray. But the cousins then gasped for at that same moment they heard earsplitting squeals.

"That's horrific," Lani said shivering and Kira nodded.

"Let's go find out if something went wrong," Wain said.

"I agree," Shaw said. "We might need to help them."

"No!" Alora said so sharply the others were stunned and stayed put. "I will ask the Fairy Queen about this first. For she promised me no one would be hurt by this and I trust her at her word which we all have seen her words been good."

"True," Rhys said. "We mustn't rush into drawing the wrong conclusion. Being your leader, I'll go see what's going on and then report back to you right away."

"No, I must go," Alora said firmly. "For though you wear the crown, I was given the Fairy Wand. That makes it my responsibility to see to this."

"Okay, but I'm coming with you."

"Me too, for the three of us have been in this battle with the Red Winkies from the start, so we do this together," Tiana said.

"Hey, we four also believe in this stick together 'All for one, and one for all' musketeer stuff. So, we're in it with you," Shaw said and Lani, Kira, and Wain nodded sharply in agreement.

"Fine," Alora said, "But you all must wait for me to decide what to do regarding the fairies. So, first we stop at the corner of 23rd street and take a look down at Garfield Park before making a decision to go any further."

"I'm sure we all agree. Right?" Rhys asked the others but the look he gave them said they had better do so and they nodded.

"I am super glad you want to stick together," Alora said, "But we can't leave our aunts so we need to take them too."

"Same as usual then," Shaw wise-cracked.

"That it is," Rhys said. "Let's go hook them both up."

They hooked them up and collected their gear then sprinted to the corner of the overpass and 23rd Street towing Gertie and Roleena along like floats, with Paris sitting on Roleena like a guard. Five minutes later, they stopped to look down the hill and gaped. They could see the Red Winkies had been removed from all the people and were floating way over their heads with a thick layer of the fairies between the two groups. Yet for no apparent reason they could see, the squealing continued.

"Fairy Queen!" Alora shouted. "I don't want anyone hurt!"

The Fairy Queen flew up to her, her wings gently brushing her cheek. "Dear girl, do not despair. No one is being hurt."

"Then why is everyone screaming?" she asked fretfully.

"Your people are not screaming. What you hear is the Red Winkie's temper tantrum in the form of high-pitched energy squeals. You see, they hate being removed from their human host's because it was an easy energy source for them."

"But it sounds like they're dying," she said worriedly.

"They are alive and well, but they are extremely unhappy about losing such an easily manipulated energy source."

"Easily manipulated?" Alora asked frowning.

"You saw them easily controlling other people yourself."

"True," she sighed. "Can we do anything to help them?"

"Not as yet, unless you wish to let them use you. Do you?"

"No."

"Then you must be patient and wait for them to calm down."

An hour later, the squeals petered out and the only sound coming from the Red Winkies was like the hum of a beehive.

"Now you can hear this huge cloud of Red Winkies is just buzzing softly as they float ten of your feet above all these human's heads. But I'll keep this thick layer of fairies between them to stay safe," the Fairy Queen said as she lit on Alora's shoulder, "Also note they are now a softer color of red."

"Yes, but why?" Alora asked and the others listened closely.

"It is because they have been mildly neutralized by the power given me and my fairies by the Universe."

"But they're unharmed, true?"

"Yes, we sedated them to keep them from reattaching."

"Oh...okay. That seems wise to me. What's next?"

"Next, you tell me how you think they should be dealt with."

"I thought you said that was decided by your overseers."

"But I also said you can have a say in what to do too."

"I'm not sure what to do. Can you give me a suggestion?"

"You could deal with them lightly and scold them or do so severely and suggest dropping them in the ocean."

"But they avoid water so what would happen to them then?"

"They would fizzle out and die," she said candidly.

"How horrible!" she gasped and they all looked revolted.

"That's too severe and would be unjust to do to them," Rhys said. "Especially without a fair trial."

"I agree," Tiana said and the others nodded.

"Me too," Alora said. "That's way too harsh."

"You are still the one who must tell us what you think should be done with them since you are the one who brought us forth to rid you of the Red Winkies."

"My goodness! I don't know. My group never discussed what to do with them if we got free of them."

"That is unfortunate, but you must decide now. For due to your Earth's heavier gravity, we fairies cannot stay here for more than this day or we will be crushed by the forces here."

"Oh no!" Alora gasped. "I most certainly don't want that to happen to your dear little people, but nothing's coming to mind as to what to do with them."

"How about we all put our heads together on this and then discuss what we think is fair?" Rhys asked gently seeing her eyes fill with tears. "We can also ask Gertie for his input since he's dealt with a lot more difficult things in life than we have."

"That's a super suggestion." Alora ran to Gertie and grabbed his hand. "What do you think we should do, Aunt Gertie?"

"Well, doggies. I don't know right off the top of head. But it'd help me a heap to do this fast figuring if ye took the stress off me by first fixing yer aunt's and my paralysis. So, missy, can ye ask yer magical Fairy Queen friend if she can undo this here rigidity them Red Winkies fettered me and her with?"

Alora turned to the Fairy Queen. "Can your magical energy restore our aunts' bodies back to the way they were?"

"Yes, I can if you wish for me to do this."

"I do! I so, so wish you to make them normal again!" Alora said clapping her hands excitedly.

"Very well, as you wish," the Fairy Queen said and she gave Gertie a tiny knowing smile realizing he was quite aware that she could so this. She flew over Roleena and Gertie waving her tiny fairy wand at them and a white light flowed through them. "There, the light has washed all the ill effects away from them."

"My gracious," Roleena said brightly as she slowly sat up and stretched her arms. "She's right. I thank you, Fairy Queen! For I feel fine now and I'm thrilled to finally be set right!"

"Dern tootin'," Gertie said. "I feel fine as frogs' hair and I'm de-lighted to be able to wiggle my fingers and toes again." He then belly-laughed so heartily the cousins and Roleena did too.

The cousins cheered and hugged their 'aunts' and each other but their revery was cut short a moment later.

"Yikes!" Tiana yelled and pointed at the western sky.

They all looked the direction she pointed and their eyes popped open wide to see enormous crackling storm clouds racing their way. Seconds later, the sky was covered with clouds so dark and thick it looked like night was on them, even though it was midday. Bolts of lightning then shot across the sky accompanied by loud booms and they all flinched.

"Are the Red Winkies doing this?" Alora asked the Fairy Queen as she clung to Gertie's hand.

"This is not their doing," the Fairy Queen said simply.

"Nope, it's not," Gertie groaned. "If this be what I fear it is, I reckon there's a heap more trouble coming our way than them Red Winkies were. So, dig down and brace yerselves, fer we might be in fer a different kind of a fight fer our lives."

CHAPTER SIXTEEN
THE ANGRY GIANTS

Tiana, Alora and Rhys gaped in astonishment as did their cousins and the crowd as five giant human-shaped beings flew down through the clouds on large glowing discs that crackled like snapped electrical lines. One male holding what looked like sticks made of lightning tossed one across the sky like a flaming spear. It boomed so loud the ground vibrated.

"I know who threw that lightning bolt," Tiana said.

"You know that giant man up there?" Lani asked in awe.

"Yes. So does Alora. That's Sir Hephaestus. He visits Aunt Roleena a lot and she told us he's a galactic level genius who's made astonishing inventions. I just know he's really kind."

"He just looks dangerous to me since he's wielding lightning like that," Wain said tersely as the discs sped toward them.

"He can be if provoked," Roleena said then glanced at Rhys. "You must all be on your best behavior now."

"Hey, I 'am' behaving," he said looking wounded.

"Actually, Aunt Roleena," Tiana said, "It might surprise you as much as it did us, but he's nice now and really brave too."

Rhys gaped in surprise to hear her defend him. "Thanks!"

Roleena brows arched up. "I'm glad to hear this, but I recall Rhys dismantling Sir Hephaestus new robot while he was away. I stopped him but I was furious he did that, and so was he."

Rhys sighed heavily and nodded. "I just wanted to see how it was made. I still feel bad about doing that. I also promised I wouldn't do anything like that again, and I haven't."

"Good," she huffed and focused on the five giants as their discs slowed down. She looked at the crowd who backed away from the giants until the wall of fairies surrounding the park kept them from going further, and noted their Chief Broomsky hid deep among them. "They're wise to move away," she said smiling knowingly as the giants set down,

"Aunt Roleena, those giants crackle with light like their discs but some have a gray tinge to them." Kira said. "Why is that?"

"It's because their emotions tint the energy they emit. Gray means they feel ill, but it's not due to the Red Winkies. It's due to the human abuse our planet is enduring," she said sadly.

"True, it is suffering from that badly," Lani whispered.

"Yes, it is, my dear…very badly."

The five giant ten to twelve-foot-tall beings snapped their fingers as they stepped off their discs which then melted into the energy veil around them. They all strode over to Roleena and Gertie and gave them a nod. To Tiana's delight, Hephaestus gave her and Alora a nod too. She nodded back noticing they were the only ones among the cousins not gaping at the giants.

"Who are these huge beings?" Shaw asked looking at Rhys.

"I only know the tallest one is Sir Hephaestus and that he's the genius inventor who designed most of their robotic units and the advanced weaponry they use."

"He sure is glaring at you," Wain said wide-eyed.

"Yeah. I noticed," he said wincing.

"Alora and I have met them all," Tiana said. "Lady Artemis has a bow and quiver of arrows slung over one shoulder and a huge spear in her other hand with a shield strapped to her arm."

Shaw shrugged. "Their weapons are big, but they would seem more threatening if they didn't look so primitive."

"Not as primitive as you think," Tiana said. "Her spear can level an army and the arrows are tipped with explosives."

"Wow! Not so primitive then. So, who are the others?"

"We met them and know their names but not much about them. We met that big male with scales covering his body two years ago when we went to the ocean with Aunt Roleena. He swam to the shore to talk to her and she introduced him as Lord Triton, son of Poseidon the sea god. The two oriental looking ones wearing orange robes are Lord Yin and Lady Yang. We met them on an archeological dig we went on with her the year after we went on the ocean trip."

"Yin and Yang?" Wain asked curiously. "I read about them in Larousse's Encyclopedia of Mythology. It was on a shelf in your library, Aunt Roleena. It said Yin is darkness, and Yang is light. But I thought they were cryptic ideas, not real live aliens."

"As you can see now," she said, "These mighty beings do exist, and if you speak or talk of them you must use their titles 'Lord' Yin and 'Lady' Yang. The water being is also a 'Lord'."

"Hey, how come we never got to go on these trips?" Shaw asked and the other older cousins looked at her questioningly.

"Ah, but I did ask you to come on these trips and more, but you were all too busy with school and friends to come away for weeks or months at a time," she said simply.

"True," Kira said sighing and the shrugs and nods from the other cousins confirmed this was true for them too.

"Aunt Roleena," Wain said, "The Chinese history book I read said Yin and Yang represent two opposing forces in the universe, not aliens like—"

"Silence!" Yin said to Wain so harshly he jerked back from the sleek, muscular giant who then turned to Roleena. "Lady Roleena, after the Red Winkies caused trouble last time why did you not use your ejector unit we gave you and repel them from this planet when they came here this time?"

"Because I was far away having gone to contact our Galactic High Council with statistics they wanted regarding an extinction event expected to occur on Earth soon. But I am surprised you asked as a member of this council you would know this."

"Yes, I am aware of this, but I do not recall in your report any mention of the Red Winkies assaulting this planet again."

"At that point the statistics were more important to report first since I knew I could easily subdue the Red Winkies later. After that report was given, I was about to mention them but was overtaken by them and my communication was cut off."

"Your transmission did end suddenly, but we thought it was due to the normal inference in that area of space. We did not know they had subdued you during your planetary report."

"I misjudged them. I did not think they could cut me off and nab me like that as they never dropped in so quickly before or in such great numbers."

"You should have engaged the Repulser as a precaution before you left to contact the High Council," Yin said coldly.

"Lord Yin, setting up that unit takes time and cannot be done in a snap. Time is critical to the extinction event, so I relayed that first. Also, if the galactic level sending devise had been set in my home as I wished and not in a hidden mountaintop cave, I would not have had to waste time taking a disc there," she said crisply. "Moreover, I did not know the amount of Red Winkies coming were triple the size of any time they had visited Earth. To my added surprise, they were able to find me in our hidden site and drained my powers before I could get free of them, so then captured me. But I knew I could count on my nieces and nephews to rescue me." She waved a hand at Alora, Tiana, and Rhys then Kira, Lani, Wain and Shaw gazing at them proudly. "They are all clever and brave, hence they did so."

Yin glanced around the park and his eyes focused on Rhys' pack. "I think these humans only did this after miraculously finding Sir Hephaestus' tracking devices which I see in a crate tied to a pack I sense was carried by the young Earthlings here."

"So, what is your point?"

"It is curious they found restricted equipment that was not authorized by our Council for any human but Sir Gertie to use."

"Yep, and it's a dern good thing this here old Earthling didn't know that restriction." Gertie said. "So, fates been kind to us. I lucked out and got hold of them fancy gizmos figurin' I might need them someday if them Winkie varmints came back. Sure-as-shootin' they did and I'm glad I had 'em. Fer that made it plum possible fer them kids to use the trackers to find me and Roleena when things started going down the toilet here."

"Sir Gertie, using an advanced species device without a proper permit is against our galactic laws," Yin said angrily.

"None they knew of. Right kids?" he asked and they nodded vigorously. "Fact is, even I'm mostly unaware of all yer fancy galactic laws. Too mindboggling fer me to figure 'em all out."

Yin reached out to grab him, but Yang stepped in his way. "Lord Yin, they are mindboggling to most beings. Now, Sir Gertie please explain to me what you meant by saying 'things went down the toilet here," the lovely Asian-looking female giant said calmly, totally opposite Yin's angry attitude.

"Well, Lady Yang, it's a crude way of saying everything went wrong in the worst possible way," he said frankly.

"Which it appears it did," Yang said sighing.

"Ye can bet yer boots it did, and I'd say that's purdy dern clear since all them folks here were lit up with Red Winkies until them good fairies plucked them off of them."

"I want a fact made clear to me," Yin said eyeing Roleena. "Did you know the Red Winkies were here when you left?"

"Yes," Roleena told him frankly.

"As one of this planet's protectors I still say you should have used the Repulser and dealt with them first," Yin said sternly.

Roleena stood up tall and put her hands firmly on her hips facing Yin boldly. "As I already told you, I had to deliver an urgent report to the High Council on critical matters here and was unaware of the vast numbers coming when I left."

"You should have checked on this before you left!"

"Lord Yin," Yang said giving him such a pained look Yin fell silent. "I ask you to stop beating her down with your angry words. For though this escalated into a serious problem, I sense the good coming from this. For it will cause some here to find a way to make this end well for 'all' our sides."

"Your eternal optimism occasionally misreads the timelines, Lady Yang," Yin said pointedly. "These situations do not always end as well as 'you' wish them to."

"That is true, but I also feel strongly this will come to pass."

"Will it? I see the Red Winkies turning all these 'humans' into another race of puppet people. It is a poor risk and—"

"Enough!" Roleena said in a deep booming voice then to the cousin's surprise, she grew to the height of the other giants. "Arguing about what has already passed will not help anything or anyone here. Let us just fix this mess by—"

"Fix the mess your lack of judgment caused us all?" Yin cut in and his eyes narrowed as he reached in his robe's pocket.

In a flash, Artemis drew an arrow and trained it on him. "Be still, Lord Yin. Let her say how she thinks we can fix this."

"Oh no! Why is Lady Artemis pointing a bow and arrow at him?" Alora asked in a hoarse whisper.

"I'm guessing it's because he has a weapon in his pocket that he's thinking about using on us right now," Tiana said tersely.

Roleena leaned down and murmured to them, "You could be right, for I sense this Winkie problem angered him greatly as his nostril's only flare like this when he's about to toss a weapon. If it's a neutralizing star, it can numb the mind of any head they hit. So, tell your cousins to hit the ground and cover their heads if I raise my fist high."

Tiana and Alora nodded and quickly passed the message on.

Yin and Artemis stared coldly at each other for a minute then Yin tilted his head up like he was listening to someone. He then stepped back and bowed, no longer looking like he might throw any weapons at them.

"Continue, Lady Roleena," Artemis said putting her arrow back in her quiver as Yin stood down.

"I was going to say I am sure Sir Hephaestus brought his mass energy collection unit with him today." She looked at him and he nodded. "I suggest we start collecting the Red Winkies before they can recharge and reactivate themselves fully."

"I will bring it down now," the brawny giant said as he began to tap a watch-shaped device on his wrist.

"Stop!" a voice bellowed so loudly everyone flinched.

Hephaestus groaned as did the other giants as they peered the direction the voice came from. The humans crowd also looked and what they saw made them gape. Coming at them from two blocks was a female as tall as a two-story house. Her upper body was shaped like a human, but she had a a whale-like lower torso and she waddled along on flipper-shaped feet dragging a Brontosaurus-sized tail behind her. As she got to the park and began crossing it, her feet slapped the ground hard making it quiver and those standing close to her path jumped to the sides. She stopped twenty feet from the other giants and whacked the ground so hard with her huge tail it rumbled.

"Is she related to Triton?" Wain asked.

"I don't know," Tiana said and Alora shrugged.

"You kids need to keep yer yaps shut," Gertie told the seven cousins, "Or this big gal will grab ye and use you fer fish bait."

They all pinched their lip shut but gasped as she lifted her tail higher to strike it again. That instant, Artemis sped over and poked the huge giant in the chest with her spear and she froze.

"Lady Eurynome!" Artemis said banging her chest plate so hard it rang loudly and got everyone's attention, "That is quite enough! You are breaking a Galactic Law you agreed to as your planet's leader which is coming here without a permit from the Galactic High Council. Worse, you are behaving like a mean drama queen. Now, stop slapping your tail before you cause an earthquake and explain your intrusion here."

The huge whale-tailed alien sneered at Artemis but then saw fire gather in her eyes and though Eurynome was twice her size she arched back. "Very well, Lady Artemis. I will hold back," she replied although coldly.

"Good. Then get straight to the point," Artemis said pulling back but kept her spear pointed at her. "Why are you here?"

"I came with all do haste to lay claim to the Red Winkies."

"Preposterous!" Triton bellowed striking the ground with the two sharp points of his fluted fishtail which pierced the ground and water gurgled up from the holes.

"Nay, it is not!" Eurynome huffed whacking the ground near Triton with her enormous tail and the water pooling around him sprayed everyone near them.

"Both of you stop this tail slapping right now," Artemis said waving her spear at them. They glared at her but both held still.

"Where is all this water coming from?" Alora whispered to her sister as they dried off their faces with their shirt sleeves.

"Well," Tiana whispered back keeping her eyes focused on Eurynome who was in a glaring match with Triton. "I read in a book called 'Everett Remembers' that North Everett is riddled with underground springs. So, it must come from one of them."

"Then I hope they don't keep doing this and drown us."

"I doubt it can do that, but we are getting a good soaking."

"Makes me wish I wore a wetsuit under my clothes," Rhys said as water dripped down his body.

"Me too," Shaw said and Wain, Kira, and Lani nodded as they as they dabbed their faces with their sleeves.

"Thinking you can claim them does not make it so!" Triton then shouted breaking the two giant's silent glaring contest.

Eurynome laughed scornfully at the smaller half-human, half-fish being. "Little fish man, just as your father was first to lay claim to the watery dominion you all rule, I am first to lay claim to the Red Winkies, so they are mine!" She whacked the ground again spraying all near her and they groaned.

"The Red Winkies are not yours unless the Galactic Courts agree to it," he said stabbing the ground with his spiked flutes again. Two small geysers showered the people again and the crowd moaned in disgust.

"You two stop whacking your tails this instant!" Artemis told the offenders. "Or I will have the Council Elders have Galactic Command's security come deal with you."

"I 'am' an Elder," Eurynome said smugly.

"You were a Council Elder but were 'retired' from that position long ago. So, though you are a member of the Galactic Order it is as a planetary leader now," Artemis said bluntly.

"True, but that does not negate my right to make a claim on the Red Winkies."

"Only if the claim is agreed to by the Galactic Court and Council. However, you first must submit a claim with this request and then wait for their judgment."

"Then until then I want to be their temporary warden."

"No!" someone roared from above them and a burly giant with muscles like a weightlifter on steroids crash-landed near the other giants and shook the ground like a small meteor. "For I will contest the matter of who should be their warden!"

"It amazes me that giant wasn't injured when he landed that hard," Wain whispered to his cousins.

"Me too," Rhys said. "What also worries me is with anymore shouting like they're doing I might go deaf."

Kira nodded. "We might all need hearing aids after this."

"No kidding," Lani said rubbing her ears.

"So, who is this blustery fellow?" Shaw asked.

"From what I read in Aunt Roleena's journal on 'Ancient Beings of Note' this big fellow is Lord Tessup," Tiana said.

"So, he's another ancient alien visitor?" Rhys asked. "Then again, I bet he is since you read every book on ancient beings you can get your hands on and likely know this. So, tell us about Tessup in the who's who book of gods and goddesses."

"Well, from what I read, he's a powerful storm god from the early days of ancient Anatolia which is now where Turkey, Syria, Iraq and Iran are and—" Tiana paused as the burly giant bulldozed his way to where Lady Artemis stood and growled so loudly everyone covered their ears. The crowd gasped to see the massive double-sided axe he held in one hand and three bound together lightning bolts in the other.

"His lightning bolts tied together at the bottom like that make it look somewhat like Poseidon's trident," Rhys said.

"Just like in the Percy Jackson movies we—" Wain started to say but got cut off by the thundering voice of Tessup.

"Lady Eurynome, it offends me you deem you have the right to be the Red Winkies warden at will and it is an appalling presumption on your part!" he growled.

"Nay, for no one else asked to do this," she said assuredly.

"True," Artemis said. "Until now, the Galactic High Council did not know or have proof the Red Winkies escaped from their confines, and without proof, they cannot act. However, their invasion on Earth is now proof and is being discussed by the High Council, and no one can be granted rights to be their warden until they decide how they wish to deal with them."

"Ha! See?" Tessup said chuckling so hard his gigantic chest muscles bulged. "You overstepped the limits of your rights once more which is why you got kicked off the High Council."

"I did not get kicked off! I was just asked to retire," she cried whacking him with her tail, but he did not budge even an inch.

Artemis poked Eurynome in the belly hard with her spear and the whale-woman winced. "You know you cannot strike anyone unless you are assaulted first. Now, lay your tail down gently, and I do mean 'gently'."

"It was just a little slap," Eurynome complained but did as she was told. "The fact is, I was first to ask to be their warden and just need the High Council's approval, which I will get."

"Will you? The Red Winkies have the right to a fair trial and so are not our prisoners as yet," Lord Triton said bluntly.

"They are held as such," she said pointing at the Winkies who floated ten feet above the human crowd's heads with a thick layer of fairies between them. "And though the fairies are holding them now, they cannot keep them contained for more than one day so will need to hand them off to us soon anyway."

"We do not know if these are the same Red Winkies that caused trouble before. If not, it will take longer for them to decide what to do as a first offense even if it is a major one."

"Until that is decided they will need is a stout guardian like myself," Tessup said pounding his massive chest with his fist.

"You? A storm god of minor repute," Eurynome snorted.

"Minor repute?" He pointed his trident at the sky and shot a lightning spear at the clouds which flashed wickedly.

"Lord Tessup, show great care when you use the lightning device Sir Hephaestus fashioned for you," Artemis said. "Or I will ask him to repossess them from you."

"Not without a fight, because these are mine now!"

The seven cousins saw Roleena, Yang and even Yin move next to Artemis and Hephaestus making it clear they were going to support them. Everyone in the crowd held their breath and hunkered down for what looked like a fight coming on.

Suddenly, to their astonishment, a big hole opened up in the clouds. Sunlight poured through spotlighting the humans and giants like celebrities on a stage. A human-like lady giant, partially veiled by a hooded cape flew through the opening on a magnificent white-winged horse, both shimmering like moonlit waters. Someone small rode behind her but their cape's hood covered their head completely so no knew who or what they were. The giant lady eased the horse, four times the size of a Clydesdale, down to where the giants, seven cousins and Gertie stood. Rhys, Wain, Shaw and Gertie moved protectively in front of the girls but they elbowed them aside and stood by them.

"We stand together," Tiana told them decisively and she, Alora, Kira and Lani all glared pointedly at them.

"Don't get yer petticoats in a twist, missies," Gertie said. "We fellas figured it was our gentlemanly duty to protect you."

"It's super kind of you to want to protect us," Alora said, "But it's like my sister said, we stand together…all of us."

"As you should," Roleena agreed firmly. She then bowed to the lady who slid off the white steed as gracefully as a ballerina. She held an ornate scepter topped by a bejeweled orb in one hand and nodded to Roleena and the other giants. They all bowed, as did Gertie. Seeing this, the cousins bowed too. The lady let her hood all the way down which revealed a stunning bejeweled crown. The three younger cousins gaped as they immediately recognized the lady's shining face.

"Why that's…why that's…" Alora stammered wide-eyed.

"Great Lady Hera," Tiana and Rhys gasped their eyes filled with wonder for she was twice as grand and twice as tall as when they first met two days prior.

"Greetings, Great Lady," Roleena said with great respect.

"Greetings Lady Roleena. You know why I am here," she said regally, each word exuding so much authority every human including the brazen Chief Broomsky was dumbstruck.

"Yes, I do, but for the benefit of all the Earthlings here, I do wish you would explain this to them yourself."

"As it is your wish, I will speak to them, but it must be brief for the urgency of this trouble preys upon us now, So, I do not have time to expand on this fully or much time for questions whether inspired by ignorance or fear. For to delay even a few hours might cause them all to lose their lives sooner than later."

"Thank you, allow me to introduce you first." Roleena then called out to the crowd in such a commanding voice, it startled even Alora and Tiana who had been close to her all their lives.

"Great Lady Hera is from the Galactic High Council and the prime overseer of this planet. You see there is critical need to end the Red Winkie invasion here quickly to save this planet. If they don't, you that have recently been freed of them, as well as all humans on the Earth, will be under their power. For their collective power is immense and if they gain control, it will hasten a worse problem…the death of our struggling planet."

The entire area the Red Winkies filled above them began buzzing loudly like millions of angry bees as if to protest and the crowd began muttering worriedly to one another.

Hera swirled her scepter in the air and the park was flooded with a warm white light. The Winkies stopped buzzing and the crowd quieted as well. She then looked at the crowd with the loving concern of a parent fearing for their children's safety.

"Earth people, I assure you that the Red Winkies will be removed from your planet thereby freeing you of their control. However, I must first inform you of the main reason I was sent here by the heavenly ultimate power. I am here to beseech you to save your dying planet. I pray you choose to do this or your lives will end sooner than you realize," Hera said waving a hand across the crowd. "So, you can more readily attain this, I am allowed to gift you with true enlightenment for those who wish to receive it. This will fill you with the knowledge and wisdom you need to achieve this peacefully. For those who wish to have this, remain standing. Those who do not wish this lie down or walk five of what you call 'blocks' away. Please realize saving your planet is a serious life-or-death decision for you all, so decide this wisely with both your heart and mind. Time is short with this so you only have ten minutes to make your decision."

"I'm certainly not going to lay down in the water here, and I can't walk five blocks in ten minutes," an elderly man said.

Hera looked to the sky and then nodded. "I have just been told by my High Council I can give you twenty, but no more. If you wish to leave, do so now. Those who find it too physically difficult to do, get onto one of the buses sitting by this park. We will then lift the buses beyond the perimeter of this event."

Hera looked hopeful but when the old man along with a third of the people in the park hurried onto buses or walked out of the area and one woman lie down on the ground, she looked sad. After twenty minutes Hera announced their time was up and the buses were lifted away by gravitational waves coming through the hole in the clouds and set down five blocks away.

"I am grateful for those of you who remained here standing and in one minute will send you true enlightenment."

"I was hoping more would remain standing," Rhys said sighing as he looked around the park. "Well, except for Chief Broomsky, though odd as it is, she did choose to remain lying on the ground rather than leaving."

"I actually hoped their Chief would go," Tiana said gravely.

"I'm just super glad over half the people stayed," Alora said brightly. "And our cousins and aunts are among them."

"So says the optimist," she said and smiled warmly at her.

"Let's just hope there will be enough to change the killer tide that's rolling across this planet of ours," Roleena said sighing.

"Enough?" Alora asked worriedly.

"What will come can be hard to change if enough people on the planet don't—"

Hera then spoke loudly to all. "Earthlings, it is time." She raised her orb high and a beam of brilliant Light shot down from the sky into the orb and into Hera's body which began glowing even more. "Earthlings, I will now send those standing the heavenly gift of knowledge and wisdom," she said reaching out with her hands. The Light flashed out her fingers into those who stood filling them with enlightenment. Seconds later, those standing looked full of joy, not fear or anger, and began smiling warmly at those around them.

"How odd, as that light touched me, I recalled us sitting by a fire in the firepit in our backyard," Tiana told her sister. "It was a cold winter's night and we were roasting marshmallows. That snarky kid next door was making faces at us again but we'd found out he was left alone a lot so we asked him over. He looked shocked but he came and we showed him how to roast marshmallows. After that he was actually nice to us."

"Yes, that made me feel good, and it makes me realize if people want to, anyone can change," Alora said smiling.

"Well, maybe not everyone. We never could convince that angry girl down the block to come play with us. So, I guess like you said, they have to want to change and for some that's hard."

"True."

After two minutes, the Light vanished and Hera stopped glowing. She waited ten minutes for the people to adjust to the change the Light brought them then said, "I must leave soon, but before I do, I brought someone for you to meet." She turned to the passenger on her horse. "Please greet the Earthlings."

The passenger pulled the hood of the cape down revealing a pixie-like lady. "Greetings, I am Pandora," she said in a soft lilting voice and she smiled shyly though tears filled her eyes.

The girls wondered why, but their attention was diverted as Hera raised her orb again. She made circles over her head with it sending out huge blue rings of crackling light which became a thin glacial-blue sheet in the sky above the park.

"I wonder why the Great Lady put an icy-blue ceiling over our heads," Alora whispered to Tiana but she just shrugged.

That moment, the Fairy Queen flit over to Hera as fast as a hummingbird and stopped in front of her face. "What are your wishes now, Great Lady Hera?"

"Fairy Queen," Hera said warmly, "The High Council thanks you for your kindly assistance. You and yours may now leave, but before you do, absorb what power you need from my blue energy sheet above us to recharge all of you and your wands."

"First, I and my people wish to know this. Can we do this without risking your safety? For we will require a lot of energy to restore what we used to pull the Red Winkies off the humans here and to keep the Red Winkies restrained until your arrival."

"Even if you need half the power in this energy sheet, we have more than enough left to hold the Red Winkies restrained after you leave. However, I do thank you for your concern and ask you to please do this now so you are not drained further."

"Of course," the Queen said bowing. She then called out, "Good fairies, we will now reenergize from the blue cloud." As she led them into the crackling blue energy layer, the crowd saw tens of thousands of tiny blue and white sparks inside the cloud that subsided two minutes later. All the fairies then emerged from the energy layer. and the Fairy Queen flew over to Alora.

"Raise your wand up high, my dear human girl," she said.

"Raise my wand?" Alora asked still astonished by it all.

"Yes. For the fairy wand is our viaduct back and forth from our home's dimension to your dimension here."

"Oh, then of course," she said raising her wand up. "Before you leave, I want to thank you ever so much, all of you."

"You are welcome. Now, brace yourself, we're coming in." She gave her a warm smile then asked, "Are you ready?"

"Yes," she said stoutly. *At least as ready as I'll ever be doing all the weird things I've done the last couple days.*

The Fairy Queen flicked her wand across her fairies then they shot into the wand like a long, thin rope of light pinging as they did. The last and loudest was the Fairy Queen who paused to nod at Alora before she left.

Hera then looked at the seven cousins and Gertie, and briefly at Pandora. "After I speak to Ladies Roleena and Artemis I will get to the serious business of dealing with the Red Winkies." Hera then went and spoke quietly to only Roleena and Artemis.

"I wonder if she's the same Pandora from our ancient myth," Tiana said to her cousins. "If so, I bet she had something to do with the Red Winkies coming here and must get them to leave."

"That would be great," Alora said excitedly but then she saw tear running down Pandora's face. "Or is it? Because she looks super upset."

"Yikes, you're right. Maybe she was just—"

At that moment, Hera cut her off. "Attention please!" she called out and everyone fell silent. "I see most humans here are shocked to be made aware of the fact you are not alone in our Universe. It is time you knew this. It is also time you are made aware of the fact we hold 'you' responsible for the poor state of this planet. We do realize you have been deceived by powerful and greedy people here telling you there is no problem. This is a lie. So, hear this warning. Repair this planet or face extinction. No one else will do this for you. The Creator of all that exists knows most of the damage here is due to poor caretaking by you humans." As Broomsky began denying this, Hera silenced her with a flick of her finger and continued. "I sped to your planet when one of our Monitors staying here went silent. The backups sent us distress messages which is why I came myself and I did not come alone."

That instant, nine big beams of white light punched holes through the blue energy layer and the beams surrounded her. The human crowd looked upward searching for the source of the lights, but they could not be seen.

"Be warned! Each beam of light comes from one of our nine galactic defense ships which cannot be found by your detection systems. I will give you a few minutes to let the seriousness of this demonstration sink in," Hera said sternly.

"Aunt Roleena, did you know about the Monitor and back-ups?" Rhys whispered without moving his lips for he did not want to draw Hera's attention.

"Yes, for I'm one of the Monitors. Lady Artemis and Sir Hephaestus are the backups. The Great Lady is the Overseer."

"Wow, I'm surprised they sent such bigtime aliens to a planet with people they think of as just primitive idiots."

"You're not all idiots,' Gertie whispered with a grin.

"Thanks, I think."

"Gertie, be nice," Roleena said. "Remember, you're an Earthling too, and so am I."

"Only on one side of your family," he muttered.

"Nevertheless, I'll say this. Not all of the Galactic Council think humans are idiots. Just backwards in their thinking."

"Some are dern scary idiots, like them crazy warmongers."

"True. But I will continue to pray for their enlightenment. That aside, I do know some off world visitors find many of us to be kind, loving, and quite amusing at times."

"I'm just a hopin' that we all get to wising up real soon."

"Me too, Gertie. Me too."

Their group then heard angry murmurs, not from the crowd, but from a few giants. Hera then glared fiercely at Eurynome as she convinced Yin, Triton, and Tessup into being furious about how lax what was being done to the Earth by humans was being handled by the High Council as was their slow dealings with the Red Winkies.

"Do not fix your fiery eye on me, Hera," Eurynome snorted and slapped her tail, but most of the pooled water on the ground had drained off so she only splashed herself to her annoyance.

"By our laws you must use my title and show respect or be reprimanded for your rudeness, Lady Eurynome." Fire flashed from Hera's eyes and struck the area by Eurynome's feet.

"Very well, 'Great Lady', since our laws require it," she said crisply as she backed away from the hot spot.

"That they do, and you are not to slap you tail here again."

"Or what?" Eurynome asked arrogantly.

"I will stop you."

"You and who else? This handful of giants and some puny humans? Because I am not alone either and you cannot use your ships without obtaining time-consuming galactic approval."

"The way you smiled as you said that likely means you brought the Furies with you," Hera said dryly.

"Yes, it does" she gloated. Her thick tail struck the ground hard drawing up its water, spraying those all around her.

"Now, I bet we 'all' wish we had on wetsuits," Rhys said.

"No kidding," Tiana agreed noticing she was not the only one as mad as a wet cat. "And I was just starting to dry off."

"We're going to need a boat and oars soon," Shaw said as Eurynome slapped her tail again. The crowd groaned, but what was worse was the anguished squeals of the Red Winkies.

"Lady Eurynome, I see spraying us repeatedly with water has now brought down some Red Winkies through the holes in the energy layer. You best not short any out and drown the beings you claim you want to protect." Hera pointed to the tiny clouds of Winkies that had been flushed down through the nine light beams around Hera and they were winking very slowly. "If any die by your doing this, it would be considered murder."

Eurynome's eyes widened and she held her tail still. It was too late. At that moment three Winkies fell into the waterlogged ground. Their tiny lights began fading and a heartrending squeal came from all the Red Winkies above and below.

"Lady Eurynome!" Hera thundered. "This will be a mass murder. The galactic data base I'm tied into says due to the electrical connection between each and every Red Winkie in each cloud, every single one will die if but one does."

"They brought this on themselves by invading this planet!" the whalelike goddess said heatedly, but the fearful truth of her bad actions could be seen in her shocked expression.

"A poor excuse for the harm you did, Lady Eurynome," Hera said sadly. "For though the Red Winkies did invade this planet a week ago, it is still a crime to meet out punishment to a being without a fair trial first. Another crime you committed is you and the Furies came here without a permit from the High Council which by Law you are required to get first. And you, Lord Tessup, you know you must get this permit too as Lady Artemis, Lord Hephaestus, Lord Triton, Lady Yang, Lord Yin and I obtained before coming." She gave the lawbreakers a fiercely disgusted look and all but Eurynome were decent enough to appear embarrassed they broke the law.

As Hera went on dressing down the lawbreakers, Tiana whispered to Alora, "I'm going to go scoop up those three little Winkies that fell in the water and bring them to you to see if your fairies can help them. I'm hoping since they revived our aunts, they might be able to revive them too."

Alora's eyes flew open wide. "But if you pick them up, they might latch on and take control of you."

"I think they'll be too weak to do that. Besides, you have gotten braver and braver, so I know I can count on you to save me from them if they do."

"But I don't know if I can do that," Alora said frantically.

"Then do your best, because I've got to go and help them."

"I know, and I wish I was as brave as you because then I'd be going right with you."

Tiana gave her a tiny smile. "Being brave takes practice and to me I think you're now actually a true warrior in the making."

"I hope so...and I'll be cheering you on all the way."

"Me too," Rhys said overhearing this. "Because Great Lady Hera is right. They deserve a fair trial. I'm also proud of you for being so willing to do the right thing. And Alora, you 'and' I will go get Tiana if they try to take control of her."

"But can you find them with their lights out?" Alora asked.

"Yes, because I've got great eyesight and I also noted exactly where they fell," Tiana said. "Plus, when their winking lights dimmed as they hit the water, I saw they still glowed a pale pink color, so I best hurry so that doesn't fade too."

"That's my sharp girl," Roleena said beaming at her proudly.

"Whoa missy!" Gertie said grabbing hold of Tiana's arm as she began to dash off. "Not so fast. Go slow and easy 'cuz as bad as this here park's been swamped with water, you'll make swells that push them away from you if you run." He then smacked the watery ground showing her it made small ripples.

"Thanks, I see that now, so I'll go slow." She kept her eyes focused on the spot the three Red Winkies went down grateful to still see their dim pink lights floating on top of the water. She then eased towards them slowly to keep from making ripples.

"Attention Earthlings!" Hera suddenly called out to the crowd. "I was just informed by our Galactic High Council our galactic judges are now deciding what to do regarding the Red Winkies. As I wait for their verdict, I will answer any questions relevant to this Red Winkie problem you might…" she paused as she saw Tiana scooping up water. "Stop! That is not safe to drink." With a wave of her hand, Tiana froze in place.

"Great Lady, she is not going to drink it," Rhys explained quickly. "So, please set her free."

"First explain what she is doing over there."

"She is trying to save the Red Winkies that fell in the water."

"Interesting…but with their spark out, it is futile to do so."

"Please show some heart and at least let her try to do this."

"Very well." Hera waved her hand again and freed Tiana.

Tiana sighed in relief and shouted to her sister. "Alora, I scooped them up in my hands but I'm afraid if I move, I'll lose them. Can you ask the Fairy Queen if she can come to me here and revive them?"

Alora nodded and quickly got her wand out. She tapped it lightly and the Fairy Queen popped out making a sharp ping.

"Is this a life-or-death request?" the Queen asked briskly.

"Yes," Alora said and told her what had happened since the fairies left. "So, though the Red Winkies caused us a lot of trouble, we still want them to have a fair trial. But first, can you please revive the soaked Red Winkies so they don't die?"

"I am sorry to say our blue energy cannot help them," she sighed. "Still, if you want to risk it, you can use your body heat to energize them, but it might not be enough to do this." With a sad wave she then zipped back up through the wand.

"Did you hear that, Tiana?" Alora asked distraughtly.

"Yes, which is unfortunate. So, I will walk back over to you to create some more body heat in hopes that will help."

With that decided, Hera spoke to the crowd again. "As I said, as I await the Galactic Judges decision, I will answer questions regarding the Red Winkies or Earth's dire state. However, you must first raise your hand and be called on before you speak or I will freeze you like I did the female human, Tiana."

No one raised a hand and everyone looked afraid to ask the powerful and enormous alien goddess anything at all.

Wain elbowed Rhys and whispered, "Okay, fearless leader, start us all off and ask Great Lady Hera a question,"

"Fine," he said albeit warily as he raised his hand.

"You may speak," Hera said softly to ease his tension.

"Aunt Roleena told me and my cousins the Red Winkies had come here several times, though most were a long time ago. So, how did you remove them from our planet back then?"

"That is an ability currently beyond your understanding. Suffice it to say we have the technology to do this."

Wain raised his hand and she gave him permission to speak. "Did they come in ships of theirs or are they able to travel through space without one?"

"No to both questions."

"Honestly, that is not very enlightening. Can you please tell us how they got here? Or are you reluctant to answer this?"

Hera looked up at the sky then nodded and looked at him. "Our galactic observers periodically investigate developing planets. Yours is a troubling concern being such a warring one so we check it often. On one of our checks, we found the Red Winkies here and looked into it. We found out they rode here on the hull of an interstellar ship doing a previous check. It was a surprise to find out they could do this and we quickly revised all our ship's detection devices to alert us of any attempt of theirs to do this again."

"But we've just learned today they need a specific kind of energy to stay alive, so how did they obtain this?"

"We found out they were able to do this by infiltrating our exhaust ports and drawing energy from our star drive."

"Move aside, move aside," Chief Broomsky said gruffly as she shoved her way to the front of the crowd. "I demand to know what gives you the right to check on us at all."

"Earth woman, you must raise your hand to ask a question."

"I do not have to do this since I am Chief of the Politically Correct Force in this section of Everett," she said snootily.

"Arrogant human, you must do so with me!" Hera flicked her finger at Broomsky and she froze. "Now, you will do so or I will keep you frozen." She flicked her finger and released her.

"Very well," she said tersely but her arm trembled as she raised it. "My question remains. I doubt we are the only planet you found wars on. So, I think you owe us an explanation as to why you check on us so often."

Those near Broomsky moved back not wanting to risk also getting frozen because of the snooty tone she was using, but to their surprise, Hera just answered her.

"I will then explain this to you clearly," Hera said bluntly. "At first, we came every five thousand of your years to check on the lives developing here. But as Homo Sapiens began to walk the Earth millions of years later, we came to see what effect you had on it and came more often. Initially, you lived peacefully in small hunter-gatherer tribes. Then you began farming and with stable food supplies you multiplied rapidly. By our next visit, you were warring upon each other, but they were local skirmishes and did not cause irreparable harm here. However, it was a concern so we increased our visitations."

The Chief shrugged. "As you can see, we can now take care of ourselves. So, I see no reason for you to come back anymore. We'll be fine without you."

"You will 'not' be fine at all!" Hera thundered so loudly the crowd quickly moved back as her eyes filled with fire. "For you have taken care of little but yourselves! In fact, a few millennia ago we saw your violence had escalated drastically. You had become destroyers. Humans calling themselves 'Greeks' had invaded the lands around them killing all in their way. Those called 'Romans' gathered in coliseums to slaughter humans and thousands of large land animals killing so many in the lands around them they wiped them out. This was not done for food or survival. It was done for entertainment! So, we then placed permanent observation posts here."

Hera took a deep breath and continued. "We were relieved when our post reported enough Romans protested this madness to stop it. But sadly, worse atrocities followed. People in lands called 'Europe' invaded ones called 'North and South America' killing the natives. In Europe and North America, thousands of women were killed in 'witch hunts'. In lands called 'Britain', they sent armies to kill thousands of native people in a land called 'India and on an island called 'Australia'. It got worse. In the land of 'Germany', they killed millions of humans in gas kilns or mass shootings. They also made the first atomic bomb, but the land called 'United States' made one first. They did not use it on Germany. They used it on two cities on an island called 'Japan' who had destroyed their ships and humans on islands called 'Hawaii'. Now you have enough destructive power to destroy the planet. So, does that answer why we need to keep a close eye on your wildly murderous species?"

"Er...yes," Chief Broomsky squeaked out in a mouse-like voice then she scurried back and hid behind the crowd.

"Good. For this is but a partial list of the murderous atrocities done here. Sadly, there are many, many more."

Seeing the horrified crowd, Rhys raised his hand to change the subject and she nodded. "Great Lady Hera, since your ships now have barriers that prevent the Red Winkies from riding on them, how did they get—?" he broke off as Alora tugged on his sleeve hard. "Excuse me a moment, Great Lady." He turned to her taking a deep breath to keep from yelling at her. "What? And be quick, since you interrupted me and Great Lady Hera."

"I know, and I'm sorry," she said wincing. "But I'm super scared because Tiana hasn't come back yet, and now I can't even see her among the crowd. What should I do?"

"Maybe she's having difficulties getting the Winkies here, so the simple solution is let's just ask her." He then shouted, "Hey, Tiana, Alora says you found the three Red Winkies that went down. So, congrats on that. But what's the problem now?"

Tiana stood up tall to be seen. "Well, as I headed back, a Winkie slipped through my fingers and I'm having a hard time scooping it up with one hand without losing the other two."

"I'm going to go help her," Alora said stoutly.

"Bad idea, because the ripples you make could cause her to lose the one who slipped away all together," Rhys said.

"I'll be careful," she said over her shoulder having already begun to slowly slog over to her sister in the ankle-deep water.

"May I proceed, Sir Rhys?" Hera asked pointedly.

"Sorry, Great Lady, I apologize for the interruption but my cousin, Tiana, is having a problem scooping up one of the tiny Red Winkies, and we feel this is important too."

"I see," Hera said nodding as she glanced at Tiana and saw she was slowly scooping something up in the water after Alora had eased over in front of her as Alora used her hands to gently direct the water Tiana's direction. A moment later, the smiles on their faces showed her they were successful and Hera looked back at Rhys and the crowd.

"With that good deed done, I shall explain how the Red Winkies got back to Earth, an event that shocked the High Council so much they sent our best investigators to look into it. They quickly found out how they did this." Hera paused then pursed her lips and frowned. After few minutes, both humans and aliens began fidgeting but she still said nothing.

"Great Lady, most of the humans here suffered unduly due to the Red Winkies control of them. Please enlighten them now so they do not suffer more by being kept in suspense," Artemis said respectfully but firmly to make her aware she needed to speak up because her audience was becoming distressed.

"Of course. I only paused because it is a sad story that must be told." Hera waved her hand at Pandora sitting on the winged horse they both flew in on. "Pandora, as we discussed, you must be the one to explain this to these humans. Please, do so now."

"Yes, Great Lady," she said blushing as she looked at the human crowd. "The Red Winkies are here because I released them from their confinement box across the galaxy. It was in an uninhabited part of space and I thought there could be no harm in doing so. Then I found out much later they knew of Earth's location from coming here before. It took a century, but they got here by riding comets and meteors going this way after learning how to store enough energy to survive long periods in space. As they got to Earth's exosphere, they rode into its atmosphere on the aurora borealis' energy bands and caught rides to the ground on your airplanes coming in to land."

People gasped upon hearing this as did a few giants. A man in the crowd then yelled at Hera, not Pandora, to her surprise.

"How could you supposedly superior aliens with your High Council and Galactic controls miss all of this happening?"

The rumblings of the crowd showed they agreed with him. As Hera waited for them to calm down, her orb pulsed out a message to her. She tapped her scepter on the ground and it flashed so brightly the crowd immediately fell silent.

"I will now give you Earthlings the verdict I have got from the Galactic High Court," Hera said in the serious manner of a judge announcing a sentence. "They came to a consensus on the Red Winkie matter and decided that since Pandora was the one who released them, she must return them to their containment box area and seal them inside it."

High-pitched squeals shot out of all the Red Winkies above and below and everyone clasped their hands over their ears. The tiny energy beings began to flicker, but instead of their lights getting dimmer, they got brighter and then flared up brilliantly.

To Tiana and Alora's dismay, tiny clouds of Red Winkies that had been washed down through the blue energy layer above by Eurynome's splashing then latched on to the two girls, Chief Broomsky, the two PCF officers, and the crowd near them.

Tiana groaned disappointedly but when the three Winkies she had scooped up out of the water began twinkling again she could not help but feel relieved and smiled anyway.

"It's creepy having them clinging to me," Alora said.

"Me too," Tiana said, "And it seems ungrateful of them after we saved these three from drowning. Now, we need to keep them from taking control of us."

"I'll do my best, but I truly don't know exactly how to prevent that," she said biting on her lip nervously.

"I don't know either, but so far I don't feel them trying to take control making this all curiouser and curiouser for me."

"Oh my, I also don't feel that, but it's creepy to have—"

Hera's voice cut her off as it thundered out as she raised her scepter high. "Red Winkies, release these humans! This is your only warning. Do it now, otherwise I have been commanded by the Galactic High Council to put all of your lights out. Pandora will then gather you all up and put you back in the containment box area across space. Now, give way to save your lives."

"Eeeee!" Winkies squealed above and below with a terror so intense it was felt by every human for blocks around them. The teeny Red Winkie clouds lifted up and gathered up over Tiana, Alora and Chief Broomsky and looked to be shivering fearfully.

Alora looked at Tiana as tears filled her eyes. "I did not feel the Red Winkie's emotions before, but I sure do now. I can tell that being boxed up terrifies them super, super badly."

"Yes, I feel that too," Tiana said and sighed heavily.

"Please Rhys, we must find a way to keep them from getting boxed up," Alora choked out as tears rolled down her cheeks.

"Why, since they've caused us a lot of harm?" he asked her but with a questioning look, not an angry one."

"No…not really," Tiana said slowly. "Even when they were on me, they didn't try to take control. So, as I think back about what's actually happened, they've aggravated us, or chased us around, but they haven't done any real harm to us."

"Truly!" he said aghast. "They kidnapped Aunt Roleena and Gertie and imprisoned them, and attached to hundreds of people here to control their movements and inflamed their feelings to get them to do what they wanted to do. I also bet they've done this to millions on this planet. Even on a small scale did you forget how upset you and Alora got when they captured Paris?"

"That scared me super bad," Alora said. "But honestly, now I'm thinking it over calmly like Tiana, I agree with her. They haven't actually harmed any of us."

"Do you truly think paralyzing Aunt Roleena and Gertie wasn't harmful?" he asked looking at them in amazement.

"Well…it did look uncomfortable, but I don't know if it hurt them." She looked at Gertie and Roleena. "Did it hurt you?"

"It was dern maddening, but when ye get down to the brass tacks of it, it didn't hurt me a bit," Gertie said but grudgingly.

Roleena nodded. "It was exasperating, but not painful."

"Rhys, I also remember the note you got on that tiny capsule with the teeny 'scales of justice' in it. It said to only take it if you wanted justice to be the ruling part of your soul, and that all items big or 'small' must be weighed according to their merit or lack of it and it did not matter how big or small the items were."

"I did agree that above all else I wanted to be just," he said.

"And I was glad you reminded us several times over about needing to be fair," Tiana said. "So, to be fair and just now, we should reach out to the Red Winkies and see if we can find another way to be free of them without boxing them up."

"I think we should do that too," Alora said nodding.

"Okay. I do agree that we need to be fair and just. But tell me this. How do you propose we do this?" he asked pointedly.

"Have you forgotten that you're the one who wears the crown and by doing that it made you our leader?"

"Only because Tiana gave it to me."

"No, what she gave you was a top hat with a note telling her to give it to the first person who earned this right. When you bravely chose to go protect us from that crazy mad Red Winkie covered crowd, she decided it was you. Knowing her that meant she felt you could justly lead us through this super harsh time. The hat must have agreed with her since it turned into a crown when you put it on your head."

"But I don't know what to do. Maybe I should give it back. Then she can find someone to wear it who has an idea of what to do to get them to leave instead of no idea, like me."

"No, I think when she chose you as leader she chose wisely."

Tiana nodded solemnly. "I saw you change for the better by light years and all in one day. I also saw you had a real knack for how to lead. Besides, I'm guessing it's too late to hand it back and that when you put it on you accepted the responsibility by doing so. Then as I saw the top hat turn into a royal crown as you did this, I knew I was right in choosing you as our leader."

"Alora and Tiana speak the truth," Roleena said. "When you chose to put the hat on, you accepted the honor and all that it demands. With this honor, the burden of being a wise leader is yours, including dispensing justice 'and' solving problems."

Rhys balled his hands into fists to fight off the panic rising up inside of him. "I want to do what's right, but I don't know what the just and right thing is for the Red Winkies or even how to go about communicating with them to do this."

A tear rolled down Roleena's cheek. "If you don't find a way to do it, the Red Winkies and this planet will be lost."

"Aunt Roleena, please don't say that!"

"I must, for this much I foresee as being true."

"You speak of truths. So, will I. The truth is you're far wiser and informed than I am. You should be the one to settle this."

"Ah, you finally realized I'm wiser than you," Roleena said with a quirky smile.

"Yes!"

"It's good to hear you admit it, but in this instance, I'm not allowed to help solve this for you. For though part of me is of this world, part is from the stars. I'm also one of the High Council members, so any solution I helped with here would be seen as prejudiced in your favor by the Galactic Court and voted down. Face it, since you accepted the crown, you must carry the weight of its 'Mantle of Justice'."

"Mantle of justice?"

"The Mantle of Justice in this instance means you must help choose what you think should be done with the Red Winkies for invading this planet or offer a better solution. Keep in mind that a leader must work on finding ways to solve serious problems."

"So, I'm stuck with no good way of bowing out even though a bad decisions could end this world?" Rhys asked fighting the urge to run for his life.

"Yes, for there's no honorable way out of this whatsoever."

The piercing look she gave him let him know he truly could not walk away honorably. He nodded and squared his shoulders now clearly realizing he must deal with this burden. He thought hard several minutes then his eyes lit up with a hopeful gleam. "Can your leaders on the Galactic High Council ask for help from their advisors?"

"Yes," she admitted and as her kaleidoscope eyes lit up. "I sense you now have an idea of how to find a solution."

"Perhaps. Can I also choose advisors to help me?"

"Yes."

"Great! So, as my wise and trusted aunt please give me what advice you can to deal fairly with life-threatened beings."

Roleena smiled. "Shrewd of you to find a way I can help and I can say this. Though you will want to resolve this with your high innate intellect, which is heavenly given, you should also run the actions you wish to take over in your heart."

"Good advice, but not much help in finding ways to fix this."

"I know," she said apologetically. "But I'm truly limited as to what I can advise you in regards to this Red Winkie matter."

He nodded then looked at his cousins, the giants, and the crowd. "Does anyone have an idea how to work this out with the Red Winkies more fairly?" He saw everyone look at each other but a few minutes later most of them either shrugged or shook their heads looking as baffled as he did. Still, he was glad to hear his cousin's throwing ideas at one another.

"While yer cousins are busy racking their noggins," Gertie said, "I'll toss in my bit in about a way to deal with the muddy mess we're stuck in. I know you'll use a heap of good sense to do right by all, but don't go soft and give the whole farm away."

"What farm?"

"The Earth, young feller, the Earth."

"Oh. Now, I get it, but I never intended to give it away."

"Then yer off to a fine start. Now, stick this under yer hat too. It's dern important to remember ye got a slew of family here willing to pitch in and help when one of ye comes up with a bright idea, which I figure ye most certainly will."

"You bet we will. Absolutely. Right on. Do or die!" the cousins called out heartily and Gertie grinned.

Rhys's face lit up as he felt the intense sincerity and strength of their willingness to help solve this problem.

"Interesting, I heard one of you said 'do or die'," Hera said surprising them all as she spoke up. "But do you truly mean it? For it might not just be a fatal decision for the Red Winkies. It might be a fatal one for all of you. So, reflect on this carefully."

Rhys groaned. "Did you really have to bring that up and put more pressure on me? Like I don't have enough seeing all the worried faces on this big crowd, your giants glaring at me, and the Red Winkies squealing in stark raving fear."

"The pressure is on you all for your planet is sick and in the beginning of its death throes regardless of the Red Winkies."

"True," Rhys said nodding. "Great Lady, as we work to find a way to treat the Red Winkies more fairly, I'd like to know this. Will you then let 'us' carry out our idea after we come up with a better solution than putting them back in that box?"

"If the majority of the Galactic High Council thinks you have a better way to deal with them than their former way, they will let me know since they are listening in on this."

Rhys sighed heavily. "Wow. Quite a prominent audience we've attracted here."

"Indeed. They are all brilliant beings in this universe with peacemaking records. So, do your very best."

"We will," he said solemnly, waving his cousins, Gertie, and Roleena over. But as Roleena went to join them, Artemis caught her arm and shook her head so she stayed put. "Our aunt's not being allowed to do more advising," Rhys told his group.

"Yes, Lady Artemis made that quite clear," Tiana said.

"True," he agreed as did the others. "Well, let's get to work on our Red Winkie problem because I truly need your help."

They kicked around ways to remove yet still help the Red Winkies but came up with none that could do both.

"Come on, no matter how crazy the idea, we have to think of a better solution than making the Red Winkies live boxed up in a containment area. And when we do, which we will, I bet the alien's will realize that we'll also work hard on creative ways to save our planet. So, let's show them we truly can do this!"

"One for all, and all for one!" Shaw shouted with a wry grin.

"Yes!" Alora cheered enthusiastically.

"You betcha, my valiant musketeers," Gertie said gustily.

I want to cheer too, Tiana thought. *Yet it's alarming to know our entire planets at stake here to save one tiny species. But for once I'll keep my mouth shut and not mention this.*

Everyone began bouncing ideas off each other and as an hour passed all too quickly no viable idea had come to them. That moment, Rhys suddenly shot his fist in the air.

"Ah ha!" he said excitedly. "This will sound crazy, but after listening to all your ideas, a weird idea popped in my head." He then told them what he had in mind. They all looked intrigued, but some were skeptical. But after the group worked to improve it, they all agreed it could work and to give it a shot.

"Now, let's show we're together on this," Rhys said holding his hand out in the middle of their group and they all placed their hands on his. "As agreed, we all stand together as we face Great Lady Hera. Then I'll give the speech we drafted outlining our 'creative' plan, even though it actually reveals little of it. Now, I'll read our final draft again." As he did, they all nodded.

"Sounds good, Rhys," Wain said slapping his shoulder.

"And more importantly, sincere," Lani said.

"Okay, here we go," Rhys said. The seven cousins and Gertie all stood up facing Hera with him in the middle. 'Great Lady Hera, and those of the Galactic High Council, we seven cousins and Sir Gertie first want you to know we 'will' devote our lives to saving this planet. We strive to find lots of others to help and work hard to achieve this. To start, we will use all our abilities and sense of fairness to find a way to free of the Red Winkies and in a way they do not need to be in a boxed area. To do so, we are counting on your wise Galactic High Council to be compassionate and let us do this in our uniquely human way. We will be grateful for this and thank you for the opportunity."

Hera's lips were pinched together and she frowned deeply. "Indeed?" she finally asked looking skeptical.

"Yes," Rhys said wholeheartedly.

"I hear your sincerity, which is good, but not any plan."

"That is because we realized we have to show you our plan in action for it is too hard to put into words."

"Then prove to me that you 'all' believe in your plan to the extent that you will pledge your lives on it."

Rhys grit his teeth and though his heart beat faster than a rabbit's he said firmly, "Yes, I pledge my life on this." He then looked at his cousins and Gertie. They all paled a bit but each of them bravely told Hera they too pledged their lives on this."

"May we now set our plan into action, Great Lady Hera?"

"I still prefer you tell me your plan," she said warily.

"From the doubt I hear in your voice, I can tell you question our abilities. That proves to me we must show you our plan. After how far we've come after the alien challenges we had to deal with, I truly believe you should give us this chance. For our ways will flex more than yours will to work with the unusual situations to likely occur while dealing with these tiny aliens. I know it's a lot to ask your advanced kind and it will take a generous act of faith, but after all we did to get past millions of Red Winkies to save our aunt and others, I feel we earned this opportunity to show you we can do this."

"You have done well to achieve what you have with your limited resources and knowledge, but some of our council thinks you have not yet earned this act of faith you ask for."

"I'm sad to hear that. I understand why, but there are many good humans and we want to prove this to you. To do so we need a show of faith as our plan uses human creativity and flexibility which will make little sense to extraordinary off-world beings as yourselves. So, like the times you told us we would not understand answers to our questions, the workings of our human plan will not make sense to you. We have now been put in a tough situation, for to earn your faith, we must quickly solve a tricky problem with tiny, terrified energy beings. In the little time we have to do it, I can't explain the flexible routes and tangents the plan might have to take or how we might need to improvise since we don't know much about the Red Winkie's lives. As we find out more, we'll likely have to flex quickly to find the right way to resolve this. Please give us the opportunity to use our plan or we can't prove ourselves in the little time we have. Worse, we overheard a few of you say any plan of ours to find a better solution for the Red Winkies is futile. We disagree. We believe our flexible plan will find one. We know this puts you in a tight corner, but how else can we give you a reason to have faith in us in such short order?"

"You have put forth a strong argument in regards to letting you do this. However, it does put me in a tough spot. What is problematic is knowing the irrational, violent tendencies of humans. It makes me wonder if I should take the chance to show this faith in mere mortals. So, give me more reasons to allow you to attempt this 'unknown' plan of yours."

"It is because we are mortal humans and this is our planet. We can and will do better. My proof is those with me can tell you I chose to change for the better. If I can, all who chose to can then they can guide others to do this. We will appeal to the Red Winkies to find other ways to live that don't cause serious trouble like they did here and on other planets in the past. That time is gone, so let us bring about a better future. One where we have the chance to fix the problems here. For we stand to lose more than you do if we fail."

"Do not be naïve," she said plainly. "This is a rare planet. Its loss would be a serious one to the Great Universe if you fail to change your ways and save it."

"But we are risking our lives for the opportunity to save it. After all, preserving life, and I mean 'all' life, is what's most important here. This includes the lives of the Red Winkies."

"Do you and the young humans in your group you call 'cousins' truly understand the life and death risk here?"

Rhys looked at his group and they all nodded sharply. "Yes," he said as he turned back to her. "Now, I beg of you, let us give this a go."

"Give this a go? What does this saying mean to you?"

"It means we know time is running out for us here. So, let us put into action what we feel will 'truly' create a better fix for us and the Red Winkies than boxes, prisons, or death."

"You said 'truly'. Will you let me look deep in your eyes which we have learned are the windows into your soul to see your truth?"

"Yes," Rhys said.

"What say the others in your group with you? Will they all allow me to study their souls too?"

"I'm sure they will, but to be fair, I must ask." He turned and gazed at his group solemnly. "Well, my dear cousins and Sir Gertie? What do you say to having some serious soul searching done by Great Lady Hera?"

No one hesitated one iota. His cousins and Gertie all nodded sharply and then each affirmed their willingness to do this.

"We are all willing," he told Hera assuredly.

One by one she stared into each of the cousin's and Gertie's eyes. To all those they explained this to later, they said they felt she truly reached into their very souls. They also all saw that as she gazed at each of them closely, her eyes widened more and more in surprise and after the last one she nodded.

"I see your truth in wishing to resolve this matter yourselves. I will now speak to the Galactic High Council privately and see what they say." Hera gazed at the sky for several minutes then looked at all the giants in the park. "I and the majority of the Galactic High Council have voted to give the Earthlings one chance to deal with the Red Winkies. Hopefully, they will—"

"No!" Eurynome screamed cutting off Hera and her Furies flapped around the park screeching so loudly everyone winced. "Does our High Council not realize this imbecilic decision on their part will start a war in the heavens! One I will back!"

"Lady Eurynome, I am shocked you would threaten the Galactic High Council with something so dire," Hera said looking appalled. "For there's no need to go to war over this singular matter here."

"Yes, there is! Tell them to rethink this decision this instant and change their vote or you can charge up your orb and Lady Artemis can start sharpening her spear!"

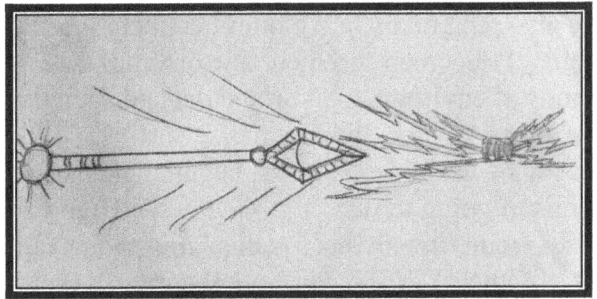

CHAPTER SEVENTEEN
WAR IN THE PARK

"Threatening war is a grave matter," Hera said pointedly.

"Yet this is what you provoke us into by being unwilling to heed the fact my allies and I feel it is the reckless action which forces us to do this to prevent it!" Eurynome bellowed.

"Our Galactic forces will then come here and stop you."

"Still, war it is if you do not stop this!" Tessup shouted.

"Wait my illustrious allies. Do not rush into this," Yin said, "For though we know how irresponsible humans are from their harm to this planet, we must first ask the Galactic High Council to put this on hold and explain why it is both wrong and unwise to let humans resolve an alien species problem here."

"Can we afford to wait since our High Council must be blind to agree to this? They seem to forget all the horrendous damage the humans have done," Tessup said shaking his head.

"My father, Great Lord Poseidon, is listening in. He agrees with you Great Lord Tessup," Triton said. "He feels humans are bad seed from the way they trash and poison the oceans for it shows they do not care how many millions of oceanic lives they kill. This sickens him. More so hearing the numerous events on this planet of their killing ways, Great Lady Hera made note of.

"Lord Triton, the facts told here today were one-sided and told to wake these humans up," Hera said. "After hearing your comment, I will add that I and the three Monitors on Earth have seen hundreds of groups of humans work to repair the damage that is being done to this planet."

"I have also seen many brave ones here help those in need," Roleena said. "Policemen, firemen, doctors, nurses, caretakers and thousands of environmental protectors and societies acting to save life on land or sea, big or small."

The cousin's eyes widened as the angered giants argued the pros and cons of going to war or talking to the High Council.

"Give my group time to discuss this," Eurynome suddenly told Hera tartly then Yin, Tessup, and Triton followed her over to the other side of the park. Hera looked dismayed to see this. Worse, Eurynome waved a hand high in the air and the Furies emerged from their roost in the tall cedars by the park and flew tightly around her group making high-pitched squeals.

"Eurynome has called in her Furies so the High Council's listening devices cannot hear what they are saying!" Artemis huffed. "But I know from their scowls alone they are angry."

"Indeed, and I thank you here for your loyalty," Hera said as Artemis, Hephaestus, and Yang came and stood by her.

"As we should 'all' be by law," Artemis said plainly.

"True. That is the law, but I feel it best to give them time to cool off in hopes they will come to realize this on their own."

"I sense they hope to keep us distracted long enough that the young humans will run out of time to work their plan with the Red Winkies," Artemis said with disgust.

Hera nodded. "Yes, and I will not allow that to happen."

For ten minutes, all they heard from Eurynome's group was the Furies cries, but a psychic on the Council let Hera know the group was angrily discussing her and the Council's ruling.

"Enough! Argue this later. These young humans will start their plan now!" Hera's voice thundered but Eurynome's group ignored her. She saw Tessup grab his thunderbolts, Triton his trident, and Yin his stars. "Do it," she told Hephaestus and he activated his weapon diffusers to ready them for their attack.

Hera also saw the humans in the park looked horrified and turned to Rhys. "Have your group pass on to the crowd they will be kept safe. Sir Hephaestus created all these energy bolts and knows how to neutralize them. I am hoping for them to stand down, but if needed, he will neutralize their weapons."

Hephaestus coldly eyed Tessup whose face showed that he knew he was outmatched. He put them away but Triton still engaged his Trident. Hephaestus quickly warned Hera it used a type of energy that by even charging them up would cause the ground under the entire park to release foul gases.

In a snap, Artemis nocked her bow with an explosive arrow from her quiver preparing to knock the Trident out.

"Not yet, Lay Artemis," Hera said. "Just stand ready."

"As you wish," she replied pointing the arrow at the ground.

"Lady Yang, can your calm energy settle any rising gases?"

"Yes, it can," Yang said raising her hands up high. A blue-green energy flowed from them over the area disturbed by Triton's Trident and settled the gases back down as they rose.

Each side stood ready. To those present it looked like a war was about to start in a little park in Everett between these huge otherworldly beings. The tension ran so high among the two factions and the crowd, the air crackled with electricity.

"Lady Eurynome," Hera called out, "Lord Triton in your group rebuked the humans for their warring ways yet you show you are no better. Think this over." Hera raised her scepter and tapped its orb to release a golden light that eased tension. It did work on the humans, but not on the angry giants. "With your link to the High Council you know I ran my decision by them first and the majority approved it. Do not lose your planet's galactic membership by ignoring this for it benefits us all if their plan works. Then properly present your issues to the High Court tomorrow which will be in your best interest."

"No, I do not believe it would be in my best interest, Hera."

"As a former High Council leader and current planetary leader, you must address me by my proper title, as I did you."

"Your title matters little right now, Hera," she said brazenly, but her eyes widened as Yin, Tessup and Triton shook their heads at her making it obvious she went too far in doing this.

"Oh dear," Alora whispered to Tiana, "It seems that not even Great Lady Hera can make Lady Eurynome behave."

"I disagree. I think the Great Lady will still handle this."

A look of fear and then anger passed over the human-like face of the whale-tailed ancient being. But they saw anger win out as Eurynome lifted her tail high to strike it down hard.

Hera quickly took Artemis' bow and arrow in hand and aimed it at Eurynome. "I warned you no more tail slapping!" A blazing light from Hera's body streamed into the bow and arrow. Eurynome froze and set her tail down gently.

Tiana nudged Alora and whispered, "You see, I recall Aunt Roleena telling me when one of them becomes a Galactic High Council Leader they're given extra powers and a fleet of ships with their best shielding and weapons. As she is one of their leaders, her powers exceed Eurynome's by far."

"Great Lady Hera, may I speak frankly?" Eurynome asked after raising her hand politely to the two sister's astonishment.

"Yes, you may do so," Hera replied with equal civility.

"Then to the major points. I and many others in this galaxy are furious how our Galactic High Council is using their power. You make decisions without getting all the planetary leader's opinions first and ignore our right to challenge these even when many oppose them. Worse, is when destructive beings like humans are allowed to kill rare life-giving planets like this one."

"A valid concern so I will set a date to discuss this critical issue with the Galactic High Council within one week. Now, let me see if the Red Winkie problem can now be solved then go to resolving the others you mentioned. Will that be satisfactory?"

"No, Great Lady. Few humans take the damage they are doing to this planet seriously. So, with two huge threats striking this planet at once, it will hasten its annihilation. We feel it must be dealt with now and severely. We insist the Red Winkies and humans be dispatched at once."

"Dispatched?" Tiana cried out. "You mean to kill us! But by your own laws you can't do that without a fair trial before—"

With a wave of a finger, Hera silenced Tiana. She looked up a minute then back at Eurynome. "The Galactic High Council heard you and set an emergency session tomorrow for your group to discuss what to do with the humans causing harm to this planet. However, an order to terminate them will not be given today as you insist. Now, the decision to give the young Earthlings the opportunity to work out a better solution to the Red Winkie problem on their planet still stands."

"Over my dead filleted body! Since you are unwilling to eliminate these two majorly destructive pests, we will!"

"Lady Eurynome, I am giving you and your group this one warning," Hera said in a deadly serious way. "Stand down."

"No!" Eurynome bellowed raising her tail and her group aimed their weapons at the humans in the park and the Red Winkies. "Stand aside, and let us eliminate them or you will be disintegrated too. Now move!" She glanced at her group and yelled, "Wide spread thermal beams on my mark!"

**

Hera raised her scepter high and a massive bolt of light shot into it from the sky. Rippling energy fanned out from it and streamed into everything in the park. She then looked around and nodded with satisfaction. No one spoke. No one moved. Even the air was still for she had stopped time itself on this small area of the Earth. She was the only one left unaffected.

"Great Universe Custodians," Hera called up to the heavens in a voice filled with the exalted light she had been given. "I, Great Lady Hera of the Galactic High Council, Overseer and Protectorate of Earth do hereby ask for your power to stop this alien act of war here on Earth which is an atrocity. Encapsulate Eurynome and the off-world aggressors with her then separately encapsulate my group and the seven young humans with us so we might deal with these off-world intruders ourselves without harm to these Earthlings."

An entity, shaped like a gigantic Man-of-War jellyfish, shot down from the sky engulfing the warring giants inside its huge dome. The forty-foot-wide entity with tentacles around its edges sunk them deep into the land like anchors. A similar entity shot down covering Hera's giants, the seven cousins, Roleena and Gertie. As both groups were covered, Hera's staff dimmed and time resumed. Everyone walked and talked again, but the humans outside the dome moved slowly as Hera tranquilized them lightly to keep them calm but left those inside the two entity domes able to talk and walk unhindered.

"Do not worry," Hera said seeing the alarmed look on the cousin's faces. "Though this entity looks like Earth's Man-of-War Sea creature, its tentacles do not have deadly neurotoxins in them. It is a Gluupi and is just using its tentacles as anchors. So, we are all quite safe and will not be its next meal."

Eurynome's group cut off any further explanation from Hera by their thunderous bellyaching as they yelled at her for pinning them in like criminals and the ground began to quiver.

"Silence!" Hera commanded them. When they did not stop, she waved a hand at them and they fell mute. "You brought this on yourselves. You will behave properly or I will have Galactic Command lock you up for attempting to kill us. Now, I will free your speech, but no shouting will be allowed. You must also raise a hand to speak to me. If I nod at you, you may speak."

The first hand to go up was Eurynome's and Hera nodded at her. "This is insanity! Do not allow this human child's plan to unfold," Eurynome said tersely but was careful not to yell it. "The result will be a disaster like everything these humans do to themselves and the Earth. They are a worse pestilence than the Red Winkies which the humans prove by their deadly ways."

"I must now agree," Yin said curtly. "For I have foreseen them continuing to wreak havoc on this planet. Still, I will agree to an emergency Galactic High Council meeting to decide what to do to the destructive humans. As for the Red Winkies, they are repeat offenders. It is best to dispose of them immediately."

The Red Winkies screeched upon hearing this and with such sheer terror the humans all shivered in horror to hear it.

"I originally wanted to be your guardian," Eurynome told the Red Winkies sadly. "But my allies insist this is for the best. Yet I believe it would greatly improve life on this planet to dispose of the human pestilence at the same time."

The collective gasp and horror-stricken faces on the humans present, even sedated as they were, showed their fear level now equaled that of the Red Winkies.

"Lady Eurynome, Lords Yin, Tessup, and Triton, I am given the sole authority to decide what to do with the Red Winkies and will allow the young humans to try using their plan today," Hera said. 'The decision of how to deal with the human abuse of Earth is not going to be decided by the Galactic High Council until they listen to your grievances tomorrow and hear your ideas on what you think should be done."

"How unfortunate to put it off," Yin said dryly.

"Is it, Lord Yin?" Yang asked softly. "For I did look into the future event you saw on the timeline and it is hazy. That means it could unfold differently than you deem it to as their fate is not a fixed one for the Universe as yet."

"Thank you, Lady Yang," Roleena said in her giant's voice. "I do believe that fate will be changed by the hard work of the young people like my nieces, nephews, and their friends. They will alter this deadly fate for there is still time for them to find a way to live here without killing this planet."

"Yes!" the cousins all shouted enthusiastically.

"Good, but now we must get back to dealing with the Red Winkies," Hera said firmly. "There will be no other discussion or work done other than this." She then noticed Pandora waving her hands high in the air. Hera sighed and looked reluctant, but she saw how badly she wanted to speak and nodded at her.

"Please, I beg of those on the Galactic High Council above, and the wise off-worlder's present, let the young humans here find a kinder way to deal with the Red Winkies," Pandora said her voice choked with emotion. Eurynome's group crisply said 'No! Their plan will fail!' and Hera's group looked unsure so Pandora pleaded directly to Hera. "Great Lady, I offer my life in exchange for you allowing these seven young humans and Sir Gertie to find a better fate for the Red Winkies. For I would rather forfeit my life than live forever aware of the anguish and torment they felt, and will feel again, to have to live out their lives imprisoned in a spatial containment box."

Hera gasped as Pandora offered this as did all the giants. "Lady Pandora, you would do this knowing your life's essence will not carry on if forfeited like this?"

"Yes," she said sadly, but without fear or regret.

Hera studied Pandora for what felt like hours to the seven cousins but was only minutes. "I see the Red Winkies plight is that dear to you to offer so much to let the humans help them. However, forfeiting your life will not be necessary. The High Council voted to allow it, as do I." Hera turned to Rhys. "You and your group have until sundown to execute your plan."

"No, Great Lady!" Triton choked out in pain shaking his trident. "We cannot allow you to set a precedent like this!"

"Great Lady, I too do question the wisdom of implementing what I see as a poor decision," Yin said solemnly.

"The final decision is my right as Earth's Overseer and I am allowing it," Hera said firmly and raised her scepter.

Again, tensions ran so high under the dome with Eurynome and her group that it crackled with static inside it.

That moment, the sky rumbled loudly and everyone looked up. Two human-shaped giants jetted down on brilliant discs and then slowed down and carefully landed between the two domes.

"Who are the new arrivals?" Tiana whispered to Roleena and her cousins leaned in close to hear her answer.

"The male is Lord Ares, one of the two heads of the War Council. The female is Great Lady Gaia, the first Overseer of Earth. Now, you must all be quiet or you might get frozen for being disruptive," Roleena said and they nodded briskly.

Ares faced Hera like the fearsome warrior he was. "Great Lady Hera, I and Great Lady Gaia beside me, feel this decision is rash. Our voices weigh heavily being I am the head of the Galactic War Council, and she was this planet's first Overseer."

"Lord Ares, it was my decision to make and it is done."

A tunnel of light shot down by Ares and two powerfully built human-shaped giants, one female and one male, appeared.

"Greetings Great Lady Hera. As you know, I am the other head of the War Council which Lord Ares 'forgot' to mention," the beautiful female giant said looking at him with annoyance.

"Yes, I am well aware of that, and glad of it, Lady Athena."

"You will also be glad that the honorable Great Lord Apollo, the only one besides Lord Hermes to return from the dark abyss alive, was beamed here with me by our Galactic High Court to remind all off-worlders here 'the Law is the Law' and when a decision is made and ratified by them it must be obeyed."

"No! We will not obey what we know is wrong!" Eurynome bellowed smacking her tail down hard. To her embarrassment the Gluupi dome around her group caused only her group to be soaked and she grimaced as she turned them. "Come my allies, let's break out of here and end this debacle and get rid of the destructive human and Red Winkie pests ourselves!"

With a nod, Tessup threw his lightning-spears at the wall of the Gluupi dome facing Hera, Triton blasted it with his Trident, and Yin threw his explosive stars at it as Eurynome whacked it with her huge tail. Ares and Gaia, caught on the outside with only small hand weapons, fired at the same spot on the Gluupi to help free Eurynomes's group. The people outside the domes huddled on the ground terrified by deafening noise and fiery explosions around them, most too scared to flee.

Athena and Apollo protected the crowd by disintegrating the fiery ricochets coming off the dome from Ares and Gaia's hand weapons but looked worried as fast as they came one might get past them and kill someone. Inside the dome, the seven cousins, Roleena, and Gertie told Hera they feared the humans outside the dome were going to get hurt or killed.

"I already contacted Galactic Command," Hera told them. "They are coming to neutralize Eurynome and those with her."

That moment, the Gluupi covering Eurynome's group cried out in pain like a whale being brutally tortured. Hera's eyes fired up, but she could not use her powers while inside the Gluupi dome without harming it. But as the first agonizing scream came from the Gluupi, a glowing Egyptian-looking female giant in a white kaftan edged in gold braid appeared in new tunnel of light between the Gluupi domes. She clapped her hands stilling all living beings in the park. Her eyes blazed like rising suns as she raised her hands and the 'Light' flowed from her fingertips over the crowd. Those injured were instantly healed, and those firing weapons found them dissolving in their hands. She then flicked her hands upwards and the two Gluupi whisked up through her tunnel and disappeared from sight.

"Was that a door into heaven that glowing being came from and then sent the Gluupi up into?" Alora asked Tiana in awe.

"I don't know, but it was amazing," Tiana said wide-eyed.

"Who is this new female giant?" Kira asked looking stunned.

"Maybe she's the head of their council," Lani whispered.

"This illustrious being is levels higher than that. Now, be silent unless called upon," Roleena told them putting a finger to her lips as the glorious giant spoke.

"I am Neith, High Judge of all Galactic Courts, and one of the Universe's Mediators. I came to inform those foreign to this planet and begat war to cease their aggressions immediately!"

Neith's voice had such authority the seven cousins trembled as she spoke as did the crowd. To their surprise, Eurynome's group of warring giants trembled too. Neith gazed at the crowd sympathetically and waved one of her hands across the people in the park. The crowd then looked refreshed and those slumped on the soggy ground from exhaustion or stress rose to their feet and moved with ease. Neith waved her other hand across the park and to their astonishment, the water receded and everyone was suddenly both dry and clean.

"This incident pained the Great Universe and humbled the Galactic High Council for Great Lady Hera was sent to tell you to cease harming your planet and your warring ways. Then four galactic members waged a war here against their High Council members. Two more joined them, the male one of the heads of the war council. They all shot at the Gluppi and harmed her," Neith said sadly. "This was an unfortunate unsanctioned event, and I apologize you humans here had to endure such appalling actions and ask your forgiveness. Know it will be dealt with."

Neith turned to the offending alien group. "Lady Eurynome, I sense you, and those with you coming without permits to this planet, forgot in the heat of your passion to pay heed to our Galactic Laws. You also seem to have forgotten Great Lady Hera is the Overseer of this planet with the right to determine the correct action to take for any invaders, including you. What is inexcusable is you incited your group to start an unauthorized war, an offense you can be put in a corrective facility for doing. I remind you to challenge a Galactic Law you must follow the proper procedures, and with a sizable number of petitioners. I am wounded you set such a horrific example for these humans. I also insist you all remember an indigenous species is allowed a time set by the Great Universe to correct problems they cause for it is the Universe, not you, that gave them this planet. Their rights cannot be negated, especially not on your whim."

"Whim! Great Universe Mediator Neith, this is no whim!" Eurynome bellowed shaking her fists angrily in the air.

Neith pointed a finger at her and she froze. "There will be no shouting, no tail slapping or using weapons. You will behave properly or I will keep you frozen. Now, I will release your speech so you can indicate that I have made this clear to you."

"Yes, Universe Mediator Neith," she replied sounding humiliated, "You have made this clear."

"Good. However, to ensure this I will keep my hold on you until I am done here. Now, for clarity, I will repeat the errors you and your group made. You broke the Law and came here without a permit. You failed to get properly signed petitions to discuss grievances with the Galactic High Council such as altering the Universe's plans for humans, which does not just affect you, but all creation. You instigated war without a permit. And on a minor matter, you failed to speak respectfully to all and use proper titles. Failure to do so in the future will land you in a correction unit. Is this clear?"

"Yes," Eurynome sighed looking sheepish. "Do forgive me, Great Universe Mediator Neith. It is true. I behaved poorly and acted rashly. As a Mediator of the Great Universe, you are right to remind me it is the Galactic High Council's, High Court's, and planetary Overseer's right to decide what action is to be taken on troubled planets like this one."

"I am pleased to sense you now realize this," Neith said and turned to Rhys. "Are you the chosen human leader here?"

Rhys was stunned to have her speak to him and just gaped.

"Hey buddy, remember 'you' are our chosen leader," Shaw said elbowing him and Roleena, Gertie and the other cousins confirmed this wholeheartedly. "Now, let her know that."

"Great Universe Mediator Neith, I'm not the leader of Earth. There are thousands of leaders here. But when I asked to protect Alora and Tiana from this angry mob, they chose to give me the leader hat. It turned into a crown when I put it on and I guess agreed in their choice for a leader…at least for that."

Neith nodded. "Thank you for being honest for I did know that, and that Tiana and Alora were involved from the start. They risked saving the drowning Red Winkies and earlier, you three bravely rescued Lady Roleena, Sir Gertie and your smart little pup, Paris. Due to this, the Galactic High Council decided you three are being designated as Earth leaders for this venture. Also, due to the loyal assistance of what you call 'cousins' and 'Aunt Gertie'," she said smiling as she glanced at him, "And for all of your group overcoming such hardship in a short time, they titled the females in your group 'Lady', and the males 'Sir'. We also saw you, Sir Rhys, learned to overcome one of the greatest obstacles for humans on your planet, Earth…yourself. For you truly became wiser, kinder and a more thoughtful listener."

Rhys blushed hearing the compliment and was speechless.

Tian poked him and whispered, "Those are really great compliments, so tell her thank you."

"Thank you, Great Universe Mediator Neith," he choked out because he was so stunned.

"I believe your Earth expression is 'you are welcome,'" she said softly. "Now, for your group's good works the Galactic High Council is also giving each of you the galactic title 'Earth Defender' which is being made known to all your Earth leaders on this planet."

"To all of them on the entire planet?" he asked wide-eyed.

"Yes."

"You know them all?"

"Not personally, but we keep a close eye on your planet so know who they are, their positions, and what they do. For some change often here and some not often enough due to their greed and warring ways. We foresee this will shock many of them, but Great Lady Hera with Galactic Command's ships and agents, will settle any problems they have with this. If you run into trouble inform Lady Roleena, and you will find it is fortunate to have an Earth Monitor in your family."

"Wow, quite fortunate indeed," Rhys agreed with gusto.

"I did see other good changes," Neith said smiling. "Tiana, you are so capable you like doing things yourself, but learned to spot and use other's skills to let them shine. Alora, you were kind but timid and became brave, and you older cousins became true and valiant team members. As usual, Sir Gertie was also helpful. I am heartened to see such heroic Earthlings as you all risked your lives to do this. It gives we among the stars hope for you and this planet. I will soon take my leave of you, but Great Lady Hera will give you guidelines on the negotiation with the Red Winkies and dealing with your planetary restoration."

"Thank you, Great Universe Mediator Neith," Rhys said. "But as we get started with our plan, will we have problems with the angry giants here?" he asked warily and for a good reason as Eurynome's group was glaring at him.

"I see why you asked that," she sighed after looking at them. "Lady's Eurynome and Gaia, Lord's Tessup, Triton, Yin and Ares, I will now give you a way to bow out gracefully or be tried for treason. The choice is yours." Neith glared at them and they flinched. "You will also pay the cost to repair the injuries you inflicted on the Gluupi, and that of sending starships and personnel here to stop your mutinous act and vow to never do this again. You also are banned from this planet. Choose this, containment or a rehab center. I give you five minutes to reply."

"They look like guilty bank robbers being called out by that big, tough movie cop 'Dirty Harry'," Rhys murmured.

"Yep," Gertie said. "I bet they didn't figure on the Galactic High Council sending in one of the Universe's big guns."

"I agree," Roleena said. "This is a small, out-of-the-way planet, so they thought they could get away with doing this."

"It's good to know they were wrong," Rhys said.

"Indeed, and now, I see Eurynome and her group are all nodding which means they've already decided what to do."

Eurynome looked at Neith. "We all agree to your terms."

"And?" Neith asked sharply as she looked at all of them.

"We all vow to not do this again and to leave peacefully."

"Good." Neith tapped her scepter and energy discs formed in front of each member of Eurynome's group appropriate for their size. They each stepped on them and zipped off into the sky.

Neith looked sad as she watched Eurynome's group leave but then looked at the young cousins optimistically. "You need not fear any repercussions from them for I have blocked them from ever coming back here."

"We all thank you for that, Great Universe Mediator Neith."

"You are welcome, Sir Rhys. Great Lady Hera will set forth the rules you must follow for your plan as I must take my leave of you. The Galactic High Council will be keeping an eye on you. I pray you fix this planet for it would pain me to hear your people had to be eliminated. Still, your group gives me hope it will be done and I will also pray you succeed. I now bid you all farewell." A brilliant beam spotlighted Neith and in the blink of an eye drew her up into the sky out of sight.

"You must first ask for the rules so you can begin your plan for dealing with the Red Winkies, Sir Rhys," Hera said as the cousins all stared at the sky in awe. "For the time to accomplish this runs out at the end of this day."

"Er, yes, and thank you for reminding me," he said blinking like he was coming out of a trance. "Please tell us the rules your Great Mediator said we must follow."

Hera sighed and turned away disappointedly when he did not address either her or Neith correctly.

"Gosh, I...I...I..." he sputtered looking totally flustered.

Tiana elbowed him in his ribs and whispered, "Don't be a nitwit. You forgot to call them Great Lady Hera and Great Universe Mediator Neith. So, do it and get us the rules we need to follow or we all might wind up in their space jail."

"Or worse," Wain said, "Eradicated from our planet."

"Hey," Rhys whispered, "I just messed up their titles because it's nerve-wracking to be under all this pressure from aliens who can wipe me out in a snap if I displease them."

"Yes, I can see that from the sweat dripping down your face and I'd give you a towel but I left mine at home," Tiana said kiddingly. "Just remember the advice from 'The Hitchhikers Guide to the Galaxy' and you'll do great."

"I'm stressed out, so just remind me what it said."

"Don't panic."

"Oh, that's right, and to always bring a towel with you, but I was never clear as to why that was."

Tiana bit back a grin. "Me either, but now with the way you're sweating I can see why it's important to have one."

"Good point," he groaned.

"Well, come on. Fix your goof up before she changes her mind about letting us do our plan since most of her higher ups are nervous to have mere humans do this. Just know she's being kind by patiently waiting for you to correct your error."

Rhys nodded and took a deep breath then turned to Hera. "Great Lady Hera, please forgive my lapse in manners. It's due to feeling overwhelmed by all this. I will be sure to give you the proper respect of using your correct titles from now on."

"Very well," she said with a nod to him. "Continue."

"Thank you, Great Lady. Now, would you please tell us the rules we need to follow for our plan?"

"Yes. First you and Lady's Tiana and Alora can decide what to do after getting your cousins input as well as Sir Gertie's."

"That's great, since we're a team but I'm puzzled by why you had already been calling Gertie, 'Sir Gertie'."

"He earned this noble title by helping us protect this planet in many different ways for many centuries."

"Wow. For centuries? How's that humanly possible?"

"You must ask him later yourself some other time. For now, tell me, what does your word 'wow' mean?"

"It's an exclamation meaning that what's said is really cool."

"Cool like it's really cold?"

"No, like it's something amazingly good."

"I see," Hera said. "Then I think he is 'wow' too. Now, let us continue with the rules you must go by. One critical rule is only one of you can talk directly to me as you carry out your plan."

"Why only one?"

"When time is limited, as it is now, it is best to talk to one leader after a decision is made to lessen any confusion. If time was unlimited, we could get everyone's input and link to the Great Universe to do tally and judge all comments made."

"The Great Universe?"

"You do not have time for me to explain this. For now, you must decide what to do with the Red Winkies as time is slipping away as you bring up other subjects. So, back to the issue. First, you should see if you can find a way to communicate with the Red Winkies. And since you three were in this from the start, stand all together to make this connection clear. But do not talk at the same time or it will be confusing for all concerned. Most importantly you must all be tactful and good listeners."

"I will do my best," he said.

"Me too," Tiana said heartily and Alora echoed this.

"May we go speak to our advisors first?" Rhys asked.

"Yes," Hera said, "But keep in mind your plan for dealing with the Red Winkies must be done in the time frame the Galactic High Council allotted you which is until sunset today."

"That does not give us much time to implement our plan," Alora said anxiously.

"Under the current circumstances, it is all the time I can give you for there are many powerful off-world beings who want to give you none at all."

"I could see that by the angry looks we got from some of the ones who came here today," Rhys said with a reflexive shiver.

"Then let's get started right now," Tiana said and they went over to their cousin's and Gertie just a few steps behind them.

The trio began getting suggestions from their group, but as Gertie spoke, the tiny clouds of Red Winkies that fell through the holes in the blue energy layer and the huge cloud above the layer squealed so loudly everyone had to cover their ears.

Hera tapped her scepter and it stopped. "Sir Gertie, it is quite evident the Red Winkies do not want you advising the cousins."

"But Great Lady, Aunt Roleena can't advise us and he has the experience we don't have," Rhys said. "So, he's the best we have here to help us deal with this wisely."

"Unfortunately, his experience is why he cannot do this."

"That's so unfair," Alora said. "Why can't he?"

Hera gave Gertie a questioning look. He groaned then he shrugged and nodded at her. She still said nothing and they all guessed from the way her jaw clenched she was deciding what to say without causing him some harm or embarrassment.

"Great Lady, I thank ye fer yer kind heart, but there be no need fer ye to stew so hard over this. I give ye free rein to spit out the bad news, shocking as it be," Gertie said plainly.

Hera sighed heavily "As you wish, Sir Gertie. To be candid, the Red Winkies want your 'Aunt' Gertie left out of this since he helped capture them the last time they were here. So, their reaction to him helping you tells me there are still hard feelings there. That means his being involved with this will keep you from having any kind of discussion with them."

"Great Lady, how can that be possible?" Tiana asked with surprise. "From what Aunt Roleena told us, the last time they were here was much longer ago than a human life span is."

"Indeed, it was."

"Then how could he have been here when even healthy humans only live on average seventy years on this planet."

"True." Hera said but said nothing further.

Tiana groaned in frustration. "I can tell from your silence you aren't going to explain how he was able to do this."

"That is also true."

"Okay, that aside, I'm guessing he put them in what our ancient Earth legends call 'Pandora's Box' making them mad."

"We call a 'containment box', and he did not put them in it, but he did find them for us and helped us capture them."

"Aunt Gertie, is that true?" Alora asked him wide-eyed.

"Fraid so little missy. I had to so's to keep folks safe here."

"I can see why after what we just went through," Rhys said.

"I know Paris sure does," Alora said and he barked.

"Enough distractions," Wain said, "Let's work on finding a way to talk to the Winkies then start implementing our plan."

"Yes, we're running out of time," Kira said worriedly and the other older cousins nodded.

"True, but rats! That stops us getting information from him. Or does it?" Rhys thought it over. "Great Lady, will you keep the Winkies quiet and let Sir Gertie quickly give us advice on handling tough negotiations with those we know little about?"

"Well, Great Lady," Gertie said as he saw her thinking hard about it. "I hope yer complex rules can allow them that much without gumming things up fer everyone in this here universe."

"Yes, they can," she said and looked at Rhys. "But you must all speak in generalities, and not refer to any past actions of the Red Winkies without a fair trial first. If you do you will be cut off and lose your opportunity to do this plan of yours. And keep it brief for you are using up valuable negotiation time."

"So, Great Lady, can I go ahead and give them some overall advise about doing these ticklish kinds of talks?" Gertie asked.

"Yes, but do it quickly. The Red Winkies are truly miffed."

"Shucks, I ain't so thick headed I don't know that." He pinched his lips together a minute then exhaled hard and looked at Rhys. "Hooey, this is a tricky one, so listen good. My best figurin' is ye need to shoot straight and not get flummoxed by slick talking or you'll get bamboozled. It's also real important yer kin here are with ye good and tight on this. So, chew the fat with them to figure what's best and then stick to it."

"What does bamboozled or flummoxed mean, Sir Gertie?" Rhys asked looking puzzled.

"Heh, heh heh! Ain't ever heard ye use that title fer me," he chuckled. "Well, doggies, as I know it, flummoxed is getting all confused. Bamboozled is when ye wind up getting conned. Ye see, I got bamboozled once when a tricky rascal stumped me with his slick talking. He conned me out of goods by saying he could give me more by selling it in his shop fer twice what I asked fer and then he'd split the profits with me. I found out later he didn't have a shop and he took off with my goods. It taught me ye have to find out about who and what yer dealing with and listen close to feel out if what they say rings true."

"Enough, Sir Gertie," Hera told him. "The Red Winkies are getting overly agitated so I must stop silencing them now."

"Well, kiddo, ye heard the Great Lady. I best stop yakking 'cuz them Winkies is getting all heated up and ye don't want them to get so mad they won't sit and chew the fat with ye." He tipped his bonnet at Rhys and went over and stood by Roleena.

Rhys nodded at Gertie then turned to his cousins. "Okay, we and the Red Winkies need to 'chew the fat' which is to have a good talk. So, I'm hoping in my absence you figured out how to talk to the Red Winkies," he said but with a wishful look.

"No such luck," Wain said and they all shook their heads.

Rhys sighed and nodded. "Let's go over our plan." They went over it looking for weak spots and pitfalls in hopes to avoid them. "So, we drew for who talks first and it seems I do," he said grimacing. "So, I'll start the plan we all worked on if you're all totally with me on this."

"Absolutely!" Alora said so wholeheartedly he smiled.

"Yes!" Tiana said crisply.

"You got this, dude," Shaw said slapping Rhys on the back.

"Yeah, we're all with you," Kira said and the others nodded.

"Then say 'all for one and one for all'" he said with all seriousness putting his hand out in the middle of their circle.

"Are we girls counted as musketeers since there weren't any girls among them?" Tiana asked with a tiny smirk on her face.

"Yes, you are and you're great ones," he said sincerely.

"Cool!" Alora said putting her hand on his. Then one by one they put their hand on Rhys's. As the last one did, they threw their hands in the air and yelled, "All for one and one for all!"

Rhys then looked at Tiana and Alora. "As the Great Lady said, we were in this from the start so we do this together. Now, who's going to be in the middle?"

"You, since you have the fancy crown," Alora said giggling.

"I agree though they won't truly see it," Tiana said then went and stood by his right side as Alora stood by his left.

"True," Rhys said. "Now, I'm reminding us all not to talk at the same time, and that as agreed I'll start out by asking for the leader of the Red Winkies to come forward. If they do, we'll follow the plan and try asking them questions to see if they can understand us and respond in a way we can understand them. If that works, we can find out more about them and hopefully find a way to get them to leave here peacefully.

"Right," Tiana said and Alora nodded sharply.

"Great Lady Hera, can the Red Winkies here and the ones up in the cloud above us hear us?" Rhys asked politely.

"Yes, I have made it so, but have you come up with a way to communicate with them?" she asked pointedly.

"It's the first thing we'll be attempting," he said.

"Very well, continue," she said and he nodded.

Rhys could not see the Red Winkie cloud above the blue protective energy layer over the crowd that Hera had placed between them and the humans, so he looked at the small clouds just above them. "I am the chosen leader now and am asking for the opportunity to speak to the leader of the Red Winkies."

"Young man, stop right there!" Chief Broomsky yelled and rushed over to where the trio stood. "I am the leader here!"

"Are 'you' the Red Winkie's leader?" he asked bluntly.

"Well…no, but I am the—" the Chief began when a tiny cloud of Red Winkies swarmed her. To even Hera's surprise, a thread of red light shot through the blue energy layer from those above it energizing those swarming the Chief. They lit up even brighter and all zapped her until she stopped talking.

Rhys grinned guessing it was the Winkies way of silencing her up so he could speak. "Great Lady Hera, I think the Red Winkie leaders are trying to show they want to communicate with me and not her. Can you let them pass through to us here?"

"Yes, and though this is rather odd, I agree. But I will only allow one miniscule group to pass through." Hera flicked her finger at the blue cloud energy layer making a tiny hole. A second later a pea-sized cloud of Red Winkies came through it and hovered between Rhys, Tiana, and Alora, and Broomsky.

"Chief Broomsky, you're not the leader they want and the Red Winkies made that clear when they zapped you when you began talking," Rhys said.

"Perhaps not, but I 'am' the leader here," she huffed.

The Red Winkies that had just come down then flashed their lights at the group swarming Chief Broomsky's head and she began babbling nonsensically.

"I think the new Red Winkies sent a message to the swarm around their Chief and are making her talk weird," Alora said.

"It seems that way to me too. I wonder why," Tiana said.

"I don't know. Let me keep trying to talk to them in hopes we can find some answers to this and get on with our plan." Rhys turned to the new Red Winkie cloud in front of them. "If the Red Winkie leader is here, my group wants to work on a way to help us both. To prove this, we wish to make a better deal with you than being put in a box. But first we must find a way to talk to each other so my people can know if you are willing to work on a way to do this," he said earnestly.

The Red Winkie cloud around Broomsky's head then lifted off of her and the Chief burst into tears. Officer's Schmartzov and Dwendoleen then quickly strode over to her side.

"Chief, what's wrong?" he asked looking alarmed that she had suddenly started crying.

"I don't know...I'm just confused and upset. And why did you call me 'Chief'? And why am I here? And why are all these people here?" she asked looking utterly baffled.

"It seemed like when that kid, Rhys, told you harshly you're not the leader the Red Winkies want you began crying," he said as he and Dwendoleen stood protectively by her. He then turned to Rhys. "Explain this, because we won't let you abuse her."

"I did nothing to abuse her," Rhys said calmly, "I just told her the truth." He saw the officers take an aggressive stance and told Tiana to run her Sword of Defense on the ground in front their group to put a protective barrier between them. "I need to speak to the Red Winkies leader. However, when she got in the way of this, they zapped her which likely smarted a bit."

"Even so, you told one of the girls by you to run her sword between us and your group which looked threatening to me," Dwendoleen said tersely.

"We did not do this to threaten you, but to protect us from you hurting us for you've already caused me serious harm." Rhys pointed to the streaks of dried blood on his face after he was hit on the head with a rock by someone in the crowd and then by Broomsky. "Now, all we want is to speak to the leader of the Red Winkies. Do you know who they are?" He then looked curious as the Red Winkies pulled off both officers.

"Well...no, I don't," Schmartzov said looking puzzled as did Dwendoleen as the Winkies pulled away from them. "In fact, I don't know why I got so aggressive about this whole situation."

That moment, the cloud of Red Winkies in front of Rhys, Tiana and Alora zipped over to Broomsky. They did not join the ones over her but flew in her tear ducts and ears. A few seconds later, she looked around and her eyes glowed with twinkling red lights causing the two officers to back away from her in shock.

"We are what you human Earthlings would call 'leaders' of the 'Western Great Voltic Grid' and are connected to all our energy beings here. We just learned from our Eastern Grid that to communicate with you we have to use a human as an avatar to do so," Broomsky said to everyone's surprise. The voice they all heard was similar to hers if she had been speaking like an old-time radio announcer on a station that crackled with static like it was out of range of a good antenna. "We are called 'Zzzzzit'."

"Zit?" Rhys asked flabbergasted knowing it was a slang word for pimples. He choked back his urge to laugh but then he heard Zach muffling his.

"Stop it," Tiana hissed at them. "That is so rude."

"Sorry," Zach said, "But Zit is such a silly name I lost it."

"Then find a way to control yourselves or leave, for we must do this with all seriousness. Sir Rhys, we three leaders must look like we are capable ones, not comediennes."

"She's right everyone," Rhys said. "We staked our lives on finding a solution. This is a grave commitment so we all must act according. Especially we three on the front line who have to find a way to negotiate with them." He took a deep breath and put on a solemn face then looked at Broomsky, the Winkie's avatar. "Do you Red Winkie leaders of the 'Western Great Voltic Grid' speak for all of your 'energy beings'?"

"We speak for all of us on these western continents of the planet you call 'Earth' but not the eastern ones. However, we will pass any information we get from you on to them."

"Before we talk about the issues between us here, I need to know if you are harming this human by using her like this?"

"No harm is being done to this human female by utilizing her like this. The only reason we did this is our 'Eastern Great Voltic Grid' told us they just recently found it was the only way they could communicate with you humans and passed this on to us. So, when we are done, we will leave her body and she will be exactly as she was before."

"Good." *Though I wish you could convince her to be nicer.* "We are glad your Eastern Red Winkies figured this out since we had no idea how to speak to you. To begin, we first need to know if you might harm the Earth again causing earthquakes, volcano eruptions, or small Ice Ages like you did here before?"

"No! Our Grid did not do those, and the results from the Grid that did were unexpected and accidental. It will not happen again. Our Grids never want to harm other lifeforms."

"I am glad to hear that. Then as we start our talks, we want you to explain why you came to our planet once again."

"We will do so gladly and are relieved someone finally asked us this before trapping us and boxing us up in what is no more than a prison to us. Now, to answer your question, we like your kind of energy. We tried hard to communicate this to the beings on your planet all five times different Great Voltic Grids were here. However, none of us were unable to do so successfully."

"You've been here five other times?" Alora asked with awe.

"Not our Grid but others were, yes."

"When did your first Great Voltic Grid visit here?" Tiana asked curiously.

"Long before your lifeform came into being. From what we gleaned recently from a human you call a 'scientist'. It was during what they called your 'Jurassic Period'."

"Wow!" Rhys said. "That's the time on Earth when there were lots of gigantic dinosaurs like they show in the movies."

"We know about dinosaurs, but not movies so do not yet comprehend that word," the Winkie's avatar said sounding baffled by this. "But yes, there were lots of big dinosaurs."

"Rhys," Tiana said. "If you'd knew that part of history, you'd know dinosaurs in movies were not all time accurate."

"Since I don't can you please help out with this part?"

"Sure, since it seems like they don't know much about our current time. In fact, if you spread out their five visits between the dinosaurs and human occupation, they've missed millions of changes on Earth. So, from the huge dinosaurs of the Jurassic period 145 million years ago and Mesozoic Time when many of the largest reptiles that people call 'dinosaurs' ruled this planet, there's been a lot of changes they have missed to this point."

"Astute of you, Earth female, and just what is a movie?"

"A movie is a moving picture of things we see with our eyes and some are true life and some made up for fun to amuse us."

"We cannot see like you do so this will remain unknown to us. However, one true comment to us was your mentioning their enormous size. We also found big dinosaurs to be quite rude," the Red Winkie avatar said sounding quite peeved.

"Rude? How?" Rhys asked his brows arched up in surprise.

"Because when we pleaded with those big brutes to let us live here, they just told us to go away and ignored us."

"Are you sure they understood you?"

"Yes, and their replies were punctuated by the Brontosaurus' tail thumping us and the Tyrannosaurus snapping at us."

"But how were they even able to understand you?"

The Winkies made crackling noises a minute then the avatar said, "We speculate that unlike your brain's current stage of development, they were at a point where they were intelligent enough to decipher our language. Evidently their brains had superior translating abilities than all those who are here have."

Rhys heard most of the giants choke back their laughter and blushed. "Hey, their comment included all of us, not just me." He then turned to the Winkie's avatar. "Am I correct?"

"Yes, what you said is true. It includes these giants with their high and mighty ways. Ones who dealt with us harshly without taking the time to understand us," the Red Winkie's avatar said sounding pained. Hearing the strong rebuff, the giants were speechless and some looked embarrassed.

"I now find this sad, but true," Hera admitted, "Though it was millions of years ago. But now, these young people asked to find a better solution than ours for your Red Winkies and we on the Galactic High Council agreed to this. They need to get to this since the price of their failure is likely death for those on this planet. So, hard as it is, this must be resolved by sunset or we will have to take care of this our former way."

"We're both painfully aware of that, Great Lady" Rhys said grimly, "But I want to hear the rest of their story." He then turned to the Red Winkie avatar. "Please continue with what happened between you and the dinosaurs."

"As I said, they bluntly told us to go away."

"And you just left?"

"Yes," the Winkie avatar said.

"It sounds like you didn't try very hard to stay. So, why did you leave without trying harder to change their minds?"

A rising and falling buzz came from the Red Winkies that was oddly like a sigh. "It was due to their epidermis being too tough for us to get through to amplify any sympathetic feelings or reach their nervous system to control their movements."

"What exactly is a tough epidermis?"

"Epidermis is the outermost layer of skin," Tiana told him, "Which I learned in my health class, and dinosaurs had thick ones which I learned from a Paleontology science class online."

"I now find I'm glad you like the sciences since it has really has helped us out, so thanks," he said and she grinned.

"Zzzzz, so this human female who just spoke likes science," the Winkie's avatar said. "We prefer this and will negotiate with her now, since she will comprehend us more than you will."

"Which is why she is also a leader, but we three in front of you are all chosen Earth leaders by the Galactic High Council."

"Seriously? Are you all necessary to this discussion?"

"Just ignore their crabby attitude," Alora whispered to Rhys and then told the Winkies. "He is super necessary. His planning and bravery have helped us get the right to try to help keep you out of your box, so you should appreciate him for this."

"That is good, but why use him now since that is done?"

"You see, in our culture, we all have our specialties," Tiana said. "Do you specialize in yours?"

"No, we are all the same."

Rhys sighed and closed his eyes to think. *Are the Winkies trying to divide us or should Tiana be our leader to appease them? She does know more science facts than I do. Or is this a trick Gertie was warning me to watch out for?* he wondered.

"Great Lady, I must be allowed to text him to clear up some confusion I sense happening here," Roleena said.

Upon hearing her urgency Hera nodded. "Do so."

'Stand firm!' she texted to Rhys. 'Science knowledge alone does not make you a leader, and altering the Council's decision to have you three as leaders here will then weaken our tenuous position with the disgruntled council members in this galaxy. Some detest any of you being in charge of bargaining with the Red Winkies. So, do not be swayed or as Sir Gertie said, don't be bamboozled. It will seem weak if you change this at the first sign of a problem. So, keep working on this together.'

Rhys heard his cell chime and was surprised but looked at it. 'Got it,' he texted back, then looked at the avatar. "You say you are all the same, but we are not. We three remain the leaders."

"Understood, but unfortunate," the avatar said. "It would be simpler to have one of the females who are more sympathetic."

I bet, Rhys thought, *and that was tricky.* "Nonetheless, it's we three or the Galactic High Council. So, isn't this better than them taking the lead? They might not even negotiate with you and just put you back in that confinement box of theirs."

The Red Winkies began chittering again then the avatar said, "We decided dealing with you three is better than risking that."

"Thank you," Rhys said through gritted teeth. *I think.*

"You may proceed," the avatar said.

"Thank you," he said politely then glanced at their group. "Any suggestions here from my advisers?"

"Great Lady, may I quickly remind Sir Rhys about his special gift?" Roleena asked.

"You may," Hera said with a perceptive look.

"Sir Rhys, just as it is done in the Galactic Court, you can use your 'Scales of Justice' to weigh everything said here."

"Okay," he said hesitantly, unsure how he should do this.

"Remember when you saw the gift of the 'Scales of Justice' you were amazed to see a tiny replica of the ancient scales. A note was attached basically saying; take it if you want justice to be the ruling part of your soul then all things big or small must be weighed by their merit or lack of it no matter their size."

"Hard for me to forget about that gift," Tiana said. "Because not long after that he sealed me and my sister under a shield that he called a 'protective bubble' which then imprisoned us."

"It wasn't meant to be a prison!" Rhys said beseechingly. "I just wanted to fullfill my promise of keeping you safe while I tried to convince the angry crowd in this park to let us by."

"That's true, Tiana," Alora said. "I could tell he was super worried about us and truly did want to keep us safe."

"But I could've helped him!" she huffed in exasperation. "And I would not have let him get whacked on the head with rocks by those Red Winkie run people."

Alora shrugged. "Maybe, or you might've gotten smacked with one yourself and been hurt or killed along with him."

"Your time is running out so I suggest you get back to work," Hera reminded them sternly. "And Rhys pay heed to the 'Scales of Justice' you were gifted with, for it will help guide you."

Rhys dug down deep to sense its presence then stood up tall as he faced the Red Winkie's avatar. "Will you keep your promise to restore Chief Broomsky to her former self when we finish with our negotiations?"

"Yes, it is only necessary to use her as an avatar to speak to you for you did not understand us until our Eastern Grid learned to talk to your kind by infiltrating your brain and controlling your vocal cords so we could speak to you."

"It's eerie, but I'm glad you learned to do this."

"Me too, but how are you able to do it?" Tiana asked.

"I can explain it but using a human host uses loads of energy and would take a long time. You see, we use so much to do this we can only utilize one subject for long conversations like ours. Otherwise, our energy would be drained away quickly. Without energy, we cease to exist, and we do not want to cease to exist. So, like your time is limited to work out a solution, our energy volume limits us. Now, what you can offer as a way for us to live and not be put back in their box?"

"Then to speed this up we would like to know what your group thinks is a just and fitting thing to do," Rhys said.

"Free us."

"I realize why you want that, but why should we free you when it would cost all my people their lives?"

All the Red Winkies gave a horrified collective squeal and the avatar yelled, "No, it doesn't! We never killed anyone on our visit here. All your people are still alive."

Alora shook her head. "Not alive in the way we were before you came here and began controlling our movements."

"Worse, your energy makes people more excitable and angrier causing them to do things they would not normally do. You affect some people so much they can't reason properly," Tiana explained.

"Are you saying we cause your feelings to become overly stimulated when we are on you, and that doing so disrupts their balance preventing you from keeping these in check?"

"Yes. That is just what I'm trying to say."

Again, crackling sounds came from all the Red Winkies then the avatar said, "We apologize. We did not realize that. Please understand we need energy to live. Humans expend so much energy that being on you allowed us to be vibrantly alive, not just to survive. We found your transportation devices cannot be counted on to get us where we need to go and your mobility to get from place-to-place filled those gaps. Now you are aware of this, can you control these thoughts and feelings?"

"No, for even the brightest and kindest of us find it hard to control these at times, especially if the feelings get amplified like you do to ours. For even without your over stimulation, our feelings and thoughts are something humans are still learning to control and have been for ages."

"We could control these for you!" the avatar gushed happily and the Red Winkies over the Chief lit up brighter. "Then our compensation could be to share your personal energy."

"Are you serious?" Rhys asked aghast. "You think it's okay to take over every being on Earth and that by controlling our feelings and thoughts it would make doing this to us all right?"

"It seems that it would then solve the problems."

"You mean it would solve 'your' problems."

"And yours too!"

"No, you would just in reality be enslaving us."

"We would not enslave you!"

"

That would not allow us to change on our own and it would take away our free will. That is an important freedom good people have laid down their lives to protect. In fact, if you think about it being controlled by you would be like you felt when you were boxed up and lacked your freedom."

The Red Winkies avatar's eyes dimmed a bit then said, "We do understand that, and do not want to take your freedom or free will away from you."

"That's good to hear," Rhys said and the cousin's all nodded.

"Then please help us some other way. We just want to live where there's lots of energy, and like you, to live freely. Can you find us a place to do that? We do so, so hope you can," the avatar pleaded in such a heart wrenching manner everyone felt their desperation. "Can you let us live on a sunny uninhabited island here? It can be tiny since we don't take up much space."

"Sir Rhys," Alora said softly as he pondered this. "Let's talk to Great Lady Hera before agreeing to anything to see if she thinks this would be okay to do."

"Lady Alora is right," Hera said and raised a finger to stop Rhys from saying more. "We will not permit them to live here for we have seen what they did time after time to planets who let them do this. They eventually left the areas they were given to gather more energy and did so without permission."

"But we only did this if we were running out of energy!" the Red Winkie's avatar said sounding wildly desperate.

"Then you should have learned to lessen your needs."

"But we must have energy!" the avatar then demanded angrily and all the Red winkies flared up sparking riotously.

Suddenly, Neith returned in a blaze of light. "Red Winkies, I heard your irate demand which caused me to return immediately to deal with this. While we know you need energy to live, all of what Great Lady Hera said is true," she told the Winkie avatar. "The Galactic High Council also heard this and were shocked by your request. You have been given many opportunities, but you siphoned off more and more energy from every planet that was shared with you to the point it damaged them. You also did nothing to pay back any of them after doing this. Therefore, we will not allow you to do this again so you best hope these kindly young humans can find another way to help you."

"Great Universe Mediator Neith," Rhys said carefully using her proper title, "We did tell them we wanted to find a better way to resolve this and a sunny desert island seems a way to give them energy and not be able to use our energy."

"Sir Rhys, we agreed to let your group attempt this but not at the expense of others. Keep in mind they behaved irresponsibly over and over again, causing great harm. In fact, many islands were donated in the past but did not stop their aggressive energy draws. The Galactic High Council will not allow this again."

"But it seems inhumane to not find them a place to live."

Neith's eyes blazed like a nova and Rhys stepped back as she shook a finger at him. "What they did time and time again was inhumane. They turned flourishing worlds into mere shells of what they were before. Some have never recovered and want us to eradicate them, not just confine them. Most claim they are an affront to law-abiding beings in the Great Universe for they have not been willing to obey laws governing this. With what we overheard being discussed now, an emergency vote was called for across the galaxy regarding these troublesome beings. The results were the majority voted to exterminate them." Neith snapped her fingers and a blazing staff appeared in her hand.

"No! Please do not kill us," the avatar screamed and all the Red Winkies squealed in terror.

"Wait!" Rhys said waving all his cousins toward him.

"The High Council feels the time for waiting has passed."

"But we're still working on a way to fix this, so why are you being so tough and rushing in so fast on this to stop us?"

"Because I must do so when I hear you ignoring the harm they have done to billions of lives," Neith said bluntly.

"Okay, we now heard the reason why so we understand the problem more. Still, we were told we have until sundown to figure out another way to do this." He then turned to his group. "My dear cousins, my 'Scales of Justice' tell me I must keep trying to try to find a way to help them." He moved between the Red Winkie avatar and Neith and spread his arms out. To his surprise and gratitude his cousins all came and stood with him.

"Is doing this still worth your lives?" Hera asked curiously.

"Yes!" the seven cousins stated firmly though they all shivered and wondered if she was ready to strike them down.

"We still do want to give them another chance and we will find a way to solve this that is not on our Earth," Rhys said.

Seeing their courageous move, Hera nodded and spoke to Roleena and the other giants. She, Roleena, Artemis, Yang, Apollo, and Hephaestus then went and stood with the seven cousins. Neith's eyes narrowed, but she did not look surprised.

"I can't believe I'm gonna help them Winkie varmints after the trouble they caused," Gertie grumbled and joined the others.

"I warn you, Earthlings," Neith told them. "We will remove you humans along with the Red Winkies if they remain here. Plus, since many in the galaxy think humans are a bad plague, it is unlikely they will ask to stop us from exterminating you."

"Great Universe Mediator Neith!" Rhys said heatedly, "If we kill this planet, we die too. Give us this last-ditch effort to solve this today. Then we will go on to save the Earth. If you don't let us, well then, that's truly a sad and an unjust attitude to take!"

"Mortal, you try my patience by brazenly scolding me. Keep in mind most in this galaxy feel allowing you to do this is sheer folly on our part," Neith said her eyes fiercely glowing. "Keep in mind, we will not let you kill this rare planet and you 'will' be extinguished before it comes to you doing that."

"Great Universe Mediator, please forgive me for losing my temper as you said those in the galaxy voted to exterminate us before we even got to try to fix this Red Winkie issue, but that truly horrified me. I know that if we don't fix this Earth that we have abused, we will all die. But I will risk asking you this for all our sakes. Can you find it in your heart as the Great Universe Mediator you must be to have such a noble position and be merciful. Please give us this one last chance to solve this Red Winkie problem then go on to save the Earth."

"So, you ask for one last chance." Her eyes narrowed again as she thought it over then she nodded. "Very well, I will give you all thirty of your minutes for this chance of yours."

"I thought we had until sundown!" he gasped.

"Twenty-nine minutes and fifty-five seconds."

"Fine, we'll take it." He quickly turned to their group. "I hope I haven't just given us all a death sentence by agreeing to do this in twenty-nine minutes. Makes me wonder if I'll be sent down below if that happens."

"I doubt it," Shaw said. "But if you were, at least you'd be dry, not soaking wet like we are here, but it's likely hot."

"That's not making me feel better at all."

"Hey, it could be worse," Tiana said. "You could get shipped off another hot spot like a volcano on one of Jupiter's moons. You know...that's an idea. What about hot spots 'off' planet?"

Other hot spots? Intriguing idea. Can the answer to this be that simple? Rhys wondered as he looked at the Red Winkie's avatar. "We have to find you somewhere else to live since I was told you're can't stay here or we will we all be exterminated."

"That is bad, so where else do you have in mind?"

"To decide that, quickly tell us what you absolutely have to have to survive."

"First and last, we need energy."

"That's it?"

"Basically...yes."

"Then why don't you just live on a star?"

"They are too hot as is your own star's 5600 degrees Celsius. We cannot tolerate more than 1000 degrees Celsius."

Rhys looked at his cousins and then at the giants. "Can any of you name any places off planet heated like this?"

"All off-world visitors must remain silent, Sir Rhys," Neith said bluntly. "Remember, you and your cousins asked to do this in your own 'unique' human way as you phrased it. True?"

"Yes," he said sighing heavily as he silently prayed for some kind of inspiration to come to him. A moment later, his eyes lit up and he pulled his cousins and Gertie into a huddle. "Talking about hot places, like the moons of Jupiter Tiana mentioned, are any of them a workable solution?"

"How about Jupiter itself?" Kira suggested. "Isn't it hot?"

"No, it's actually cold at minus 110 degrees Celsius," Tiana said. "Though a few of its moons are hot."

"That won't work since they plan to send more satellites to Jupiter and its moons in the future," Wain said. "So, the Red Winkies might be tempted to attach to one returning here."

"Dern good point," Gertie said nodding vigorously. "Way too tempting. Best try to think of some other one."

"Think fast, you have twelve minutes and thirty seconds left," Neith said pointedly.

"Yes, yes! Keep thinking," the avatar said. "A hot moon would do, and we would love, love, love you all for finding a planet of our own for us!"

"Love. That's it! Like that song of John Lennon's Auntie likes, 'All you need is love'," Alora said pulling her sister, Lani and Kira close and whispered a word to them and they gasped.

"Great! That's got to be the answer," Kira said cheerily and Lani nodded vigorously then they all began laughing.

"It 'is' indeed a great idea," Tiana said grinning.

"Okay, what is it?" Rhys asked as patiently as he could manage knowing they had very few minutes left to solve this.

"VENUS!" Alora shouted merrily.

"Venus? Are you sure?" he asked doubtfully.

"Yes! Venus is hot, but just 464 degrees Celsius so it's not too hot for the Red Winkies," Tiana said. "Plus, few satellites go there and it's too hot for them to land anything yet."

"Then that's a fantastic suggestion," Rhys said excitedly.

"It is," Wain said, "But as a precaution, can you ask Great Lady Hera to tell all the space agencies and governments it's off limits for everyone else if the Red Winkies move there?"

"Sure, but let's share our idea before we run out of time." Rhys sweat profusely as he turned to Neith knowing they had only six minutes left. "Great Universe Mediator, our idea is to move the Red Winkies to Venus."

"That is an excellent idea," Neith said and for the first time since they had met her, she smiled. "I am pleasantly surprised you young humans were willing and able to come up with a solution. Now, I must ask the Red Winkies if they are willing to do this." She looked at the Winkie's avatar. "Do you all agree to this plan of theirs of moving you to the planet, Venus?"

After a short pause the Broomsky avatar said, "We have just communicated with the Eastern Voltic Grid and they are all in agreement with this plan, as are we," the avatar said cheerily.

"Good, I am glad you all agreed. Then it is settled, and we will handle this immediately. Great Lady Hera will now let your planet's governments, space agencies, and other rulers know Venus is off limits to all due to this Red Winkie relocation."

"Great Universe Mediator Neith, some of our rulers are not cooperative," Rhys said. "Will she be able to get them to take this seriously and cooperate instead of retaliating violently?"

"If they refuse to cooperate, Great Lady Hera, backed by Galactic Commands personnel, will show them why it is in their best interest to do so. As for your planet, remember failure to repair its environment will still result in your demise. We give you one of your decades to fix this. If needed, for any reluctant or ignorant leaders on this world that want proof we can and will exterminate you if you fail to do this, we will give them a demonstration of our power. Now, I must speak to Great Lady Hera." Neith then drew Hera up through a tunnel of light. A short while later they came back down and looked hopeful.

"Relocating the Red Winkies and dealing with your various governments is being dealt with now. It will be settled faster than they realize is possible. Great Lady Hera and Galactic Commands counselors and enforcers will handle issues with resistance to healing your planet and will set up educational programs to enlighten your people to the critical need fix the harm they have done. Now, I must go. I bid you to strive to be learned and wise." With a regal nod to all she lifted her staff high and, in a flash, went up in a tunnel of light and was gone.

"Wow!" Rhys said wide-eyed. "That was amazing."

"It sure was," Alora said nodding.

"I must say that she knows how to make a flashy entrance and exit," Tiana said smiling.

"That she does," Roleena said with a twinkle in her eyes.

"Yep, just like the star she truly is," Gertie said chuckling.

*

Silence filled the air after Neith left, but a few minutes later, the genius inventor, Hephaestus looked at Hera quizzically and she gave him a nod. He snapped his fingers and a disc formed under his feet. He nodded at Roleena, Gertie, and the seven cousins, giving Tiana, Alora, and Rhys each a salute. He then whisked off on his disc into the sky drawing the blue energy layer up with him and disappeared from sight. Artemis and Yang then bid Roleena, Gertie, the seven cousins farewell and with a snap from each, a disc formed under them and swiftly flew up to the stars they came from.

"I'll be watching all of you," Great Lady Hera said warmheartedly as she spread her arms out towards the crowd. She then went and touched the forehead of Roleena, Gertie, Tiana, Alora, Rhys, Lani, Kira, Shaw and Wain. "My eye will be especially close on you." She smiled then snapped her fingers and her winged horse came to her. "Time to go home, Isis," she said slipping up on the steed in front of Pandora and with a huge whoosh of the steed's wings, they vanished from sight.

**

"The Red Winkies are gone!" an elder woman shouted in surprise after Hera left and everyone looked startled as they searched around for their red winking lights or listened for the buzzing sound they made. But no one could hear or see them.

"She's right," a man by her said. "They've all disappeared."

"Where did they go?" Alora asked Roleena worriedly then looked at Tiana curiously as she bit back a grin.

"Venus, of course," Roleena said matter-of-factly.

"Just like that?" Rhys asked with astonishment.

"Yes. The Great Lady had the power to do this," she said with a tiny smile, "Given to her by the Great Universe."

"Wow!"

"That concise word you often use does sum this up nicely," she said chuckling. "Now, gather up all your special gifts and let's go home before the people here start asking us questions most of them are not ready to hear the answer to."

"But Auntie Roleena, we can't go home yet. We must first find out where our parents are. In fact, I'm afraid they might have been taken by the Red Winkies like you and Aunt Gertie were," Alora said then her eyes flew open wide. "Oh. My. Gosh. What if the Red Winkies had them when Great Lady Hera sent them to Venus? Then our parents might've been sent there with them!" she gasped in horror as she realized what might have happened to them and Tiana and Rhys gasped too.

"They most certainly were not sent to Venus," Roleena huffed. "Great Lady Hera would not make a mistake like that."

"But if the Red Winkies disguised our parents like you were, Auntie Roleena," Alora said, "She might not have noticed they weren't just manikins in their rush to get them off our planet."

"And mistakenly taken to the planet Venus!" Rhys choked out with tears in his eyes.

"Which means they've been burned to cinders!" she cried.

"They weren't taken so they're not burned up! She is quite capable of sensing a living being under any disguise," Roleena harrumphed shaking a finger at them and her hair writhed like snakes. "You're all being utterly foolish, and besides that, do you truly think I'd ever let that happen to them? Now, I'm so upset you would even think that I need to take a minute to calm down." She then looked at Gertie. "Talk some sense into them for me before my hair bites someone."

Gertie nodded. "Listen up right now!" he told them sternly. "Don't let yer wild imaginings get the better of ye. Fact is, lines must've got jammed up fer some time now which is likely why we haven't heard from them. But things have changed since I jest got a slew of messages from them wondering why no one has answered any of their messages. From what I can see, it seems they're all fine as frog's hair."

"They most certainly are," Roleena said with a sharp nod.

"Are you sure because I haven't heard from them," Rhys choked out.

Before Gertie or Roleena could say more, Alora, Tiana, and Rhys got multiple pings on their smart phones and a flood of texts messages came in over them.

"Hey!" Rhys shouted excitedly. "I've got a boatload of texts from my mom and dad. One says they are having an amazing adventure. The next one says they'll call me in a few days since their guide says they'll be near a good cell tower and have better sending capabilities then."

"I just got a bunch of messages too," Alora said jumping up and down and giggling gleefully.

"Me too," Tiana said cheerily.

"I knew mine were on vacation but when I hadn't heard from them for days, I thought they were kidnapped," Rhys said.

"They most certainly were not," Roleena said seeming like she had been insulted.

Gertie looked at her closely then his eyes narrowed and then he scowled at her. "You set this up," he muttered in her ear.

She ignored him as he mumbled under his breath about someone doing a snow job and looked at Alora and Tiana. "I got some texts from your parents too saying they had trouble with their cell phones. They also said they're doing a tour of some ruins in Guatemala for two more weeks and not to worry if their calls are sporadic. In fact, the connections have been so bad they couldn't get any messages out until today."

"I bet they couldn't get calls out because the Red Winkies messed up the lines and blocked them," Rhys said angrily.

"Good point," Tiana huffed, "I also think it was due to them. That way they wouldn't know we were all in big trouble here."

"It does seem like it could be that," Roleena said with a shrug, glad the kids had not noticed Gertie roll his eyes at her and groan as he lightly shook his head.

"What a naughty thing to do," Alora said with a pout.

"Yes, it was," Tiana grumbled.

"Look at the bright side," Roleena said. "At least all your parents were safely out of the way while this was going on. Otherwise, they'd have been sick with worry about all of the harrowing things you were doing to save this world."

"True," Tiana said. "So, I guess it did work out for the best."

"Hmmm...I guess it did at that because this would've really spooked them," Rhys said and Alora nodded sharply.

"It certainly would have! It makes me glad it all turned out so well," their aunt said cheerily, looking with great affection at all seven of her nieces and nephews.

"Dern tootin', I guess it did turn out fer the best at that," he said with a shrug and stopped frowning at her. He then chuckled and gave her such a big knowing wink that she chuckled too.

**

CHAPTER EIGHTEEN
ROLLENA'S TRICK

"It's so nice to be back home," Roleena Bloodstone sighed gazing warmly at Tiana, Alora, Rhys, Lani, Kira, Wain, Shaw, Gertie, Paris, Pythia, Dodona, and Harold all sitting with her in the parlor. She smiled as she sat back in a cozy Early American oak rocker taking a sip of delicious African Nectar tea. Gertie began snoring loud as a Grizzly bear in the recliner by her and everyone grinned. She then turned to Tiana who sat near her.

"I'm so very glad that you, Alora and Rhys wanted to stay on with your old aunties until your folks get back," she said cackling lightly to see Pythia draped around her and Dodona wrapped around Alora. Rhys had her talking fly Harold, resting on his shoulder and she was glad to find they were now friends. She then looked at Lani, Kira, Shaw, and Wain. "I'm delighted you four also arranged to stay for the weekend. So, now, before the caterers come with the food I ordered for today's festivities, let's get any serious questions you have out of the way. Then we can just enjoy a relaxing day with good food, fun games, and silly movies and just enjoy each other's company."

"No questions here," Wain said. "Since the trouble was clear to see from the second the four of us flew into Garfield Park on the two enormous ravens that picked us up and took us there."

"True," Kira said. "Which was quite exhilarating in itself."

"Really rad," Shaw agreed. "Especially with the Red Winkie crowd surrounding our cousins looking like a deranged mob."

"I'm just glad we got there in time to help," Lani said.

"So were we!" Rhys said gustily.

"Absolutely!" Tiana and Alora said applauding them as Paris wagged his tail and barked as if agreeing with them.

"Auntie Roleena," Alora said with a tiny worried frown, "After meeting all those giant aliens from the stars at Garfield Park, I do have a serious question to ask you."

"A serious one you say?" she asked curiously. "Go on."

"Well, I'd like to know is this truly home to you or is there another place you'd rather live?" Alora asked biting on her lip.

"This is my home while each of you dear ones here have need of me," Roleena said smiling at all of them fondly. To her delight, they all looked relieved and smiled back at her.

"Are you sure you want to count me in this group after all the rascally things I've done?" Rhys asked wincing.

"Oh my, definitely yes. With the self-improvements you made and good works you did during this harrowing time of ours you are unquestionably part of my favorite group now."

Rhys blushed to receive such high praise from her and it took him a moment to speak. "Thanks, Aunt Roleena…a lot!"

"You're entirely welcome, my dear," she said then looked at the group. "I sense a few others are dying to ask me a question. Oh, goodness me…I didn't mean to put it that way, but eager enough to be squiggling about like puppies waiting for a treat."

"I guess I do want to ask something that puzzled me a lot," Tiana said looking at her quizzically.

"And just what would that be?"

"It's just that it totally shocked me the Red Winkies were able to capture you. 'You' of all people, with all your amazing gifts and gadgets! How could they possibly do that to you?"

"Because I let them," she said simply with a slight shrug.

"What?!" Alora and Rhys choked out.

"Why?" Tiana gasped.

"Because knowing you all as well as I do, I knew it would inspire you to do great feats! Remember, this was also a battle for Earth. One you had to win for us, and it's not the last. This Red Winkie invasion forced all of you to quickly grow braver, more aware, and more just. Not only with humans, but with alien beings. It was necessary for you to do this and succeed with the abilities I perceived within each of you and why I knew

I could count on you to find me. For I knew the Red Winkies would not expect humans as young as you to be such tough opponents. Even better," she said grinning, "You astonished the Galactic High Council by fixing the Red Winkie issue so fairly. Great Universe Mediator Neith told me if you actually did this, I could tell you she was the one to put the time pressure on you. You see, two gifted Seers on the Galactic High Council told her they foresaw you must succeed or we would lose the Earth. It's that close to dying here. I was angry she did this to you, but she insisted she knew you would then work harder and faster yet still make wise decisions to resolve this. Now, in your doing this, it has positively affected our future events here."

"From the way Great Universe Mediator Neith spoke to us, I thought she didn't like humans," Rhys said.

"Actually, she is a fan of humans like you and your cousins who strive to do better and better. She hoped you, your cousins, and Gertie could pull this off. Then you did. Due to your efforts to save the Red Winkies, the Galactic High Council postponed what they intended to do to save our planet. It was drastic but they felt they would soon have to…" Roleena paused.

"Eliminate humans," Tiana said finishing the sentence.

"Yes, that means you all saved everyone on this planet."

Alora huffed. "So, she was going to kill us and the Red Winkies right away and not even give us until sundown like the Galactic High Council said we could have."

"She was not going to extinguish both of you right away."

"Was she lying to us about that?" she asked gaping.

"No, she told the truth. They were discussing the final stage removing all the humans on Earth if our damage to this planet was not stopped soon. So, she brought this to your immediate attention to get you moving faster on it. The High Council saw the Red Winkie problem as a trial test to see if you could solve tough problems, which you passed with flying colors."

"Good to know, but I'm still puzzled," Rhys said, "You said you 'let' the Red Winkies capture you, but I feel there are still some pieces of this puzzle missing to this story."

Kira nodded. "I agree, Auntie, I also think there's more to this, and though I'm glad you knew you could count on all of us, Earth was a lot to risk. You must have had another reason to do things the way you did them."

Roleena cackled and her hair wiggled and giggled with her. This would have surprised most humans, but the cousins were used to her odd attributes. "You got me on that. I did know there were a few ways to fool the Red Winkies."

"Come on, Auntie. Tell us what they were," Alora said.

"Yeah, spill it," Shaw said eagerly.

"Well, my dears, I had an odd feeling the Red Winkies were coming back. Fortunately, I'd become aware they could detect familiar energy signatures. So, having run into them before, as have most of my off-world friends, I realized they knew my energy signature, as well as any others they had come across. They were especially aware of those who caught them last time. It's why they'd been able to elude us for centuries and some even millennia. So, I had to get all of you ready for this."

"So, that's why you gave me, Kira, Wain and Shaw all these miraculous gifts a year ago," Lani said nodding.

"Yes, and it's why I had to quickly get these gifts for Tiana, Alora and Rhys. Still, it was hard to think of everything you'd need to stop the Red Winkies, but I did my best to give you lots of special gifts to use for any tricks they might pull on you."

"Auntie Roleena I can see why you chose us to fix the Red Winkie problem, but what about Paris?" Alora said frowning. "He's just a sweet little dog and they zapped him around a lot."

"But he wanted to help you, so I gave him a gift too."

"Yikes!" Tiana said. "I did find a small gift for him when I found ours. I put it in my pocket but I forgot to give it to him."

"Ah, but my furry friend is a brilliant little fellow. He nosed it out of there. Right, boy?" she asked and Paris barked loudly.

"What was it?" Tiana asked grinning as he wagged his tail.

"Treats."

"It was just a few treats?" Alora asked frowning again.

"Not just. They were two yummy treats I made to help him. One had a Winkie nullifier in it. The other had a tiny beacon that sent signals to the Red Winkie locating units you found."

"Those units did help us find the Red Winkies hideout but the nullifier didn't help since they zapped him a lot."

"True," she sighed. "But it kept them from controlling him and is why he could battle them for so long. That way you could use the units to track him to their hideout. He then let them pen him in so you could follow him to that games store's dungeon to find Sir Gertie. But you know that since Sir Hephaestus explained how to use the units in his instruction book."

"What book?" the trio all asked so loudly Gertie woke up.

"Oops!" Gertie sputtered and smacked his forehead.

Roleena's hair twisted into a long snake braid and leaned towards him. "What do you mean by saying 'oops', Sir Gertie?"

"Well, I rushed to the cemetery with Sir Hephaestus' two tracking gizmos after ye asked me to hide them there quick like after them Winkies invaded again and plum fergot to stuff it in the box with them. Then ye had me come guard Tiana, Alora, and Rhys and I wound up having to lead the Red Winkies away from the three kiddos there and fergot all about that book."

"Oh dear...then I'm glad it all worked out anyway."

"Whoa, doggies, me too, pun intended," Gertie said swiping his brow. "Good thing yer pup Paris was able to get their attention down in that creepy dungeon."

"It was at that," Rhys said nodding. "I'm also glad you gave Paris a Winkie nullifier, Auntie, but shouldn't you have done that for all of us in case one of us was taken?"

"Actually, I did," Roleena said cackling lightly. "I put one in each of your flavored multi-vitamin capsules."

"What vitamin capsule?" Rhys asked looking puzzled

"Didn't Gertie make you both a sandwich before you left to come over to my house? Then didn't you both take a vitamin after that with your glass of milk?"

"That's right! I forgot all about that."

"The fact is, you were all given this 'special' vitamin."

"I didn't think anything about it since you always had me take a flavored multivitamin every day," Alora said.

"Sneaky," Tiana said grinning. "And smart of you to do."

"Thank you," Roleena said smiling. "That wasn't the only sneaky thing I did to the Winkies. You see, I knew they would expect me, Hera, or Artemis to come for them when we learned they were here. But having met us, they'd be able to evade us. What they wouldn't expect was the fine sleuthing from all you clever young people. And I was right. You were brilliant!"

"Why didn't you just tell us why you were doing this so we wouldn't worry?" Rhys asked scowling.

"Because the Red Winkies would've sensed you being more at ease with them then you should've been. Then they'd have swarmed you relentlessly giving you no way to find us at all. Add to that, they can erase a phone or computer message if attached to any open line. So, if I left you a message, they could delete it. For though they can't see you, they can sense tension or the lack of it. So, if you were tense as you read a note, they'd set fire to it and 'poof' it's gone."

"But our note from Aunt Gertie was in his wood burning fireplace," Alora said looking puzzled.

"Was the fireplace still hot?"

"No, the ashes were cold."

"Then it was brilliant of him to hide it in such an outlandish place as there was no heat to attract them to it," Roleena said grinning at Gertie and he chuckled. "More importantly, it worked perfectly since they never knew you found it."

"Since heat and stress attract them, why when we raced all over the cemetery to find what Aunt Gertie left us didn't the Red Winkies get us since we were both of these?" Tiana asked.

"You had a little help to get the time you needed," she said cackling. "An intentional pun, for though Paris is little, he is smart. Since you hadn't come for him and Gertie yet, he kept the Red Winkies distracted by escaping from the dungeon cell under the game store. Then they had to work hard to find him and put him in the cell again."

"But this was all super hard for us too!" Alora said.

"Yes, and I'm so proud of you for learning to be so brave," Roleena said cheerily. "I'm likewise delighted you all chose to do this because you're big hearted and want to help others. But know this, it was scary for me too. For though I expected the Red Winkies to set their radar for me, Gertie, and the off-world beings here, I knew as my family they would then aim for you!"

"Then why did they nab Gertie?" Rhys asked. "Technically, he's not actually family."

"Ah, but he's been the only human able to find and trap the Red Winkies. Due to this, they know he's an exceptionally skilled tracker and he would likely find their hideout again."

"Skilled in wit, years or miles?" Rhys asked jokingly.

"All of those," she said and her kaleidoscope eyes twinkled.

"Auntie, how come Aunt Gertie could still speak after the Red Winkies paralyzed him, but you couldn't?" Alora asked.

"Because they knew my alien side kept me resistant to anyone trying to force information out of me so they shorted my entire body out. But since Gertie is all human like you, they thought they could zap him enough to get this out of him. But they were wrong, so very, very wrong."

"Sure as shootin' they were, but I still hope they don't ever have a chance to do that to me again."

"We should be fine now the Red Winkies are on Venus."

"Are they?" Kira asked warily and Lani looked worried too.

"Yeah, are 'all' the Voltic Grids of the Red Winkies on our planet truly there now?" Shaw asked and Wain nodded.

All the cousins held their breath as they awaited her answer.

"Yes," Roleena said assuredly. "Great Lady Hera confirmed they are indeed all there and seem to be enjoying it immensely. So, I believe that this time they will stay put."

"Are you absolutely positive?" Alora asked biting her lip.

"No, because there is no absolute. Still, I do think they will. Now, I'm just worried about fixing our dear planet Earth for the Galactic High Council was serious when they said if we don't fix it, they'll get rid of us. Keep in mind, most think we are just acting like a virulent plague on this planet."

"Wow," Rhys said. "We really need to get to doing this fast so we can change their reason to think this."

"Yes, we do, and I truly believe with your help, we will."

"I hate throwing water on our parade of successes," Tiana said apologetically, "But I have another serious question."

"What is that?"

"You mentioned this was a battle for Earth that we needed to win for ourselves. Then you said that it won't be the last one."

Roleena sighed. "True. You see, the battle here in this tiny park on Earth between different Galactic High Council factions and Earthlings drew some serious attention our way from some rather bad scoundrels in the neighboring galaxy. So, we might not have seen the end of this yet."

"Yikes!" Tiana said her head snapping up sharply as did Alora's, Rhys', Kira's, Lani's, Wain's, Shaw's and Gertie's.

"My goodness, Auntie, that's a scary thing to say," Alora gasped.

"It certainly is," Rhys added heartily.

"Calm down, it may never happen. Still, it's best to keep your gifts close at hand and a sharp eye out for troublesome extraterrestrials. As for me, I'm just happy knowing I have all of you with your special gifts and abilities to protect us!"

***

Greetings! I hope you enjoyed 'Attack of the Red Winkies'. If so let me know and tell your friends too!

Dear readers,

I thank you all whether you are ten or ninety years young for picking up and reading my first young adult novel 'Attack of the Red Winkies'. If you found it enjoyable, I would truly appreciate you taking a moment to mention this to Amazon or Amazon's Kindle. Plus, if you have time please write a review, short or long as you wish. As authors, our books all live or die on these reviews. They don't have to be lengthy. Even a few words help others decide if my light sci-fi fantasy book would be fun for a young adult approximately or for yourself as an adult if you like good hearted adventure books. This encourages authors to continue a popular scrics. Also, if there are certain characters you'd like to see again in future novels, let me know because I do seriously take such requests into consideration.

Once again, I thank you and as the Epherean's would say in my adult genre fantasy sci-fi book series, 'The Books of Epherea' which starts with the first book, "The Angels Return'.

Be well, and may the Light of the 'All' fill and surround you with its warmth, vitality, and goodness!

G. E. McCurry